MAX AND

A STORY OF LOVE AND DESTRUCTION

Mrs Stroud

MAX AND MRS. STROUD
A Story of Love and Destruction

Copyright © 2015 Mark Bondurant, All Rights Reserved
http://www.markbondurant.com
Cover design and illustrations by Mark Bondurant
Cover art by Claude Monet

Published by Bongo Books
http://www.bongo.net

Publisher's Cataloging-in-Publication
(Provided by Bongo Books)

Bondurant, Mark.
Max and Mrs. Stroud / by Mark Bondurant. –
1st ed. p.292 ; 16x23cm.

ISBN: 1940995051
ISBN 13: 978-1-940995-05-2

1. Espionage. 2. Steampunk fiction. 3. Science Fiction. 4. Alternative histories (Fiction), European. I. Title.

Dedication

I dedicate this, my third book, to the
children of my parents. May they find
peace in their lives without resort
to bloodshed.

Table of Contents

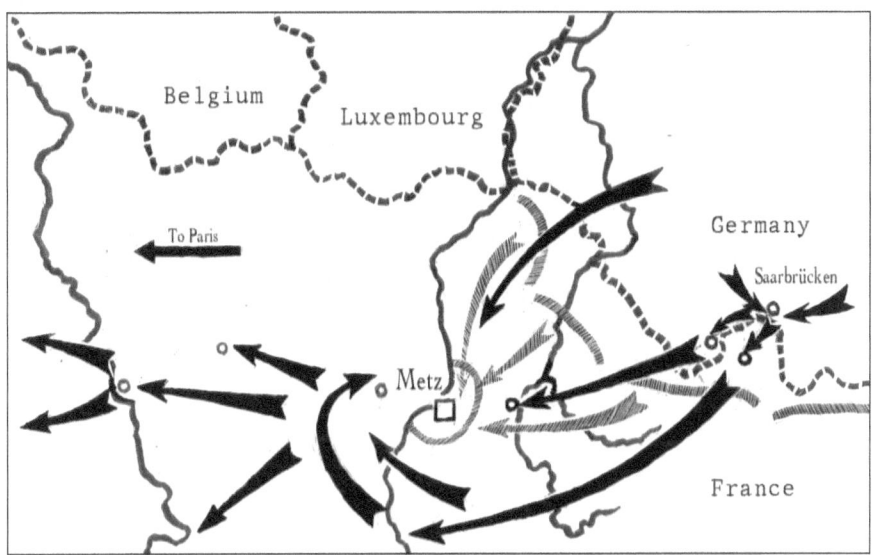

Metz

Max hid behind a pair of empty barrels in a stinking alley, ravenously wolfing down his prize. He'd managed to grab nearly a third of a loaf in the fight. The mob had fought over the broken supply cart, killing the soldiers who pulled it. He grabbed the rolling loaf just before ducking into the alley. More soldiers had arrived, wielding gun butts and bayonets, only slightly less crazed than the mob. He would have had a whole loaf if that crone hadn't spotted him and grabbed at it, but he was grateful to have gotten something.

A dark shape loomed at the top of the alley, then the crunch of gravel behind him. He should have hidden in one of the barrels, he thought. There was no escape, so he tried to eat faster. Faster until he started hiccupping.

He saw the soldier's feet as he curled around his bread. The soldier had worn shoes and stained white spats.

"It's a kid," the soldier said to his companion, who was still walking toward them down the alley.

"What did he steal?"

"Just piece of bread."

"Just a piece of bread? That's my ration!"

"He looks like he hasn't eaten in a week. Here lad, drink this. If you're going to eat, you should at least keep it down."

"You're giving him water too?"

The soldier was holding a canteen out to Max, who looked back at it suspiciously. He knew they could take his bread any time they wanted to, but hunger had driven him a little crazy and he wasn't sure what he was thinking. Finally, he took the canteen and slurped water greedily, then started in on the bread again. They could change their mind.

The first soldier shook his head as he looked at Max. "This can't last much longer," he said.

"Maybe, maybe not. Bazaine will never give up."

"Even Bazaine has to eat."

"Last I saw, he still had his horse."

The first soldier snorted. "So very, very, true."

Max swallowed his last bite, took another swig of water, and then held the canteen up for the soldier to take.

The soldier took it with nod, then looked up at his friend. "We better get back."

"Look, they're pulling the cart apart!"

"Hell!" Then they took off at a run.

Max watched them as they ran back down the alley in their dirty torn blue. The sound of the cannon had picked up. They were hitting the hill forts. He found a crumb in the dirt and ate it, before falling asleep.

ഇരുജ

Max woke in pitch darkness. There was little wood left to burn anywhere in Metz, and none for warmth and light, the houses having been stripped to bare stone. The first thing he noticed was that it was quiet. The cannon had stopped. Too dark to shoot, he thought. His joints creaked as he slowly stood. He was thirsty.

Walking slowly, he made his way back to the square, past

the spot where the cart had been, and then the dry fountain, toward the Moselle. It was October and the wind sent rattling shivers through him. He pulled his blanket closer around him as he walked past the shapes of bodies, just shadows and blood. Dead or asleep, he couldn't tell. A shot, then two more, then quiet, barely noticed.

Too dark to shell. He said it again to himself in a whisper as he walked. "Too dark to shell, too dark to tell," he piped. There used to be cats, he thought, as he staggered down the dry empty street, his feet almost numb in his too large stolen socks and shoes. He remembered there had always been cats. "All gone," he sang to the corpses.

At the river he sat down on the steps that led to the water to untie his tea cup from his belt. He had found it sitting all by itself on a low wall. Someone had left it. It was gilt with pink flowers, the colors dazzling in the sun. His fingers worked the knot slowly. A shape floated by in the current, and then another. He didn't look. Just more shadows.

The water was cold and it hurt to touch it as he skimmed away the surface slime to dip his cup. He was grateful he could barely see. The end of his blanket had fallen in the water and he sucked on it after he pulled it out, sucking out the water and the salty dirt.

∞

Dusty orange sunshine. It was afternoon. They were shelling both hills again, Kameke and Manteuffel. Max sat with his back to a wall, his head in the shade and body in the sun, trying to stay warm, watching the shells falling in the distance. It was quite a show and something to fill the time. Then rifle fire rose in the valley between them. An enemy attack.

In the early days this would have alarmed Max, but he was beyond caring. He felt only his dim existence, the world completely separate. A thing of its own, like his cracked lips that no longer bled.

The tops of the hills were lost under the explosions, which gave way to quiet as he watched the sun slowly drift across the sky with the smoke and dust. The sky was a river and the sun floated within it, he thought, as he drifted along with it into sleep.

Daylight. Another night had passed. He was sitting, leaning against a wall a little ways up and across the river from the Prefecture Palace. Across the bridge he could see the soldiers milling about the square. They had the general's horse out and saddled too. Something was afoot. He wanted to see, but found he couldn't stand, so he sat and watched the tiny figures in the distance. The general in his best gold uniform, painfully bright, was helped up on his horse. Then he a rode off followed by his men, line by line. Gone. Until the square was empty. He watched them go, staring with dry eyes, drifting in and out of consciousness.

"Mein Gott. Es ist eine andere!"

A face loomed over him, another behind that. He couldn't make them out. It took him a moment to understand what they were saying, so used to French he had become. They had put a cup to his dry lips, so he drank with his swollen tongue. It was sweet water.

Then he was in a wagon under a cloudy sky, their passage marked by trees slowly passing. Max was confused. The trees had all been cut down for the trenches.

"You're awake. Here drink."

Another man with a cup speaking German.

"Danke," Max managed.

"They were right. Definitely one of ours," then man said.

"Now this," the woman handed the man a cup.

Tepid broth.

"Take your time. Drink it all."

They were in a line of wagons on a road he didn't recognize.

The man smiled. "It's a wounded train. We're heading to the railhead at Saarbrücken. Can you talk?"

"Yes," he said.

"We need to know about you. Is there anyone we can notify?"

Max shook his head, immediately regretting it. "No. All dead."

The man's face twitched, but forced its way back to a smile. "Well. You're among friends now. Do you have a name?"

"Max."

"Max?"

"Max Schuster."

"Well, Max Schuster. As one veteran to another, it's an honor to meet you."

Then he set Max's head carefully down.

"Rest now little veteran. We have a ways to go."

❧

The shells were landing around them, soldiers running from the artillery. The line had collapsed. A house went and then another. They were running and running, the shells sweeping them away one at a time, until a wave lifted him into a forest of hands. Hands grabbing him and pushing him and screaming, faces looming over him with bayonets. Screaming that turned into whistling. And then finally, a train.

He had been screaming.

They were holding him down, down in his stretcher. Their silhouettes turned into worried faces. A man and a women. The man in the wagon. They were on a train platform, next to a big black train, stretchers and wounded everywhere.

"Settle down little veteran," he said.

"Night terrors," the woman, a new one said. "So young."

"We picked him up in Metz. As best as I can tell, he's German."

"Then, little one, you're in the right place" She tried to smile. "Do you need to pee?" she asked.

Max shook his head.

"Then it's sleep, broth, and water for you. No food until you can pee."

They pinned another note to his shirt. Max was surprised to see that he had two. And put him in a box car, still in his dirty clothes, his stretcher side by side with soldiers bloody and bandaged. Women in blue grey dresses with white aprons brought him water and broth.

It was three days to Berlin.

❧

He had been riding in a seat the third day, able to walk. His notes still pinned to him.

They had nothing for him to wear, so they had tried to wash his rags at one of their frequent stops, but they were torn and worried and the shirt had to be thrown away. He wore a stained soldier's shirt, hastily mended, the sleeves rolled up, sleeping despite the cigarettes and conversations of the men in the seats with him. He felt only the rocking of the train and his inability to fight his own weight.

In Berlin, he had tried to climb down from the car on his own, only to faint on the landing. The bright sun light scattered and broke around him as he fell down into darkness. He had no memory of hitting the worn wood planking below. A darkness clawed him down. He fought it, but it drew the life out of him and wouldn't let him wake.

"He's perfect." A man's voice. "We'll take him." It was a man. Max opened his eyes. He was in a bed in a long hall filled with beds. His eyes were dry and slow to open. A nurse in grey was talking to a man in a suit and cane. The man's hair was oiled back and he had a lens in his eye. Max thought he looked silly.

"You're awake," the man said, looking down at him. "Perfect timing."

"Please," the nurse said. "He shouldn't be moved. Not yet." She looked worried.

"Nonsense," the man with the monocle said. "He's survived this much. I don't think a train ride will kill him. And we have our own nurse." Then he looked back down at Max, an odd expression on his face, almost thoughtful. "Besides," he said quietly, almost to himself. "It's a matter of natural selection. He's a survivor. After all he's been through, I don't think anything could kill him. He fits the requirements perfectly."

"But you have no idea what it was like there!" the nurse said. "I was there!"

The man with the monocle looked up at her with an amused smile, "Oh, but I do. And so does the king."

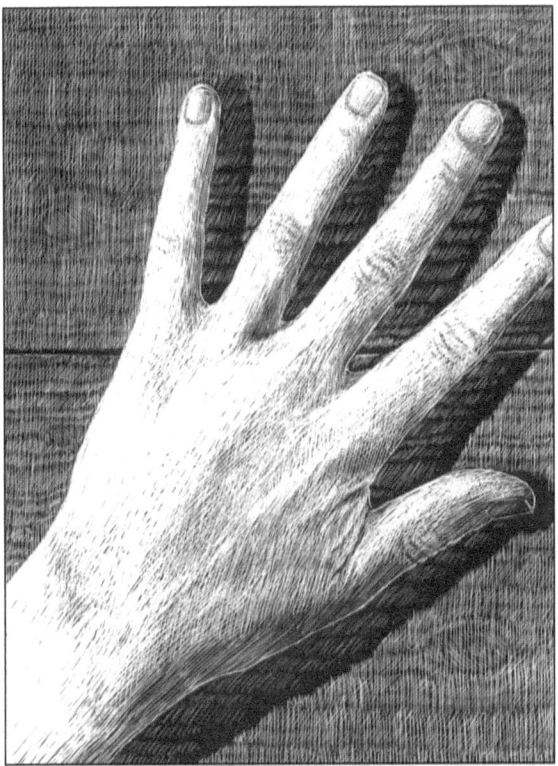

The Royal Institution for Young Women

She held her knuckles out in front, flat on the desk. They already throbbed. It took all her will to hold them out again. The ruler came down, harder this time. The pain blinding. She gasped.

"Class, it's allowed to recognize pain, even show it. But you must never cry."

She wanted to cry, but instead tried to think of the pain as an abstract. Somewhere else, outside of herself.

"Very good Emelia," Mrs. Dabney said. She gave her a light rap on the top of her head. "Class?" She said. "What is the rule?"

The girls recited.

"Anger will not sustain you through adversity. Unrequited it leads to despair. Tears are gold to the oppressor. They are a coin we can choose to mint," they intoned.

Then she continued on to the next girl.

None of them had laughed nor showed any sign of care. They knew the punishment for doing so. The classroom held twelve girls. Two years ago they had been twenty two. No one knew where the others went. They simply, one by one, failed to show up for breakfast.

They were all orphans with no memory of their parents. one had been outside the school's walls. What they saw of the outside world they learned through books. Emily loved books. She read stories of lands far away, magical places, and people doing amazing things. She longed to see the outside world and drained each one, asking her teacher one day if, when they graduated, she would see Paris.

"Someday Emilia, if you do well in your studies," her teacher said. But ten year old Emily doubted she would live to see it.

The girls had just come from dinner. It had been a test, as always. They had been given desert spoons instead of soup spoons. Some of the girls had protested, but Emily had had taken a chance and ignored them, choosing instead to skim her soup with the incorrect spoon.

"What are doing Emilia?" the mistress scolded, which brought the class brought to abrupt silence.

Emily felt a spike of dread. She knew an incorrect answer would bring trouble, but she had started the play and now had to see it through.

"It's lovely soup. Is it borscht?"

"Beet soup yes, but not borscht. Why, may I ask, are you eating with the wrong spoon?"

"Well," she paused as she had been taught, placing her spoon to the right side of her saucer for added effect. Make them wait just a little. "I didn't want to embarrass you."

The mistress looked at her oddly and said nothing more, which was as much of a victory as she could expect.

As always, neither tea nor desert were served. There was the matter of keeping teeth perfect and waists trim. Instead they spent the last course practicing with empty dishes.

"You must watch your figure," they repeated constantly. Hunger was their constant companion.

Tonight the class was doing flash cards and she had brought her box with her from the shelf to her desk when she entered. The cards changed every few days. When she opened her box, she noticed that this batch was ink-stained. She almost cried out, but caught herself. It was another test. They meant to remind her of Abby.

Friendship at the school was nothing like it was in books. There were no games. No toys or dolls. No possessions at all beyond their uniforms. Not even free time for walks or trips to the country. Friendship was just another secret, she thought grimly, and secrets were all they possessed.

She looked at the first hand-tinted etching. A Rubens. Fat women, Romans, and cherubs. Awful really. Emily generally disliked the Italian Renaissance.

Abby's real name had been Abigail, but friends traded their secret names. It was all they had to give each other. Abby had disappeared last winter. She had spilled her ink well and ruined her dress. An amazing feat really. The things were practically impossible to tip, but Abby had managed it. She had never been good at physical things. Emily could always beat her in self-defense and she was terrible at fashion. She tried to help her and Abby, in turn, had helped Emily with her math. Abby had been a wizard at math.

Emily flipped through the cards, reminding herself of the artists and their significance.

"Three minutes," Mrs. Dabney called. The sand had been running down the hourglass and she had been daydreaming! Emily picked up her pace. Luckily it was review.

Mrs. Dabney called time and then started pulling cards out of her deck, picking girls to recite. Emily breezed through. She had always had a knack for memorization. She excelled at the memory room.

The memory room was just that. A room. Sometimes it was a study, sometimes it was a parlor, or even a bedroom. You were sent in and then called out. The time always varied. Then they'd asked you questions about the contents, even the contents of drawers and underneath furniture. You had to search quickly, but most of all quietly.

She had gone to sleep that night thinking of Abby, only to be rudely nudged awake. Her time disappear had come. What had she done wrong, she wondered? She should have felt fear, but could muster little more than resignation.

Two men loomed over her bedside, which was strange because Emily had only seen men four times, and then only in passing. Twice it had been the gardeners when she had managed to exit through an unlocked door left open by mistake. Once, a man waiting in the school office with briefcase. The last was a man caught wandering the school grounds. He and, of course, the men who had clubbed him bloody and carried him away.

"Come on charming. Time to wake up. You have a date," said a Cockney accent. She had risen easily, yet they still seemed inclined to help her. She detested their touch.

The men's footsteps echoed in the hallway as they walked towards the school office. Emily made no sound at all.

Down the hall, as they approached, she heard a voice. "It's too soon!" It was Mrs. Hollins. She ran the school. "She's just beginning to show aggression."

"It's been decided. She fits the role."

"Who decided?"

"Lord Hudnall of course. You know how this works."

"It's, it's just that she's . . ." Then she stopped. Emily wanted to hear more, but they had heard her guards' footsteps.

They walked the rest of the way in silence. When they entered the office she faced Mrs. Hollins, standing in her night robes, and a man with a grey mustache and a Savile Row suit sitting in her chair.

"Ah. There she is," the man said, giving her an appraising look. "Come over here and let me see what we have." The chair creaked as he turned to the side so she could approach. But Emily stopped first and looked at Mrs. Hollins, who nodded to her.

She approached warily. Sitting, the man's eyes were level with hers. She thought he looked a bit stiff, probably age. It would be easy to push him over.

"Turn around."

She did, but she didn't like turning her back to him.

"Smile."

She did.

"Like you mean it," he said, then nodding thoughtfully when she complied. "Good." He looked up at Mrs. Hollins. "No marks, nice teeth." Then he looked in her eyes for an uncomfortable length of time.

"Her name?" he asked Mrs. Hollins.

"Emilia," Mrs. Hollins replied.

"I bet that's not what you call yourself is it?" he said to Emily, as if she were a child.

"My name is Emilia," Emily replied coldly.

"Well Emilia. What do you make of me?"

"We haven't been introduced. It would be forward."

"I'm afraid we'll have to skip that," he replied, perhaps with a touch of impatience.

"How should I address you then?"

He chuckled and looked up at Mrs. Hollins.

"I think she's aggressive enough. Did you teach her deflection?"

Mrs. Hollins didn't reply.

"Again. Tell me what you make of me?"

Emily looked up at Mrs. Hollins, who nodded.

Emily looked the man in the eye.

"Savile suit, Stafford shoes. You took off your ring and pocket watch. You're due at your barbers. You have a man who helps you dress. You rarely walk, but don't normally sit at a desk, and you're hiding your hands."

"Very good. You noticed the ring when you came in didn't you?"

Emily said nothing.

"We need to work on that frown," he added.

"Relax your face Emilia," Mrs. Hollins said.

"Good," the man said, watching her face. "She's perfect," he smiled up at Mrs. Hollins. But Mrs. Hollins looked worried.

She was riding in a real steam carriage still in her night dress and slippers but wrapped in the too large cloak they had given her. She'd left her uniforms behind. Moon lit the snow dusted countryside that rolled past the carriage windows, the car lurching occasionally as it hit ruts in the narrow Hounslow country road. It seemed unreal to Emily, who had never seen anything of the outside world but pictures. Like a great rolling painting. She could see no lights. Their speed seemed dizzying.

Sir Killam, as they had finally been introduced, kept trying to make conversation. He seemed nervous. He sat in his pool of moonlight on the other side of the seat, occasionally checking his watch. She could see the driver and his accomplice in front through the window that separated them.

Sir Killam seemed to come to a decision. He reached over to put his hand on her knee.

"We should be more comfortable with each other," he said.

Emily wasn't sure what to make of his hand.

"Please remove your hand," she said.

"You need to get used to it. Where you're going, it's part of the job."

"Please remove your hand," she said again, with greater firmness.

"You must eventually. Why not with me?" he asked.

Emily wasn't sure what he was talking about. She thought he was speaking more for himself, deciding it was rhetorical. She said nothing. Her school lessons rolled through her mind as she looked for scenarios that matched the situation, but she could think of nothing. She could think of nothing except she should avoid enclosed spaces with no exit. Finally, she came to a decision.

"Sir, we are hardly on speaking terms." And she put her hand down on top of his and, grasping his little finger, pulled it back, peeling his hand off her leg. She had hardly started when he shook loose and pulled his hand back. He looked angry and twice her size. If she were in the open she might stand a chance, but in the closed cabin his brute strength would be impossible to counter.

He began to rise from his seat, she thought to come at her.

"Unmarked wasn't it?" she said, guessing at his orders.

He sat back down, as if knocked back, frowning at her

before turning his attention back to the window. After a quiet moment, he muttered, "Aggressive indeed."

೮ಂಐ

Woods and farms turned to villages and city. The road improved. They stopped to stoke the boiler.

Sir Killam, a man with no soul

It had then been three hours of silence when finally, after rolling through park, they pulled up to the gate in a tall brick wall topped by a high iron spiked fence. The brass gate plaque, lit by gas lamps, read "Danson House." Watchmen, rough men in solid uniforms, inspected the carriage and Sir Killam's papers.

She heard them talking, catching words here and there.

"Late . . ."

"Damn roads . . . winter damn it!"

A runner was sent to the dark house.

Danson House stood alone, isolated in the center of a wide bare lawn, crossed only by a stone carriage way. Square and blockish, with little decoration, and no light, Emily thought it looked a bit forbidding, but she had no place else to go. At least, she thought, it looked likely to possess a water closet.

The runner returned, lights appearing in windows, the gate finally opening. The car pulled up at the foot of a long wide run of simple stone steps ending in a wooden door and two windows. A face peered out a window for a moment as they ascended, the door opening at their approach.

Two servants met them in the hallway, still in their nightshirts, candlesticks in their hands despite the house clearly having gaslight.

"Milady is dressing. Please follow me," one said.

They were led into a small parlor, just off the hall. The other servant had gone ahead to light lamps and a fire.

"Would either of you care for tea?" the he asked.

"Yes. It's been a long day," Sir Killam replied.

The servant looked at Emily, eyebrows raised. This presented a dilemma for her. She dearly wanted to try real tea, but she wasn't allowed to have it. Was this a test?

"May I have water?" she asked.

The servant smiled and replied, "Yes, of course. We've no ice though. They won't deliver it for hours."

"Water will be lovely, thank you."

Then they were left to themselves. Since Sir Killam was distant, sitting in a worn chair scraping out his pipe, Emily took advantage of the moment to examine the room.

The fireplace had lit correctly, having been properly banked in preparation for visitors. The mantel had several figurines, a clock showing 3:12 AM. She saw a piece of folded paper. Above was a still life of the Queen in her blue Order of the Garter sash. Beside her sat a lamp, brass, white glass shade. On she went, inventorying and evaluating each item in the room.

She decided the owner was rich, but not noble, despite her being called "milady", mostly due to age of the objects. Most were relatively new. A true noble would have centuries of accumulation. There were rings left from previous furniture on her table top as well which indicated that the present owner was not the first. The room was more like the school memory room. Objects assembled temporarily and underneath it all, the room itself was rather dingy.

When Milady finally entered, Emily faced an elderly but still striking woman. She seemed to be dressed in Egyptian or Middle Eastern costume with her hair in a wrap. She looked more like a fortune teller than a lady, Emily thought. Her jewelry, tended nails, and silk though spoke of wealth.

"Ah, Rodney. I see you've brought our girl, late as always."

"The roads were appalling."

"I'm sure they were." She managed to sound unconvinced. "I hope she is undamaged."

Sir Killam grunted in outrage. "Of course she is."

"We will see." She looked at Emily. "Nice bone structure. Good posture. Perfect features."

"My pardon ma'am, but I don't believe we've been introduced."

"Brave too." She cocked her eyebrow and asked, "So tell me. What is behind your chair?"

Emily thought the expression unwise as it promoted wrinkles. Then again, perhaps this woman was beyond that.

"The furnace vent," Emily replied. "Nothing is tied to it, although I couldn't look at it closely."

"Well trained."

"May I know your name?" Emily asked.

"If you stay."

"Did you make this room for me?"

"Like the memory room?" She laughed. It was genuine. "Oh, I remember the memory room. No child. This is just another government building. It's for training. Perhaps even yours."

"And what do I have to do to enter."

"A small task. You have to steal something."

"When?"

"You leave in seven days."

"Leave?"

"All in good time."

℘℘℘

They gave her a small room with a simple bed. Already in her night dress, she crawled in to bed and closed her eyes against the dark. When she opened them it was light. She had a window, light leaking in through the curtains. Outside she heard a lark. She decided the room had probably been meant for a maid. But what time was it? There was no clock! Her breath fogged as she rose. Folded on the dresser she found an ill-fitting shift, bloomers, a light bodice, and new slippers. There was no chamber pot under the bed. Rising, she dressed. Opening the door as quietly as she could in the echoing uncarpeted room, she found a lush carpeted hardwood hallway with paintings and flowers. No one was in sight so she set out to explore. The hallway was gas lit and lined with doors. She didn't know which to pick. Which one was the water closet?

A rattle! A door opened. A young woman at the end of the hallway emerged dressed in lovely winter wool. Behind her, she could see a maid folding the woman's night dress. The woman's hair was wrapped to protect it. She had just had it done.

"Pardon, where is the water closet?" Emily asked.

"A new girl," the woman said with a forced smile. "The end of the hall." She pointed.

The door she pointed to looked like the others, but when Emily opened it, it led into darkness. She needed a candle and there were none in her room. But the woman had been correct. It was a water closet. She looked at the room with the light from the hallway and memorized it, then walked in and closed the door.

℘℘℘

Emily counted the steps as she descended, marking each creak. Downstairs they were serving buffet. Buffet Emily knew from

16

school and walked in. The plates had been warmed, which was interesting. She picked carefully, certain this was a test, and then sat down at the long table away from the others. She could hear their conversation.

"Are we playing discover the title again today?"

"This dress has been seen too much. When am I going to get a new one?"

"Oh, Lord Ailesbury is fine for a tryst, but really."

"You used the wrong fork dear."

Their experience and age were beyond her, so she concentrated on her eggs instead, which were quite good. She thought perhaps the cook had used garlic and thyme.

"So we have a new girl," a voice taunted. She looked up at them.

"Yes," she replied.

There were smiles all around, mostly mean, but one not, or perhaps well faked. The woman of note was thin beyond question and her gaze sharp. Her features at present were not pleasant, but Emily was sure they could change at will. On further thought, Emily decided the smile had come from greed. Perhaps she thought Emily might be of use. If the woman had needs then perhaps there were grounds for negotiation. She might be useful to Emily as well.

"They treat the new ones so poorly. I'm so tired of seeing new girls in that dress."

Where were the new girls who had worn it before? She thought. Or were they trying to panic her?

Then one tossed down her spoon. "Why does she get a mission?" she hissed. "I'm fit for more than marriage."

The sly one hissed back, "Silence. That's why."

The first paled, stood, her chair tipping back, and almost bolted. But then she just stood there, lost, her eyes darting about, trying to collect herself. Panic, Emily thought. What had scared her? The room was quiet after that. They all picked at their food.

Emily had orange juice! She avoided the coffee. A servant offered her some despite her lack of cup, which made her suspicious. Just another thing to put her off her food. She excused herself, retiring back to her room upstairs. She heard whispers behind her as she climbed. She managed to avoid the spots that creaked, passing through the hallway in silence.

She was laying in her bed, thinking about trying to venture outside. That had always brought trouble before, but she had new boundaries and they had to be tested, when she heard a tap at her door.

"Pardon, Miss?"

She opened it and saw a young man. His perfect smile was beautiful, dashing in livery. A foolish test, she thought. She was only ten. This was wasted on her, she laughed to herself.

"The dressmaker's here," he said. "If you could follow me downstairs?"

"Yes, of course," she said, and followed him downstairs to a library filled with intricately rigged wooden ships, each with their own brass plaque.

The dressmaker was an old man, with a young assistant in his late twenties. The table behind them was piled with sample books with cloth instead of pages. They had Sedwell & Son on their covers.

"Good morning," he trilled, then glanced at her with a critical eye. "Let's look you over." He walked around Emily while his assistant stood ready at the books.

"Good. Uh hm . . . yes," he mumbled, as he walked, sometimes tisking.

"Do you think her colors will hold?" he asked his assistant.

"It's a difficult age sir," his assistant replied.

"Yes it is . . ." his voice trailing off. "Well. Let's begin with number three." The assistant picked up a book of cloth and handed to the man, who began holding up pages to her face.

෧෮ඐ

Class began that afternoon. She was called down soon after she returned to her room. It was about New York City. The boroughs, the people, the tensions. It was given by a man with a strange accent. She tried to mouth his words as he spoke, but it was like having a mouth full of marbles. The worst was the humor. Every other sentence ended in a joke. She listened and learned, but much of the humor escaped her.

Thanks to class she missed afternoon tea. She started dinner that night alone, the women gone, only to be replaced later in the meal by a new set of strangers. These were older men who asked her questions. Questions like "what's west of the Brooklyn?" or "Where do the fish come in?" She didn't know the answers, which made her afraid. She didn't know so she made up answers. Their faces revealed few clues.

That night she went to bed afraid. Afraid she had failed and that she wouldn't wake. But wake she did in the early morning, by a tap on her door. When she opened it, the dark hallway was empty, lamps yet to be lit. She heard the steps creak as someone descended. It was first light so she dressed and went to breakfast, buffet again, alone. She risked a piece of fattening bacon. She would regret it.

After breakfast, on her way upstairs, she was pulled aside by solid men in livery. Men who were clearly not servants.

"Why the bacon!" they asked.

"Because I've never had it before," she lied with the face of a saint, a scared saint.

There were questions. Had she been taking food before? Had she been sharing it with others? What other rule violations was she hiding? They threatened and she knew their threats to be real. She spooned her terror out carefully. She even cried. Eventually, they grew tired and let her go.

Her afternoon class was on cable car routes in New York, the location and use of the harbors, zeppelin aerodromes, and the use of cabs. She was relentlessly quizzed.

That afternoon, the tailor showed up for a first fitting, simple girl's dresses and shoes that didn't fit. The clothes were ridiculous. She was beyond bonnets, but she kept her opinions to herself.

As the days passed, her knowledge of New York grew as did her wardrobe. The day came when they presented her with her last delivery, her finished clothing.

"These are your blades," the tailor bowed and intoned with his son standing behind as he passed the paper wrapped bundle across the table to her in the centuries old tradition of the Knight Companions. She had yet to know of the Companions or the weight of those words. Emily thought them merely odd, but thanked him anyway. They were the last of her only clothes, beyond the throwaways she had been lent at school. She packed the bundle that night unwrapped in her new travel trunk.

℥℥

The great leviathan hovered over the grass field, a monstrous grey ghost that looming in the thin morning sunlight. Its size was all out of proportion to anything she had ever imagined. Their car chugged towards it across damp grass. Around it stood teams of men, waiting on anchor lines tied to blocks of concrete buried in the earth.

"Mutti?" she asked. Her new parents were Friedrich and Gisela, new immigrants to the U.S. She had yet to meet Friedrich. He was already in the U.S. making preparations for their arrival.

"Ja, liebe?" she replied. Her smile was less than perfect.

She paused in thought, then said "Nichts." Emily couldn't think of way to express the incredible size or the majesty of the zeppelin to her. It was simply the biggest thing she had ever seen. So she chose instead to sit quietly and watch. She wanted to remember it and began memorizing its details.

The people in the seats in front of them seemed to have no problem finding words. An elderly couple and a young man. They pointed out details, the elderly man espousing his knowledge, the driver nodding and saying, "Yes sir," and "That's about like it."

Emily had come to understand, at least so far, that there were three classes of people in her world. Teachers, bystanders, like those sitting in front of her, and people like Gisela. Gisela was a member of The Institution, as was she. But she was different from her. Really, a completely different animal. When the subject came up, they referred to Emily as one of the *schooled* and apparently, Gisela was not.

Her new parents' job was to deliver her to the target and to give her support while there. They were to provide a home. But Emily doubted their abilities and guessed they had been a choice made in desperation. She found Gisela to be disorganized and scattered in her thinking. Their instructors often had to repeat things before she would remember and then, when Emily surreptitiously tested her later, she found Gisela sometimes had forgotten. Perhaps Friedrich would be better, she hoped. Neither

Friedrich nor Gisela had had children. No experience at all. She certainly didn't know how to act with parents and could have used their help.

And then, there was the problem of the fear. For some reason, though she tried to hide it, Gisela was afraid of her. It was foolish and a bit confusing, but then there many things she had encountered since leaving school that confused her.

Gisela's German however, was impeccable. Emily, on the other hand, spoke only a little German, which was a huge hole in the plan. If the theft was to be blamed on Germany, then she would have to pass as German and there were a lot of Germans in New York. Better, she thought, to blame it on the French. Her French was quite good.

"She's a beauty isn't she?" Their driver called back. "The Atlantic Falcon."

"Der Atlantikfalke," Gisela replied.

"Yes. That's what they call it. Written on the side over there." He pointed.

"It only flies back and forth between here and New York," the old man said.

"That's about it," the driver repeated again.

Other cars and several trucks were parked near the gondola cargo doors, passing bundles up ramps through large doors in the side. The side of one truck was marked Post Office. Emily liked the picture under the words. It was a picture of a lion and unicorn flanking a shield. It made her think of fairytales she had read. Their driver parked in a patch of empty grass amongst cars, pulling levers to bring them to a stop, venting steam. A car pulled out in front of them, rolling by, showering them with damp cooling vapor.

"Careful!" their driver called out absentmindedly ducking a bit as it passed. Then he sat up and slapped his hands together, rubbing them. "Right!" he said, and hopped out. "Please allow me to help you down."

"I can do it myself," the old man grumbled.

"Of course you can, sir," the driver said, as he made sure the man's foot met with the step rung.

When he got to Emily he said, "And the pretty little lady."

Emily showed embarrassed amusement, which she hoped

was correct.

There was a girl at the door to airship in Lufthansa blue. She was no bigger than Emily and didn't look to be much older. She had a carefree air about her and a strange lack of control in her face. All her thoughts and emotions were out in front. How can she survive like that, Emily wondered? Emily had been plucked from school early and had no practical experience with the outside world.

Gisela found their cabin, their bags already there.

"Do we have maids?" Emily asked.

"No. I'm afraid we have to help each other, or at least you can help me with my corset. Speak quietly too. The walls are very thin."

Emily winced inside. Gisela was not using her German accent as she should. There would be no privacy until the mission was over. And, besides, Emily already knew about the walls, but nodded anyway just to get her to be quiet.

There were Germans on the flight, which was bad. They would see right through Emily, so she had to stay in the cabin and plead airsickness. It meant throwing up her food. To her credit, Gisela added her own occasionally. Sadly, their cabin was small, even with the beds up. Emily used the room she had to exercise and practice eastern meditation. The cabin was also on the wrong side of the gondola to see anything but ocean and sheep when they landed in Brooklyn Aerodrome. Some idea of the city's layout from something other than maps would have been helpful. And Emily just wanted to see it! She tried not to be disappointed, but it had been for Emily, a very long flight.

Brooklyn Aerodrome was big field on the edge of town. She had only seen two aerodromes so far, but she expected they were going to all look alike. This one had horse carriages and a few cars. She had to continue to play sick while she rode through the morning dew to the terminal. Friedrich was there to meet them. Emily flew into his arms, hugging him. He smelled strange.

Brooklyn, to Emily, was all mud streets, dung, and rotten wood tenements, none over four stories. Dogs and filthy children, some shoeless, played in the streets, mixed with cart vendors and traffic. There was no order to it. On one corner she saw a milk wagon with a dead horse. The driver appeared to be crying. On another there was a fight surrounded by a crowd. So many people! The closest she could come to it was the pictures of Bombay, which she had only read about.

They entered an industrial area and the streets quieted. Gisela had her map out.

"Driver, take the next left," Friedrich said.

"Left it is, Sir."

The street looked no different than their last, until they passed a fenced factory yard. Gisela tapped Emily's knee and pointed. That was it.

Emily focused. Two buildings, one with two stacks with smoke rising. One gate, no gaps. A bell for entry. Barbed wire on top. The driveway heavily rutted. No visible guards. Street completely bare and exposed. There wasn't much she could see! Perhaps there was access in the back. She would have to come back on foot. To that end, she began to concentrate on the route between the workshop and their house.

Their new "home" when compared to the earlier tenements, was a reasonably decent three story row house. They were met at the curb by an unliveried manservant who introduced himself as Daniels. Clearly untrained, he met Emily's greeting with a smile and a slight dip of the head. Friedrich had hired the manservant, an Italian maid named Maria, and a cook, Mrs. Ferguson. She was a woman of Germanic origin but without the German language.

Friedrich, after hearing about their trip, suggested resting, but Emily had had all the rest she could stand in that tiny cabin. She set out to explore, first the house, then the streets. She was met in the dining room by a plate of biscuits.

She stopped and frowned at them. Was this a test?

Friedrich entered behind her.

"They're from the neighbors. The neighborhood has been dropping by since I arrived." Then he continued in German. "The Harveys are only two doors south of us. Mrs. Harvey will be visiting for sure, perhaps with their son."

Hayward Harvey, a screw manufacturer, had developed a new concept in armor plate which, according to reports, could revolutionize naval warfare. If he could patent it and bring it to market then the world's naval ship builders would be at his beck and call. England had to have those patents. England had to patent it before Mr. Harvey could. To that end she was to steal the process.

She was to befriend his son, Thomas. Friedrich had told Harvey's wife and son, when they visited, about Emily and when she would arrive. It was Mrs. Harvey who had brought the cookies.

And, as predicted, they came calling that afternoon.

"Emilia!" Friedrich called. "Daniels, could you fetch Emilia?"

"I'll go look," he replied, heading for the coatroom with Mrs. Harvey's and Thomas' coats first.

"Ja, Fatti?" Emily called from upstairs.

Thomas, waiting with his mother in the hallway, snickered, followed by a "Shush!" from Mrs. Harvey. Mr. Harvey was not present.

"Was ist los?" Emily said as she descended the steps.

"We have company," Friedrich replied.

"Oh." She stood at the bottom of the steps, staring at them. "It is a pleasure to meet you," and she gave a little curtsey. "I am sorry first for my English."

"No. Please," Mrs. Harvey replied with a smile. "Your English is fine."

"Thank you," she said with a smile and another curtsey.

"Please, dear," Gisela said. "Let's go to the parlor. Daniels, please tell Mrs. Ferguson that we have guests."

"Yes Ma'am."

Emily held back to see where Thomas was sitting. Though she knew its layout, it was the first time she had sat in the room. Her parents had avoided the seat next to him so she plunked down in it.

Mrs. Ferguson entered with the plate of biscuits. "The tea's coming dears," she said.

Emily eyed the plate. She had had a biscuit precisely once and it had been different than these.

"Emily?" Friedrich said.

"Yes?" She realized they had been talking.

"Would you like a cookie?" He was holding out the plate. Emily noted the word.

"Yes," she said, uncertain.

She looked at Thomas. He was halfway through his, so she steeled herself and took one.

It was round, light, and flat on the bottom. She took a bite, like Thomas had done, and was immediately assaulted by sweetness. She wasn't sure what to do! Where was the tea? She had nowhere to go. She chewed and swallowed and gave a wan smile.

"Thank you," she said.

"What a polite girl," Mrs. Harvey said.

She said, "Thank you" again. This could go on forever she thought.

"Does Thomas go to the city school?" Gisela asked.

Emily looked questioningly at Thomas, who nodded back.

"Yes he does," Mrs. Harvey said.

It went on, with both Thomas and Emily being at a loss as to what to say. She supposed this was how parents communicated with each other. They had taught her how to conduct herself at a proper tea and even some suggestions as to how to proceed at an improper one, but never once did they talk about how to be a child at one.

After they left, she went out and sat on the step in the afternoon sun. Unlike the tenements they had passed, there were no children playing in the street. She thought that she might walk to the workshop to look it over and got up and started walking towards it. It was only eight streets over.

"Emilia!" someone called from behind her. She turned and up puffed Thomas.

"Hello," she said.

"Sorry about my Mom. She loves to talk."

"You call her Mom? That's very English." She smiled, which seemed to give him courage. "Mine likes to talk too."

"Did you come from Germany?"

"Ja, yes. Fatti intends to start a business."

They had reached the corner. Emily looked around.

"Where are you going?" Thomas asked.

"I don't know. I wanted to look. You have no kinder playing."

"Kids?"

"Goats?" Emily was enjoying this. Thomas was easy to lead.

Emily and Thomas on the front steps.

"Children?"

"Yes, children," she replied.

Thomas laughed.

"There are only a couple and they're older. Most of the people here are older."

"Oh." Emily sounded disappointed.

"Don't worry. You'll see lots at school, only it's summer. There're two, next street over. Mom lets me go there sometimes."

They started walking back down the street the way they had come.

"Can I go too?" Emily asked

"Sure."

"Sure?"

"Sure thing?"

"Sure thing?" Emily asked, genuinely confused.

"A sure thing," he replied, then added "Yes!" and laughed again.

"Oh," Emily said, laughing with him.

They walked up the street together and back down again, then went over to Thomas' house where he showed her his toys. They were completely alien to her and quite fascinating. Soldiers, spinning tops, jacks, and a music box which had a horribly painted man pop out of it when cranked. He played baseball during school, a game involving clubs, hard leather balls, and padded leather gloves. Emily listened intently, trying to sort through the rules and play of the game.

"Maybe we can get Pa to take us to a game!" he said.

"He would do that?" His enthusiasm piqued her curiosity.

"He likes baseball too, but he probably won't. He's been very busy lately."

"Oh," she said with disappointment. "What does he do?"

"Our family makes screws," he said, his enthusiasm rising again. "We have a factory." They'd been sitting on the floor, looking at his toy soldiers, so he had to hop up to pull a small box down from a shelf. "Here, look. It's my collection."

He handed the box to Emily. When she looked inside, she saw tapered pieces of threaded metal than ended in notched tops.

"What do they do?" she asked.

"What do they do?" he replied, incredulous. "You really are a girl. They hold things together, like wood and metal. Here. Let's go out back and I'll show you."

He took the box and led her downstairs through the kitchen where they encountered their cook, an elderly black woman.

"Hello Nana," Thomas said, as he opened a drawer.

"What are you up to Thomas?" she asked.

"I'm going to show Emilia how screws work," he replied, pulling out a flattened rod of metal with a handle on one end from the drawer.

"Emilia? I don't believe we've met."

Emily had never seen a black person before, outside of books, and she wanted to stare but chose instead to curtsy. "Emilia

Sommer. It is a pleasure to meet you."

"So polite," she smiled. "But you don't have to do that to an old granny like me."

"Yes ma'am."

"You aren't from here, are you?"

"No ma'am. We come from Essen."

"Emilia just arrived today. She came by zeppelin."

"A zeppelin! My, my. That must have been an adventure."

"It was . . . Spaß?" Emily lied, then looked bewildered.

"Fun?"

"Ja, yes, I think. Fun? Like play?"

"Yes."

"Oh."

Nana smiled a caring smile and asked, "So, would you two like a cookie?"

Emily quailed, but Thomas jumped in, "Yes!"

They each got to pick a cookie from a big clay jar that Nana kept on the counter. Thomas was halfway through his before they made it to the back door. Emily's eyes were darting about, looking for a place to get rid of it.

Finally, she had to take a bite. She could find no privacy. It wasn't as bad as the last, but she still desperately wanted water.

Out through the back porch with its sinks, clothes wringer, and washtub. Through the insect screen door and down the barely painted wood steps, they went out into the flower ringed packed dirt backyard. Emily wanted to look at the flowers but Thomas was heading towards the shed, darting between clotheslines. A rough plank and shingle room attached to the carriage house.

"Do you have horses?" Emily asked.

"We used to, but Dad bought a car. We had to put in a well in the back just to have water for it. Dad says we're getting electricity next."

"Ooo, sehr schön," she said.

Inside the shed it was dark with only the light from the doorway and a cobwebby window to light the workbench. Thomas dug carefully through a pile of junk in the corner, finally teasing out a piece of tin.

"Darn spiders," he said, knocking it against a wall beam.

Then he pulled a block of wood from under the bench.

Emily looked up at the wall beside the bench. It was covered in tools. She walked closer, fascinated. She had never seen their like. People use these to make things.

"So many," she said, half to herself.

"Hardly," Thomas said, as he cranked down the block in the vice. "You should see Dad's real workshop."

"I would like to," she said, as she reached up to run her fingers down the worn smooth wood block of a wood plane.

ꙮ

"Wo waren sie?" Gisela asked. Where were you?

"Ich spielte auf Thomas Haus," she replied. There were servants near, so she stayed with German.

"You will tell us when you go out," she scolded.

"I will."

The conversation had been in German, but its content had been plain to anyone watching.

They had dinner together for the first time in their dining room. Friedrich had, she thought, perhaps lectured her too much on her table manners, especially since her manners were impeccable. But, she knew it was for show.

They tucked her into bed that night, then left to go downstairs. She had moved the room's clock so she could see it, and fell asleep to its gentle ticking, 9:00. Outside, it had started to rain.

She fought her way to consciousness in the pitch dark. As expected, someone had come in later that evening to turn off her lamp, while she pretended sleep. Finding the box of matches on her bed stand, she lit one. Glancing up, she saw the clock showed 3:28. Lifting the chimney carefully off the lamp, she lit and trimmed the wick low. There had to be an excuse for the lit match and lamp, she thought. She had been trained to worry about details and she had no place to dispose of it where the maid might not find it. So she used the chamber pot to provide an excuse.

Her luggage was there. Friedrich had told the maid that it was her responsibility to put away her own clothes. Opening the largest, she found, among other things, her new toys. She had never actually seen what they had given her, but it wasn't the time. Her eye caught sight of dolls and a tea set still in its box, but she moved on to the lid.

Slipping the pull wire from its hooks, she loosened the cover slip and back board. Sandwiched between it and the lid top were her work clothes and a rope and a folding grapple. Dressed in thin grey, she slipped from her darkened room, carefully skipping the steps that creaked, leaving through the front door.

It was cool outside. A sea breeze drifted down her street. She took a moment to enjoy the coolness and the sense of freedom. It was the first time she had been on her own. Their plan was to first try direct assault. A probe of their defenses. If they were lucky, they might get away with simply stealing the plans. They could be on their way back to England tomorrow. Emily didn't question why she was doing this alone or what waited for her back in England.

She drifted down the street through the thin moonlight, a small grey ghost. Drifting until she met the corner. There were no police in sight but the street itself was churned mud. This had been unforeseen. She could cross, but she would be a mess. She would leave footprints and it would make it difficult to hide her clothing afterwards. She looked at the street, and thought about all the streets that would come after. What she needed were rain boots she could dispose of.

&)(&

She was woken by a knock on her door. She allowed herself a noisy moan.

"Wachest du!" Gisela called.

"Ja Mutti."

She looked at the time. 7:10. Had she slept that long? She quickly donned her morning dress.

Mrs. Jackson brought her eggs, potatoes, bread, and tea. She eyed the tea. It couldn't be a test, she thought. She ate sparingly and sipped her tea. It was strange, different than what she had tasted before. More bitter. It couldn't be doing her teeth any good.

Mrs. Jackson tisked at her plate. "A growing girl like you needs to eat more than this."

"Try to eat some more," Friedrich chided.

"Have you had milk in your tea?" Mrs. Jackson asked,

watching her.

"No Ma'am," she replied.

"Well, may I pour you some?"

Emily looked up at her and saw an honest smile.

"Yes Ma'am."

"You are the most polite little girl I've ever seen," she said, and poured a dash of milk from the creamer into her cup. "Now stir it around and tell Granny what you think?"

Emily sipped, and then sipped again. It was good. She smiled and nodded.

"Thank you," she said.

"There," Mrs. Jackson said, and headed back to the kitchen.

After breakfast, Emily took a walk with Friedrich around the block. Ostensibly it was to explore, but mostly to request boots.

"I can see how this would be a problem," he said. "They sell rubber boots. I'll get you some today, but where should I leave them?"

This was a problem. They would be hard to hide. The logical place would be in the carriage house, but Mrs. Jackson slept in the back of the house, next to the kitchen. A kitchen with a squeaky floor.

"Leave them in my room if you can, when I'm there. I'll hide them."

"You still have to put away your clothes," he said, with half a smile.

"I will. As soon as we get back."

As they passed Thomas' house, he stepped out and called to them.

"Hi Emilia,"

Emily turned and called back, "Hello Thomas." Then she waved. The morning sun had come out, the trees that lined the street making spots of light on the sidewalk that danced in the breeze. Thomas came jogging up.

"Can you play today?" he asked.

"I have to put my things away, but after maybe." She looked up at Friedrich, who nodded.

"I could help," Thomas added, hopefully.

"They are girl's things," she said.

"Oh." He frowned. "Yeah. That's right. OK, then after."

"But I will come after," she promised.

When she returned to her room, she was confronted by her luggage. She had no idea what most of it contained. She started with the toys.

She had three dolls, two with ceramic heads and one soft. What was she to do with them? She pulled out the tea set. The pieces were primitive and a bit small, but still pleasant. Underneath she found a wide flat box. It contained a table top and four legs. All she needed was a tablecloth. There were things that she thought must be puzzles. Two sticks linked by string and a spindle, and another pointed spindle with a stick tied to another string. She turned them in her hands, but couldn't fathom their purpose.

At least the tea set she understood. She needed a tablecloth. Looking around she found doilies, but they were too small. Perhaps a towel. On the way to the WC cupboard she ran into Maria.

"Hello," Maria said.

"Hello. Do you have a towel I could use?" she asked.

"Did something spill?"

"No. I need it for my tea set."

"You have a tea set?" Maria asked, brightening. "What do you need it for? So I can get the right size."

"I need a table cloth."

"Oh, a table cloth. A towel won't do for that. We can do better. How big is your table?"

They ended up sitting down together in her room, setting out tea. She found another box that contained blue and pink disassembled chairs. They sat the dolls in them at the table. Maria poured and they pretended to drink and made up stories about the dolls. Before she knew it, it was time for lunch.

Mrs. Jackson had made sandwiches, which were delicious, and she thought might work well for tea, but then she remembered Thomas.

"Oh," she said. Friedrich and Gisela looked up. "I've forgotten about poor Thomas."

"That's right," Friedrich said. "You were to meet him."

She realized she hadn't put her things away.

"May I go?" she asked.

"Yes, of course," he replied.

She excused herself, and started to run to the door.

"No running in the house," Gisela called.

Emily shivered inwardly at her lapse. She was glad this wasn't school.

At Thomas' doorstep, she stopped and knocked. Which brought no answer. She tried the pull, which did. She heard heavy footsteps across a wood floor inside. A big man in a waistcoat, with a great bushy beard answered. He stared at her for a moment, blinking.

She stared back up at him.

"You must be that new friend of Thomas'" he said.

"Yes sir," she replied.

"German, they say."

"Yes, sir."

"Good workers, Germans."

"Yes, sir."

"Dad! Let her in," Thomas called from behind him.

He started, almost as if waking. "Yes. Yes, come in." And he stepped back.

She saw Thomas standing in the dimly lit hall.

"Hello," she said.

"Hi Emilia," he said.

"Did you finish unpacking?"

"No."

"Are you going to get in trouble?"

She blushed, "I don't know."

"You sure you don't want help?" he asked.

Emily thought for a moment. His father was home. There might be opportunity. But then again, she wanted to show him her tea set.

"No. I will finish it."

"That's the spirit," Thomas' Father said. "Germans are good workers son. Remember that." Then Mr. Harvey walked back into the house.

They went up to Thomas' room. Emily almost laughed. It was a mess. In just a day!

She went to his bookshelf. She had no books of her own and

they might make the evening easier, so started looking at their spines.

"Grandma likes to buy me books," he said. "She brings them over all the time."

"May I borrow some?" Emily asked. "I need to learn to read English. I need to learn before school starts."

"You can't read English?"

"Not well."

"That will make school hard. You need to learn."

"Yes."

"You can take whatever you want, but the library isn't far. It's just next to the park. You can take the train."

"Perhaps you can show me how to do that?"

She heard a board creak behind her. When she turned to look, she saw Mr. Harvey looking in the doorway. He nodded to his son, who was smiling.

"Sure. We can go to the library. It'll be fun."

"Sure," she said.

಄ೲ಄

That night she was pleased to see she had woken a little after two. Perhaps last night, she thought, she had been tired after all.

Friedrich had purchased three pairs of boots. Two for missions and one for the day. They were black rubber with ridged soles and high tops. Lacking any other place, she had put them in one of her suitcases and stacked it in the closet with the others.

At the street corner, she turned right. It was dryer there. Despite the lack of rain that day, the mud still stuck to her boots as she worked her way across. She heard a police whistle in the distance. A reminder to be careful. There were police about. On the other side, she took off her boots. They made too much noise and she couldn't run in them. She planned to carry them between streets.

The next street, posed a problem. It was twice as wide, with a great latticework of iron running over it. The overhead railroad Thomas had talked about. It made useful shadows in the moonlight where she could hide, but those protecting shadows were across a long wide moonlit stretch of street. Anything could already be

34

hiding in those shadows as well. Most especially policemen. Looking up and down the length of the street, she could see no place with cover to cross.

There was nothing for it, she thought, and she started towards the curb. But she heard a whistle come from down the street. A dark figure in a light helmet appeared from the shadows right across from her and began running down the street toward the noise. She watched his back as he sprinted away. She felt neither shock nor fear at her narrow escape.

Across the street, she ran into a wall. From the maps, she knew that it was the graveyard. She had to follow it three blocks south then one block west towards the harbor, but there was a train stop in between and almost certainly another policeman, so she decided to cut cross the graveyard.

Unfolding and tossing her grapnel, she scaled the wall, dropping into dark brush on the other side, thanking the stars in the sky they weren't roses. Working her way free into a moonlit meadow scattered with gravestones, statues, tombs, and sheep, she skirted its shadowed edge to a large pond. She heard voices and the glint of a cigarette reflected in its smooth silver surface.

Night watchmen.

But they were easily avoided in the bountiful cover and brush. Her feet drifted across the sweet earth until she saw the south gate ahead. She was off course and stopped to get her bearings.

She had just turned left when a hand reached out and grabbed her arm.

"Got you, lad!" the guard said.

She turned and broke his hold, pushing him down. He hit the grass with an "oof!" A shaft of moonlight lit his surprised face. Emily saw a glint at his neck. His whistle. She grabbed it from his neck, breaking the chain, and ran towards the wall, dashing straight across an open meadow. She made the wall before she heard his first yell. Answering whistles lit the night here and there, but it was too late for them. She was already climbing. The far side was garden to the street and gave her cover as she ran, but she needn't have worried. She met no one else until the workshop.

They expected the Harvey's to have dogs, so she had been

given a packet of drugged meat. What they hadn't expected was the workshop to be lit, its furnaces running, and men at work.

She moved down the length of the street next to the workshop, checking both cross streets. It was dead quiet. That was until she paused at the neighboring fence. A wet nose poked out through a hole and snarled. The neighbors had dogs.

She tossed her meat and backed away across the street to wait, counting fifteen minutes. This time, when she approached the fence, she met no snarls and climbed it easily. Down in the shadows under the fence, she found the dogs. They weren't breathing. She cursed Friedrich for overdosing them. If they had been Harvey's dogs who had died they would have known someone had entered. Around her loomed great piles of scrap metal. Sprinting down a trail, past twisted bent shapes in the darkness, she reached the fence that abutted the workshop. Sparks rose in the smoke high overhead from the Harvey smokestacks.

The fence tilted as she climbed, but she made the tin roof, flattening and rolling over the barbed wire. She tested the roof carefully as she crawled over it. Iron and tin, difficult footing, but there was a skylight ten feet away. Coiling her rope, then spreading her weight, she edged out across the warm metal towards the skylight, wincing at every creak and pop.

She needn't have worried. Inside was a world of noise.

The shop floor was crowded with tools, wood, and crates. There were two big brick boxes, ovens, with railroad track leading out of them. She felt sure they were significant.

She saw two men in dirty clothes sitting in old wood chairs in front of them, one smoking a pipe and the other absentmindedly peeling paint off his chair leg. They were lit by a single lamp.

"Temperature check," the older one said, looking at his pocket watch.

"I checked them last time," the younger man said sullenly.

"I'm too tired to check. You came on later. My shift's almost over."

The younger man growled, got up and headed towards a table. "You shovel then," he said over his shoulder.

Emily needed to be on the ground. She couldn't draw while holding on, so she worked her way back down to the rickety fence and dropped like a rag inside the compound.

In front of her was a large pile of loose black stuff. Her grey would stand out against it. She needed to stay away from it. The first building was a workshop, but she needed to get to the second. To this end, she decided to go around the outside of the yard, the path furthest from the workshop.

Working her way around the yard, she was just approaching the front gate, when it gave a great rattle. Emily turned and ran for the shadow under a wagon.

"Fucking hell, Larry!" a voice yelled. "You locked the gate. Let me in!"

Needlessly vulgar, Emily thought! She could see Larry and his friend in the shop through the big doors, looking over their shoulders, out into the darkness over the pond of water that sat in the center of the compound. That was when she noticed that the rail tracks from the big brick things went into the water. She felt that must be significant as well.

"Ha! Well, I'm out of here," the old one said.

"Lucky bastard," the younger one said.

The old one got up and went somewhere out of sight, then left the building holding an empty cloth sack and a ring of keys.

"Have fun shoveling," he said with a laugh, over his shoulder.

"You're a damn mean bastard," the young one muttered.

"And lucky!" he laughed as he made his way around the pond.

"Hurry up Larry. I've got to piss."

"Piss on the fence. No one's lookin."

"Larry!"

"Hold on." Larry jingled through the keys until he found the right one, then rattled the lock. Emily heard the chain part, then the shadow of the fence broke to reveal two men framed in moonlight.

"Thanks Larry," the new man said, and started to dart inside.

"Take the keys," Larry said, annoyed.

"Oh yeah." He reached back and grabbed them from Larry's outstretched hand.

"Goodnight children," Larry said and then popped through

the gate, leaving it open.

Emily looked back at the workshop, then dashed across the gap. As she neared the office building, she heard a wail from the outhouse, and then another.

"What the hell's the matter with you?" called the man in the workshop.

"They slipped!"

"What slipped?" he replied impatiently.

"The damned keys."

"The keys?"

"I said we needed a hook or something."

"You're kidding." His head popped out of the workshop door, peering into the dark.

"They're down the hole."

Emily caught herself. She had almost laughed, but instead concentrated on maintaining focus. The door to the office building was open. Inside, she found a storage room filled with nothing useful and a small disorderly office. Carefully picking up and replacing papers, holding them in the moonlight, she quickly came to the conclusion that it was all bookkeeping. Their materials purchases might be useful, but she had no time to go through them and no way to copy them. Any theft would be the end of it. She would be discovered. The Institution would have to be satisfied with a drawing of the furnaces.

She sat back in the shadows in the yard, moving from place to place, memorizing the furnaces. When she decided she had seen all she could, she left, drifting through the unlocked gate, a silent spot of grey in the moonlight.

৪০৫৪

She was nagged about the shape of the ovens. She had drawn them accurately and yet they persisted, Emily enduring with diplomatic cheerfulness. There had been no signs of plans nor calculations and the general consensus was that Mr. Harvey must have a study in his home.

But Emily felt odd about breaking into Thomas' home. It was the nicest place she had ever seen and breaking in would be a little like crushing a flower. To be honest, Emily liked Thomas, and his family as well. She had never realized that life could be that happy. It made her think about things, like parents and homes. She was, for the first time, questioning her upbringing.

She managed another half hour of sleep before she was woken for breakfast. After breakfast Friedrich left to take the drawings to the embassy and left Emily with instructions to search Thomas' house. She was tired, but it never occurred to her to take a nap. Instead, she went outside to look for Thomas.

She found him sitting on his front step playing with one of those spindles.

"Hello Thomas," she said.

"Hello."

"What are you doing?"

"It's a top."

"A top?"

"Look." He carefully wound the string around the spindle from the pointed end up and tossed it on the ground. It bounced, then stayed.

Emily watched, fascinated. It stood there, on the tip of its point, without falling!

"Look, you can pick it up," Thomas said, and scooped it up still spinning, balancing it in his palm.

"Can I do this?" she asked.

"Of course. Don't they have tops in Germany?"

"No. At least I don't." Then she thought. "Oh, but I do. Someone gave me one, but I didn't know what to do with it. But mine are different."

"Really? I'd like to see them."

"Sure," she said, and they ran off to Emily's house to play with her tops and tea set.

At lunch, Friedrich could say nothing with Thomas there, but gave her a sharp glance to remind her of her duties. For some reason, Emily felt a spark of anger. The weakness disturbed her. As though there was anyone here to punish her. She smiled an honest smile at herself.

Afterwards, Emily asked if they could play at Thomas' house.

"You have better toys."

"You hardly have any," he replied.

"Yes. Most of my things are coming by boat," she sighed.

Upstairs, in Thomas' room, she was looking at Thomas' soldiers, thinking how they charged bravely into danger. Sometimes to certain death. They reminded her of all the girls who had failed to show up for breakfast. So many had fallen. She thought of Abby and found that her cheek itched. She scratched absentmindedly. Her fingers came back wet.

"Emilia. Are you OK?" Thomas asked.

She was crying! Oh please no, she thought. She was suddenly afraid. She couldn't be crying. Not her too. She looked around in a panic.

"Ma?" Thomas called, then stood up and went to the door to call again.

Emily's sobs grew worse, marching lockstep, carrying her towards death. The tighter she tried to grip them, the more escaped.

"Oh you poor dear." Thomas' mother's arms were around her. "There, there. A new land, a new language."

"I was thinking of a friend," she sobbed.

"You had to leave them all behind didn't you?" She looked up at Thomas. "Please get me some kerchiefs, could you?" Her arms were warm and soft.

Later, they were sitting in the kitchen, drinking milk and eating cookies, when Emily saw that the door to the cook's quarters was open. Inside she could see that it had been converted into an office. There was a drafting table, shelves of books, and a desk littered with rolled drawings and paper.

The idiot! She thought angrily. On the first floor, with a window no less. She supposed that he liked the light and the view of the garden.

"Thomas," she whispered.

"What?" he whispered back.

"You must never tell anyone."

"What?"

"My secret name is Emily."

ⅎϱⅎ

"You are so quiet today," Gisela said, as she dug through

her travel trunk looking for her slippers.

Outside, Emily heard the steady drone of the zeppelin engines as they climbed away from Brooklyn. She didn't reply. She had actually gotten to see their takeoff, but had made no effort to remember it.

"I suppose we haven't given you much time to rest. You've been out every night."

"Yes," she said, her voice dead.

"Well, I'm glad it's over, and we don't have to pretend this time. Would you like some tea?"

She weakly shook her head no.

"Then try to get some rest."

"I will."

When Gisela had finally left, Emily decided to go to the WC. Perhaps a nap was for the best she thought.

She settled on the seat, finally alone. She thought of her toys, left behind, and then Thomas and wondered what she had done to his family.

A wet drop landed on the back of her hand.

She was crying again, but this time she didn't care.

She watched the drops fall in the dim electric light, each one hard and bitter.

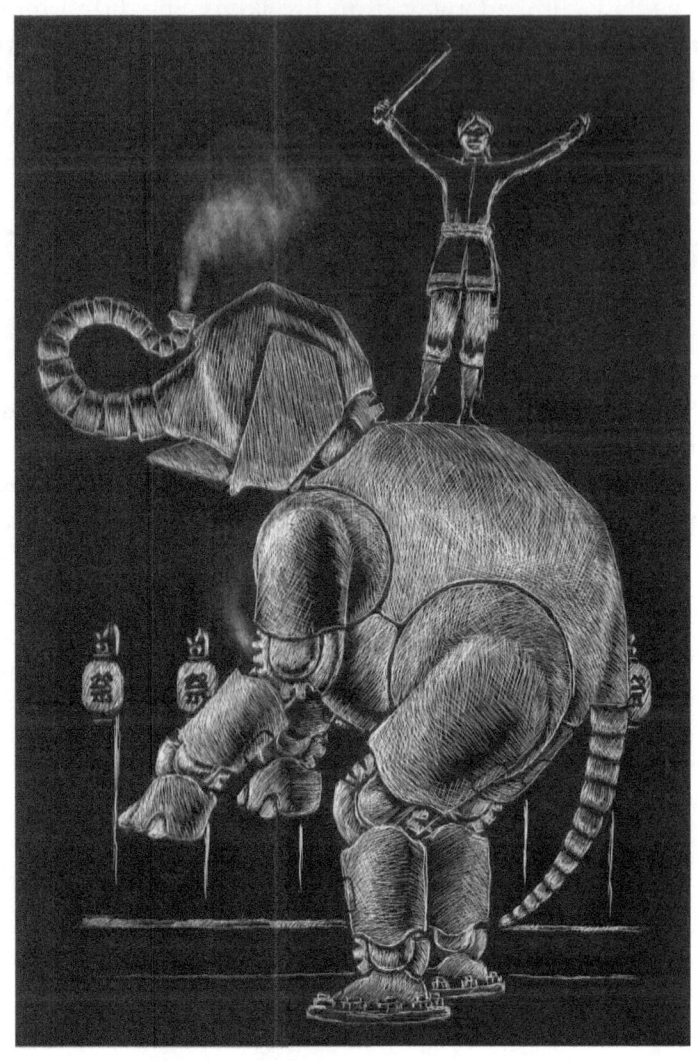

Moulin Rouge

Maximilian Schuster sat in his padded seat, at his tiny table, two uncomfortably close rows back from the stage at the Moulin Rouge in Paris. His drink barely touched, he stared at the stage in disbelief. The dancing women lifting their skirts he could understand, but standing in the limelight now was a man in evening dress pretending to play the violin. What was remarkable was that the invisible violin made sound, much to hilarity of the audience. Max was at a loss until he realized that the sound of the violin was issuing from the seat of the man's pants.

"He's farting!" he heard himself mutter in German. "How remarkable." Then he frowned at his indiscretion. He needed to avoid German.

Max had purposely arrived early. The Moulin Rouge's reputation was such and his tastes not yet so jaded, that he actually wanted to see it. The meeting, if his superiors in the Königsespionagebüro were correct, wouldn't be for another hour. He checked his watch, pulling it out by the fob. Fifty three minutes to be precise. He needed to learn the crowd and the club's floor plan. Neither the thief nor the agent would advertise. They may have already arrived. All Max knew was the time they were to meet, eleven o'clock. He would have to wait to see who had reservations if he were to intercept them. Ah, but reservations to what? The club was large, with many diversions.

Leaving his drink and the tiny table, Max rose and threaded his way between crowded seats to the dark smoky theatre aisle and worked his way back through the laughing crowd. He doubted the meeting would occur in the theatre. The lobby, lined in red velvet and carved gilded wood, was cooler and less crowded. He could breathe, the absence of smoke refreshing. There were two lounges which sometimes also had acts, a bar, the gallery, the dining room, and the very famous Japanese garden.

"Herr Schuster," said a female voice behind him. English.

Max foolishly turned. Before him stood a startlingly beautiful young woman. Thin, clear skinned, her shining auburn hair fashionably pulled back in a flowered bun. She was thin, not yet come into the full bloom of her beauty, but carefully crafted dress, a pale green, conspired however to accentuate the assets she already possessed.

To be honest, Max was stunned. Not just by the sight of her, but also by the fact that she knew his name. In the years to come, he would learn to feign ignorance.

"I don't believe we've had the pleasure of being introduced," he replied, stalling, trying to remember her.

"No," she laughed. "We haven't. I apologize for being so forward. I'm Miss Linford," Emily lied. Girls from the school had no last names until they married. "Emilia Linford."

"A pleasure," Max said, slightly dipping his head.

Max was not tall and she only slightly shorter than he, but her hair and perhaps her shoes gave her additional height.

"Sometimes one cannot wait for society," she continued. "One must step forward on one's own."

"Yes. I suppose that's true." Who was she?

"Don't fret," she sang. "We've never met."

"I wouldn't have forgotten you if we had," he replied, almost stopping himself midsentence, realizing the rudeness of the statement.

She laughed again. What a sound.

"I was wondering if I could convince you to walk with me?" she said. "I would like to see the garden."

"I'd love to, but I'm afraid I have a prior engagement."

"I think that would be me," she said, with a touch of mischief in her eyes.

Max could hardly be called handsome. He was short, thin, with a pale round face split by a wide thin mouth. Was this woman propositioning him?

"I thought it would be best if I found you first," she continued. "Then we could relax and enjoy the evening."

"You have me at a disadvantage," Max replied.

"I do," she said. "Really, that is the point."

"The Royal Institution," Max said flatly.

"Yes," she smiled again. "My partner recognized you."

"Do I know, her?"

"My partner knows of you," she replied. "Come. Let's walk. We haven't much time. I really do want to see the garden."

She took his arm. Max allowed himself to be led. He detected the slightest hint of flowers mixed with the scent of her hair. They proceeded at a gentle pace across the lobby. Max's eyes darting about, looking through the suited men and silk and jeweled women. Some fool had left his hat on a gilt statue of a naked cherub. Where was the partner, he thought?

"Please don't worry. The game is over. My compatriot is a senior agent, an unlikely spot. Armed as well."

"Do they allow juniors weapons," Max asked as they walked into a short corridor.

"No more than they do in Germany I'm afraid. Nasty things. They lead to nasty business. We would be better off if we all had nothing at all."

The corridor to the garden had two paintings, one on each side, lit by gas light. They were large, ragged and colorful, both flat and bold. He wanted to stop and look, his eyes couldn't help themselves, but Emily led him on.

Noticing his attention, she said, "Street artists. They can be fun, but hardly worthy of a proper parlor." Then she sighed. "But the French seem to like them," she trailed off, eyes already on the garden.

Ahead, through an arched doorway, was the garden, its trimmed hedges and walkways lit by streetlamps and endless strings of paper lanterns. Emily stopped at the gate.

Max smiled, despite himself.

It spread out before them, much like a Roman garden, was an ambulation. A long courtyard ringed by a portico roofed in Chinese tile and spotted with glowing windows and closed doors. In front of them was the famous animated elephant. Behind the equally famous tea house. In the center under the colored lantern light was a great open party. It was still spring and there were flowers in bloom.

She led him forward through the portico, past the steam

heaters and the hedge. On the other side was a ring of shallow pools dotted with floating candle lights. They passed a couple, arms unseemingly entwined, heading in towards the lobby. Emily pulled Max a little closer.

"Come along," she said, tilting her head towards him. "I want to see the tea house." She led Max down the path, into the revelers. Ahead was music, the thin reedy whine of the Orient.

They were in time to see the end of the elephant's act. A young Oriental woman, a girl really, was dressed in silk pants and a long tunic, her straight black hair pulled back in a ponytail. She wielded a long crop, which she applied to various parts of the great iron elephant, forcing it to grind into new poses. At the moment it was sitting back on its haunches, legs in the air rampant. With a flourish she leapt under it, rapping its belly sharply then sprinting back around to the front.

The great machine slowly began to lower back to the ground. Halfway down it let out a great jet of steam into the air and a trumpeting screech, like the bending of rusted metal. The crowd stepped back with indrawn breath, but the woman stood her ground without worry, the steam falling as a fine drizzle on the crowd. Max could almost feel the earth depress as the weight of its feet settled. The girl caressed the machine's trunk, which it wrapped around her in seeming affection. Then it reached down and snaked under her raised foot, lifting her up over its forehead. She gained the top with a tumble and stood with beaming smile and arms outstretched.

The crowd erupted in applause as she bowed, then with a giggle of joy, she slid down its back to land with a flourish and another bow to more applause. Leaping the fence, she scampered off towards the teahouse. The elephant itself did not stop, but slowly raised itself back to a standing position. It never stopped, which was part of the charm. It was always in motion in little ways, as if alive, even between shows.

"Come," Emily said. "We'll be late." And she pulled him onward.

"You're bringing me to the meeting?"

"Of course," she said. "I can't leave you. If I let go of you now, my partner would probably do something foolish like kill you."

"Somehow, I find your concern to be less than reassuring."

"Besides, a dead body would bring the gendarme and spoil everyone's evening," she added with a brush of theatrical wistfulness.

Max, despite himself, liked her.

The crowd was dispersing back to their drinks and conversations at small polite tables in hedge shielded nooks, but a sizable group was making its way towards the tea house, along with Max and Emily. It glowed, lit with gas light lanterns, towering above them three stories tall, each smaller than the one below. Its roofs sagged as if its tile were merely draped across its tops. The topmost story could be seen from the street, over the Moulin Rouge's iconic windmill in front.

The music was coming from the first floor.

"We have reservations. We must be prompt. They will not hold them." And she quickened her pace.

The outward facing walls of the tea house were all sliding panels, the rooms behind open like stages facing the garden. In the one facing them were three women, their black hair wound around their heads, held in place with sticks, their faces painted white with red lips. The patterns on their silk robes glistened in the lantern light. They sat on the floor without furniture, only pillows and a very low table, playing instruments, one stringed, a drum, and a small shrill flute.

At the steps up to the first portico, they were met by a man with swords, who looked at Emily's card and nodded them through. Max noticed that she moved silently across the wood floor, despite his certain knowledge that she was wearing high heels. Another man, this time without swords, met them at the top of the steps. He bowed and led them around the side. Max had to stop himself from bowing back. They stopping at a panel at which, the man bowed again and slid back. They had to duck through the low door. Inside was a small paper walled room with a stone floor, almost crowded with the two of them. A stream of water issuing from a bamboo pipe poking through the wall, quietly pouring down in a perfect steady stream into a stone basin.

"We must wash," Emily said. When Max looked confused.

"It's part of the ceremony," she continued. They washed their hands, and at Emily's insistence their faces. A low panel in the next wall slid back and they had to stoop again to pass through.

The next room contained more round cushions, a table, and a small open very clean charcoal pit. Suspended above the glowing charcoal was an iron water pot. The coals warmed the room.

The door had been slid open by an elderly Japanese woman, sitting on her knees, who bowed as they passed. Emily stopped to bow back. At the side of the room sat a pretty young woman cradling another long stringed instrument. Sitting on a cushion at the table, looking uncomfortable, was a tall man in evening dress. He frowned as he looked up at them.

"You were to come alone. Who is this?" he hissed. The Japanese women looked alarmed.

"He's my bodyguard," Emily replied, with amusement.

"Unger," Max said flatly.

Anger flashed in the man's eyes and he started to rise.

"Be still!" Emily snapped, her voice suddenly sharp. The man fell back, off balance, behind his pillow. "Let me make proper introductions."

Max had taken a step back as well.

"He's German!" the man said.

"And so are you," she replied.

Then her mood shifted again suddenly. She added cheerily, "He's here to arrest you."

Unger drew breath.

"Fear not. He's my prisoner," Emily continued. "But he needn't be if things become impolite so let's enjoy our tea before we move on with business."

Then she looked at him directly and addressed him. "Herr Unger, may I introduce Herr Maximilian Schuster of the Königsespionagebüro."

Unger replied with an indecipherable mumble. Emily frowned at him. Then she turned to Max.

"Herr Schuster, may I introduce Herr Gerhard Unger, formerly of the Dieselmaschinenwerke."

"A pleasure to meet you at last," Max replied, with a hint of a smile and a slight bow.

Unger scowled back.

"I suppose I should introduce myself as well. Gentlemen, I am Miss Emilia Linford of the Royal Institution." Then she breathed deeply and added to herself, "I can smell the tea. Sensha I think." She looked towards Max. "Shall we sit?"

"Please," Max replied.

Emily tilted her head towards Max and smiled. "I shall be sad if we are forced to kill you." Then she took the seat across from Unger, lowering herself down with fluid grace onto her pillow, sitting cross legged beneath the ample folds of her dress. This left Max with the third seat between them.

"I would be as well," Max replied, half to himself. He took a moment to decide as to the best way to sit on the pillow, deciding to take his lead from Emily, sitting cross legged.

Emily nodded to the elderly woman to begin, who bowed back.

"I should point out that neither of these women speaks English or German," Emily continued. "Our conversations will be private. Japanese tea is almost as advanced as English. The ceremony began when we entered. I suggest that we observe and appreciate." Then she looked at Unger, "Or at least remain quiet out of respect for a venerable tradition."

Unger scowled.

Another panel opened, startling Unger, but it was a pair of girls carrying a basin and a tray with small dishes and towels.

Dishes and towels were placed precisely in front of each guest. On each plate were small colored objects. Max noticed that the passage of the girls left a sweet scent.

"Candy?" Max asked, looking at Emily.

"Of a sort," she replied. "Do not touch the towel," she said to Unger, who was reaching for it to put on his lap. "It's for later."

"May we eat them?" Max asked.

"Of course," Emily replied. "But take your time. Enjoy the taste."

The old woman had moved to the hearth and began to wash shallow cups and a shaving brush in the basin. The woman with the stringed instrument plucked a string, which, Max noticed, seemed to bring the quiet of the room into focus. The revel outside seemed distant, despite the paper walls.

Max picked up a candy. She was right. It wasn't exactly candy, but he decided it was pleasant. Then the woman began to play.

Max looked at Emily. "It reminds me of American banjo, although perhaps not as enthusiastic."

"You were in America?" she replied.

"Recently," Max replied.

"Were you successful?"

"We are always successful," Max replied, looking at her sideways with a slight smile.

"Of course," she replied, amused by their shared joke.

"How long will this take?" Unger interjected.

"As long as it takes," Emily replied airily.

"I have a train to catch," Unger said.

"Fear not," Emily answered. "Try a candy."

Unger looked at his bowl with annoyance and picked a candy. It was clear that it wasn't to his taste as he chewed, but Emily took no notice. She was watching the old woman whisk tea in a small bowl. Max took his eyes off of Unger for a moment to watch as well. Her movements were smooth and practiced. The light from the hearth fell across the folds of cloth, her bowl, and the dry wrinkles in her skin. The clink as she put the brush down was singular.

She placed the tea cup in front of Emily carefully with both hands. Emily again bowed to her.

"Do as I do," Emily said.

She turned the cup a quarter of a turn, then lifted it and took a sip. Max watched fascinated. She spent a moment savoring the tea, then replaced the cup in exact same spot on the table. She then picked up her napkin and with a single careful movement wiped the edge of the cup where she had drunk.

She then slid the cup over to Max. Max looked at it. The tea was green yellow with remnants of froth from the whisk. Not black at all. He took a breath exploring its aroma. He turned and then lifted the cup, as she had, before taking a sip. Different, but definitely pleasurable.

The next part was more difficult. He tried to wipe the cup

edge, but instead settled for several thorough wipes. He looked up at Emily. She seemed amused. Then he slid the cup to Unger.

Unger was not having it. He reached in his pocket, pulled out a yellow envelope and slammed in down on the table. Max recognized the Diesel factory stationary. The envelope, at least, was real.

"Give me the money now."

The musician missed a note.

"Try the tea," Emily replied.

"Give me the money or I'll ring your neck," Unger growled back.

"Try the tea," she replied again, still perfectly calm, but her handbag was in her hand, clutched close, in plain sight before him.

He lunged across the table, reaching for the handbag. Max lunged as well, trying to grab him by the shoulders to pull him back. One of the women screamed. The table collapsed.

Unger rolled and backhanded Max, then lunged again for Emily, who was hampered by both her skirts and the hot charcoal next to her. He grabbed the purse and began a pulling match with her. Max rallied and lunged again, pulling both Unger and Emily's purse free of Emily. Then Max's training took over. They were rolling on the floor, Max looking for pressure points, bursting through the flimsy panel into the corridor beyond. Women screamed and ran. Max caught Unger's fist before it could land and broke two of Unger's fingers, then tried to gouge his eye, but the larger Unger brushed him aside. Unger's hand was at Max's throat. Max was going for his ear when he heard running footsteps, then more. They rolled on the floor. There were male voices speaking in Japanese. Unger used his size and strength and pushed Max on his back, ready to bring his fist down, when suddenly, he dropped flat and limp on top of Max.

Max looked up at the unconscious man on top of him. A trickle of blood was making its way down past Unger's ear. Max rolled him off before it could drip and stain his suit. Standing over him was a large Japanese man, the man with the swords from the front. In his hand was a kosh. He said something in broken French, which Max understood to mean, "Are you going to be trouble too?"

Max chuckled and shook his head no. Holding up his empty

hands he called, "Miss Linford. Miss Linford, are you all right?" But he received no answer. He picked up her purse, ignoring the man with the kosh, and crawled back through the hole in the panel under the watchful eye of the Japanese man, but she was gone, as was the envelope.

He was, for a moment at a loss, but then began to laugh. He'd been had. There had never been a senior agent!

Jean-Pierre "The Fist" Legrande of the French Deuxième Bureau, confronts Max in a café.

Old Friends

Legrande spitefully thumped down the steps as he exited the gondola. It had been an uncomfortable trip. He had been forced into a state of constant vigilance in the fragile Air Union zeppelin.

His large fingers were a menace amongst the zeppelin's china-like weight saving fixtures and paper thin dishes and walls. Legrande was not a subtle man. He needed substance and weight. The sky was not for him.

Vienna aerodrome stretched around him, damp and cold. The morning rain had fought becoming sleet, the grass already asleep in anticipation of snow. The steam from the waiting cars drifted silver in the thin sunlight, rolling and curling in the slightest of breezes. Twenty meters away grey uniformed men were pulling luggage from the cargo hatch, loading it in long ramped trucks. He did not see his bags. He had nothing to rely on but Austrian bureaucracy, the one thing they excelled at.

A member of the Deuxième Bureau, France's external military intelligence agency, Legrande was in Vienna to secure the work of a certain Dr. Arturo De Varda. An Italian by birth, German trained, Dr. Varda had followed opportunity, coming to roost in Austria at the University of Vienna. Until recently his work was of minor consequence, mostly constituting minor improvements in crop rotation and chemical composition of soil. That was until two weeks ago.

Today was Tuesday. On Thursday, the next issue of Ungarische Zeitschrift für Landwirtschaft und Zuckerindustrie, a Hungarian agricultural journal, would be released containing an article that could change the world. Sig. Varda had discovered a new alloy of aluminum having to do with the isolation of nitrates, vital to both agriculture and explosives. Legrande had no pretentions of intellectualism. He knew nothing of chemistry. All he knew was that the metal would be light and easily crumbled with the fingers. The doctor's laboratory would need a furnace. He should look for the stack. He was to steal all notes on the process and if possible, obtain a sample.

Look for the stack. Legrande chuckled to himself. Vienna was a forest of stacks. All he had to go on was the university itself and an address, Dr. Varda's home.

He took a cabriolet from the aerodrome, his bags in the coffer. Varda lived near the university, which was city center on the loop, der Ringstraße. The city loop was a ring of parks and roads, land cleared with the removal of the city's original walls to ease access to the city center.

But hunger tugged at him. A civilized man might stop to eat, but Legrande was proud of his strength. He was the fist of the Deuxième Bureau. The thought of finishing the assignment early appealed to him. He would strike, win, then eat! So he let the carriage carry him onward through the narrow streets, dark under the heavy sky. He ignored the food vendors, restaurants, and coffee houses, their street tables sparsely attended due to the weather. He had a mission.

The carriage turned down a narrow side street, the cab passing better terrace housing edged in gold and marble, the streets swept clear of dung. There were no street vendors here, no homeless. Ahead, though, he saw the street was blocked by crowds of people. There were police vans trailing thin rolling clouds of steam and smoke in the cold air.

They were forced to stop in a line of carriages and cars. Legrande paid the driver, leaving his luggage and instructions to find a place and wait. He made his way through the crowd. Polizei in their black uniforms held the crowd away from the steps of a house. Detectives crouched next to a body. The victim had been middle aged, just starting to grey, drying blood pooled under its red soaked coat. A man, almost certainly Dr. Varda. Judging by the smeared trail, he had dragged himself out through the front door, apparently looking for help. Legrande couldn't tell if it was a stabbing or a gunshot. Varda, though, was clearly dead. Searching his house at this point would be useless as well as dangerous.

The body was fresh, blood not yet dry. The murderer, he thought, could still be close. He scanned the crowd, running through their faces until his mind began to numb. Then he saw him. It was Schuster! A German agent. So much for love between Austria and Germany.

Legrande fell back into the crowd and began making his way around, hoping to approach from behind.

"Mister," said a small voice. It was some hopeless street rat pulling on his pants leg. "Spare a penny? I'm terrible hungry."

"Not now," he growled in accented German, pushing onward, eyes on his quarry. He heard laughter somewhere behind him but couldn't be bothered by it.

Searching the crowd, looking for Schuster, he threaded through the throng, working his way around to the front – and then nothing. The bosche was gone! His eyes frantically darted about. Then he spotted him. He was back where Legrande had first been standing, giving silver forints to two boys!

Merde! Legrande cursed and felt his pocket. His wallet was gone. His money, his tobacco! Starting forward without thinking, he was stopped by a policeman.

"Halt! Back up. You cannot cross."

"Yes, yes, of course," he mumbled.

By the time he had made it back to the other side, Schuster and the boys had vanished and he had no money for the cab driver which left him no choice but to go to the French embassy to request more.

∞⳺

A quick lunch is almost, but not quite as bad as hunger. Schuster had left him little choice. He had to stop at a tobacconist as well of course. One had to have civilized priorities. That left him with the now dead doctor's university, his last lead. Pointless really. Schuster had surely already been there.

The cab let him out on the Ringstraße itself, in the city's center. Across the street stood the just completed New University, a huge edifice, a five story block of stone columns and domes. Steady streams of students and staff came and went, like lines of ants crawling through its doors.

The entry hall was large and airy, ringed in offices and a great staircase. Behind, spilling in through a row of glass framed doors, was daylight from a large central courtyard.

Stopping a student, he asked for Dr. Varda's office, but received a shrug. And then another. And then another still! It was a big school. Then at last, a useful answer.

"Do you know where I can find Dr. Varda?"

"No, try the doorman."

"Can you tell me where to find the doorman?"

"The windows there. Read the signs."

Legrande growled. He might have killed the rude strutting brat for his insolence, but they were in public and, of course, France

56

came first.

At the doorman's office they gave him a map with a third floor office circled. He ventured off into the labyrinth of hallways and stairs. He only managed to get lost twice. Down a quiet corridor, outside Varda's office, a dejected looking student sat on the floor in front of the office door.

"Is Dr. Varda in?"

"No. I was supposed to meet him, but he hasn't shown."

Legrande needed to search the office. The student had to go.

"I'm afraid he's dead," Legrande said. "Someone killed him."

The student looked up, eyebrows raised in surprise.

"Really?"

"Really."

The student brightened. "You aren't joking?"

"No. I'm with the police."

The student smiled. "Dead is he? That's too bad." Then he rose. "I guess my appointment is cancelled."

"Did he have a workshop or lab?" Legrande asked.

"Oh yes. Across the street on Scholttenstraße."

"Thanks."

As the kid walked off he replied with a genial "No, thanks to you!"

Legrande watched him go, shaking his head, thinking Varda must have been a tough teacher.

With the student gone, he pulled out his lock picks and went to work on the door. It was an easy three tumbler design and he had it open in two minutes. Inside, he found a mess. Schuster had been there already. It was pointless as he'd anticipated.

But something was wrong. It was strange, he thought. Schuster was tidier than this. Then again, he had never heard of Schuster killing anyone when a sound thumping could achieve the same end. He closed the door without searching.

Walking down the front steps, he was confronted by the arrival of a police car. It came chuffing up, followed by a van full of police, bells ringing. He was only a step ahead of them. He would have to hurry.

At the corner, he passed a café. A man behind a newspaper,

coffee cup steaming, said his name, quietly, almost as if it were an afterthought.

Legrande stopped and turned.

There were three couples, a businessman, and a man with the newspaper. The corner of the newspaper drooped slowly, revealing the man's face. He looked up at Legrande with a genial smile.

It was that little hun Schuster!

"Ah, Jean-Pierre," he said, flipping to the next page. "Won't you have some coffee? You might as well." Max liked keeping his competition close where he could see them.

Legrande walked around through the gate, taking the seat across from Max, his face red with anger.

"If we were alone I'd kill you Schuster."

"Perhaps, but I think in this case we are both losers. Really, have some coffee. It's quite good here."

"You didn't kill Varda?"

"No. It was Yakov. I saw him leave. He didn't even bother to wash his hands."

"That's Yakov," Legrande agreed. It made sense.

"Oh. Here's your wallet. I just wanted to slow you down."

Legrande frowned at it. "Thanks, but I have a new one."

"Take it. I don't smoke a pipe."

He grunted, "Very well." Then absent mindedly palmed it, it almost vanishing from the table. "So Yakov has the notes?"

"I don't think so," Max replied. "I think he killed Varda out of frustration. I suspect the workshop and office had already been burgled."

"Then who has them?"

"Who indeed? It wasn't the Russians, Germans, or French."

"Maybe it was the Spiks?"

"Or the English."

"The Institution."

"They're next on the list."

"Then they're gone," Legrande grumbled. "They'll be in a diplomatic bag on the next zeppelin out."

Max frowned at Jean-Pierre. "You give up so easily. I'm sure Yakov will be on that zeppelin."

Legrande marveled at how Schuster had put him at ease. Perhaps, he thought, he should kill the little pest anyway. He was dangerous.

"That's true. He wouldn't care if it was a diplomatic bag or not. But it's a big city. If, assuming it's the Institution and they aren't at the embassy, where can we look?"

Max snorted. "That's easy. It's the Institution. At the best hotel in town."

ଞଠଓ

Emily sipped her tea in the red parlor at the Palais Colburg, a waiter standing at the ready behind her just inside the doorway. It was a blend of elderberry and roses. She admired its color, the placement, how it blended with the tint of the flowers on the cup. The aroma drifting upward.

The Palais Colburg, a former Austrian palace converted to a hotel sat just off the circle, connected by a long statue strewn plaza that was kept free of the poor by the regular sweepings of the local police. The shops that lined it were as exclusive as the water of its fountains pure and unclouded. To stroll was to experience peace. It was the one of the few places in Vienna where she could be sure of walking undisturbed by manure or the homeless.

Her assistant, Roko Nosek, was upstairs making cyanotypes of the stolen notes. He was Bulgarian but well paid. Still, she didn't trust him, thus he had exactly the sheets needed to make the copies and no other paper. He hadn't the education to memorize anything let alone understand the formulas. Thus she felt safe leaving it to him, the smell of the chemicals being unpleasant. Although he was officially unknown to the hotel, he managed to make his entrances and exits through the servant's quarters using an empty room window.

Once she had a copy for the currier when he arrived, to be whisked out of the country, she intended to forge a new version of two key pages, the equations altered, burning the originals. The altered originals would remain as a decoy. She would allow them to be stolen. She had but to wait for her contact and, of course, the others. Every country's spy agencies monitored the journals, keeping track of the competition's discoveries. They all knew. She would sit here with the originals, apparently stranded. She smiled. Britain had struck first, but the game had only just begun.

She smiled and took a sip, then frowned – carefully. One mustn't wrinkle. Her cup had cooled.

"A fresh cup please," she said.

"Yes Milady."

The cup arrived warmed, clean, empty, along with a fresh pot. She looked down, admiring the cup. It was purity awaiting distinction.

œ•ℂℂ

Max moved his hotel from the Imperial to the Palais. He had only to ask. His record and reputation in Berlin justified almost any expense.

France, on the other hand, after the revolutions following the Franco-Prussian war had neither the patience nor the budget to cover the astronomical cost. Legrande had to wait outside, which made him second to Max and even more determined to kill the little Prussian. What were Prussians anyway but uppity Poles, he thought. He had asked for and received a pistol, an aging Lemat, along with twenty rounds. They came in a little paper box deftly packed by the nimble fingers of French factory children.

He was watching the hotel, a block away down Schellingstraße, sitting in a café, his bladder awash in coffee. It was then, when he was sitting at his little iron table in the weak afternoon sunshine, perhaps because of the coffee, that he had an idea. Both he and it felt brilliant.

œ•ℂℂ

"Mr. Schuster," said the servant, his uniform a perfect black, gold trim brilliant. "Your valet has returned with the rest of your luggage."

Max was confused, but determined not to show it. "Yes?" he said. He took a draw on his cigar, enjoying the curl of the smoke in the last of the day's sun. "Send him up to my room."

"Of course," the servant beamed and bowed.

"Oh," he added. "You do have quarters for him? I forgot to ask."

60

"Of course sir." Then he bowed again, backing away.

It had to be Jean-Pierre, Max thought. He chuckled to himself. It was a brilliant move from an opponent he had discounted. It made the game all that much better.

Only three had made it this far. Three that he knew of, he reminded himself. The very clever Stroud, Legrande, and himself. And then, of course, there was the Austrian Intelligence Bureau. They had to make a show, heavy handed and pathetic though it would certainly be. There were no signs of the Spanish, Italians, nor the Turks.

The Japanese and Chinese were major players as well, but distance would put them out of this game. They couldn't know about the journal article yet.

The cigar smoke curled in the thin fall light. He could taste its overtones in the air. A symphony in curling rococo color. He was at peace.

ഇരെ

His room was bare and sparse. A bed with squeaky springs. A chest of drawers. A mirror. A pitcher and basin. The WC was at the far end of a long cold tile hallway. His new uniforms barely fit. The worst was the bell.

But that paled when he considered the bonus, he thought, smiling to himself. The hotel was connected by a second set of corridors. They ran behind every room through hidden doors. True, there were keys, but locks were no barrier to him. He couldn't watch, but he had access to everything. He only had to know where.

The bell rang. Oh, the bell, he thought. He'd break that when he came back.

The very coming at the junior Prussian pipsqueak's call put him at disadvantage. The gun loomed large in his mind. He arrived through the servant's entrance.

"May I congratulate you on your brilliance," Max said.

Legrande frowned.

"Trust me," he added, templing his fingers. "I will make no demands of you."

Oh! Legrande thought. Now I owe him!

"Naturally, we need to keep the pretense when there are

others here. I will, however, expect reimbursement from the French government for your expenses. I have to justify my budget."

"As do we all," he said, catching himself. He almost bowed!

The tinge of a smile on Max's face told Legrande that Max had noticed. This would end in death, Legrande raged under a thin veneer of calm.

❧❀☙

Sergey Yakov grabbed the stripped body of the cargo loader and, with a great heave, rolled it head first over onto his back. Then with slow effort, he gradually stood, carrying the limp strangled body on his back. His target, the laundry bin, loomed ahead. Sergey walked quickly. The bastard was heavy.

He found though, that when he tried to put the body in, the arms flopped forward blocking a clean entry. Cursing to himself, Sergey stepped back, letting the hands dangle just outside the lip of the bin. Then he slid the body in head first, first tucking one knee and then the other in before, with a pained grunt, he tipped the body inside.

He had to love Russia, he thought, to put up with such as this.

The mechanics uniform he had stolen followed the handler into the bin, his new uniform fit well enough. His German would pass if questioned, though he didn't think he could fake an Austrian accent.

Outside, he saw the baggage trucks waiting, still loading last minute baggage from late arrivals. He trotted towards them. A man, a supervisor hailed him.

"You there? Where's Ernst?"

"Took ill. Probably his breakfast," Yakov yelled back.

The supervisor grunted, then said, "Well look lively. Time to go."

Sergey hopped up and grabbed on to the side of the second truck as had the others. Almost immediately it lurched and began to roll forward. Steam, damp and cold, condensed into drizzle that floated back across their faces as the truck turned in the weak morning sun.

They bumped and rolled across the turf towards the waiting

zeppelin. He looked back at the terminal. They were still doing their before flight toast. A foolish German tradition, Yakov thought.

Under the looming grey bulk of the airship, the crew had popped the cargo hatches. They gaped wide six feet above the ground. The trucks pulled up to them and men immediately let go, scrambling up the loading ramps affixed to the sides of the trucks to form human chains. Then luggage began to follow, passed hand to hand up to the waiting zeppelin.

Yakov passed box and bag up while trying to watch for the pouch. He tried to hide his impatience. Then he saw it. A diplomatic pouch. It had been on the other truck. He watched enter the hatch.

"Switch with me," he said to the man above him, and miraculously the man did! He did it again with the next man and was standing at the hatch. So cooperative and unquestioning the Germans, he smiled!

Inside there were men stacking bags. He spotted the heavy canvas diplomatic pouch just before it was covered by a box. Sergey stepped inside and began to move bags. He switched with the man in front of him to get further in. He was inside but he needed a place to hide. He was so close. He just needed a moment of privacy.

"That's it!" called the supervisor. "Back to the trucks."

His fellow workers stacked the last few bags and turned to the ramps without looking back. Sergey lagged behind, then hugged the bulkhead between the doors. They didn't check, he chuckled to himself! How did they ever beat the French?

The doors slammed, one, two. Before they had even finished dogging the latches, he was at the bag, his knife was out, lock-be-damned, worrying at the stiff canvas. It cut with great difficulty.

"What do they make these things out of?" he muttered.

He finally worried a hole in it and started sawing at it, but it wouldn't tear!

The floor lurched under him as he finally split a seam, the bag's contents spilling on the floor. The airship was taking off! Pawing through the contents, he could see nothing. Letters, forms, reports, nothing! They weren't there!

He climbed back over to the nearest hatch and began to undo the dogs one by one, the hatch finally bursting open to wind and sun, the cold air an assault on his face, the grazed grass twenty feet below and picking up speed. He had no choice. He jumped.

ଓ୦ଓଔ

Luncheon was served in der Rotspeisersaal. Emily's table sat under a shaft of sunlight. The color pattern of the tea cup, the unbroken gold gilt rim reflected and played in the sun across the table cloth. It all framed the sensuous golden brown of the tea. Her first cup, she sighed.

Her contact, the currier, hadn't shown. Was he delayed or dead? She sent Roko out early that morning to make inquiries, but she had to wonder if it was time to run for the embassy with the notes?

"Is this seat taken?"

Emily frowned for a moment. There were many empty tables. Then she recognized him. He was a German agent. Unlike her currier, the enemy was on time. It had been two years since she had last met this one, at the Moulin Rouge, but his name had appeared often in briefings. He had become a very active and successful field agent.

"I'm sorry," she said, "but have we been introduced?"

"Yes we have," the man said with a smile. "But I must apologize if I have you at a disadvantage. Surly you must remember me. I remember you so well." Then he looked at the seat. "May I sit?"

Did she have any choice? Then she brightened. "Please excuse my lapse and do sit. I believe you are Herr Schuster."

"Please call me Max. We shared tea two years ago."

"Yes, I remember. Please, call me Emilia." She laughed then. It was the light music he remembered. "We were at the Moulin Rouge. How can you call that having tea?" Emily relaxed. Any pretense was foolish.

"But it was. I wish we could have finished. I was devastated when you disappeared."

"I had to put duty before propriety." Emily radiated empathy.

"So must we all," Max sighed, choosing resignation. A waiter appeared.

"May I bring the gentleman anything?"

"Tea as well," Max said. The waiter bowed and left. They had over forty kinds of tea, but he knew there would be no confusion. The cup arrived warm.

Emily watched him pause over the cup. He was drinking in its light. Then she looked up at him. He seemed a studious man, mild natured. It was a mask of course, and yet still the truth. She tried to remember him that night two years ago. It was his laugh, she thought, as she had fled the tea house. He had seemed genuinely amused by her betrayal.

"May I pour?" she asked, now intrigued. He promised to be an interesting opponent.

"Yes, please," he replied. He watched the tea spill across the white porcelain. She could see the quiet intake of breath as its scent drifted.

Yes, she thought. This will be interesting.

Max, for his part, remembered the girl he had met and then marveled at what she had become. Her porcelain skin, the curve of her lips as she smiled. Her hands moved with the precision of a ballerina as she poured, the practiced silence of her movements. He had decided, he would not let go of this thread. He too was interested. Like two moths around a candle, both dangerous, they each loved to dance with death.

"I was assigned to Japan for a short time and managed to finally experience the full ceremony," he said.

"You did?" Emily suddenly forgetting herself, envious. "I've tried to get assignments there, but they insist on keeping me close to home." It was her turn to sigh. "I do wish to go."

"I resented the assignment at first. It was a long way to go, even by airship." And then he began to tell her about Japan, wondering at how good it felt to relax with honest conversation with an experienced colleague.

≈∂≪

"My employer has asked me to deliver a note to a Miss Linford," Legrande asked at the desk. "Do you know the room number?"

Legrande had watched Schuster at tea from the servant's alcove. He was with Linford, an English agent. She certainly had the notes. If not on her person, then in her room. Ah, but which room? He had to find it. He smiled to himself, he might search her as well, even if he found the notes in her room.

"We will deliver it for you," the manager said curtly, as if he should have known. "We do not give out room numbers. Hand it over."

This took Legrande by surprise. He didn't actually have a note to deliver. Not even a piece of paper. "He asked me to do it," he replied.

The manager just stood there waiting.

"I'll ask if he wanted it delivered by the hotel." And then Legrande made a hasty exit. He could hear murmuring behind him. Damn it, he seethed! He knew nothing about being a servant. He felt sure he had damaged his cover.

Back in his room, he paced. Linford had the notes. She was trapped. If she left the hotel, if she fled, she couldn't get far. It was a long way to England and the embassies were surely being watched by the Austrians. They had to suspect the reason for the murder. He yet again cursed Yakov. All he needed now was her room number. Then there was a knock on his door.

"Who is it?" he called.

"The house detective," came the reply.

"Merde!" Legrande cursed. A little tin house cop. What else would rain on his day? He would take care of this quickly. But no sooner had he unlatched the door when it banged open, knocking him back and in spilled four big men in suits.

They said nothing and he didn't try to fight. They knocked him back and flung him painfully face first against the wall, handcuffing him. Then they searched his room and found his gun and papers.

Another entered, obviously in charge. "Georges Legrande," he said, as he thumbed through his passport. They had gotten it from the front desk.

"Yes, that's me."

"French."

"Yes."

"Why would a German of no social standing have a French valet?"

"Because he's rich?"

The man tisked as he walked over and punched Legrande in the back. They let go of him as he sank to the floor choking for breath.

"Georges, Georges, you are known to us, as is your employer." He said "employer" as if it were a joke. "Why would the French and German's be working together?" Legrande couldn't breathe, let alone answer. But then, they really hadn't expected him to. "Could it be what was stolen from Dr. La Varde? Hmmm?"

They were Intelligence Bureau, Legrande thought. He managed to cough, tasting blood.

"Tell us all about it and then we'll send you home."

What had tipped them off?

"That's it. Breathe in, cough, then we'll start."

"Linford," he managed. There was no point in not talking. Holding out only gave the English the notes.

"Linford? You asked about her at the desk."

"She has everything."

"We're searching her room. If she has it, we'll find it. Did she kill La Varde?"

"Never with a gun," he managed, and then began coughing again. "How did you know?"

"A Russian with a broken hip."

"Yakov. Schuster saw him. Says he killed La Varde."

"The Russian won't be going home. You though. You are a good boy. You might make it." Then he kicked Lagrande in the gut.

෴

The elevator cage rattled upwards. Max waited quietly next to the elevator boy. As they rose, he scanned each floor, one after another. As his head topped his floor, he could see his room down the hall. The door was open. A man in a suit stood outside, legs spread, arms crossed.

"Don't stop," he said to the elevator boy. "I've forgotten something. I've decided I want the fifth floor."

"Yes sir."

They rolled past. At the fifth floor the boy pulled the lever back, expertly stopping within a quarter inch of the landing. Then he reached out and slid back the gate.

"Please watch your step," he said, as Max stepped out into the carpeted hallway.

Max had to work fast. The Austrians had arrived far too quickly and in force. Something had tipped them off. He had to rescue the notes. She almost certainly had them in her possession. He headed for the stairs, listened, and then ran down.

Emily was just leaving the tea room when Max found her.

"Emilia," he said, trying to hide his need to catch his breath. "I think we need to take some air. Perhaps a walk."

She looked at him calmly. "Do we have visitors?"

"I'm afraid so."

She laughed gently, as if he had just told her a joke, then blushed and said airily, "We must find a side door."

Max chuckled.

He was impressed by her composure. No one looking could have known that their situation was dire. The Austrian police were crude and brutal. They made their way towards the end of the wing, away from the lobby. The first thing they had to do was to lose the servants that were always watching.

₨₩

Chief Inspector Leo Mosele watched the damage unfold as they took apart Emily's room. They had found the notes almost immediately, pinned to the backside of a curtain, but they could have been a decoy. He had to be certain. To this end his men were breaking apart the furniture and inspecting the pieces. Behind stood the hotel floor manager, who flinched and whined to himself as each piece hit the floor and shattered.

"Sir, sir," a young voice called running down the hallway outside. Turning, Mosele and the floor manager were confronted by a boy in hotel uniform.

"Sir," the boy started again, out of breath. "I'm instructed to tell you that they are in the Red Tea Room." Then the boy's eyes went wide as he saw the room. "Oh!" he said.

The boy's reaction only encouraged the floor manager to whimper more.

Mosele rolled his eyes and called, "Christoph, Jonathan,

Nico, with me. The rest of you keep looking. She made copies. I can smell it." Then they ran for the stairs.

It was only after he made it to the first floor that he realized that he had no idea where the Red Tea Room was. So they ran to the lobby, catching stares from guests and staff all the way, and grabbed a bellhop to lead them. By the time they had made it to the Red Tea Room, the doorman there said that they were ten minutes gone, pointing down a hallway.

ಬಡಚ

Max paused in the hallway. "Do you have any money?"

"In the hotel safe. Do you?"

"In the safe as well, and the desk has our passports."

"There can't be that many of them," Emily smiled. "They can't be everywhere."

"True." Max looked amused. "Shall we then?"

"Let's," she said, and they departed. The hallway stood empty.

Mosele and his men thumped down the now empty hallway.

"They could slip out any window. Nico, Jonathan, start searching the rooms. Christoph, follow me. We'll check the service passages. Whistle when you find them."

They all took off at a run, Nico and Jonathan knocking on doors then breaking them in when they had no answer. Once they had passed, Max and Emily walked back to the lobby. The desk was mobbed with people asking questions, exclaiming when they got answers, some demanding to check out.

"Herr Brunner. They're here." The desk clerk had seen them approach.

"What is it? More trouble?" the manager said, looking up from his checkout forms. "Oh, it's them! The police are looking for you."

Max and Emily looked confused and surprised. "For us?" Emily said.

"We wanted to complain about the noise and running," Max said.

"Why would they want us?" Emily looked worried.

"They probably want to question you," the manager said. It was punctuated by a scream and exclamations of guests as two men in suits dragged the limp bloody form of Legrande through the lobby.

Emily looked at Max in panic.

"We want to check out," Max stammered.

Emily, looking pale, turned on the manager, "Yes. We want to check out!"

"I don't blame you one bit," the manager said. The police were not popular in Austro-Hungarian Empire. "They didn't say to detain you," he added with a sigh of exasperation, sliding over two forms and gold fountain pens.

೧೦೦೩

They sat together in the jitney as it clopped over cobblestones worn smooth by centuries of feet and wheels, winding its way through the weaving maze of cars, carriages, and wagons. They had requested that their things be sent to the aerodrome.

Max sighed. "Any suggestions as to how this can end well?" he said with exasperation. The AIB had arrived too quickly. They were all trapped. He had the plans sitting next to him, but how to get to them? And how was he going to get out?

"It does look grim," she replied wistfully. "Still, the day is young."

They were speaking French for the benefit of the driver, whom they hoped did not.

"Embassies or the border," Max said.

"The embassies are always watched. Now, doubly so, but if we move quickly. . ."

"There's the small point of which embassy and which border. I believe my dear that you have the notes," Max said tiredly. "I have no desire to fight with you, but my duty is clear."

It was Emily's turn to sigh, but she said nothing.

"If they were left back at the hotel," Max continued. "Then they are in the hands of the police, or the cleaners, but I don't believe you would allow that to happen. A decoy perhaps, the real notes still in your possession. I have to check." He looked sad.

They were interrupted by two men running beside the

carriage horses pulling them to a halt.

"Hey! What are you doing?" The driver yelled just before he was pulled from his seat by a third man and beaten in the street.

Max was on his feet, but was confronted by a common dark skinned man with a black mustache. "Sit!" he hissed, showing a short barrel revolver under his coat, pushing Max back into his seat. Another man in better clothes pushed in next to Emily from the other side, another revolver in hand hidden by his coat as well. His dark well-trimmed hair and beard set off his blue eyes.

"Ah, my Tatlim. It has been far too long," the blue eyed man said.

"Hello Yusuf," Emily said. "Yes. It's been a long time."

The carriage bounced as two men climbed up into the empty driver's seat, pulling the carriage back into the road's center. They felt a third climb on to the back.

"Max, may I introduce Yusuf Avci of the Teskilati Mahsusa, the Turkish Special Organization. Yusuf, this is Maximillian Schuster of der Königsespionagebüro, the Kings Espionage Bureau."

"It is a pleasure," Yusuf said with a smile, reaching over Emily with his free hand to shake.

"It's no trouble at all," Emily said, as she leaned back to give him room. It was clear she felt the gesture had been rude. Yusuf didn't seem to notice.

One of the men in front of them had picked up the driver's whip and flicked the horses back into motion.

"We have the greatest respect for your organization," Yusuf said to Max. "I hope our relations will remain cordial." Then he looked at Emily. "I was broken hearted when you stood me up in Budapest. You could have at least left me a note."

"Yusuf, I was kidnapped."

"Kidnapped? Who!" he said with outrage.

"The Bashiazouk."

"The scum. Tell me who and I'll have them killed!"

"I already killed him," Emily replied, wistfully.

He grunted. "I hope it was slow," he said, gesturing with is gun. He reached in his pocket and handed Emily a cigarette case. "Can you get me a cigarette? My hands are busy," he said, glancing at his gun.

Max watched this exchange with fascination. "I take it you're here for the notes as well," he said.

"Of course!" Yusuf said. "Why else would I be here. The food is terrible and the women are cold." Emily put a murad in his lips, then lit it with a match.

The intimacy bothered Max.

"The hotel is crawling with AIB," Yusuf continued, the thick smoke from his cigarette swirled around them. "You are the only two who escaped." Then he laughed. "Poor Legrande. They got Giovanni too."

"Giovanni was there?" Emily said, with a look of surprise.

"You didn't spot him my Tatlim?" he said with a look of worry.

"No," she said. Max noted a fleeting flash of embarrassment.

"Have you seen Yakov?" Max covered.

"Yakov's here too?" Emily asked.

"Not at the hotel," Max said.

"They got him as well," Yusuf growled, with a dismissive wave of his cigarette.

"Well," Max sighed. "He was a poor player."

They sat quietly for a bit, cigarette smoke trailing from Yusuf's mouth.

"What do you plan to do now?" Max asked.

"It's simple really. Either the AIB has the notes or one of you two do."

"Yes," Max sighed. "That was my thought too."

"Must I call you Maximillian?"

"Max will do."

"Max. We have a house. We will take you there. Then we will settle it." He frowned at Emily. "I hope you will cooperate. If you fight, you will lose. There are too many of us."

Emily rolled her eyes and sighed. "Yusuf, you may search me personally."

Yusuf tried to hide a slight smile with another draw on his cigarette. "I will enjoy that," he said quietly.

&&

The "house" was a wreck of a medieval two story side by side down a short rutted dirt alley, crisscrossed by laundry, almost blocked by a broken wagon. The street was crammed with dirty children, dogs, out of work men, and old women. They all seemed to be Turkish.

Yusuf seemed to feel that he needed to explain.

"They come here with promises of work," he said, tipping his head towards a sagging balcony. "But it's just filthy Austrian lies. They treat them little better than slaves. So now they are stranded."

"They're poor," Max said. "What if they talk?"

"Never. We are the only ones who help. These children wouldn't be alive but for us."

Max frowned. This will make escape difficult, he thought. If they ran, the whole street would be after them.

A boy, almost a man, ran over and took the horses, holding their bridles as they stopped.

"Elmas!" Yusuf called to him. "Take the carriage where it will be found by the police. The man we stole it from was not rich."

"Yes Yusuf."

"Let's see what Dicle has made for lunch," he said as they climbed down.

As they entered, an elderly woman at the door, her body draped in cloth, reached out to take Emily's arm.

"No, no," Yusuf chided. "She will eat with us."

The woman scowled, but bobbed her head and left.

It was a European house with the normal entrance hallway, its floor foot printed by dirty boots, but a parlor off to the side had been expanded by knocking out a wall. The room was filled with cushions and long low tables. Lamps were lit to supplement the dim light from the single front window.

"I'm not supposed to be in here," Emily said to Max, with conspiratorial glee.

"Ha!" Yusuf laughed. "If I let you out of my sight, you'd overpower our women and be gone over the roof tops."

Emily smiled at the complement. It was true, she thought.

They had meat rolled in cabbage leaves, soup, borek, and sour bread, while laying on cushions picking food off the tables. It ended in coffee in little cups, which Emily only sipped. They talked of past adventures, the fates of known compatriots, and the doings of royalty. It all would have been very pleasant except for the screams and breaking glass.

They came from the street end of the alley.

"Bok!" Yusuf spat, putting his coffee down. "It's the AIB. We must have been spotted."

"You left a witness in the street," Emily chided.

"I am too kind hearted," he said. "It will get me killed someday." Then he leapt up, pillows scattering.

"Follow me," he said, sprinting for a door at the back. They were up, running through the kitchen, women already crowding through the far door. Emily and Max started to follow, but Yusuf stopped them.

"No, not that way." He dashed into a dark pantry with no door. Pushing aside a barrel, he exposed a small trap door which he kicked aside, jumping down the dark hole. "Quickly," he called from below.

Emily gathered her skirts and jumped, and then Max. It was only five feet down, but a low tunnel sloped away downwards. Max pulled the trap door closed. It had an inside latch. A match was struck in the darkness. Down the tunnel they could see Yusuf lighting a lamp.

"Very nice," Max said, admiring the tunnel.

"The neighborhood has many of these. There will be Turks climbing out of the woodwork everywhere. Hopefully, we will be lost in the confusion." The he picked up the end of a rope.

"Ah, but today is special. This isn't the police. It's the AIB. We will not be coming back. Are you ready to run?" he laughed. Not waiting for an answer, he took off into the darkness pulling the rope along with him. They followed, Emily's dress sweeping dirt down from the sides of the tunnel.

They heard the trap door behind them. A thump, then a crash as wood splintered.

"Damn they're fast," Yusuf said. "Max, help me pull." He passed the lamp to Emily as she squeezed by him, and held up the end of the rope for Max. Together they pulled and something gave in the tunnel. Figures were advancing down the tunnel. Someone yelled "Halt!" but he was cut off by falling timber and dirt as the tunnel fell, crushing the men beneath it, blotting out the light from the trap door. Then the three of them ran, crouched down, dust and dirt at their heels. The tunnel ended in hole knocked through an old brick foundation, covered by a wooden wall. Yusuf pushed the wall, which gave way, turning out to be a large crate. Coughing in the dusty air Max and Yusuf pushed together, shoving it in little jumps until they could squeeze out into a dark basement.

"Help me push it back," Yusuf said, nodding at Max. "They will be searching this house soon."

Upstairs, they ran through the house, Yusuf pausing only to yell, "AIB is coming. Run, now!" They sprinted out through the back door into alley, following Yusuf. Soon the street filled as people spilled out doors, men and women carrying children, dogs barking and dancing, everyone looking to escape. The alarm spread through the neighborhood.

A police van stopped at the head of the alley, venting steam and policemen. Yusuf turned to the right down a narrow branch that ended in a wall. He kicked in a door in that led to a dark hallway with light spilling down from a narrow stairwell. He shut the door behind them by wedging it with a splinter of wood broken from the door jamb. Then it was up the stairs to the window and the roof. The window's eve was well worn. People went that way a lot.

There were men sitting on landing under the window smoking. They heard music upstairs. It was, perhaps, a mandolin, and a baby crying.

"The AIB is coming," Yusuf said. "Spread the word."

The men groaned and stood, one sprinting upstairs.

They helped Emily through the window, tossing away their cigarettes lest they burn her dress. She thanked them graciously.

Climbing and hopping over the roof tops, grabbing clothing from clothes lines as they passed, women following, yelling at them, only to quiet as Yusuf waved them to silence. Through another window, at the quiet top of a stair landing, they stopped and rested panting.

"We need to change," Emily said, stepping to the center of the landing. Not waiting for them, Emily pulled two wires from the back of her dress and literally stepped out of it. Max and Yusuf almost fell down the next flight. Standing there in her corset, stockings, and bloomers, she picked up a dress, stolen from the clothes lines above, and pulled it on over her head.

"Help me," she said, turning her back to show the buttons.

The men jumped and began to pull the dress down, doing the buttons. Emily appraised it.

"Close, but large," she said. "My shoes are wrong too." She looked at the men. "How does it look?"

They were still in shock, but nodded their heads.

"It needs a belt," she tisked. "My hair still up?"

They nodded.

"And a hat." She smoothed her dress. Then she looked at them. "You both are a mess. Change!" she commanded, and they jumped again.

They emerged in a more "Austrian" part of town, now in common clothing. They hailed a jitney, putting distance between themselves and AIB.

⟡

Emily insisted on shopping, landing them in Kärntner Strasse, spending some of their limited funds to finish their wardrobes. Then they stopped for tea at a café on the shore of the Danube, the evening light painting the far shore orange.

When they had settled and ordered, Emily addressed them.

"Gentlemen. This must end tonight. I'm not falling asleep unless I'm alone. I intend to have a good night's sleep."

"Then I propose we search each other," Max said.

"That won't do," Emily sighed. "I'm afraid I have the notes. They're in a pocket in my corset. Really, I'm at a loss as to how to proceed."

"We could burn them," Max suggested.

"What?" Yusuf snapped.

"Burn them," Max continued. "No one wins. Blame it on the AIB."

"You would do that?" Emily said, puzzled. She realized he meant it. It had been a long time since she had been surprised by someone. She was impressed.

"It's out of the question," Yusuf said. "It would be

dishonorable."

"It's practical," Max said. "I doubt the winner of any contest between us would be in any shape to escape the country."

The waiter came with their tea and they had to wait to continue while he left them spoons, sugar, crème and napkins. Emily looked at Max again and then poured the crème and spooned the sugar. An odd feeling stole over her. After a moment's thought, she decided it must be regret. A cold evening breeze blew in from the river. She was glad they had bought coats.

"Bah. Your tea is too weak," Yusuf mumbled, taking a sip and then another. "And you drink it made of anything. I'll find it has woodchips in it next."

Emily laughed. Max grinned, but said, "Yes, possibly. But that's not the point. The tea doesn't matter. It's the same as your coffee. A point of commonality."

"Yes," Emily added. "It's a basis for conversation, or in our case negotiation."

"I can see that, but then we should have ordered coffee," Yusuf said.

"You would have complained about that too," Emily said, putting her hand on his arm.

Yusuf laughed, then said, "Yes my Tatum, I suppose would have."

Emily looked at Max, eyes smiling. "Max, you haven't tried your tea."

"This milk is off. I think I'll ask for more," he replied.

"I'll do it," she said, and she waved to the waiter.

"It has been a long day," Yusuf said. "I'm very tired."

Max looked at Yusuf and smiled. "Don't worry. It's almost over."

"Yes madam?" the waiter said.

"The milk is off. May we have some more?"

"Of course."

At that moment, Yusuf's head hit the table, spilling his cup.

"Yusuf?" Emily looked alarmed. The waiter stepped back in surprise.

Max shook him, squinting at his face. "You know? I think he's ill."

"Oh my," the waiter quailed. "Is there a doctor in the house!" he yelled, still staring at Yusuf.

Max looked up at Emily with concern. "I hope it isn't contagious!"

"Contagious?" Emily yelped.

"Yes. He just came in from Turkey!" Max exclaimed.

"Contagious?" echoed at nearby tables. "Turkey?" Chairs scraped as people stood to look.

Max stood and tossed some coins on the table.

"I think we should leave," he said.

"Yes, quite." Emily stood clutched her purse to her chest, looking down at Yusuf in horror and distaste.

Coins were hitting tables, chairs scraping.

Max took Emily's arm and they left quickly, their waiter just inside the café door, arguing with the manager in panic. They made their way towards the strand and the river, laughing. Another strange feeling. She rarely honestly laughed.

"That was very clever of you," Max said, amused. "I almost didn't see it. If I had any, I would have used it too."

"It was the best solution I could think of," she said wistfully.

"It's been pleasure. I'm actually sad it has to end."

"Yes. It's strange, but I feel the same way too." The sound of her own voice confused her. It worried her that she wasn't her usual self. She began to doubt her judgement.

They stood together for a moment in a small alley, the evening twilight painting the world blue and black. The lights on the far bank shimmered in water as it swirled by. A quiet moment as they gathered themselves.

She struck first, a simple flat handed jab at the throat. He blocked, aiming a palm punch at her chest to knock her off balance. She turned in the Japanese style, brushing his arm aside, stepping in to trip him, but he continued to turn, countering in the Japanese style as well, catching her arm in hopes of a throw. She tried to hook her leg under his to reverse it, but lost her balance in her skirts and ended up against the wall, somewhat amazed and winded. No one beat her!

Max punched, but she brushed it aside and perhaps because Max was thinking the fight foolish, his counter was ill prepared and failed as well. She pushed away from the wall, turning away from his next attack, tipping him off balance into a throw that ended up with him against the wall. He hit hard, winded, admiring her technique and to be frank, the look in her eyes.

Emily, curiously found she didn't really want to hurt him. Confused, her punch was slow and so he slowed his block. She closed in reaching for his neck, but he brushed her hand away, following through, reaching for her hair. And for the first time in Emily's life she let go, falling forward instead, their lips meeting, his hand caressing her neck, her arm dropping as she lay in his arms in the gathering darkness. They had reached consensus.

∞∝

The notes were never recovered.

Toria and her dog, Mack.

Lady in Waiting

After thirty one successful field assignments, at the ripe old age of seventeen, Emily was put out to pasture. Stationed as Lady in Waiting to Princess Beatrice, the youngest daughter of Queen Victoria. Schooled girls were in great demand in the top echelons of English society. They collected and deflected gossip and intrigue, acted as bodyguards, and kept errant royal children in line. "It was, after all, for the good of the crown," she had been told. But for Emily, it was a tedious and boring assignment that, short of

Beatrice's death, looked to be her last. Most of all, she hated wearing black.

Surprisingly, she found a companion in Beatrice herself, who was as much a prisoner of her mother as Emily was of her. The Queen's youngest, her last link to Albert, the queen kept Beatrice locked by her side, always on call, working as her personal secretary. Far worse, at the ripe old age of 21, the queen refused to allow her to marry. Every suitor had been rejected. The last, a German prince, had been killed by a Zulu! It looked to be a dreary end for them both.

At least, she thought, they were on their way to the Mediterranean, out of that cold wretched sooty London winter, on the train to the Riviera. Not that there still wasn't discomfort to be shared. The royal entourage took up four cars, their end of the train being closed off from the rest. This didn't, of course, block royal visits forward, much to the discomfort of the train's other passengers. Prince Edward, travelling with his family, practically took over the smoking car displacing the rest of the train's males, and the dining car was awash in royals and their little princes and princesses.

Emily reported to the Queen's assistant, John Brown, a big Scot; he was an honest manageable man who constantly wandered the corridors trying to keep order. He was, as well, bedding the Queen. Everyone had standing orders to always be on the lookout for evidence, which the Institution removed – one way or another.

Her Institution contact was Alfred Kinsey, Prince Edward's secretary. Thin and balding, he was not among the schooled. Emily couldn't help but respect him anyway. He exuded a practiced professionalism that marked him as a difficult opponent should he choose to be. As to others, Emily was sure there were more, but members of the Institution were difficult to spot, even by their own kind.

Emily was not an aristocrat but sat suspended in the uncomfortable grey area somewhere above the servants and below the nobles. The train held many of her class, doctors, advisors, aids. They were the trusted professionals who made life easy for the royal family.

She shared a cabin and maid with Victoria, or "Toria" as she was called by all. A princess, a daughter of Prince George, seventeen like Emily, and probably the most vacuous woman Emily had ever met. She was sitting on her bunk across from Emily with her dog, an aging scotty who she rescued daily from the baggage car and practically crippled with love.

"Who's a good dog, a good dog," she cooed. "My Mack is. Aren't you my furry boy?"

The dog groaned as she scratched it, his tongue bobbing along with her scratching

Emily eyed her and wondered. Why had she be sentenced to this cabin? Had it been their ages? Or perhaps she was there to make sure Toria didn't hurt herself. She grunted as their maid Nance pulled on her corset strings.

"You have hair all over your dress," Emily said.

"You can see it?" She looked down. "No you can't. My Mackie's black, besides Nance will brush me won't you Nance?"

"Of course my lady."

Emily sighed as Nance helped lift her dress over her head, wondering if the queen would relent and let them wear something besides black at the beach. She could smell the dog.

"May I go on ahead, my lady?" Emily asked. "I need to see to the princess."

"Hmmmm?" She had been rubbing her nose against the dog's nose, growling and making woo, woo, woo noises at him.

Emily tipped her head towards the door.

"Oh yes. Go," she said, waving her hand at the door.

"Thank you," she said, curtsying.

Emily gratefully retired to the narrow corridor and wandered towards the dining car, leaving Nance reaching for the clothing brush. Ahead, Ducky and Missy, were huddled together whispering, which could only mean trouble. Ducky and Missy were the daughters of Alfred, fifteen and sixteen respectively. They had tried to make Emily's life a living horror, forcing her to constantly curtsy, spilling things on her dresses, and trying to trip her at inopportune moments. That was until they found that Emily could inflict pain without leaving a mark. Everyone, even the royals, looked forward to the day they were safely married, preferably in separate corners of the empire.

They edged to the side of the corridor to let Emily pass, eyeing her with alarm as Emily continued on to the next carriage; an endless stream of dreary rain soaked French farms rolling by the train's steamy rain streaked windows. The bridge to the next car was tented, but still cold and windy. They were barely out of Paris and still had days to go until the sun shone.

Inside, the dining car was filled with cacophonous laughter, Edward having just told a joke. She found Beatrice by following the queen mother's cackle. Beatrice was, as always, sitting next to Her Majesty, who sat in a big leather chair that had been brought in from the smoking car. Dressed in black, the venerable ancient sat cupped in her comfort, sipping tea, surrounded by her children. Most of the car was dressed in black, like a pack of coal miners coming up from the deeps, Emily thought.

Emily glanced towards the teen tables. Thanks to forced breeding, most of Her Majesty's grand children were around her age, the dining room currently sporting six young princes and princesses. Unsurprisingly, most of the empty seats were next to them. She chose a seat across a small table from Dr. Smith, the queen's dentist.

"Pardon. Is this seat taken?" Emily asked.

"Nae, lass," he said, putting down his newspaper and nodding towards the seat. "Take it."

Dr. Smith was a balding man in his mid-sixties, whose square face shunned facial hair, unlike the turbaned Indian Sikh bodyguard seated behind him who seemed to sprout hair from every pour. Emily noticed the date on the doctor's newspaper. Only three days old. He must have picked it up in Paris.

"Have I missed anything important," she said, lifting a finger to summon a waiter.

"Nae. Another damned war in Burma. Boer trouble. Oh, here's something. Jumbo the Elephant died. Sad that. Put on a good show. Did you see Barnum?"

"I'm afraid I was in Constantinople."

"Heavens! With your parents?"

"Yes," Emily lied.

The waiter made a wide circle around the teen table with a roll of his eyes and approached, towel over his arm, menu card in hand.

"Nae been farther than Berlin myself. German food is nasty stuff," Dr. Smith continued. "The food gets worse the further you are from England."

"Oui madame?" the waiter said.

"Le café s'il vous plait," Emily replied.

"Bien sûr," he replied with a smile.

"Damned French. Can't understand a word they say," the doctor mumbled.

They chatted while Emily watched Beatrice work her needlepoint, the queen laughing at another joke that Beatrice clearly didn't get. They brought her coffee. She added milk and stirred. When she looked up again, she saw that Beatrice was making her way towards her table.

"Emilia?" Beatrice said.

"Yes Beatrice?"

"She wants an audience."

"Her Majesty?"

"Yes."

Emily sighed.

"Better go lass," Dr. Smith smiled.

Emily left her untouched cup and followed Beatrice. She suspected the queen needed diversion. The smelly old bombast required a lot of it. A chair had been brought for her to the queen's table. Emily curtsied low, waiting permission.

"Your majesty," she said.

"So this is your Emilia," the queen said to Beatrice.

"Yes mum."

"Sit," she to Emily, waving back handedly towards a seat.

"Thank you, your majesty," Emily added. It was the first time she had been asked to sit at the queen's table.

The core of the British Empire stood around her, staring, curious. What was the old woman up to? She supposed they were waiting to see, as was she, what the queen would do.

"Beatrice has been telling me about you," the queen said. "She feels you've become friends." The queen looked at her slyly. "But you're one of our special girls aren't you."

"Yes ma'am."

"You're a trim thing," she said, eying her. "They always are Bea," she said to Beatrice. "You've done well keeping your dresses clean while staying with Toria." The queen sighed, "She and that dog."

"Yes ma'am," Emily replied, with a small kind smile in deference to the queen's joke.

"But it couldn't be helped," she replied. Emily was surprised at the apology. "Beatrice and I worked on the assignments with great care."

Emily thought that Beatrice wouldn't have put her in with Toria, so it had to have been the queen's decision.

"It's good you're there to look after her," she clucked away. "She needs it." Then she focused on Emily directly. "I'm told you're quite accomplished for someone so young. Perhaps even a prodigy," the queen continued.

"I wouldn't know ma'am."

"That is almost certainly true Beatrice," the queen said with a smile. "Listen carefully to her."

Emily had no answer to that, choosing instead to radiate pleasant attentiveness.

"And I don't believe you've had your coming out have you?"

"No ma'am." It was a rhetorical question, Emily thought. She had neither family nor sponsors and the queen would have been there if she had.

"A pretty young woman like you should be married," she said thoughtfully. "It's not proper."

"No ma'am." Inside, Emily quailed. Marriage was the end of it. A better end than dead, but still – an end.

"See Beatrice? Look at the control." She looked at her daughter and lectured. "You mustn't be fooled. The last thing she wants is marriage. You must get to know them. They're the backbone of the Empire."

She turned back to Emily. Beatrice had put down her needlepoint as well. She looked worried.

"Still. You must be married," The queen said. "It just isn't proper."

"Of course," Emily replied, matter-of-factly. And then to

herself, "Someday."

"No soon," Victoria scowled at Emily, contradicting her, eyeing at her closely. "It's decided. You must wed. We are not through with you yet. You are dismissed." And she waved her away.

ℬℭ

Emily and Beatrice were sitting in Beatrice's cabin, Beatrice still working on her needlepoint. Beatrice had been telling Emily about the Riviera when she abruptly changed the subject.

"You really don't want to get married?"

Emily paused for a moment. How honest should she be? Beatrice was, after all, a member of the inner circle, the Royal Family, however naive. She would have to play this carefully.

"Her Majesty is correct," she said.

"But don't you want a home of your own? Don't you want children?" Beatrice sounded confused.

"A home," Emily replied wistfully. "I do want my own place. Somewhere where I can be alone." She looked out the window. "With a garden." Then she brightened. "And unlimited travel expenses!"

"No children?"

"No."

"I don't understand."

"Listen to your mother."

Beatrice frowned. "Not even a husband?"

"Don't frown. It makes wrinkles," Emily lectured.

Beatrice looked surprised.

"That does too," she chided. "If I had a husband, there every day, I suspect I'd eventually be inclined to kill him." Emily assessed Beatrice critically. Surprise and perhaps fear. Good, she thought. Beatrice was taking her seriously. "Which is why I'm curious as to what Her Majesty is up to."

"I'm certain she's thinking of nothing but your welfare."

"I'm sure you're right. That and England. But what is she thinking?" Emily replied, half to herself.

"You would kill your husband?" Beatrice was still back thinking about that.

"It's likely. Eventually."

"Dead?"

"It'd be an accident." Emily replied, as if that excused everything.

"Emilia." She said with disbelief. "This is so unlike you."

"Perhaps," Emily answered, smiling to herself, referring instead to her telling the truth rather than murder. "But Her Majesty seems to feel that you need to understand us. I suppose, since you're to be her secretary, you need to know."

Beatrice stared at her.

"I'm being honest," Emily said. "Consider it a complement." But Beatrice had turned away from her, furiously working on her needlepoint.

Emily stared out the window for a bit, watching the French countryside, thinking about the Queen. What she didn't tell Beatrice was that she wouldn't kill her husband if she were ordered not to.

☙⊗ଷ

Alfred Kinsey bumped into Emily in the corridor as she was making her way to the WC. It was innocent, the corridor narrow. They apologized. When she had closed the door, she checked the accustomed pocket and found the note. They were to meet on neutral ground where there could be no possibility of impropriety. In Edwards's cabin.

He said nothing as she entered, waiting instead for her to close the door. He was thin, tailor dressed, his treasured mustache and hair carefully trimmed and oiled. He waved her towards the opposite seat.

"Sit," he said.

She sat in silence and waited.

He had his portable desk out and was writing. He was always careful. The desk had folding shields that could be lifted to provide privacy. She couldn't see what he was doing.

"Apparently the queen likes you," he said, still writing.

"Oh?"

"You are to be married."

"So she said."

"She told you and you didn't report it?" He looked up, his

eyes boring into her.

"I didn't think she was serious," Emily replied levelly.

"She's serious. It means you can continue."

"I can continue," Emily replied, as if she were discussing laundry. Inside she felt a spark of excitement. She could continue! The alternative was unthinkable, a real marriage or even death.

"It will be in name only. They'll pick a suitable match. In the past, it's usually been an officer, or someone from the foreign office. Someone with an excuse to be absent. If his job is risky and he dies, so much the better."

"I see."

"I'm glad you do. It means promotion as well."

Emily nodded.

"When," she asked.

"Not until the season. There are forms that must be followed. You are to be presented and claimed."

⊗⟩⟨⊗

The train curled and snaked its way through the foothills of the Alps, working its way toward the coast. The weather was still chilly, but the sky was blue and the air dry with altitude, all moisture having been scraped off in its passage over the rocky mountain tops. Emily gazed through the clear window in Beatrice's cabin, enjoying the lack of humidity.

Beatrice, her mother now trusting her with more important tasks, had written up the orders for Emily's marriage. Apparently it meant promotion for them both.

"It's positively unholy," Beatrice said.

"It's the best I could expect," Emily replied.

"You should stand up to them."

"It's what I want Beatrice. I don't want marriage. Best to get it over with."

"Will you have to bed him?"

"I don't know."

"What will you do if you have to?"

"My duty." Emily sighed.

"What if you have a child?"

"I won't."

"But what if . . ."

"I won't."

Emily had returned to staring out the window at the hills when she noticed an airship pacing them. It had to be a fast ship. They were making at least 20 miles per hour. Emily's heart skipped a beat.

"Beatrice, I have to go."

"Where?" Beatrice asked, but Emily was already opening the door.

"Go to the front of the train. Be brave," Emily said as she dashed out.

"Be brave? What does that mean?"

Emily ran down the corridor towards the back of the train. Crossing the bridge, she could hear the airship's engines laboring to catch up over the whipping wind and the surge of the train engine.

In the quiet of the car she ran around the corner, past the WC, only to run into a Sikh, one of Her Majesty's bodyguards.

"Airship pacing us, closing," she said quickly.

His head bobbed as he tried to follow her. Then he blinked.

"Where," he asked.

She pointed.

"I will spread the word."

She found Edwards door, knocked and burst in. Edward and his wife looked up at her in surprise. He was sitting on a seat, the other folded up. Apparently he had been watching his wife undress.

Emily couldn't care less.

"Airship, pacing us, closing," she said. "Where is Alfred?"

His eyes went from shock to anger and then to fear.

"In the dining car."

Emily rolled her eyes. That was two cars away, in the opposite direction of her gear.

"Arm yourself, spread the word," she said as she closed the door.

She ran for her cabin down the hall. Toria was there with one of her endless romance novels and, of course, Mack.

"Oh, Emilia." as if she hadn't slammed the door open and run in. "How is Beatrice?"

Emily shut the door and pulled the back of her dress loose, the buttons rattling against the wall.

"What are you doing?"

"Toria," she said, using the familiar. "You need to go to the front of the train."

"Oh but Mackie and I are happy here," she trilled. "Aren't we sweet'ums?"

Emily pulled the wires that held the seams of her corset and shoes, dropping the whole of her clothes on the floor, stepping out of it in a single smooth motion.

"Emily! The window is open. Someone will see."

"Get to the front of the train," she said again, this time with emphasis. Reasoning with Toria was pointless.

She pulled one of her cases from under the bed and dropped it on the seat. Inside the lid the covering pulled loose, then the panel, to reveal her night gear. Pulling on her grey jumper, then her rubber climbing shoes, she took out and hefted her grapple and knife.

"Emily?" Toria squeaked, sudden dawning panic lighting her eyes. Mack jumped up from Toria's lap, spinning in confusion.

"Go to the front of the train," Emily repeated.

She buckled her knife belt and grabbed her grapnel and rope. She could hear shooting. Rifles. Probably the Sikhs, she thought. The engines of the airship thrummed through the cabin roof.

Reaching up, she grasped the latches of the window, raising it open. The wind drowned out Toria's exclamations. Above her, the airship loomed, only fifty feet away. Emily leaned out and threw her grapnel into the wind, over the top of the train and pulled it back until it caught. Then she was out the window, Mack barking after her.

On top of the car, she saw ropes dropping from above, dark shapes, men, clinging to them. One of the Sikh's killed one, the man's body twisting as he hit the ground, bouncing away behind them, but their fire was largely ineffective as they were firing from the train bridges, at a bad angle.

As she crouched down on the top of the train car, she realized that they hadn't noticed her yet, the grey of her suit

Emily deals with an anarchist.

blending with the train top. She had the first move. The Sikh's kept up a steady rain of bullets, but the underside of the gondola was steel. They were probably doing no harm other than to make slow leaks in the airship envelope. More figures followed the first wave, the first wave having just reached the train top, the engines of the airship drowning out everything except the rifle shots.

As the closest man's foot touched the train's roof, Emily gave him a push which sent him tumbling down, dashed over and over against the rocky slope. Grabbing the rope before it blew loose, she began to climb, the next man's feet above her.

He kicked at her, but she grabbed his foot and began to climb over him, trusting him not to commit suicide by letting go.

"Dimmit . . .!" he cried in French as she neared his head. He could do nothing.

She grasped the rope above him with her left, drawing her

knife with the right, and, dodging his desperate hand, slit his throat.

Her eyes were on the gondola above as his body tumbled down, blood spraying in the wind.

The other climbers only realized what was happening as she cleared the airship railing, firing from below with their pistols, too late to catch her. Only two men were left on deck. She threw her knife. She had been aiming for the head, but a shift of the deck left it in his neck, his blood arcing as he turned.

She approached the man at the wheel, the captain, hands open. He was no anarchist. He was probably their prisoner.

"Take off," she said in French.

He nodded in a panic and reached over and pulled back on the throttle. The engines roared, the airship surging forward.

Retrieving her bloody knife, she edged back to the railing and glanced down. Most of the men were climbing back up the ropes to rescue their ship. She laughed and then with her razor sharp blade, she slit the ropes one by one.

৪০৫৪

They landed in Grasse. With no anchor ropes, the airship could only bounce across the turf, the ground crews chasing after it. Emily pushed out the captain and followed, rolling on the grass laughing, the airship came to rest broken in the rocks and trees at the edge of the field. The gendarme caught the captain, but couldn't find the girl. She disappeared despite her blood stained jumpsuit.

But when the train finally pulled in Grasse station, she was waiting with new dresses and luggage. They were stolen or store bought, but all of reasonable quality. Best of all she had found beach dresses. None of it black! The queen's tailor could alter them for her. This much at least, she felt, they owed her.

Tesla's coil, lighting Paris.

A Simple Matter of Power

Maximilian Schuster stood staring at an eight foot tall block of pure steel. It was standing squarely and immovably in the center of the English exhibit hall in the Exposition Universelle in Paris, the 1890 World's Fair. He was there as part of the delegation from Krupp Industries. And, incidentally, Max was also a spy.

He preferred to be called Max. It set people at ease, and setting people at ease was important in his line of business. Max was short with a wide face. His hair fashionably greased back. No one would say that Max was handsome, but he was impeccably dressed.

This block, a product of Bessemer Steel in England, was a challenge. A clear attempt to put a thumb in the eye of his employer, Krupp. But that really depended on its quality. Just pouring a block that size was a major achievement, but if its quality was good then Krupp would have no choice but to tip its hat, and lose a great many contracts.

Really, Max thought. There was only one way to tell.

Walking slowly around the exhibit, he waited for the moment, that moment when all backs were turned, then he stepped over the rope, up to the corner of the block, opening his pocket knife with his gloved hands as he moved. Reaching up, he dug the blade into the edge of the block.

"Arrêt! Qu'avez-vous fait?" came a voice from behind him. He didn't stop, but worked his knife further into the block's edge." Arrêt!" Hands pulled him back from the block.

It didn't matter, he thought, as they escorted him to the exhibit hall office. He'd found out what he needed to know. It was soft, barely better than iron. He had pried a piece loose. It was safely in his pocket.

The guards finally let him go and left him in a pavilion office seat. He had barely managed to straighten his clothes when he was confronted by the hall director. He showed his ID and accepted their lecture about respect for one's competitors. Then he was politely booted out.

Outside the building in the cold morning air, standing on the street between pavilions, the morning sun shining, he watched the crowds of visitors dodging the marvelous electric trolleys that rolled back and forth down the street.

Towering over the fair, still covered with workmen, was the great tower, the front gate of the fair, being built by Gustave Eiffel. A monumental work of genius. Already the tallest structure in the world. A plum contract for Krupp by the way, who supplied a large portion of the iron.

But the real prize was coiled around its towering top. 3.2 miles of sheathed copper cable. A great coil. The promise of wireless transmission of electrical power. If it was successful, entire cities could be lit with no need to modify existing infrastructure. The genius behind the device was a diamond in the rough, a Serb by the name of Nikola Tesla.

Tesla had been a first tier engineer of Edison Machine Works, but had broken with the company and formed his own, Tesla Electric Light & Manufacturing. Word was that Edison, known for his stinginess, had reneged on a verbal contract with Tesla and now Paris was about to witness the result. Tesla had vacated his Menlo Park laboratory and moved straight to Paris and the fair. Max's orders were make sure that when Tesla finally located his new labs, after the successful demonstration of his coil mind you, it would be in Germany.

Blue black in the gathering morning coal haze, the polished sphere at the top was taking shape, the basic structure of tower itself firmly defined. But there was clearly much still unfinished. Much of the tower was still bare iron, without primer or its final coat of red. The tower itself would not be finished by the opening of the fair and Max couldn't see how Tesla could possibly make his expected test date in two weeks as well. But tickets had been sold. Bleachers and outdoor tower view cafes were being built. He didn't think they could afford to postpone.

A female voice behind him quietly laughed. "My dear Max,"

Emily said, Lady Stroud now. Her marriage was common knowledge, though she had told no one of her knighthood, a Knight Companion. "If you wanted near it then you should have asked."

At eighteen, a year younger than Max, she was fashionably dressed even for Paris. She worked for the English delegation. Emily too was a spy. A spy for the Institution and the British Crown. She had married in name only to a British colonel. A pretense which left her free to move about alone in proper society.

He turned to face her with an embarrassed smile. "The point was, my dear, that you weren't to know," he said.

"Then you should have waited two hours for tea."

Max could only shrug his shoulders and smile. "It seemed an opportune moment."

"I'm sure it must have," and she laughed that sweet laugh again.

"Would you care to walk with me?" he asked.

"It would be lovely," he said, and they began to stroll, their breath fogging in the December air.

An electric cable car hummed by, its pantograph arching, leaving ozone in its wake. Next to it, on the roof, was the coil housing and battery boxes for Tesla's demonstration. They had to dodge it and in the process she dropped her umbrella. It was Japanese. They both stooped to pick it up, accidentally bumping, her hip soft and warm. Max picked it up, dusting it slightly, handed it back.

"Here you are my dear."

"Thank you," she said with a smile and a slight tip of her head.

Max looked up and squinted at the tower. "The tower is taking shape."

"It is magnificent! Have you met our amazing Mr. Tesla?" she asked. She took his arm and they began to walk.

"No. Not yet. I saw him at the fair's opening ceremony."

"I have, at a party given by the French delegation," she replied. "He's an odd one."

The French were ahead of them both, providing Tesla with complete funding for his fair demonstration.

"Ah, the French," Max said.

"Yes, quite."

They walked together down the lane always towards the tower.

"Our government is under a great deal of pressure from the coal industry to stop Tesla," Max said. "They feel that houses powered by steam should be the future."

"They've been very active in England as well. Have you seen them here?"

Max smiled. "No. I'm afraid not, but I'm sure they are here someplace, just out of sight."

"Who else have you seen?"

"My dear, I have seen too many. We should throw a party for all of us and invite M. Tesla," Max replied with a chuckle.

And then there was that laugh of hers again. Men had been ruined by that smile.

"The world is begging for his invention," he said.

"As long as it works."

"It works. I've seen it."

"Where?" She looked squarely at Max.

"I saw his original proof of concept demonstration."

"How brave of you to cross a war zone."

"I didn't. I was in China when the orders came through. I went by zeppelin, der Pazifikclippershiff. I got to stop in Hawaii."

She smiled, "I'm envious." Then out of the blue, "Will you give me that piece you took from the block?"

"No," he replied. She had already tried to pick his pocket, but Max had palmed it and moved it to his sleeve pocket. He looked at her and said, "Emily. I owe it to Krupp. It's simply the truth." He smiled and continued. "Besides, this isn't our game. Our game is up there." Max looked up again at the tower. "In two weeks."

⁊ಅಈ

"Nikola, why don't you come to bed," said Mme. Leclair. Tesla had met her at a party the previous night and she had been great fun. It was amazing luck to meet someone who spoke Serbian, even if she did it with a French accent. Only now, she had become somewhat tedious with her constant hints at the wonders of France.

As was often the case, Tesla had found himself awake at 3:00

AM, full of ideas. But the formerly fun Mme. Leclair only wanted to drag him back in bed.

"The equations are not correct," he said, sitting nude at his desk. "Thanks to the budget, we are short of cable. This will alter our voltage. It has to fall within the receiving coil's normal variance or the whole experiment will fail." He scribbled equations on a sheet of paper, trying to remember the constants. "It's a matter of motive power," he mumbled as he wrote.

"I don't understand you Nikola."

"If I don't do this, it will fail," he said, flatly.

"Oh," she said, shifting around and laying at the edge of the bed, her chin propped up on her arms, her ample breasts pressing over the edge of the mattress.

"I can't think when you sit like that," he snapped.

"Oh?"

"I can't think!" he yelled. Tesla stood up knocking the chair back. He grabbed a handful of paper and threw it at her. "Stop it!"

She pulled back onto the bed, pulling the covers over her. She had misjudged.

"Out! I have to work!" Tesla yelled at her.

"Please, Nikola," she said.

"Out!" he yelled.

"Nikola!" she cried.

"Out! Out! Out!" he yelled.

Mme. Leclair crawled off the bed, scrambling for her things. "I need to dress."

"Out!" cried Tesla, and shoved her towards the door. She tumbled naked into the hotel hallway. Tesla threw her things out after her. Then slammed the door. Several doors opened in the hallway to see what the commotion had been as she began to pull on her dress. One of her shoes was still inside. She would have to walk barefoot.

Tesla picked up his chair and sat back down at his desk. Numbers dove at him from his notes. He needed more cable and he needed it quick. Damn them for cutting his budget! This was a bad as Edison.

ဆာcs

98

"Honestly Giroux, this whole thing has been a waste of funds," Allard Marion said. He twirled his pencil thin mustache with his fingers nervously. Allard was the head of the French General Confederation of Labour, and a favored Whist partner of Rèmy Giroux, Directeur D'Exposition, the fair director. Allard was having lunch with Giroux and the very quiet Dr. Roland Blanc, a French Canadian employee of Edison Electric.

"Dangerous too," Allard continued. "Who knows what effect all that electricity will have on people and . . . and things!" He waved his hands through the air. Today's lunch was more about business than friendship. Today, Allard was working as an advocate in defense of the pipe fitters union and coal interests. A non-official, but still well paid position. His friend Giroux was not unhappy with that, at least as long as he received his share. The democracy of bribery was common in France.

They were sitting at a table in the French exhibition hall café, sipping wine, waiting for their lunch to arrive. The huge hall above their heads, a latticework of glass and iron, echoed with the sounds of people and machinery. The café itself being its own building within the hall, had "outdoor" tables like any street café. It even had pidgins that had found their way in and were begging at their feet.

Both men thought Blanc a cold fish, but a potentially powerful ally. They had met at one of the multitude of parties that revolved around the management of the fair.

"Allard, enough," Giroux replied. "I've done what I can. I may already be in trouble."

Dr. Blanc had so far, been staring over his spectacles at his glass, but seemed to rouse himself. "You've done well. Your diversion of funds has left him short of cable. This will force him alter his design, to add compensations, which will introduce chaotic eddy currents."

Giroux and Marion stared at him blankly.

Blanc stared back for a moment, looking puzzled. "Harmonic distortion," he said. Still silence. "It will make his electric field unstable."

This seemed to break the spell. "This is good?" Marion, offered tentatively.

"We have a plan and this can only help."

"A plan? Edison?" Girox asked.

"Perhaps," Blanc replied.

Girox, suspicious, eyed Blanc. "Involving . . ."

"A secondary coil."

"Which would cause . . ."

"A very annoying noise, possibly vibration."

Girox visibly relaxed. "Not something catastrophic."

"No. But it will be very unpleasant. Tesla must fail, but he must not be damaged professionally if we are to reunite him with our fold."

Marion lit up, "Oh! I've seen it haven't I? It's in the American exhibit. That display."

"Yes. How observant you are. I'm being forthcoming with you because I need a favor for this to succeed."

Girox squinted at Blanc. "My neck is already too far out."

"We need a man near the Tesla's control room. We need to know when he throws the switch. Timing is important."

"Oh, I could do that," replied Girox.

"No. You are too important. You could be called away or distracted. This job does not require anyone of consequence. Just proximity."

The complement brought a hidden smile from Girox. "Of course."

"Like a workman or a janitor," added Marion.

"Precisely. But he must be one of ours," replied Blanc.

"Why?" Girox said.

"There is a communication device involved. Its operation requires training."

"Not only would he be foiled, but we would be rid of him as well," Marion said with a smile. "This is brilliant!"

It was Blanc's turn to hide a smile. "We think so."

§⊙CR

Tesla was desperate. The parameters of his design were very strict. In order for the Earth and the atmosphere to operate in harmony to carry power to the streets of Paris he needed precise frequencies and power levels. His voltages were going to be too low for a reasonable level of ionization in the upper atmosphere to occur. He had to have more cable, and for this he was willing to make a deal with the devil. Ah, but which devil? They were all chasing after him, France, Germany, the US, even Belgium. It was France who had shorted him. To hell with them. But then they were the closest. The Germans or the Russians might not be able to get the money to him quickly enough. His vendor had the cable. He just needed the money.

Suddenly he found that he had collided with someone. He had been walking down his hotel hallway. Why? Oh yes, breakfast, he thought. He'd quite forgotten.

"I'm very sorry," said the little man.

He reminded Nikola of an owl. He had a German accent too. Nikola was immediately suspicious and checked his pockets. His billfold was still there. "It's nothing," he replied, and continued towards the elevator.

At breakfast, several people tried to engage him in conversation. And then, there was that very pretty English woman, but he was no longer in the mood for that. On the way back to his room, two more people bumped into him. This hotel is populated by drunks, dolts, and Punch and Judy clowns, he thought!

By the time he had arrived back at his room, he had decided that he would ring all the local embassies to ask them to send someone around for lunch. Then he could take his pick. It would be at one o'clock, downstairs.

He stood at the door and felt around his pockets. He had misplaced his room key! He felt around again to no avail and then tried the door itself. Locked! But there, in the keyhole below the knob, was his key. He had left it in the door. Breathing a sigh of relief, he opened his door and entered. Everything was where he had left it and no one had come to clean yet. He threw his coat on the bed and lay down with the house phone and began to ask to be connected with the embassies, one by one. Then to fill the time until lunch, he sat with his equations, trying to adjust the variables to work with the smaller coil.

Come lunch, he had almost forgotten the time and had to run. Down in the dining room, it was crowded. He had no idea how he would find his appointments. He wandered back and forth between the lobby and the maître d'hôtel, until finally a well-dressed silver haired fellow in a bowler hat, who had been sitting watching him with a bemused smile, stood and walked over to him.

"M. Tesla?" he said.

"Yes," Tesla replied, quite relieved.

The man put his gloves and cane in one hand and held out the other. "Donald Roland, first secretary, British Embassy."

"A pleasure," Tesla said as they shook. "Have you seen any of the others?"

"Others?" Roland replied.

"Yes, apparently so," said a German accent behind them.

They turned and there stood a dapper thin man with dark brown oiled hair and moustache. He lifted a brass monocle to his eye and blinked at Tesla.

"Emil Kappel, undersecretary to the German Embassy" he said.

Nikola looked around the crowded hotel restaurant. "Are there any more."

Roland looked at Tesla squarely. "There might be more?"

"Well, yes," Tesla replied.

Kappel cleared his throat and said, "Well, it was very short notice. We will just have to see. Shall we sit down?"

By the time they had been led to their table, the waiter leaving them with menus, two others had arrived and had to squeeze in, Deter Rauffenburg of Austria and Felice Abella of Italy. The Italian tried to shake everyone's hand, but this proved to be impractical at the crowded table. Then he then raised his index finger to call the waiter who, being French, thought it rude and ignored it.

"Allow me," said Herr Kappel. He called to the waiter, "Herr Ober."

The waiter scowled at Kappel, but made his way over to them. Kappel thought that he must not like Germans.

"Qui?" the waiter asked.

"We will require a larger table," Kappel said in dry thickly accented French.

Tesla frowned at this exchange. He was uncomfortable with the situation. Now that they were all here, he was uncertain how to proceed. It didn't help that he hadn't thought about asking for a bigger table.

"Bien sûr," the waiter replied.

"I hope he understood," Mr. Roland muttered to himself. He had picked up, for lack of any other choice, his meat knife to slice off a piece of bread from the table loaf just as the Italian, sig. Abella had reached over to tear off a piece. Sig. Abella snatched his hand back, scowling at the knife. Roland stopped, his knife poised over the loaf, the others all looking on in horror.

Then everything came apart. They all started talking at once. Tesla finally focused on the German, Herr Kappel, primarily because he was the only one who didn't seem angry. Tesla had always felt an affinity with Germany.

"Please gentlemen, let M. Tesla tell us about his problem," Kappel said, clearly amused.

The problem! That's it, thought Tesla. "Yes, the problem," he replied. "The problem is that the French have cut my budget and I find I am unable to complete my project. I find myself at wits end, unable to proceed. I'm out of cable and the receivers are coming and I will not be able to pay for them as promised. Time is very short."

This brought silence. They all were staring at him, which unnerved Tesla even more.

"Are you proposing that we supply you with alternate funding?" asked Herr Rauffenburg.

Tesla looked embarrassed. "Well, yes," he said, sheepishly.

"And in return," the Englishman, asked.

"In return, you will have my good will." And after thought. "And of course, my lab."

"We are to bid?" the Italian, exclaimed.

"I don't know," Tesla replied. "I didn't expect so many to show up."

"M. Tesla. I must remind you that you have an agreement with the French," Herr Kappel said.

"Which they have violated!" Tesla replied, with fresh energy. "They have endangered everything." He chopped the air with his hands.

"You didn't pad your budget?" S. Abella asked, incredulous.

The waiter interrupted.

"A table is being prepared. If I may, I can take your orders now."

"Wait," said Herr. Rauffenburg. "If Mr. Tesla has no money, then who's to pay for lunch?"

"M. Tesla. We would be honored to help," Herr Kappel said, cutting off Herr. Rauffenburg.

And then the bidding on who would pay for lunch began.

₧₨

"Max," Emily said, as she lifted her tea. "You've heard of course, about M. Giroux?" They were sitting in the tea room outside the English exhibit, across the street from the Negro Village, a popular human zoo attraction. She looked at their grass huts and wondered how they were dealing with the December cold?

Max looked at her with raised eyebrows. "The fair director? I suspect he hasn't cleared out his office yet," Max replied, guessing. Max always found tea to be annoying. He never drank it fast enough and he detested tepid tea, but English etiquette required he drink it rather than pouring it out and getting fresh.

She frowned. "How did you find out so quickly?"

"I didn't. But it seemed likely after we won M. Tesla's trust."

"The French won't let him go." She took a sip of tea and then frowned. "Too sweet," she said, to herself and reached for the cream. A trolley rolled by, its pantograph spitting sparks, the rumble temporarily stopping conversation.

Emily gave the trolley a cool stare as it passed.

"You know," she said. "I think the French had our tea house put on this corner on purpose."

Max shook his head, smirking. "They'll try to seize Tesla's equipment next. We're already moving to block that. Then we expect them to attempt to reduce power to the tower."

"You are, as always, logical."

"Thank you. But I'm far more worried about the Americans." Max drew a breath over his tea cup before tasting it. "You know, my dear. I think they put roses in this."

"Yes. I think they did." She tried another sip and stared across the street at the crowds milling around the human zoo exhibit's huts and their semi-naked occupants. They had been shipped in with unwritten promises on boats from Africa. Speaking little or no French, they were practically slaves to their employers.

"Yes, The Americans have nothing to lose," she said, looking back at Max. "Our lawyers tell us he hasn't created a will yet."

"And he has no living relatives," he replied, eying the biscuits.

She smiled. "American patents, American probate courts, if he died who would get the patents?" she added.

"Edison most likely, which means we all need M. Tesla and his patents alive don't we," Max stated flatly.

"All of us but the Americans," she replied coldly.

ଅଠ

Tesla paced the tower floors one by one, inspecting everything. He had been away for days and work had only just resumed. He wouldn't tolerate any further monkey business from the French. They had already tried to pry loose his precious oscillator. It was practically to the lift before the workmen and police were stopped by an out of breath barrister waving a stack of paper. The delicate instrument would require extensive testing, and probably even repair. He paced the coil mounts, looking for breaks in insulation. They were still sound.

At the top of the tower, just below the terminal cupola, he ran into workmen eating their lunch. They weren't his! Then there were stacks of iron, torches and tools. At first disoriented, he roiled livid. This was a parting shot from Giroux!

Stalking forward, bumping aside workmen, he climbed the stairs to the next level. He felt sunlight where there should have been none and caught the whiff of forges for the heating of rivets. The structure of the tower had been altered. Standing there aghast, staring at the tunnel that had been bored through the center structure of the tower. The walkway to the cupola had been breached by a rail that cut right across the width of the tower top. He would have to duck under it every time he wanted to get to the top. What if he had equipment to move? The rail extended some twenty feet out the side of the tower into empty space. A great trestle had been added to the tower's structure to support it.

Tesla was stunned. His anger forgotten, he stared at the iron trestle. What kind of train uses only one track, he thought? And what kind of track ends in a thousand foot drop?

"Who is in charge here!" he cried, but he could find no one who had a clue. Just the plans for the track and nothing else.

§∞℞

Emily sipped her champagne carefully. She was at a German delegation party at the German pavilion. Time had grown short. M. Tesla's test was only two days away and she was at her wit's end. The Germans had him in their pocket, unless the Americans killed him first, all because the fools at her embassy had failed to recognize his importance.

She didn't have his equations or plans either. Out of options, she had finally been reduced to picking the lock to his hotel suite door. She finally gained entrance to his rooms only to find his work desk had been moved.

Now the Germans were her target. They had it all. The Americans were a German problem. To this end she was attending a reception for Rudolf Diesel in the German pavilion. Stumbling along with her atrocious German, pawed at by dreary overly attentive aristocrats, she hunted for information. Max was nowhere to be seen, which made her wonder what he was up to.

Diesel's engine was amazing to be sure. More powerful, and safer than kerosene and oxygen. Airships all over the world would be scrambling to switch. But the designs and equations had already common knowledge, their patents already secure. What she really wanted to see were the workshops next to the exhibit offices.

The German exhibit had long since been finished. That was until three days ago when crates had begun mysteriously arriving. She had stood in the crowd watching the train of steam trucks deliver them. Then yesterday, she caught a whiff of welders from the vents behind the building. The Germans were up to something.

But the doors were locked and the locks too exposed to pick. She mingled, working the crowd, looking for a tour, which she got. A tour of everything except the workshops. Apparently, even the exhibit director didn't have access. He apologized profusely, lingering over her hand far too long. She smiled anyway.

She'd come back later, after the party. Dressing as a cleaning woman and attempted to break in. There were only four guards in the quarter mile long hall. Easy! But then she found that the door lock was brand new, six pin! She had no training on it and lifting the pins had taken forever. She twice had to leave her tools in the lock and duck for cover. Then she found the door operated mechanically, the switch being a second lock twenty feet away, covered in a wood box in plain view under a light.

It had taken all her fortitude and willpower not to scream in frustration! Time wasted, lost sleep that would have to be covered with makeup, and she was reduced to rummaging through the trash! But it was then that she found the most curious things. There amongst the sessile and paper were several pieces of thin cut fabric, silk, and metal tubes. Tubes made of aluminum!

That same evening, Max was pacing the outside of the American exhibit. He had seen no strange vehicles, odd crates, or even comings and goings. No indications as what their plans were. Short of brute assassination, he couldn't see what the American's had in mind. Tesla was protected and his machine was sitting eight hundred feet up at the top of an iron tower. Short of using cannon, no one could touch it.

He was walking along the street, straining to see what he could be missing, when he came to the exhibit generator house. Most exhibits made use electricity generated by the power station near the base of the tower, but the Americans, specifically Edison, had seen fit to build their own. He stood across the street from it. The building was two stories tall with two tall brick stacks rising from its roof, one belching black smoke and the other steam. It had windows, but they were high up and revealed only a network of piping. Down a short dark alley, against its side, was a great iron coal bin.

Max stared at the power plant. It seemed rather large, but then he could only see the building. It also seemed to be putting out a lot of smoke, which spoke of large boilers, but steam was used for many things. Max had to dodge a trolley as he crossed the street. The plant shift would change in a few minutes. The alley door was locked so he palmed his key ring and waited beside it, leaning against the wall. He waited until he heard the shift change bell, then stood in front of the door. He noticed snowflakes on his sleeve.

Most workers entered and left through the front entrance

but Max got what he hoped for, a worker leaving through the side. The door banged into him as he was jingling his keys.

"Ow," Max exclaimed.

"Oh, sorry," the workman said. "Let me get that," he said, holding the door for him.

"Thank you," Max replied, holding his nose.

Once the door had closed, Max let out a small chuckle. Sometimes he found great satisfaction in his profession.

Inside the power plant it was hot and damp, the boiler towering over him. Steam hissed through dozens of pipes, drowned out by the steady whine of the electrical generators arranged in rows on the other side of the shop floor. Max took a deep breath and felt his nose again. He really had hurt it.

Setting off towards the generators, he passed an indifferent worker checking pressure gauges. Max looked across the powerhouse floor and counted ten generators, but only three in operation. How odd, he thought. It was night and all the lights were on. They should all be in operation. What were the other seven generators for? They should be running. But there was nothing else to see, so he left back out through the side door.

Whatever it was the Americans were planning, it would require a lot of electricity and had to be in the main exhibit hall. He would need the help of someone with a technical eye.

❧☙

Tesla rattled his newspaper at Kurt Meyers, his new German liaison. "This is nonsense!" There had been a fire last night in the trolley house and the paper blamed his "new electricity."

Meyers wondered where Tesla had gotten the newspaper. The last thing the unstable Tesla needed to see was the news. "I agree," he said. "Especially since the trolley in question didn't have a receiver. Only the usual pantograph."

"No receiver? Who told you this?" Tesla replied.

"I was down there this morning to see for myself. There was no receiver. It was just a fluke."

"But it can't be. All the trolleys have been fitted with them. Every trolley and streetlight for the entire two square miles of fair!"

Tesla was growing agitated again. Meyers found him to be a

disagreeable man and this, a very disagreeable assignment. "Well, you missed one. And lucky we are that you did. This has nothing to do with you. The papers will be set straight."

"I must go and see for myself." Tesla rose from his seat.

"You will not! You are to stay here, under our protection, until after the demonstration."

"I need no protection!" Tesla declared and began to walk toward the door.

"If you don't need protection, then you might at least consider clothes," Meyers said.

Tesla looked down at his bathrobe and groaned in frustration.

It took an hour to get from the hotel to the trolley shed. Black soot stained the top of the bay door and wet burnt wood littered the ground around the shed where the trolley had burned. There were workmen climbing through the wreckage, pulling out pieces to be examined by men in suits and gendarmerie. One of the men in suits looked up and began to stride towards them, followed by two more. "M. Tesla! M. Tesla. Do you have anything to say about this?"

"Say nothing!" Meyers said under his breath.

"M. Tesla, could your new electricity have had anything to do with this?" called one.

"M. Tesla, tell us why it burned."

But Tesla was no stranger to reporters. Self-promotion was an important part of his work. His manic ego always burned brightly in the spotlight. He smirked and replied, "It didn't have my coil installed yet. It must have burned out of jealousy!" That drew a laugh out of the reporters and a look of surprise out of Meyers, but then Tesla strode past them frantically eying the wreckage.

"Then why are you here?" a reporter asked.

"I want to make absolutely sure. This test is too important to leave anything to chance," he replied.

"Could it have jumped from one of the other cars?"

"I wish it could. Then I'd only have to install half as many coils," he replied. More laughter.

Meyers frowned. He had underestimated Tesla. It only made him harder to control.

"M. Tesla, we would like to ask you a few questions as well," the police detective said, standing next to a gendarme. The other gendarme shooed the reporters back.

"And I you, but not in front of these gentlemen," Tesla replied.

"Then perhaps we could go to the fair security office?"

"Yes, of course." Tesla's eyes darted around the inside of the bay. It really didn't have a coil. He was confused. He had supervised the installation of these coils personally. Walking quickly over to a workman who was pulling out a burnt piece. "This is all of it?"

"Yes sir," the workman replied.

"Very well then," he said, frowning and clearly distracted.

"Shall we go?" said the police detective.

They walked in silence the two blocks to le Poste de Gendarmerie. The facility was not large. Meyers had to wait in the outer room while Tesla was shown into a tiny office.

Tesla was waiting in the office alone, the policeman having gone to get tea, when into the office from the other door came a tall thin man with thinning hair and spectacles. "M. Tesla, I'm Dr. Roland Blanc."

Tesla scowled at him. "I know who you are," he replied.

Blanc was an Edison enforcer. His job was to make sure employee effort stayed focused, organized, and most of all - loyal. This was the last man Tesla wanted to see, especially not alone.

"I'm not going back," Tesla said flatly.

"Perhaps, but I'm here to make you one last offer," Blanc replied. "Close this foolish project down, come back with me to California and we will double your salary and provide guarantees to maintain your project funding."

"No! I've had it with Edison. He wants me to sign over my patents while time and again stalling my projects with his penny pinching. He says he will support me and then he's not there. He wants everything, but gives nothing."

"I haven't much time. Is that your last word?"

"Absolutely!" Tesla replied, with finality.

"Then I will spare no more worry for you or your safety. You have made your choice." Blanc rose to leave.

"What does that mean?" Tesla asked, frowning.

Tesla thought about the trolley fire, his mind racing. Did they have something to do with it? He was sure it had had a coil, which meant that someone had stolen it. What use was the coil and why burn the trolley after it was stolen? A bomb! They would use the coil to trigger a bomb. Tesla sat back in his chair, his hands beginning to shake. They were going to make a bomb that would go off when he turned on the generator!

"You stole that coil!" Tesla yelled.

"Nonsense," Blanc said, turning back. "We have stolen nothing. We are perfectly capable of making our own coils."

"You don't know the frequency."

"But we do, M. Tesla. You have never been very far from us."

"You're going to make a bomb!"

"Now you have disappointed me. To think us so crude." Blanc frowned. "We want your patents and your future work."

"You would, to prevent a competitor from gaining them."

"How coarse." Blanc paused, frowning. Then he turned back to the door. "Thank you for your time M. Tesla," He said.

"Then what did you mean?" called Tesla, as Blanc closed the door.

ଽଠଓଷ

Emily stood with a group of reporters in the equipment room, a pencil and notebook in her hand, listening to a very nervous M. Tesla explain his apparatus. His behavior and attitude were most uncharacteristic. In the past, he had always seemed to enjoy being onstage. Never a moment of self-doubt. But this was a different man, worried and unsure. Perhaps it was opening night butterflies, or was there something new she didn't know about?

Climbing the steps, above the coil room, they looked up the neck of the tower. She could see the elevator descending down the center, the coil wires blocking the sunlight for half its length. At the top she could see the cupola and something new as well. She could just barely see something sticking out the side of the tower.

"M. Tesla," she asked. "What is that at the top of the tower, below the cupola?"

"I don't know," Tesla replied, bitterly. "Someone else's project. I want to know myself, but no one will tell me."

"May we go up there?" she asked.

"It's not . . ." Tesla stopped mid reply, and then continued with a growing smirk. "Yes, of course."

The elevator wasn't big enough to hold them all. It would take two trips. Emily made sure she was in the first with Tesla.

"Since we will be near it, I can show you the cupola as well," Tesla continued. Girders and ironwork rolled past as the elevator climbed first through sunlight then in shadow as they passed within the main coil. "All motors and lighting in the tower are electric. We went through hell with the steam and gas lobby, believe me, to do it." A chuckle passed around through the reporters. "But steam would not travel this high or this far. We would have had to have had four separate boilers along with four separate pumps for the gas spaced along its height to do it." Then he stopped and looked at them all. "Electricity is the future gentlemen," and then to Emily, "and madam." This was the old Tesla, she thought.

At the top, she saw the trestle and track. He seemed surprised by the stack of crates in the middle of the landing. It made the place very crowded and they had to move out onto the catwalk to make room for the others. The drop from the railings was dizzying and the wind bitterly cold. She buried her hands deeper in her fur muff. The crates were new, the nail heads still shiny. There were no markings, no dents, or scuffs in the new wood. They couldn't have been shipped far and no clue as to their contents. Perhaps they had been shipped only as far as the German exhibit, she thought. How very strange. She would have to find some way to get a look inside.

⁜

The next morning Max walked through the quarter mile long gallery of machines towards the American Exhibit Hall with Hans Ziegler, a middle aged engineer with bad teeth and a shabby sense of fashion. The Americans had felt it necessary to build an entire hall dedicated to Edison alone. The ironwork and glass ceiling arched hundreds of feet over their heads. Water dripped occasionally from above as the steam from hundreds of machines condensed. It was a long walk to the American Hall. Max wished the trolleys ran indoors, but it had snowed last night and it was a choice of an interesting walk or a damp freezing ride.

Herr Ziegler specialized in the working of electricity and had been flown in by zeppelin from Berlin, landing early that morning. He was bubbling with anticipation at the prospect of meeting M. Tesla. His eyes darted everywhere, trying to take everything in as they hurried past.

"I fail to see why I must go back tomorrow. I've requested an extra week to see the fair." He stammered for a moment. "At my own expense, and they turned me down."

"They are bureaucrats and see only complications and trouble."

"They gave me no time, even to pack. I was rudely hurried to the aerodrome," he replied.

"The experiment is tonight. We have very little time, but I will see what I can do tomorrow. Staying will do you no good if none of this is left standing after tonight."

"Yes, at least I will see the experiment," he gushed. "I think I have a general idea what he is going to try, but your notes were practically unreadable. Ionize the upper atmosphere." His voice trailed away in thought. "Amazing. I really don't see how he could expect to succeed."

"I've seen it," Max replied. "It works."

Hans' gawking excitement was infectious and Max couldn't help a smile as they passed through the short corridor between buildings. Where the Hall of Machines was iron and glass, the American Exhibit was brick and wood.

"Is there any reason why they might have built this with wood instead of iron?" Max asked.

"Not particularly, although a grounded iron frame would insulate them electrically. Perhaps they want to draw power from Herr Tesla's machine?"

"Would the insulation work both ways?"

Ziegler looked at him, clearly perplexed. Max supposed it was a foolish question.

"Yes, of course," Ziegler replied.

"So perhaps they might want to have access to Herr Tesla's

machine instead of it to them?" Max asked, trying to be patient.

"Yes, possibly. Or maybe wood is cheaper."

There was a loud bang and Max went immediately into a crouch, looking for cover, but Ziegler stood there transfixed, staring at a large cage.

That was silly, Max thought. There could be no gun play in here. He stood and looked at the cage. The sign read, "Lightening Cage."

"They've caged lightening?" Max asked.

"No. It's a high voltage discharge. Those big drums in the back are the capacitors. I've never seen an arc so big! I wonder what the voltage is." He was grinning like a kid.

"Could this cause Tesla problems?"

"No."

They inspected the exhibits one by one, Max wincing at every lightening discharge. It was too much like the war. Finally they came to an exhibit set back in the corner. A large copper coil mounted next to a smaller one. "High Voltage Transformer," the sign read.

"This could do it, if it were managed properly," Ziegler said.

"The coils?"

"Yes. Use the smaller one to pump up bigger one using high frequency alternating current at a dissonant frequency."

"Wouldn't that take special apparatus?" Max asked.

"Yes, quite a bit actually. Oh!" Ziegler stopped in thought. "We passed a big tuning capacitor didn't we?"

"Where?" Max asked.

"Back there. The thing with all the plates of metal sandwiched together. And over there there's an alternator, and over there is a spark gap. They've got everything they need."

"And how do we stop them?"

"That's easy. Break the machine or shut off the power. The oscillator or perhaps the tuning capacitor are probably the most fragile."

Max looked around the exhibit. They would have to close it first if they were to do this in secret which meant Max had to find a way to get in, either here or into their power station. At night, after they closed.

$\text{\small ∞}$

Fenced private gardens had been built along the Champ de Mars, filled with potted plants and warmed with gas flame, for the elite and those who could pay to view L'Illumination, as it had been billed. It would be greatest New Year's event in history and mark the official opening of the fair to the public. The snow gone, the fair that evening had begun to fill with ladies in fine dresses and men in suits, delivered by stately steam carriages that stretched along the Avenues de la Bourdonnais and Suffren. Champagne and coffee were served. Stately meals and banquets laid out, silverware sparkling in the colored electric lamplight. Everywhere, there was a festival atmosphere with street performers, orchestras, and great electric arc lamps shining beams of light into the sky. The great red tower itself was draped in light, each level ringed with lamps and lit by a glow from within.

Tesla himself stood in his new room, fumbling with his tie, until an assistant to Herr Meyers turned to help him. Tesla looked down at his hands. They were shaking. His hands never shook. Ever. But then no one had ever threatened to kill him before. Meyers had assured him that the missing coil had been found but Blanc had threatened him just the same. Who knows what mischief Edison may have cooked up, he thought. The aid helped him into is waistcoat and coat, Tesla obviously unable to manage even he buttons alone.

Then Meyers stood in front of him and looked over with a nod. "Well then," he said. "Shall we go?"

Tesla nodded.

They filed out of his rooms into his new hotel's hallway, Meyers locking the door behind them. Tesla had at first resisted the change of hotel, but he had to admit that it had brought him a bit of peace and quiet. No more idiots bumping into him. No more unwanted guests at dinner. The elevators were bigger too. Even still, with Meyers' crew, it was a tight fit.

The elevator operator slid the door shut and took them down towards the lobby. The hallway they left behind was, for a moment, quiet. Then the stairwell door opened and out stepped a beautiful English woman in evening dress. She paused in front of M. Tesla's door and pulled out a handful of metal tools from her handbag. Gracefully stooping down, despite her heels and corset, she began to work on the lock.

Down on the street, in front of the hotel, a line of three steam carriages were waiting for Tesla and Meyers, one of them already full of tough looking men dressed in evening suits. Meyers helped Tesla into the second one personally, followed by himself and three of his aids. They pulled away into the crowded gas lit streets of Paris, already lined with spectators waiting to see the evening's demonstration.

Meyers hadn't allowed Tesla access to newspapers since he took over and his route to the tower always seemed to avoid news vendors, but they passed several that evening and Tesla was shocked by the headlines. Words like "Tesla's Fireworks Display" and "Will Paris Burn?" leapt out at him. It was insanity. Clumps of revelers crisscrossed the streets, often causing their cars to stop. Every once in a while, someone would recognize him and shout and point, "Hey, it's him!" But the guards were menacing and people kept their distance.

In the fair itself, they drove down roped off streets, passing through barricades and checkpoints, past richly dressed revelers, many cheering. Occasional flashes of blitzlicht left afterimages as reporters took pictures of their procession. Tesla was under the impression that he was to give a speech, but Meyers shook his head grimly no. Instead he said to the driver, "Take us straight to the tower." Under the tower, the driver turned left towards the elevator, taking their escort by surprise, forcing them to turn back in order to follow.

Parking under the tower with ease, which had been kept clear of revelers by a ring of ropes and fair security, they gained the elevator with no difficulties. At the top, on the first landing, Herr Meyers shut off the elevator power.

"What are you doing?" Tesla asked.

"It's to prevent unwanted guests," Meyers replied.

"But who would want to bother us?" Tesla stammered.

Meyers answered only with a grim chuckle and turned to the next lift, ordering half the men to guard the landing. The ride up the second lift was much less crowded. At the top he held Tesla back as his men fanned out to check the landing. After he was sure it was safe, Meyers shut off the power to the second elevator.

ℬↄℭ

The American Hall in the Hall of Machines had been closed for over an hour when the runner came panting up to the side door.

He banged on the door. "Let me in, we've got trouble!" he called, in thickly accented English.

The door opened a crack and then wider as a man stuck his head out, his breath fogging in the light from the door. "Walther, you're supposed to be at the tower!" the man in charge of the door replied.

"They changed the plans. I'm locked out," Walther replied, between breaths.

"Damn. Well get on in and report. Quick." Walther was practically dragged through the door. Inside it was warm, the dark displays made a fantastical cityscape of silhouettes. The far end of the hall was brightly lit were the engineering crew worked to assemble the apparatus. He stumbled on, dodging down aisles, until he saw Dr. Blanc, leaning against a work table directing the assembly.

"Dr. Blanc!" he called.

"Walther, what is wrong?" Blanc replied, in German.

"They've changed the schedule. I'm locked out."

"But there are the speeches, the presentation, the procession. We are not ready!"

"It was that damn Meyers," Walther replied.

"Well, we are not yet foiled, but I should have anticipated this. The Kaiser doesn't care about the fair or French speeches. He only cares about the experiment. Does it work, or not." Blanc stood up and addressed his technicians in English. "Gentlemen, we've run out of time. Our timing is shot. However, even though we can't discredit Tesla, we can still destroy him. We have perhaps fifteen minutes to get this thing working and we will need to double the power output."

A general wail rippled through the technicians and their movement became frantic.

ℬↄℭ

Max watched Meyers deliver Tesla to the elevator at the base of the tower and cursed under his breath. It was a good move on Meyers' part. He didn't know about Max or what Edison had planed. Sometimes secrets cut both ways. Max's men weren't supposed to gather for their assault on Edison for another half hour. It was only twilight. That meant that Max was on his own.

He tossed his hat and umbrella in a trash can and began to sprint towards the Hall of Machines. Halfway there when he ran across Helmut, one of his men, on his way to the rendezvous point. Max stopped next to him, hands on his knees. Helmut steadied him as Max tried to breathe. "The timetable has changed," Max said. "We must move now. Take the Avenue Anatole France. Hurry any you find to the rendezvous. I'll take Pierre and Loti."

The man whispered a quiet, but crisp "Jawohl" and ran for the other side of the plaza. Max continued on. The fair was huge and it was two thirds of a mile from the tower to the Hall of Machines. It was another seven hundred yards to get around it to the side with the American Exhibit wing. On the way there, he found two more of his men.

They were all out of breath as they met in the alley beside the Korean Exhibit. It was, like everything else, closed for Tesla's demonstration. Helmut had found another man and there was another already there, waiting, early. Six out of twelve, and then of course himself. Not a good start, Max thought.

"Gentlemen, we are going to have to begin the assault early," Max puffed.

"We're not all here yet," said one.

"They've advanced the test time. I'm sure Edison is scrambling as well." Max looked at them all. They each nodded. "Helmut, you will wait here for the others to arrive. When you feel you have enough, go for the hall side door. Don't wait too long. The rest of you will come with me to the power plant."

ജ

A runner appeared and whispered in Meyers' ear while he was watching Tesla tinker with his equipment.

"What is it?" Tesla asked.

"We've run out of time. You must be ready to start at any

moment," Meyers replied.

"But I haven't gone through the pre-start checks yet."

"It must be now or not at all," Meyers replied, sternly.

"What's wrong?" Tesla said, beginning to panic.

"Nothing we haven't anticipated and planned for, but you must be ready to throw the switch when I get back."

"You're leaving?"

"Just for a minute. I need to make some preparations myself."

Meyers followed the runner to the tower platform side. A man stood there looking down with binoculars.

"They're at the Rue de Monttessuy gate," the lookout said. He handed his binoculars to Meyers.

Looking down, Meyers could see a line of police vans crossing the gate, their trail of steam marking their passage. It glowed white, lit by the fair's electric street lights.

"Tell them to fire the rocket," Meyers said to the runner, who took off again at a run. Alone, he looked down again with the binoculars. "It's time for the big show," Meyers said to himself. Then Meyers trotted back to Tesla, only to find him curled up on a stool.

"What are you doing?" Meyers shouted

"I'm going to die. Edison is going to kill me," Tesla sobbed.

"Nonsense. How could he possibly get to you?" Meyers was annoyed, they didn't have time for this.

"I don't know, but he will."

"He might I suppose," Meyers said. "But I certainly will if you don't start this machine." Tesla looked up and saw Meyers pointing a gun at him. He yelped and fell over backwards off the stool.

"You wouldn't!" Tesla squealed.

"I will. We have no time left for childishness. You are no use to us without your machine." Meyers normally friendly patient face had turned cold and alien. "Throw the switch."

Tesla shook himself and then stood unsteadily. As he walked over to a bench to get his gloves, he noticed that it had become dark outside. The power to the city had been cut. It was Tesla's turn to deliver it. He pulled on his elbow length rubber

Max, wounded, silences the power plant manager.

gloves and walked slowly to the big knife switch in its nest of cables, bolted to a beam. With a sob, he reached up and grabbed the big wood handle and lifted the switch. Electricity was already arcing across as the handle neared the contacts. The switch slammed home with finality. Behind him, he heard his alternator wind up.

∞CR

Max was attempting to pick the powerhouse side door lock, a vexing four pin design, when it suddenly went dark. The streetlights had gone out. "Damn," he cursed. "We are out of time." He lifted the last pin and turned the lock barrel. The deadbolt slid free. He stood up with sigh of relief. "Gentlemen, we must hurry. Once the workers are neutralized, you must block the corridor to the exhibit and let no one through. I will take care of the generators."

Max drew his revolver with one hand and pointed at one of his men with the other. "You, open the door." As the door opened, Max darted in first expecting guards, but there were none. The building was its own independent power supply and well lit despite the rest of fair being without power.

"They're going to turn on Tesla's machine in a minute," Max said. "Everything in the fair with a coil will light up. That's when Edison will strike. Find all the powerhouse workers and bring them to the generator area. Kill any who resist. We have no time for games."

They fanned out, moving around the boilers along the walls. Max edged around the wall, past the generators, to the main office. The light was on inside. The office walls facing the generator room and its door all had windows, but the blinds were drawn. Max edged around the wall, staying below the windows. At the door, he stood and kicked it in. A shot rang out and Max felt something tug at his arm. Blinding pain shot through it. There was a man hiding behind the desk. Max shot him as he stuck his head up to look. There was a shot out in the powerhouse floor. Max twisted the light switch, shutting off the office lights and rolled through the door to the opposite side of the hallway. He had left blood on the floor. Nausea gripped him. Looking down at his upper arm, he could see blood soaking his coat sleeve. Max cursed.

Behind him were a set of double doors that led to the exhibit hall. They were shut, but Max could see no way to bar them. Back in the office, pocketed his pistol and rooting around through the manager's pockets with his good arm. Fishing out a key ring, he grabbed a chair on the way out. He had just locked the doors and was wedging the chair under the handles when he noticed a change in the timbre of the generators, a low pitched drone. Then he got shocked by the door handles, like he had been scuffing his feet on a carpet. They had started their coil!

In the middle of the floor in the midst of the generators, his men had three prisoners sitting flat on the floor, with their hands on their heads. "Oberhaupt, you're wounded," one of his men said.

"Yes, but we have no time for it. You, watch the prisoners. The rest, watch the door. Kill anyone who comes through." Max looked around. There was a fire axe amongst the tools hanging on wall pegs. Max ran over and grabbed it. The generators seemed to be connected in series along a central trunk line running along an elevated track. It went through the wall at a point about two feet above his head. Perfect. He grabbed the axe with both arms, the pain searing, and swung the axe at the cable. There was a bang and a flash, and then could remember nothing more.

୨୦୯୫

Tesla stopped to check his equipment, but Meyers would have none of it, science be damned. "Throw the second switch!" he said, and waved the gun at him. Tesla shuttered and ran the second switch. Saying a little prayer, he grabbed the wood handle and swung it upwards. Only a few sparks this time. Gradually, the hairs on the back of neck rose and the world turned strange. It was almost as if there had been a sound, but now it was gone, but he couldn't remember what it had been. He yelled, "It's working!" and ran for the railing facing the Champ de Mars, forgetting all about Meyers and his gun. There below, the lights of the fair were spreading outwards from the tower, gradually rising in brightness as the upper atmosphere ionized. A cheer drifted up from the stands below.

Behind him he heard the clockwork of his music player crank into action. A gramophone tube fell down the shoot and into place on the spindle, the needle dropped, and music began to spill out. Simultaneously, all over the fair, on speakers mounted to light poles, his music began to play. People stopped dancing and cheering and looked up. Across the entire fair, there was only one song, one sound. It was Tesla's song, *You'll Miss Lots of Fun When You're Married* by John Phillip Sousa, one of Tesla's favorites.

As the light and his music spread across the fair, Tesla noticed a purple blue glow rising from the Hall of Machines. Meyers had come up beside him. Tesla pointed and yelled, "It's Edison! I told you." Meyers nodded that he understood. Then things began to shake. It began as a sick feeling, like he had lost his balance, but increased quickly to a rattling tremor. The whole tower was shaking. Meyers gave Tesla a questioning look.

"They're generating a dissonant signal. We have to shut down," Tesla yelled over the racket. They staggered back to the work area, but things had moved around with the vibration. The cables were physically hot and Tesla couldn't get close to the main switches. "It's no good," he yelled. "We have to run."

"What's wrong?" Meyers yelled.

"The capacitors will blow if the tower doesn't come down on us first!" Tesla yelled back.

"Follow me," Meyers replied. He headed for the elevator. The wrong elevator.

"No!" Tesla yelled. "We can't go up."

"We can't go down. It's full of French police! They'll arrest you."

"Better that than dead."

"Trust me!" he yelled back, this time grinning.

Tesla paused for a moment, gathering his wits, then nodded. They ran for the elevator, but its doors wouldn't open all the way. Meyers pushed them until they gave. Inside, not bothering to close the inner doors, he pushed the control handle over and they began to rise. Above, Tesla could see orange sparks of vaporized iron as insulation failed and the coil arced to the tower.

ഇൽരു

Emily stood on the roof of Tesla's hotel. Under her arm, she carried a leather tube filled with Tesla's notes and drawings. She had left Tesla's rooms just before Max's men had arrived. Now she was watching the tower, the roof opened to hotel guests, sipping wine. The hotel had set up a bar and iron basins with open fires. She gasped along with the onlookers as the tower cupola began to glow purple blue and the fair lights climbed back to their former brightness. Then came the music, drifting through the air, so unexpected. Once again, she cursed the embassy staff for being outbid. But still. She had the drawings and equations, the French his actual equipment, and Germany had Tesla himself. The world was still in balance.

Then the music stopped in mid song and she could see little

orange pinpricks of light here and there, down the coil, starting below the cupola. Something had gone wrong. The Americans must have made their move.

☧)ℂ

Max awoke across the street from the powerhouse, sitting on the sidewalk leaning against a wall. He was still holding the smoking axe handle, but the top had been burned off. He stared at the smoldering piece of wood for a second. Two of his men crouched near him.

"Careful Oberhaupt, you've had a rough time. We are bringing a car."

"Did we get it?" he asked, his voice horse.

"They are all dead. Their machine burned up everything, even while you were stopping it."

Max could see the tower. The top was glowing purple. Then he realized that the streetlights were still on. He looked down at his hands. "Why am I still holding this?"

"Because we couldn't get you to let go of it."

"You're right. I can't get my hands to let go." Then he chuckled. "Then again, since I have to take it with me, it might make a good souvenir."

☧)ℂ

They were inside the coil, halfway up, when the shaking stopped. The elevator continued to rise, much to their relief. Tesla realized that he had been clinging to the elevator cage and forced himself to let go. At the top, Meyers again shut off the power to the elevator. They heard commotion from the deck below, echoing upwards. The police had broken down the stairwell door and were pushing past the barricades Meyers men had erected to slow them down.

"Almost there," Meyers said. "Come on." He pulled Tesla along to the catwalk. Where there had only been the rail and trestle, there was now a contraption of pipes and cloth, and another of Meyers' men. The man stepped forward with a smile and handed Tesla a pair of goggles and a coat.

"Here, you'll need these," he said.

124

"Why? What are we going to do?" Tesla felt a stab of fear as he looked at the machine. "What are those? Wings?"

"You're going to escape of course," Meyers said with a grin.

"In that?"

"There's no going down. We're going to use your own invention," Meyers replied.

"It'll power the motors," the pilot added.

Then he saw his coil, mounted dead center amongst the pipes between two motors with propellers. "That's the missing coil. Wait, it needs to be on top. The pipes will distort the field."

The man with the goggles shook his head. "No, everything is aluminum. Please, get in. We must leave before they shut down your generator."

"It can't happen. The switches are fused."

"They may gain entry to the power house though," Meyers said, as he drew Tesla towards the machine. "Put on the goggles, that is unless you want the wind to ruin the best view of your machine on earth."

"So how does this work?" Tesla asked, as he settled into the seat.

"You're going to soar like a god," replied the pilot.

"But what if my machine fails and we lose power?" Tesla stammered.

"Then you are no use to us," the pilot laughed, and the catapult flung them forward.

Aloha Max

Chapter 1 —Max Tests the Waters

Honolulu bars, when I was at a loss for stories, had become a bit of an addiction and let me tell you Hawaii has some fine ones.

That afternoon I was sitting in the *Aloha 'aina*, an airy clean establishment with big windows, up in the hills overlooking the beautiful blue of Pearl Harbor, sipping a beer, considering again for the thousandth time the possibility of immigrating to Hawaii. As the last American bureau employee of the New York Times, the rest having all been drafted for the war, in all of the Kingdom of Hawaii, I held a special a special place in the islands. The last American reporter. I had the run of the islands. Everyone knew me, even the king. I kind of liked that. The only reason I hadn't been swept away with my fellows, drafted or shanghaied depending on your point of view, was because of my employer's bribes. At least that was the excuse they give me each time I mentioned my ridiculous salary, better suited to 1842 rather than 1892. It was an ace job, but unless I came up with some stories soon – those bribes might stop.

If I immigrated, become a Hawaiian citizen, I'd escape the draft, miss the slaughterhouse and the ire of my paper, but I'd lose the one and only reasonable job I'd ever find here in the islands. I could always live on the beach, a prospect that sometimes seemed inviting. Go native, get a sun tan. Maybe learn to surf. Bribes or not, someday that letter would come and once it did, there'd be no escape. Hawaii had a very explicit extradition treaty with the U.S. The war was going badly for both sides and able bodied men were getting scarce.

So far, the war between the North and the South had been a stalemate. Not the stalemate of the newspapers, a battle fought with honor and valor, a gentleman's duel. No, being a newspaperman has many benefits, and one of them was access to the truth. This was a war like no other before. A war of machines. A bloody festering scar of blackened land stretching from Saint Louis to Washington. The whole world, every country, generals and aristocrats, were watching. A mechanical holocaust waiting for each nation. Waiting for their next war.

The thing was, even if I did immigrate and miss the war, I could still get caught in the next. It was going to happen here, maybe soon, which was why the Times kept me on their payroll and why I declined to go live on the beach. Hawaii might not be the sanctuary it seemed. It was also why I had no stories. Everyone was sitting quiet which kind of gave me a cold feeling when I thought about it.

Why a war here? The world runs on coal, especially ships, and Hawaii sits in the middle of the vast Pacific Ocean. And it isn't just ships. It's zeppelins as well. Everyone needs a place to rest in the middle. The great powers agreed that a neutral Hawaii was in everyone's best interest, an important place to stop, refuel, and repair ships on their way between the Americas and Asia. But owning it might be a better deal to certain parties. The Japanese, for instance, had been showing the flag a lot lately. Control of Hawaii would give them control over half the world's trade.

I smiled as I sipped my cold beer. Oh, I had taken a shine to cold beer. That's one of the many things to love about Hawaii. Nothing in Hawaii ever gets cold of its own accord so they chill everything. Honolulu had twelve icehouses just to make sure there was plenty of cold to go around, and a coal ship every week to make sure they stayed running.

So that was my problem. The reason for the bribes. Hawaii sitting smack dab in the middle of the Pacific Ocean for no good reason other than to be "the" coaling point for the entire Pacific Ocean. To be honest, there was also Midway Island. Every major power's ships stopped here or there too, but Midway didn't have Pearl Harbor, Honolulu Aerodrome, or the Kingdom of Hawaii to back them up. Hawaii was the key to South and Central America. And with the U.S. busy cutting its own throat, the world's great powers were climbing all over themselves to divide the spoils. Bananas, rum, rubber. Ships heading east from South America docked every day in Pearl Harbor. Rum was cheaper than water in Honolulu, and Hawaii has a lot of water.

Hawaii was a free kingdom, at least officially. In reality, it was controlled by the British, a protectorate they called it. They had a fleet in harbor that said so. I could see it through the bar's big window, between the palms, great huge iron ships, bristling with cannon, which came and went with alarming frequency. I'd report their comings and goings to my paper, but I'd wind up with a broken hand or two.

But there were other great iron mountains in the harbor as well. Some of them were Dutch, some German, some French, some Spanish, even the occasional Portuguese or Italian. But by far and away, lately, the most numerous were the Japanese. Their ships were bright and shiny, their guns bigger, their sailors more arrogant. The city was full of them. With them came Japanese immigrants bringing businesses and money that the British, halfway around the world, couldn't match.

But perhaps you were thinking that Hawaii is just a gathering of the big boys. There are lots of rats in the corners too. Everyone's navies play and strut about in the day, but there are others who only play at night in dark back alleys. They don't need dreadnaughts. Chinese cartels, Siamese traders, and even the occasional dhow, junk, or even unnata from India. Their cargoes often unload in the dead of night. They trade in goods best left under the table. Opium, slaves, guns, art, and a steady stream of their own immigrants. I love their restaurants. Their cooking is to die for.

That's why the New York Times wanted someone here, even if it meant shelling out bribes. It couldn't last and someone had to be here when the guns started going off.

The beer was German by the way. It was the Aloha 'aina's specialty. Pretzels too, which fit with beer just fine. All beer in Hawaii was imported. Grain is about the one thing Hawaii can't grow. You'd think with all the sugarcane we'd make great rum, but the best Hawaii had was local hooch, rotgut rum, *halalurama*, and some pineapple liqueurs. Vile stuff fit only for novelty collectors. One had to appreciate one's beer, and what it took to get it to Hawaii.

A slight man in a white suit entered the bar. We all wore them. They were supposed to help keep away the tropical diseases. I casually glanced his way. He was an odd looking fellow. He was small with a round thin lipped head and brass glasses.

He sat down at the bar in an empty seat halfway down. Not difficult at that time of day. When he spoke to the bar tender, I noted that he had a German accent.

"I'm told that you have German beer," he said, when the bartender, a big Hawaiian, nodded at him. The bartender's name is Luke by the way. I suppose that made him a Christian.

"We sure do mister," the bartender said. "We have Ettaler and Andechs, just in. Ship arrived last night."

"That would have been my ship," he said.

"Weltenburger Kloster and Füchschen Alt as well," the bartender continued.

"Ettaler," the man said. "I feel an affinity for it, having ridden so long beside it."

"He mea iki," the bartender said, and turned to pull a pint. He set it on the bar in front of him, the glass frosty.

"It's cold," the man said, eying the dripping glass.

"Try it," I said, smiling down the bar at him.

"It isn't natural," he replied, grimacing. Then he took a sip, and then another.

"Cold is to be treasured here," I said.

"You're American." He looked over at me, clearly unsure about his beer.

"Yes sir, born in the hills of Kentucky, land of horse and bourbon."

"I've never been there," he said, staring again at his beer.

"No sir, and you won't be either, at least for a while. The war runs right through it."

"Oh, the war," he said. He frowned. "Most inconvenient."

"Inconvenience is war's middle name," I replied lightly.

"Yes." He chuckled. "It's certainly one word for it."

"So what brings a man like you halfway around the world to Hawaii?" I was a reporter after all.

He looked up from his mug and said, "Beer. Although I wouldn't have come if I knew beforehand what they do to it here."

"Spend some time here," I replied. "I think you'll grow to appreciate it."

The bartender, wiping a glass, turned to the man and said, "That'll be ten pence."

"Ten pence!" the man said.

"It followed you here," I said. "We've got to pay for the ticket. Welcome to Hawaii."

"Maybe I can get you to warm it," he said as he paid. The bartender laughed.

"My name is Carl Burgess," I said, scooting down a few stools and holding out my hand to shake.

"Max Schuster," the man replied as he shook with no

thought, then went back to fishing through his purse counting his coins.

Why did a beer company send someone halfway around the world? Maybe there was a story there.

"Really, what brings you from Germany?"

"Trade," he said. He looked down at his beer. "Beer, among other things. I'm here to discuss trade with the king."

"So you're going to the party tonight?" I asked.

"Yes," he replied, and tried another sip frowning. "That's why I'm here. I represent Der Königehandelsministerium. I represent our Kaiser. Honestly, that ship was horrible, a Chinese steamer, but there was no zeppelin service from Manila. I didn't think I would get here in time. As it is, I have less than a day to prepare." He shook his head slightly in disbelief. "They chill our beer."

"You seem distressed."

"Well yes. We'll have to take this into account. Tests perhaps." Then he thought for a second, "Although, who would try it?"

I laughed. "I'm sure you can find somebody."

"Maybe Poles," he mumbled.

"Maybe," I replied. "So what else besides beer are you peddling?"

His body said casual, but his eyes focused and for a moment locked on me. "Oh, anything and everything we make," he said. He lifted the mug and admired the light shining through it, and the harbor full of British ships behind it. "I represent Krupp as well." There was definitely a story here. Krupp, among other things, was the biggest arms manufacturer in the world.

"I'm here for trade. So tell me about yourself," he said.

"I work for the New York Times. I'm their foreign correspondent here in Hawaii."

"That's why you know about the party," he said.

"Yes, I often attend these things."

The bartender asked if I wanted another beer. I answered yes without thinking. "I suppose you haven't met the king yet," I said.

"No. I would have liked to have arrived earlier. I've had no time for preparation."

"This doesn't count?"

"We'll yes, I suppose it does," he replied, and smiled sheepishly. "It would normally. So how does one dress for these events in Hawaii?"

Chapter 2 —Carl Finds an Enemy

I caught a ride with friends to the party, the Kekuku family. They were entertainers and always hungry for press, so they had no problem with me hanging around. Their son Joe was going to play and sing at the party. It took two carriages to carry us all with Joe, still working on his playlist, sliding away on his guitar sometimes accompanied by his two sisters singing along.

When we arrived, we were met at the driveway by servants in livery. They looked hot. Believe me, they didn't dress like that normally. They helped Mama Kekuku down carefully like the fragile old matriarch she was. She didn't really need it, but the sly old witch likes the attention.

"Hey Carl," Joe said, still leaning back in the carriage with his guitar, strumming a tune while he waited for the carriage steps to clear. "You going to see Miriam? I hear she's taken up with some guy from the Japanese delegation."

Joe always did have a mean streak. "No Joe, you know Miriam and I are history."

"Nobody thinks that but you and Miriam," he said, and started playing Kuu Ipo i ka Hee Pue One. It's a song about lost love. The ass.

I gave a chuckle back that was clearly not felt. Then his sisters, Anouha and Miliani hopped forward and each took one of my arms.

"You leave him alone iki," called Ana.

"The man has a broken heart," added Mili. "Don't you worry Carl. What you need is to make a proper entrance. Then that Miriam will see sense."

"That or one of us will get you!" Ana leered.

"Tut tut," Mama said, as she huffed up the steps.

And up the steps we went, straight through the front doors with a girl on each arm, and believe me they're definitely worth looking at. I couldn't help entering with a smile.

We surrendered our hats and shawls to servants as we

entered, my claim ticket slipping easily into my pocket. I could hear music from inside. All strings. It was probably malamalama o ka mahina, who I generally like. You haven't heard anything until you've heard Strauss on slide guitar.

Then it was through the double doors to the house's front atrium which served as the ballroom, its glazed ceiling arching over our heads. When the lights were out, you could see the stars through it. The central parquet floor was surrounded by double doors that let in the sea breeze from outside. It helped to clear the heat from the gas light and so many people. We faced a sea of white cotton and linin suits and dresses. People were still arriving and guests were mingling, sipping white wine imported from France. Ladies fanned themselves, wearing too much silk for the tropics, flaunting dance cards looped around their wrists with colored yarn. In the back, I could see a knot of people clustered around one man, undoubtedly the king himself.

Standing just far enough away to be considered disinterested, stood the British delegation, milling about in their own less sizable circle of followers. They sported the normal mix of facial hair, red uniforms, and white dinner dress. You can tell the new arrivals from the mother isles. They still have their beards and insist on buttoning their collars.

We had always had a sizable Japanese naval presence at Pearl and you could generally expect to see a fair number of glowing white uniforms at any official party. Tonight though, their numbers had doubled. They had a corner of the room to themselves. Down in the harbor, there were floating mountains of iron that went with each of these men.

Standing among them with a glass of wine in her hand was Miriam, laughing, talking to several officers.

"Don't look at her Carl," Mili said, tugging on my arm. "Let's say hello to David." That's the king by the way, David Kalākaua.

"Good idea," I mumbled.

We made our way across the room, maneuvering between the usual characters. When you've been to enough of these things, they start to feel like Sunday dinner at home. There was Griswold, sugar plantations. Pilotte, pineapple plantations. Keyes, an opium distributor. Hasakawa, warehouses. Miller, an island shipper, actually a smuggler. Everyone comes to the tropics to make their fortune. These are the blessed few who did. I snagged a wine glass as we passed a server with a tray. French wine is far too rare in the tropics to pass up.

King Kalākaua, probably the world's only elected king, stood among his followers, his hair as white as his suit. Despite the wrinkles and the stiffness of his stance, he was smiling and joking.

"Aloha ahiahi Joe," the king said, noticing our approach. "I see you're working on getting over Miriam." He smiled at Ana and Mili.

Hawaii really is like Sunday dinner. Nobody has secrets.

"Hi David," the girls said in unison.

"Where's Joe? He's coming isn't he?" he asked with a frown. But then he looked up towards the door. The tone of the crowd had changed as Joe made his entrance, guitar in hand. He seemed to draw the women from the crowd like a magnet.

"Oh, there he is," David said with relief. "I was afraid we'd lost our entertainment."

"We don't count?" Mili pouted, bumping David with her hip while still holding my arm.

"Nani, I could never replace you," he said and touched his wine glass to her's with a gentle ring.

Mili giggled.

Ana pouted. "Come on Carl, we'll leave these love birds to sing," she said, and pulled me away.

"Oh no you don't!" Mili said, pulling back.

"Let's stay here for a bit," I said. "I have some business with David."

"Oh Carl no, that sounds boring," Ana said.

"It is," I replied. "But it needs to get done."

David eyed the girls and gave them a wink. "You girls run along," he said. "Hey, isn't that Kea Lani over there?"

"Where?" They both looked before realizing they were being tricked.

"Oh David!" Mili said.

"It is, Mili!" Ana said, looking at someone in the crowd.

"We'll go David, but we'll be back Carl," Mili said.

"We want to see the sparks fly," Ana added, over her shoulder.

Then they were off. Kea Lani, by the way, was the son of Ahe, the best surfboard maker in the islands. His son was a rising star on the waves and had the good looks to match.

David chuckled to himself.

"So tell me about this business Carl," David said, wine glass in hand.

"I met a man today at the Aloha 'Aina."

"They get that beer in?" he asked.

"Sure did," I said, and gave him a smile.

"Good is it?" David said.

"It's Maika'i," I replied.

"So who's this guy?"

"He's a German, representative of the Kaiser."

David's eyebrows went up.

"He was looking for you. Said he'd be here tonight."

I knew David well enough to know his surprise was genuine. If he had a need to deal with Krupp, then he didn't expect it to come tonight.

"Did I hear Kaiser?" came a voice from behind us.

It was Oliver, the last person we wanted to overhear. Sir Oliver Audley, High Commissioner to the British delegation and a nosey guest at parties. Behind him was a white woman, strikingly beautiful, which was strange because I didn't think Oliver's tastes ran in that direction.

"The new load of German beer came in," I said, deflecting Oliver. "Oliver, we were about to toast the Kaiser and his brew masters."

"Good is it?" Oliver replied.

"Give it a try," I suggested.

He snorted. "The last thing the empire needs is a picture in the newspapers of its ambassador drinking German beer."

"Don't give me ideas," I said, and laughed. We were both lying. He had heard what we'd been saying, but I appreciated his willingness to be led away from the subject.

"A German?" asked the woman, nursing a practically undrunk glass of wine. Young, but oddly sure of herself. Judging by her dress, she was expecting a dance. We would, but I doubted it would be what she was expecting.

"Can you describe him?" she asked

I was about to describe him when I saw Herr Schuster himself make his entrance. I had only had to glance his way for both David and Oliver to look too. Their gazes lingered on the little man. He was so obviously German. Who oils his hair in the tropics? And the cut of his suit. I tried to point out a good quick tailor back in the bar. It was far too tight. Loose and baggy is best in the tropics. It lets the air in.

Max was standing just inside the door, clearly at a loss as to how to proceed.

"I better go and help him," I said.

Oliver snorted. "Yes quite."

As I made my way through the crowd, I spotted him talking to the server. Apparently there was a problem with the wine.

"Are you sure it's French?" I heard him asking the waiter.

"Ma'i 'oia," the waiter replied.

"I sorry, but I don't understand."

The waiter frowned, then spat out, "Truth."

"He doesn't know English," I said as I approached.

"Savez-vous français?" Herr Schuster asked.

The waiter blinked back at him then said, "¿Sabe Español?"

Max, confused, shook his head.

"There're no French missionary schools here," I explained. "He went to a public school. They only speak Hawaiian and take other languages as second subjects."

Herr Schuster frowned. "This is going to be most difficult."

"He namu Kelemānia," I tried to tell the waiter that Schuster only spoke German, but my bad Hawaiian didn't fly, so now we were all confused. What is the Hawaiian word for German?

"It's French wine," I said. "I suggest you take a glass. It's quite good."

"Is it?" He took a glass tentatively.

The waiter bowed and said, "Mahalo," while backing away.

Herr Schuster watched him go with a frown.

"You know," he said. "The Rhine region produces some excellent vintages these days. The quality is far more predictable than French. We blend vintages to produce a . . ."

"Herr Schuster, would you like to meet the king?" I asked, trying not to laugh.

"Yes. Very much. I apologize as well. I enjoy my work. Please call me Max," he replied.

"Max it is. You can call me Carl."

He tasted his wine, then frowned. "It's good," he said, with some distress. "You chilled it too."

"As I said. This is Hawaii."

"I would like very much to meet the king."

"We can do that."

So I parted a path through the throng for him as I led him across the dance floor. As we approached, I could see David and Oliver looking him over. I could understand their confusion. Max was, even for me, difficult to pigeon hole.

"Maximillian Schuster," I said. "I would like to introduce you to His Highness David Kalākaua and High Commissioner Sir Oliver Audley of the British Consul."

"Please, call me Max," he said, clicking his heels and giving a small bow.

"Call me David as well," David said, and reached out to shake hands.

"I suppose I should make it Oliver then too," and he shook hands with Max as well, clearly amused by what the competition had sent.

"And this delightful young woman?" Max asked, bowing again to the woman.

"Mrs. Stroud," she said with a smile. "Emilia Stroud." She held out her hand and Max took and gave it the barest touch of his lips. Then he looked up at the king.

"I represent Der Königehandelsministerium, the German trade ministry," Max said. "There are issues of trade we would like to discuss with you."

"You came all this way for that?" David exclaimed.

"Well yes," Max replied with a smile. "That and to better understand the markets here in the Pacific."

"Die Handelsflotte here?" Oliver asked. He no longer seemed amused.

"Perhaps." It was Max's turn to smile. "We're hoping to make solid business connections first. But we must know the market before we can invest. It's true, our merchant fleet is small compared to yours," Max looked at Oliver. "But we are always striving to improve."

David seemed pleased. Oliver did not.

"I know we've had some discussions at a low level," David said. "But I didn't think anything would come of it."

"You are more important than you think," Max said. He frowned at his sip of wine. "I was asked to drop my work in Manila to visit you." Then he looked at me.

"You know Carl," Max said. "I think wine may be better chilled."

"We'll make a Hawaiian of you yet," I said smiling.

I caught a fleeting frown on Stroud's face, but then felt a tug on my arm.

"Carl! Kea Lani is boring." It was Mili. They'd returned.

I glanced at Stroud to see her reaction to them, but she seemed preoccupied with Max.

"Come on Carl," Ana said. "Let's go somewhere and have fun."

I could see Kea Lani. He was surrounded by girls. I suppose there was too much competition. There are some advantages to a competitive market.

"You go on," David said. "I'll tell you about it later."

"Thanks," I said sarcastically, as they dragged me away.

"Don't you be boring too," Ana said.

As I was being pulled away I heard David say to Oliver, "So she still works at the base?"

"Yes, I'm afraid so," Oliver said. "But if she keeps her new friends very long, that will have to change."

But the girls had me by the arms, leading me towards the food.

Trade with the Americas and Asia had brought in a cornucopia of new foods. We cultivated bananas, coffee, sugarcane, and cocoa locally now. Farmers were even experimenting with curry and peanuts. Combined with cultural migration, Hawaii had turned into a competitive culinary warzone with cooks and restaurants jumping through hoops to outdo each other. David's table was a major battlefield. It was all practically unrecognizable. Why, for instance, was that that corn dark grey blue with red flecks?

"Carl, you have to try this." Mili lifted a cracker with a red paste on it towards my mouth. "It's Lani's newest."

If it was Lani's, then it was going to be hot. I was taking a bite when someone bumped into me. I don't know if it was that or the fire in my mouth, but I choked, spitting the bite out on my plate. Thank goodness we cooled our wine, I thought.

"Hey," Mili yelped.

It was lucky I missed getting it on my suit. I turned and looked behind and saw a Japanese officer. He had pushed me aside to get to the table. He looked at Mili like she was a slab of week old meat, then turned back to the table and began picking through the food without a word.

"That wasn't nice," I said.

He ignored me.

I tapped him on the shoulder.

He gave me a squint. "Fugainai banjin," he said, and turned back to the table.

"You should apologize to the lady," I insisted, and then repeated it again in Hawaiian, but he ignored me and kept picking through the food. "Now listen . . ." I was about to get forceful when a voice barked behind us.

"Nobutomo!"

It was another officer, this one with more braid on his sleeves and grey in his hair. Our man frowned in annoyance at his plate, but his face turned passive when he turned and snapped to attention.

I wasn't sure what to do as our man was berated by his superior officer. It was only a few words, but they had an effect. Frankly, it was embarrassing. I was turning to take the girls further down the table when the elder officer addressed us and those around us.

He gave us the slightest of head nods and said, "I must apologize for his rudeness. Disrupting the party is unforgivable."

I nodded back. "It's nothing," I replied.

That seemed to satisfy him. He dragged the junior officer

back to their group.

"They can be so mean," Mili said.

"They're not all mean," Ana said. "They can be fun when they've been drinking."

Mili sighed, then picked up the cracker again. "So Carl, you have to try this."

"I tried it!"

"You spit it out," she said.

"For good reason," I replied.

The evening progressed and everyone got drunker. Max had vanished. I suppose the introduction was all he wanted at this point. I had no clue what kind of trade he was looking for. He couldn't have come all this way just for beer.

The Brits and the Japanese kept their distance each other. I found out from Henderson that he was going to try mulberry trees, aiming to raise silkworms. He was old. I doubted he'd live long enough to see any silk. And then I heard from the chief of police that there was another hopeless crackdown on opium coming. I think he only mentioned it to give all parties concerned time to lay low. Still, it was a story. All together it looked to be an unproductive evening.

The girls had abandoned me, claiming I was boring, saying something about no sparks. I was left to talking to Mr. Zhang, a man of considerable entrepreneurial talent, under the table connections, and a heck of cheater at cards, when I heard a disturbance. It was between Miriam and one of the Japanese officers.

"I can't," Miriam said.

The officer hissed something at her that I couldn't understand. Joe was playing so the crowd wasn't looking. There was only me.

"Absolutely not!" She replied.

He grabbed her arm, and she pulled away. Then he grabbed it harder.

I was starting towards them when Zhang grabbed my arm. "Not your business Carl."

"They can't do that," I said.

"She's not your girl anymore," he replied.

He was right. So I stood there hating myself, doing nothing as Japanese officer pulled Miriam out on the patio.

"So tell me Carl, how is the war going these days," Zhang asked. He was trying to distract me but it wasn't going to work.

"Sorry, but I have to go. Just to keep an eye out."

Zhang looked at me with a look of resignation. "The candle has a heart for this parting night," he quoted half to himself.

I looked at him confused.

"Go," he said, and waved me towards the patio.

He didn't have to say it twice. I was moving towards the doors. They had gone out on the right so I took the leftmost door. Standing in the corner of the patio I looked around the various couples walking in the garden moonlight. Strangely, I thought I saw Max walking with that Stroud woman. It was difficult to tell in the lantern light. But I couldn't see any sign of Miriam or the officer.

I was heading down to the garden, taking the steps two at a time, when two Japanese officers caught up with me. They came up on either side. When I turned to look at one, the other slugged me. I'm not made of iron nor am I any kind of hero. I went down seeing stars. The pain was searing. They watched me fold and walked away as if nothing had happened.

I was laying on the steps, gasping for breath, counting the cracks in the stonework, for I don't know how long when I was found by Max.

"Emily," he said. "Go find the king."

She glided up the steps without a word while Max tried to help me sit up. To be frank, we weren't having much luck. Moving only brought more pain. He kept trying to talk to me, but it was hard to focus. I finally did eventually manage to sit up. It was that or piss my pants.

I was leaning against the stone step railing, trying to stand, when that Stroud woman came back with David.

"Carl, are you OK?" he asked.

"No," I moaned. It should have been obvious. "Can somebody help me up?"

"You sure? You look bad." He called to someone to start his car.

"Kidney?" Stroud asked, to no one in particular.

"I think so," Max replied. "You are going to need rest Carl."

I put my arm around David's shoulder and with the help of Max I stood.

I was trying to get the stars out of my eyes when David asked, "Who was it?" I think he knew, but he had to ask.

"It was nothing," I replied. "We can't talk about it here."

At my request, they took me to the WC. Even by the dim lantern light, I could see my urine came out mixed with blood, which wasn't good. Then David had his doormen load me in the back of his car to puff down the hill to the hospital.

Chapter 3 —Carl Avoids Hope

The morning sun slanted in through the open window, the morning breeze stirring my mosquito netting. I assume it must have been a lovely morning, but the beauty of it was lost on me. I'd slept fitfully, the pain in my back and side throbbing with each beat of my heart. The bed didn't help either. The springs squeaked with every movement.

They had brought me mangos and green tea for breakfast, and a newspaper to pass the time. Unfortunately, I had stopped in yesterday to drop off a story and ended up helping to set up most of these pages. The setter had apparently decided after I left to change my normal column spacing, adding slugs to use more space. They must have been short copy. It looked bad. Better to have ended short on the page or at they could have asked me. I could have come up with something.

It would be days before I was back on my feet, a long stretch of immobility and boredom. The sheriffs had showed up to question me that morning. I told them the truth. I didn't know the officers in question. It was dark. I was busy collapsing in pain. Then they came by with the book cart. I recognized nothing on it but Tom Sawyer, which I'd already read.

I'd resigned myself to purgatory when who should drop by but Max.

"Do you mind visitors?" he called tentatively from the foot of the bed.

"Not at all," I replied. My smile was genuine. I was desperate. I put down my book, something called *The Brothers Karamazov*.

"I'm sorry about your accident."

"I was sucker punched."

"Very unfortunate," he said, coming around the side of the bed and pulling up a stool. "I'm surprised someone should want to hit you. I've been reading your stories in the newspaper. You seem both polite and discreet. Very unusual in a reporter."

"It's a small island. I've built my trade on friendships."

"Which makes the act surprising." He shook his head in distaste.

"We're not prone to violence here. Even the criminals. It doesn't pay to step on toes unless everyone agrees they deserve to be stepped on." I decided I needed to shift. The bed squeaked and pain shot through the side of my body. Max looked on with sympathy.

"Don't worry. These sorts of wounds heal quickly. You should be up in a couple of days."

"That's what the doctors say." How did Max know about kidney punches?

He looked at my book and frowned.

"Russian," he said.

"I'm afraid so."

"It will be depressing."

"It is," I said with resignation.

"Do you know who hit you?" he asked.

"A couple of Japanese officers. I couldn't see them. It was dark."

Max nodded. "They're an arrogant bunch, peasants mostly. They think their promotions make them samurai."

"Samurai?"

"Warrior class. Class is important to them."

"Apparently so," I said, shifting and wincing again.

"Best to steer clear of them."

"Unless you can't."

Max looked at me questioningly.

"They were hurting a friend," I said.

"That would explain it," he said. "David is giving me a tour of the docks, the day after tomorrow. It will include the Japanese zone. Would it interest you to go?"

"Very much."

"Think you will be up by then?"

"I'd go now."

"Good." Then he looked at my book again. "Do you really want to read that?"

I shook my head no.

Carl gets an unexpected visit from Miriam.

"Do you mind a suggestion or two?"

I shook my head again.

He held out his hand, so I gave him the book. The stool fell over as he got up. He stooped to put back upright before he left. I watched him as he walked down the rows of beds, lit by morning sunlight, towards the book cart. When he returned, he had two books.

I looked at the first, a plain brown cover. "Doyle? Never heard of him."

Max shrugged. "It's only a suggestion. I'll get your other book if you want."

"No, no," I replied. I looked at the cover again. *A Study in Scarlet*. It sounded like a cheap romance.

ഇൻരു

I had several visitors that day, David, even Anouha and Miliani, but the big surprise came just before the end of visiting hours. I saw her walking down the aisle. Her eyes were darting from bed to bed, looking for mine. She was wearing a simple dress in tropical white, a small hat, her parasol furled. When her eyes found me, she stopped for a second. There was still that electricity. The Kekuku sisters called it "that spark." It could see it in her eyes. My heart skipped a beat.

"Hello Carl," she said. She stood at the foot of my bed. She seemed worried and uncomfortable.

"Hello Miriam."

"I told you to stay away from me. You shouldn't have followed."

"I had to. I would have followed if it were any woman. He was hurting you."

"Carl, you're too nice for this."

"For what?"

She frowned for a second, then changed the subject.

"Did they hurt you badly?"

"I'll get over it."

"They said you had kidney damage."

"They're exaggerating. It's nothing. I'll be up in couple of days." Thinking about it though made me want to change positions, but I didn't want to show her how much I hurt.

"You should stay in bed and rest."

"I don't have much choice. They have my clothes."

"Please. Take it easy Carl," she said. She turned to go. "And don't follow me." There was a catch in her voice.

There was nothing I could do. I had to watch her walk down the aisle to the door.

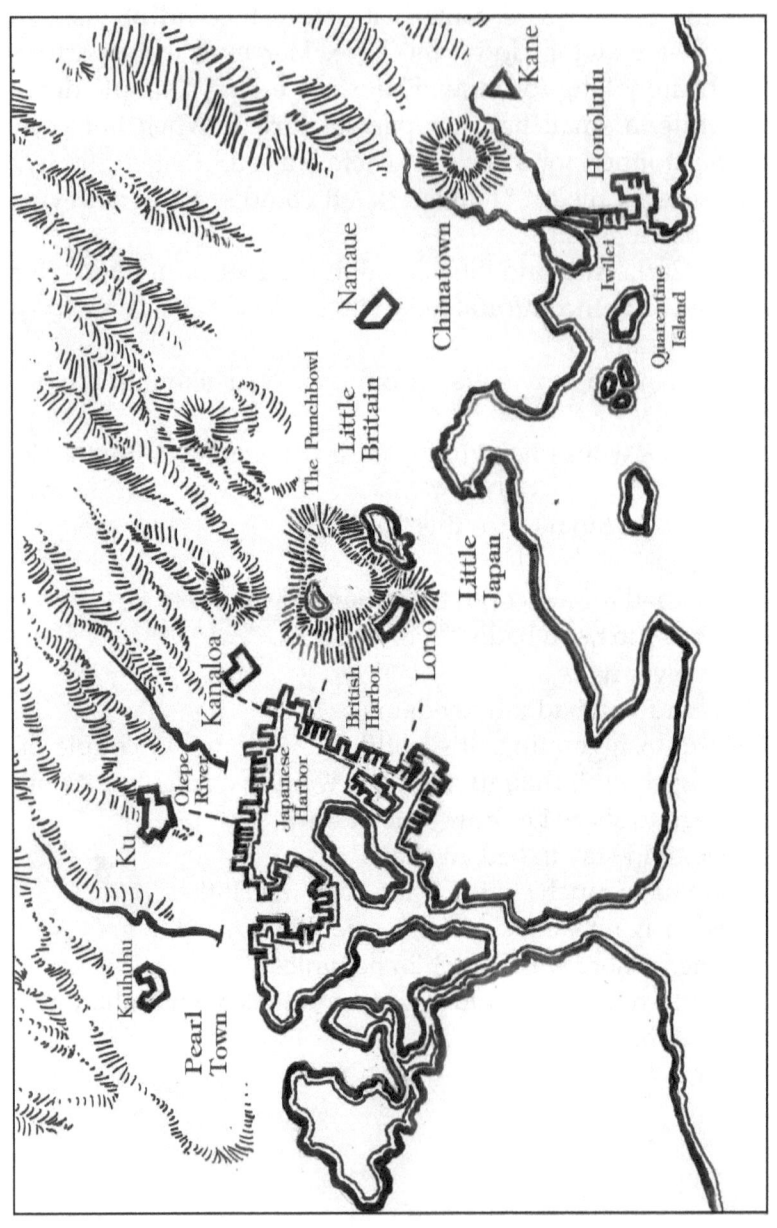

Honolulu and Pearl Harbor, showing the British fort network.

Chapter 4 – A Tour of the Docks

I was still a bit unsteady and to be frank, walking didn't feel nice. It was the contact with the ground. That little jar that sent pain up my back. But I wasn't about to let anyone know that it still hurt. Hospitals can get boring quick. Besides. I couldn't pass up a chance to get a closer look at the Japanese. I owed them.

Max, David and I were riding in David's car towards the harbor trailing puffs of steam as we chugged and bumped down the road. David's chauffeur was good, but he couldn't avoid all the ruts, each one sent shooting pain up my back. It's a sad fact that most roads in Hawaii are still dirt. Even in town.

We had occasional stops to stoke the boiler, horses and carriages balking as their drivers tried to force their horses past. Our chauffeur donning long gloves and walking back and forth from boiler to scuttle with shovelfuls of coal.

"David. When are we going to get paving?" The pain was making me grouchy. I was sitting on the side and had to hold on sometimes to keep from falling out.

"When we can afford to buy the equipment. I want asphalt. It takes trucks, graters, steamrollers, and the paving itself. The U.S. is the closest supplier and they're a little busy at the moment." Then he smiled. "What? You don't like crushed pumice?"

"It lasts about a week."

"It's what we have. You sure you should be out of the hospital?"

I growled at him.

"Suit yourself, but don't make me carry you back."

"I've been looking forward to this trip," Max said. "What I've seen of your dock facilities is very impressive."

"They're built and maintained by the countries that use them," David replied. "Die Handelsflot will have to do the same, or lease space from another power."

"Lease to begin with, or pay with use," Max replied.

"It's what makes the docks interesting," I said. "Each power has its own area with its own language and rules. It's almost like the concessions in China."

"That's a poor example," David said, with an annoyed frown. "The Hawaiians are not unhappy with the arrangement."

"I have to admit," I said, "it beats paying for it all with taxes. But it also makes it impossible to regulate trade. We get everything from walnuts to slaves."

"It's a free market," David said, with a tired wave of his hand.

"The problem," I said to Max, "is the goods that leak in, like opium."

"Opium and slaves?" Max asked.

"There are a lot of people here illegally," I replied. "Field workers, kidnapped girls. It hard to keep a lid on things when you don't control your own ports."

"Hawaii has a strong coast guard and police force. They do a good job," David said. "But we don't have a real army or navy."

"We depend on the British for that," I added. "It's cheaper than building an army."

"Britain is a long way from here," Max said.

"Sometimes too far and sometimes too close," I said.

"Too far I think," Max said. We both looked at him. "That is if you intend to have an argument with the Japanese," he added.

Pearl Harbor is a long drive east from David's house, down wide straight streets. Electrification had yet to take hold in Hawaii so the sky overhead was smoke free blue and clear of wires. Hawaii didn't have access to enough coal to run a big power planet yet. Personally, I liked dark nights and lamplight, and I preferred my coal being spent on making ice. Dark is nice. There was something comforting in walking on a beach lit only by the glow of the surf and stars. Which, of course, brought my thoughts back to Miriam. But I shook it off and took to watching the carriages trying to avoid our great chugging monster of a car instead.

Past downtown and the punchbowl we headed into Chinatown. It doesn't look like much up front other than most signs being in Chinese. It's what goes on in back that's important. Gambling, opium, and trade in the strange. You can find just about anything there, from parrots to gold and jade. And I mean anything. I kid you not and swear on my Mother's grave that once I ran into a man selling elephant penis'. They were dried and he had a basketful of them on the counter.

"They will make you good with the ladies," he said. His wrinkled face and tea stained smile were, as best as I could tell, up front and honest. He was serious.

Looking west from Chinatown, just across Kuwili bay and a short walk over Iwilei Bridge, is Iwilei itself, the city of prostitutes. The police had given up trying to contain it so they made it official. If you wanted to practice prostitution, you put up your sign in Iwilei. Iwilei had its own special pecking order based on distance from the bridge, its main connection to Honolulu and the Pearl. The best entertainment is at the front and I'm not talking about shacks. Some of these places had grown into regular pleasure palaces. Gambling, music, bars. We even had two burlesque theatres and a mirror maze you could chase girls through.

Everything in Iwilei is controlled by one of three gangs. The Hawaiian Lani, whose head Palani was at the party by the way. The American Tong, who had a tendency to buy and sell women, mostly from China or the Philippines. You can shop for and even try out your bride. And lastly the equally unreasonable Gokudo from Japan.

Beyond Iwilei, across the bay, is Quarantine Island. Hawaii gets a lot of visitors from faraway places. People were always coming in with unfortunate diseases. When they catch you, that's where you get sent, most often to die. People occasionally try to swim back to shore, but there are some places in Hawaii that seem to attract sharks. No one knows why. The water between Honolulu and Quarantine Island, a submerged sacred site, is one of them. It's a dwelling place for family spirits, *'aumākua*, and the bones of dead prisoners.

Past Chinatown we threaded our way between the British and Japanese districts, the British naturally living back against the hills and their forts full of soldiers. They likely found them comforting. Honolulu Military District is a network of six forts or redoubts that overlook Pearl and Honolulu harbors. Their cannon cover the water around both harbors. To be fair, the Brits probably like the hillsides too because they get a nice breeze.

Down below in the flats are the Japanese who seem to prefer the shoreline and their fishing docks. They eat a lot of fish and care a lot about the quality. They have the best markets. They also put on some nice festivals.

In between, facing the boulevard, which we were driving down by the way, sits the opera house, "The Thespian." Around it stretches the opera district, the only area in Honolulu with gas light. It's where the best clubs and most exclusive theatres are. You can eat Pilipino for dinner, attend a kabuki theatre performance, and then finish up in a pub. This is the deep water where the big fish hang out. There is startlingly little crime there. A perhaps too oft told joke is that we have more sharks in the Opera District than in the water off Quarantine Island. No one wants to get bitten.

Which was why the murder came as a bit of a surprise.

The streets are generally straight down in the flats so we saw the commotion long before we reached it. We could see a crowd being held back by cops, police wagons, and an ambulance. I looked at the crowd longingly. It could be a story. I think David must have noticed.

"Pull over Kale," David said.

"'Ae Luna," Kale replied, and began working his way over to the side, looking for space to stop.

"Thanks David," I said.

"It's nothing. I'm kind of curious myself."

"What do you think it is?" Max asked.

"I suspect someone did something foolish," David replied.

The sight of the king parted the crowd for us, some even bowing, muttering "Aloha Ali'l." The constables in sight immediately stood to attention, the crowd stilled.

The chief constable strode forward in his blue coat and immaculate white pants and snapped to attention. "Ali'l!"

I translated for Max.

"Good morning constable. Please, tell me what happened."

"A murder, a British officer," he replied stiffly.

"Was it a fight?"

"No. It's most strange." Then he grimaced. "He was tortured, we think to death, and the body left in the alley behind the pub."

My ears perked up.

"May we see?" David asked.

"It's not seemly," the officer said. "The sight is beneath you. He was very brutally handled."

"Nevertheless, I will look. We will be visiting the British today and I may want to bring it up with them."

"As you wish," he said, and then bowed.

He led us towards the alley. They were right. Judging by the lack of blood, he'd been dumped and judging by what was left of his uniform I took him for some sort of officer, but he had some odd insignia I'd never seen before. Looking around the alley I could see nothing else. Just the back door of the tavern. I recognized the place of course. It was *The Three Tuns*. Miriam and I used to go there after shows.

"Why here?" I said to myself. "Why not feed him to the sharks?"

"Perhaps he knew someone connected to this place?" Max replied.

"A warning?" I asked.

"Or retribution," Max said.

"This isn't right," David said. "A broken arm or two if the family owed money, but . . ." He shook his head and turned back towards the street.

"It's very crude," Max said to me as we walked back to the car.

"That is a mild way of putting it," I said.

"No, I mean the technique. They weren't professional, despite the use of a scalpel."

"They?"

"It would have taken at least two to carry him. He was dead when they left him."

"Why a scalpel?"

"Size of the cuts. Did you see where they peeled back the skin on his arm?"

I had actually been averting my eyes. "OK. Why was it unprofessional?"

"You don't work on arms. They aren't sensitive enough," he

said. He looked up at me and smiled. "You work on the feet. They probably had him tied to a chair. And from the look of him, the fools spent most of their time hitting him. It's no wonder he didn't talk."

I was afraid to ask how he knew the guy didn't talk, or why talking was the point of the torture. We were back to the car anyway and I had to climb in, which hurt.

David was in his seat thanking the chief constable. As I took my seat it came to me that I had misjudged Max. Who was he really?

David's Car

Chapter 5 –Everyone Meets an Untimely Death.

David was quiet the rest of the way to the dock district.

We passed a dozen other enclaves each with its own spice and color. Hawaii is the hub of the Pacific after all. People blow in from all over the world to settle.

Pearl Harbor is our international port, as opposed to Honolulu harbor which is just for Hawaiians. It's divided into zones, areas leased by different nations. Naturally, the areas around these zones tend to reflect those who run the docks. There's no gates between them by law but there are definite borders. The signs on one side of the street might be in Hawaiian and the other in Russian. Clothing changes. You tend to stand out when you walk the streets. And the streets themselves are policed by soldiers in foreign uniforms rather than Honolulu police.

David knew each zone and its people. He'd been present as each nation negotiated their contract. That was the basis of his power. That's why he'd been elected king. He was the only man everyone trusted. And we were there to see what David could do for the Germans, his next new friend.

We started our tour from the south progressing north from Haole Point, beginning with the Dutch. A strong presence in the Pacific. Did you know they were our primary importer of coal? I didn't. It knocked me flat. But there it was. Great black piles. Apparently they get it from Indonesia. Seriously, I was impressed, but this has nothing to do with this story. I sold it though. I sold the story to the Hawaiian Times.

Max and the Dutch didn't seem to get along. Apparently there was bad blood left over from one war or another. We didn't even try with the French, probably for the same reason. The Russians seemed friendly, but their operation was too small.

Max expressed interested in visiting the British, our next stop. I was inclined to skip them. It was unlikely they'd help a growing maritime rival with anything having to do with shipping, but David wanted to see them about the murder as well. The British zone takes up a whole mile of the East Loch, its length puckered with dry docks, cranes, and concrete lagoons, all lined with railroad tracks. It's sad that they hadn't extended their tracks outside their area. Honolulu could use a good rail system.

We were stopped by a British checkpoint at the edge of the harbor. There was a line but they waved us over to the side before the car could cause trouble with the horses. The soldier who walked over to talk to us had his rifle slung over his shoulder, but his two friends didn't. They all seemed edgy for some reason.

"G'Day Sir," he said. He seemed young, beaming with honest determination. "Please state your business." Did I mention that the local British regiment was Australian?

"How long have you had checkpoints out?" David asked with concern.

"That's not for me to say, Sir. It's just that we've been having trouble. If you want, I'll ask my sergeant. But, could you please state your business first?"

"David Kalākaua, here to see Admiral Arterberry, if he can find the time."

"The King?" He looked at David carefully.

"Yes."

"Bloody hell!" His eyes went wide. "Oh, sorry sir."

David smiled back.

"Anthony, it's the King," he yelled to his friends. "What do I do?"

"Fair dinkum? You're not having a go?" One friend started forward, trying to see. "Stuffed I'll be! Call the seargent. Call the seargent!"

They let us through with the addition of two guards for escort who had to cling desperately to the car's sides as we bounced along, riding on the running boards.

Admiral Arterberry had a spacious office with wood plank floors, bookshelves lining one wall, a globe, and big windows that looked out over the harbor. The Admiral had come out from behind his desk to meet us and ended up sitting in a much used leather cushioned chair. He wasn't alone. That Stroud woman from the party was there. She seemed like she knew her way around the office. Max and I had the sofa and David an armchair. An orderly poured us tea. Through the window behind the desk loomed the upper housing of a British dreadnought moored at the docks below. It looked like a blue grey mountain.

A little cloud of melancholy drifted by. Miriam worked in this building, in the maps office, somewhere downstairs.

"I still can't figure out how those things float," I said, accepting my tea cup and saucer with a muttered, "Thanks."

The Admiral chuckled. "To be honest, neither can I. In my time we still used wood." He nodded towards a plate of cookies. "Try the biscuits. The orange ones especially. You have, of course, met Mrs. Stroud."

"Yes, we have," Max said.

"We were introduced at David's party," I added.

"Excellent. That will save introductions," he said. "Mrs. Stroud is here to help us with some trade issues."

"This is new. Why haven't heard about this?" David asked.

"I'm so sorry, but I've only just arrived," she said. "I'll require an appointment at some point in the near future." She smoothed her dress, spreading it carefully as she sat.

"Yes of course," David said. "This wouldn't have something to do with the Bank of England?"

"I'm afraid it does," she replied. She stared over David's shoulder as she took a sip of tea.

"We're not borrowing money again," I said to David. "We owe too much already."

"We need infrastructure." David gave me a sharp look.

I groaned. "David." But then I sighed. "Whatever you want."

I looked at Mrs. Stroud. Since when did White Hall send women diplomats representing banks? It seemed that all sorts of odd people were turning up. She was definitely hiding a story. It looked like the news business was going to take a turn for the better, or perhaps things might finally coming to a head here in Hawaii. Maybe both.

"They are amazing," she said, tipping her head towards the ships.

"They most certainly are." Admiral Arterberry was clearly proud of them. "Sadly, I'm afraid they're obsolete. Another ten years and they'll all be gone. Another age passes."

"Obsolete?" I said. "How can something like that become obsolete?"

"There's a new class of ship," The admiral replied.

"Bigger?" I asked, incredulous.

"Quite the contrary. Small. Very small."

"A bit like the end of the dinosaurs," Max said to himself.

"It's all hush hush. Secret you know."

"We call them Zerstörer, destroyers," Max said. Everyone turned to look at him. He looked back at us, as if everyone knew but us. "Everyone's building them."

"Well, ours are secret," he said, slightly annoyed. And then looking directly at me, "We expect them to stay that way."

"You can't hide a ship," Max continued on to himself, which left pause in the conversation. "We can sell you some," Max said, looking at David. "With approval of our king naturally. I have catalogs."

David ignored him and continued with business. "I'd like to talk to you about a murder," he said.

"Yes."

"Apparently, he was one of your commanders."

"He had this on his sleeve," Max said, pulling out a sheet of notepaper from his coat pocket. He had drawn the officer's arm insignia.

The Admiral took it and frowned at it with distaste. "Well yes. We do have a man missing." He passed the paper to Mrs. Stroud. She barely looked at it before handing it back to Max. "Part of all the trouble. An observer from White Hall."

"We found him dead in an alley," David said.

"A common end for sailors," the Admiral replied.

"He'd been tortured," David continued.

The Admiral frowned. His grey moustache drooped. "Tortured?"

"To death," Max added, with relish.

For a second, I thought I saw Mrs. Stroud glance at Max, but I couldn't read the look.

"Oh?" The Admiral said. He took a sip of tea, then glanced at Mrs. Stroud, looking for support, but met silence. "Well then," he said, turning back to us. "This will be difficult." He put his plate down on the side table and got up. "Someone in the community must have been upset."

"No one does this. Not here," David said.

"No, not here," the admiral said. He had wondered to the window and looked out. "Not in Hawaii," he added with finality.

"Being as you're British," I continued. "We thought you might have an idea as to who would do this to a British officer."

"Not a clue," the admiral replied, tiredly. He stood with his back to us. "But be sure. We will investigate."

"You will cooperate with our police?" David asked.

"As always," he replied.

"Thank you."

Then the Admiral turned and looked at Max. "But you're here to talk about trade." He stepped over to his desk and sat down. "I'm afraid I must apologize Herr Schuster, but the British government cannot be of aid to the Handelsflot. As you can see, our sector of the bay is quite full and always in use."

"Naturally," Max replied.

"Since we're here," I said. I'm always angling for more. "And since I can't write about destroyers, would it be possible to tour a dreadnought? Someone should write about them before they're gone."

The admiral thought for a moment, then broke out in a smile. "You know? You're right! Someone should."

಄ඦ

The Admiral decided to give the tour himself, which caused tremendous consternation throughout the corridors of the vessel. Sailors were constantly dashing about, not quite out of sight. Brass hastily polished. The occasional cleaning rag dropped in haste. Gun sights and munitions too quickly covered with rags and tarps. The Captain of the ship accompanied us, his eyes always darting about, his brow furrowed in worry.

Mrs. Stroud stayed behind, claiming an errand. I doubt she could have made it through the narrow corridors without ruining her dress. We were in the depths of the ship, looking at the steam turbines, when the news came. An officer came down the steps and walked out on the catwalk above us. He pulled the clapper stop off a bell and rang it.

The engine crew, who had been standing at attention in their sweat and grime, black coal soot and steam everywhere, stopped and looked up. The officer gripped the railing above us, clutching a wrinkled torn piece of paper. His voice breaking, he began to read.

"On Tuesday, 22nd of January, in the year of our lord 1893, at 6:35 in the evening, our beloved Queen Alexandrina Victoria, Empress of India, Queen of England, died peacefully in her sleep at Osborne House. She was attended by her children." It had taken two days for the news to reach us.

There was a collective intake of breath and muttering. The man near me said, "Dear God!" to himself.

It took the officer a moment to rally, struggling to continue. He finished with a hoarse, "God save the Queen."

"God save the Queen," shouted the crew, voices unsteady.

At which he turned quickly, shielding his eyes as he rushed back to the steps. He hadn't reset the bell.

When I looked about, I saw that the Admiral had fallen back against the turbine housing, his uniform probably ruined. He looked stricken.

Max looked up at David. "I think we should leave," he said.

David looked worried. "Yes. We should."

David said goodbye to the Admiral, but he just waved us away. I thought I saw tears.

"I'll take you up," said the deckmaster. He had just wiped his eyes with a dirty rag leaving long smears across his cheeks.

"Thank you," David said.

The deckmaster showed us to the dock with no challenge from the deck watch. We walked back to the car. The entire base seemed to be in morning. Somewhere a church bell was ringing. Word had spread fast. At the perimeter, they were turning away carriages. Things were going to become complicated for the British.

Chapter 6 –Tea With the Enemy

After the British, across the bend in the bay, were the Dutch, but Max shook his head and waving for us to go on by. He seemed sure it would be a waste of time.

"We recently invaded them. I doubt they feel like talking to us," he said to me with a shrug.

After that came the Japanese. They too had a mile of bay front, theirs looking just as busy as the British. Like the British as well, their docks sported a line of dreadnaughts.

To be frank I was, at that point, a bit hungry. Cookies and tea are great, but not filling. I hoped the Japanese had a place we could eat lunch. But then again, it would probably be raw fish and rice.

Unlike the British, the Japanese checkpoints were alert and always on guard. Today, they were curt as well. The message this time was a clear "you aren't welcome."

"Apologize, not allowing entry today," said the only guard who seemed to know English. His bow was rudely short.

"I apologize too, but this is sovereign Hawaiian territory, and I'm king," David replied firmly.

"Very sorry. I cannot let you through,"

"Are you going to shoot the king of Hawaii?"

He frowned and looked confused. "No."

"Then I'm afraid you can't stop me." David laughed and waved his driver forward.

Max was laughing too, but when I looked back I saw one of the guards raise his rifle to shoot only to be stopped at the last second by the guard who had been talking to us. Instead they took out a flash lantern and began sending a message to someone ahead of us.

"Damn these straight Hawaiian streets," I said to myself, and then to David, "I think we should change direction."

"This is fine," David said.

"We'll get caught."

"I expect so. I just wanted to make a point."

Max looked at me with amusement. "They won't respect you if you cooperate," he said.

Sure enough, they had thrown up another checkpoint in our path, this time the street was blocked by wagons.

They didn't raise their guns. Just a lone officer raising his hand for us to stop. An officer with the button on his holster undone. He was followed by a line of soldiers, who trotted out and flanked our car. They were all navy, with their white uniforms and those ridiculous murata rifles. With the bayonets attached, the things are as long as they were tall, which wasn't very.

David looked at them with impatience. They stared back.

"Do any of you know English or Hawaiian?" David asked.

The officer, some kind of petty officer I think, just blinked back then barked something back in Japanese.

"It seems not," David said to himself.

Then the officer started motioning to us to leave the car, but David wasn't having anything to do with it. He kept shaking head no, looking annoyed. The officer had turned to one of his men and I got the feeling that they were going to pull us out, when there was a shout that caught everyone's attention. Up trotted another officer, quite out of breath. This one was obviously commissioned and army.

"I apologize for the misunderstanding," The officer said between breaths, apparently bowing properly. Really, I think he was bending over, out of breath. "We didn't realize you were coming." The navy soldiers didn't seem pleased to have him there.

"I accept your apology, although I find it strange that I can't drive through my own city," David replied.

"Yes, it's regrettable. These are common soldiers who sometimes take their orders too literally. I'm afraid Admiral Fujioka is away. If it's acceptable, you may see Commander Mori."

"Commander Mori?" David said. "I don't believe I know him."

"He arrived recently. He replaced Commander Akiyama."

"I hope Akiyama-sama is well"

"He is. He took a fleet assignment."

David looked at Max, who nodded back.

"That will be fine," David said.

"May I direct you?" A polite command.

"Yes, that would be very helpful," David replied.

We ended up driving down the street towards the docks passing wagon after wagon, our guards holding on to the side of the car. The wagons heading towards the docks were full of crates, bags, and shells. The ones coming back were empty. All around us, through warehouse doors we could see soldiers moving supplies, piling them in wagons. There were marching lines of solders as well.

"That's a lot of supplies moving," David said. "You could have hired Hawaiian labor."

"Yes, we must apologize, but we are in a hurry. We are having surprise maneuvers soon and two of our warehouses are going to be rebuilt, enlarged." He had to yell over the noise of the engine. "They must be emptied."

"When are your maneuvers?" David asked.

"I cannot say. You must ask the Commander."

We turned along the docks, passing a line of Japanese dreadnoughts. We don't mind warships stopping by for coal and repairs. But they aren't supposed to be based here. Most seemed larger than their British counterparts. Supplies were being carried up ramps, lifted over with cranes, coal spilling down chutes from the docks through doors in the great hulls.

"Ammunition," Max said under his breath, not quite looking at David. But David stared forward stoically, his face unreadable. We were driving by row after row of neatly crated shells on pallets. We don't allow the storage of ammunition on the island. We're neutral.

Admirals everywhere like harbor views and the Japanese are no different. We pulled up to a three story dockside building with more windows than wall, many open to let in the breeze which, thanks to the choice location of the Japanese dock area, was clean and free of smoke.

The building had an ornate steel and iron elevator, which meant they had, at some point, electrified at least part of their zone. Sadly, it hadn't yet extended it to streetlamps. It was funny, but I didn't remember seeing any wires overhead. The elevator operator was a navy seaman in his pristine whites. He said nothing as he pushed the lever forward to two at a word from our escort.

The commander's office was on the second floor, a number two view. Our guide entered first, then came back to tell us we could go in.

Mori's office didn't lack for spaciousness or amenities though. The floor was polished koa wood. If you follow the old religion it's sacred, normally being reserved for surfboards and musical instruments. Objects with a soul. For some reason I felt reluctant to walk on it. Mori was sitting behind his desk, the Japanese fleet visible behind him though his window. Our guide took up station beside him. Mori didn't speak English and needed translation.

"I apologize for any inconvenience," Mori said. "If you send word before you visit next time, we can be sure of a proper reception and that amenities are provided." He waved to three chairs in front of his desk. "Please, be seated. Tea will arrive shortly."

"We were not inconvenienced," David replied, smiling. "Although we were confused. Your security is unusually tight."

"We're holding maneuvers which means we have supplies and ammunition out of warehouses where it's difficult to guard. We don't want theft or accidents."

"Of course."

There was a knock on the door and in came an orderly with a tray. The tea set was English and when he poured, the tea black.

"Living abroad broadens one's tastes, don't you think?" Mori said.

"This isn't abroad for me," David replied.

Mori laughed. "Very true."

"I can understand why many of us want to settle here. I've noticed that Japanese isn't a language option in your public schools."

"If parents demand it, we will add it. And you have your new private schools."

"Yes, but perhaps these things can change. Japan can be a great benefactor for Hawaii."

"Komo mai, we welcome all immigrants equally."

"Someday, you may even see Japanese as the new Hawaiian."

David's a smooth character. He didn't even blink, but kept his smile warm. Mori stayed polite and our talk progressed from there without incident. He turned Max down but apologized profusely.

"We have always had the greatest respect for Germany and your Kaiser, but we haven't enough dock space for our purposes." He looked at David. "This is something we hope to change in the near future."

"There's Ford's Island, or we could discuss dredging the west channel. Ewa would welcome better harbor access."

"Yes, of course," he replied curtly.

We said goodbye, Mori bowing a slight tip of the hips. We were led by our guide back to their perimeter in silence. I could tell David was brooding. Max was simply unreadable. Me, I was hungry.

I was about to suggest a restaurant when Max piped up.

"He didn't bow low enough," he said. "Most disrespectful. He thinks he already owns the island."

"I must have a talk with our British protectors," David said.

"Soon I think," Max said. "Those soldiers. You allow them to base them here?"

"Most definitely not!" David snapped.

"They'll probably say they were in transit," Max said.

"They are not welcome on the island," David said flatly.

We said nothing after that as we drove on. David was about ready to boil over.

Max found his dock space. He found it in the Spanish district, despite their docks being very cramped. The admiral, the first Pilipino admiral in the Spanish navy, Admiral Solos, greeted us warmly as if he knew we were coming. Max and he shook hands and called each other *Katipunan*, whatever that is. I had the feeling that Max had known he would settle on the Spanish all along. I think he just wanted a chance to look the British and Japanese over. We had Burmese for lunch, by the way. Chicken with mango and mint, and David paid, which was great.

Chapter 7 – Max Drives his Message Home

Let's be clear, once we found Max his berth, I was ready to go home. My side still hurt, and I needed time to think. For once I had too many stories. The death of Queen Victoria and the Japanese arming their ships were both big. The last one might even get me killed. But David was all for going back to the British to demand something be done about the Japanese ammunition.

We were stopped again at the British checkpoint. This time they were turning away all traffic. Apparently the harbor and forts were closed in mourning.

"Crikey, it's the king again," the first guard said.

"You big wally, you don't talk to him like that."

"You still on guard?" I called.

"The bludgin relief didn't show," the first called back. "No word, just bugger all nothing."

"No food either," someone called from behind.

"Your lordship," his friend added quietly, frowning and nudging his mate with his elbow.

"Your lordship. Sorry sir," the first piped up.

David was chuckling, but Max looked worried.

"Their relief didn't show."

"Apparently not," I said.

"David, we need to go in," Max said. "This is important."

That got a thoughtful frown out of David. "Yes, you're right." He called to the guards, "Mind if we go in?"

"You sir? No worries."

They waved us through.

Chugging down the road we passed idle trucks, some half loaded, gear and crates just sitting in the empty streets.

We had no trouble walking in the front door of the port admiral's offices. The guards we met before on the wide porch were missing, as was the Admiral's secretary upstairs, and finally the Admiral himself. I don't think he had come back after we left. Our cold tea cups were still there.

We split up. I was looking through offices when I ran into Miriam. She was coming out of an office with some rolls of papers in her arms. I think I was the last person she wanted to see.

"Hello Miriam," I said.

"Carl," she said. She looked embarrassed.

"Any idea where everyone went?"

"They're all at the service."

"Service? Of course, the Queen, but you aren't?"

"No. Someone has to stay behind. I'm not British." She was trying to put the papers on the table inside the office door. I got the feeling she was trying to hide them. "I'm glad you're better."

She might have been glad, but she couldn't seem to muster a smile.

"Your Japanese friends are good, but not that good. I still hurt though."

"They aren't my friends."

"No?"

"Carl. You have to go. Go anywhere, just as long as it isn't Hawaii."

"Something's coming?" I asked.

"Yes, something bad," she said. It was almost a sob.

"Like Japanese are going to attack?"

She lit up with fear.

I smiled and shook my head. "We're not all idiots. That's why we're here." Looking around at the empty offices. "But the British seem to be indisposed."

She stared back at me. I'd never seen that in her before. The complete absence of hope.

I looked at the papers on the table behind her. "And you're spying for them."

She took a step backward, but I grabbed her by the arms before she could run.

"What did they do to you?" I said.

"No Carl, I can't tell you." It came out a sob mixed with panic.

I turned and began to pull her along the corridor.

"Then we'll have you locked up."

"Please no!" She began to fight and pull back.

"Why?"

She stared back at me saying nothing.

Perhaps it was something in her eyes, pleading for me to go away. It came to me in a flash! What they had done. Those bastards!

"Where's Martha?" I asked. Martha is her sister.

"No!" she shrieked and pulled harder, but I held on.

"They've got her," I said.

"Please don't, they'll kill her."

"I'll see them all dead first!"

"One hopes," said a voice behind me. It was Max.

"Max, stay out of this!" I snapped.

Max held up his hands palms out in front of him smiling.

"Oh I intend too. You're doing very well without me."

He looked at Miriam who had broken down, falling back against the wall sobbing.

"This explains much," Max said.

"Where are they keeping her?" I asked.

"I don't know, we meet in Ililei," she sobbed.

"It figures." I thought hard. Where could I get the kind of help it'd take to get in there?

"If you don't mind my interrupting again, but where is Ililei?" Max asked.

"It's our red light district," David said, walking towards us down the hall. "Sorry Carl, but I couldn't help overhear."

I shrugged, then said to Max, "It's a maze of alleys full of kidnapped girls and it's one of the few places the police won't go," I added. "It'll be difficult to find her."

"Yes. But very few of them will be white with blond hair," David said.

"We have that going for us," I said.

"Please don't. They'll kill her," Miriam pleaded, breaking down in heaving sobs. She was still beautiful, even in tears, I thought.

"I don't see how we have any choice," I said. I wished I could have held her. She needed comfort. Perhaps we both did.

"Let me go meet them," she pleaded. "The last meeting is tonight. They said they would let her go."

"Tonight," Max said. He frowned, which got me worrying even more. "We need to find the British," Max said, half to himself. "This is going to be very difficult."

"They're at a service." David said.

Miriam nodded.

"It'll be at the chapel square," David said.

We practically had to carry Miriam downstairs. She was halfway between running and fainting. We all piled into David's car, David in the front, Max and I on either side of Miriam. She sat there warm against my side. It took a while to start the car. The chauffeur had let the pressure drop. He didn't know when we were coming back. We sat in the back while he walked back and forth with the coal shovel, Miriam sobbing to herself. I suspect she thought that the world had ended.

"I've been thinking," Max said. "These Australians might be useful. Foreign soldiers in a red light district wouldn't be noticed."

"That's true," I smiled. "But they couldn't go armed."

"No. At least not in any obvious way. Perhaps pistols."

"Please, please don't," Miriam pleaded.

"They probably intend to kill you both tonight anyway," Max said, with a casual wave of his hand. "It will prevent possible trouble later. You will no longer be of any use to them."

Miriam stared at him like he had already killed her sister, then wailed.

"It makes sense," I added.

The driver climbed into his seat and pulled a lever. We vented steam, jetting it upwards behind us. He seemed satisfied with his gages and pulling a big lever in the floor we took off with a lurch that hurt my back.

Chapel Square isn't very big. Space is always at a premium in the harbor districts leaving little room for parade grounds. Men were packed into side streets as well as the square. Besides being a safety hazard if there was an emergency like we thought, one Japanese shell in the middle of it would take out the entire base. The service would have made a great picture though. A sea of dress reds and blues dotted with white caps.

That's when I saw him. It was Lono, balancing his tripod on the canvas top of a truck. He must have been standing on the steel support stays. Lono Kekoa was a freelance photographer. He worked primarily for the Tribune, but also on occasion for us at the New York Times. Heck, he worked for anybody who would pay. He'll take pictures of your baby.

Behind the crowd was the chapel, tall, narrow, and gothic. Its bell tower in front needling skyward. Crowded on the steps in front, too far away to hear, were the officers and clergy. I could see the admiral amongst them. He had changed his uniform to all blue with a white topped cap. Gold practically climbed up the cuffs of his sleeves.

There was no possible way to drive the car through that crowd. The driver went as far as he could, but from there we had to make our own way. We couldn't have done it without David. As it was, I had to break the way. I called out "Make way for the King of Hawaii!" breaking path through a sea of exclaimed *crikeys, blimies,* and *bloody noras.*

"Turn it up you galah!"

"Shut you gob. It's a funeral!"

The crowd looked angry. I was trying to apologize, when the admiral saw us and told the crowd in a booming voice to make way for us.

When we reached Lono's truck, he had pulled the cap from his camera, counting the seconds to himself.

"Hey Lono!" I called, as quietly as I could.

He waved me away. I just laughed back at him. Then he popped the cap back on his camera.

David and Max had pushed on ahead, but I whispered as loud as I could up at Lono in Hawaiian instead. "Hey Lono, you want a shot from the chapel steps?"

That got his attention. He looked down.

"Carl!" He picked up his camera and threw it over his shoulder. "You bet!" he replied in English, laughing.

He hopped like goat forward to the truck cabin then down to the street. Together we worked our way forward to catch up.

"Hehena the queen dying," he said. He handed me a couple of his bags, which I took. I always like pictures with my stories.

"You have no idea," I said. "How many plates you have left?"

"I've got eight," he said, looking serious. "You think I'll need them?"

"I think you'll want a dozen more before the day's over," I said.

"You got a story?"

"I've got more stories than I know what to do with!"

Lono shut up after that. He looked worried as we worked our way to the front.

Up on the steps the admiral shook David's hand, followed by many of his staff. The admiral's and many of the officer's eyes were red, their cheeks flushed in the afternoon breeze with unshed tears. Then David, the consummate politician, stepped forward and delivered a eulogy off the cuff to the crowd. He expressed sorrow at England's, Hawaii's, and the world's loss, then gratitude for the help the Queen and England had given Hawaii. Me, I stood in the back, scribbling furiously in my notebook. It was great copy. Lono took a picture from behind. It was gold.

When he had finished, David left the steps to a clergyman and went, after a few words with the admiral, to the church atrium. This was something I had to hear. I'm a reporter. I could see Max and Meriam heading that way as well.

Lono was going to set up another picture, but I told him to save it.

"You're crazy Carl. The admiral and the king."

"Trust me," I said.

When I joined them, they were hard at it.

"You can't be serious!" the admiral exclaimed.

"I am. We've seen it!" David replied.

"We think they plan to attack tonight or perhaps tomorrow morning," Max said, almost as if he was talking to no one in particular.

"Nonsense. It's just maneuvers," the admiral said, wiping his forehead with his handkerchief. "They sent us proper notification."

"They're loading way too many supplies and too much ammunition, that is unless they're planning on practicing for months," Max said.

"And how would you know?" the admiral snapped back.

"I work for Krupp as well as the Kaiser. I know what it takes to outfit a warship. I can make a list. I have catalogs back at my hotel. I can even give you prices."

"I'll send someone to investigate."

"You don't have time for that," David said. "How about the troops? Regular army. Lots of them."

"Maneuvers," the admiral replied, crossing his arms.

"Admiral," said a woman's voice. Mrs. Stroud had come up behind him. "I think you ought to listen."

The admiral frowned. It was plain he didn't like her intervention and it was strange that he listened. "The Queen's representative tortured to death and the Queen herself dead," he muttered in frustration. "And now you're asking me to spend hundreds of thousands of pounds to ready ships with no evidence."

"Nigel," Mrs. Stroud cautioned him.

"The time for spies is past," Max said. "The Institution's work here is done," he said, glancing at Stroud. "It's your turn Admiral."

The admiral scowled at Max. "How do you know about that?"

"I represent the German government and the Kaiser," Max said.

"You're a bloody spy," he sputtered, suddenly angry.

"No more than any representative of any government. But you do have a spy problem."

"No," Miriam said quietly.

"Max," I said, trying to intercede.

"He must to be convinced," Max said with an uncharacteristic growl. "We have no time. The whole of the Pacific is at stake, including Hawaii."

"We have a spy?" The admiral asked.

"Max!" I tried to reach for him but he turned aside.

"Miriam has been forced to spy for the Japanese," he said quickly. "They're holding her sister hostage."

"Please, no." Miriam started to pull away, but I caught her. I hated myself for it. I wanted to run with her.

"Miriam?" The admiral looked surprised. "Not possible."

Mrs. Stroud just sighed.

"I know you told me," he scowled at Stroud. "But Miriam . . ."

Miriam started to answer, but it came out a sob, followed by another. They came falling out of her one after another. We all stared for a moment.

"Is that why you broke up with David?" the admiral finally said.

What can I say? The place is like a big family.

Max looked annoyed. "The point is that her last meeting with them is tonight," Max said. "I expect them to kill both her and her sister."

The admiral ignored Max. "You should have come to me," he said.

"They have Martha. They broke her leg and told me they would keep braking bones if I didn't cooperate."

"They broke her leg?" the admiral said, aghast.

Max frowned, then exclaimed in frustration, "This makes things very difficult," he said, shaking his head. "She will be unable to move on her own."

"Were the men holding her Japanese?" the admiral asked.

Miriam nodded between sobs. People around us were trying to be polite, trying not to listen, but Miriam's crying was drawing attention.

"Soldiers?"

She shook her head no.

"Were they covered in tattoos?" David asked. We all looked at him. He'd been so quiet.

Yes. "Necks and arms."

"Gokudo," David spat. "Japanese criminals."

"I'm sure they're very useful to their homeland," Max said to himself.

"I suppose I'll have to lock you up now," the admiral said with a frown.

"No," Miriam sobbed.

"You can't," I snapped.

"I wouldn't," Max said. "You'll need her at the meeting or they'll be suspicious."

"Yes," the admiral said. "Yes. You're right. Of course." He

sounded relieved.

Behind us, facing the sea of British soldiers, the minister was finishing up. People were glancing our way, looking for the admiral to step up.

"I have to finish this," the admiral said, and started towards the front of the steps.

"How long will it take to fire the boilers on your ships?" Max asked casually. "Four, maybe five hours?"

The admiral stopped, then turned back.

"Without steam, you cannot aim or load your guns, and they're right next to you," Max continued.

"They wouldn't, not in a neutral port, not without a declaration of war." The admiral frowned at Max.

But Max only stared back. They both knew their history.

"Think of it as a precaution," Max said.

He frowned, sighed, and reluctantly turned, heading back outside into the late afternoon sun to the steps.

"The time has come for us to continue our work. Each of us must morn in our own way. We, the instruments of her will must continue for the sake of all. The empire must endure. All staff officers to the steps!" he barked. "All others return to your posts!"

Noise rippled through the crowd as the order was passed back.

David looked at each of us with a sly smile, while the admiral spoke.

"I think I know who we can go to for help."

"We need to hurry," Max replied. "When were you to meet them?" he asked Miriam.

"Seven this evening."

"Before the Iwilei gets crowded, while everyone is at dinner," David said.

"Four hours," Max grunted. "It will take half an hour just to get there."

We were heading out the door when the admiral and two MP's blocked our way.

"I'm afraid you can't leave," the admiral said.

"If we don't go, they'll kill Martha," David said.

"And I can't risk losing Miriam. We have to know what

she's given them."

"Perhaps we can compromise," Max said.

Everyone looked at Max.

"It's just that you need to arrest Miriam, and we need muscle."

"Out with it," the admiral said.

"Arrest Miriam, but send her to the meeting. Send her with a squad. . ." That ended with a frown. "I'm sorry, section of soldiers." He smiled. "Sometimes I forget which army I'm talking to. And a clerk to record what she knows."

"We need to hurry," David said. "We have to make a stop."

"Will you take responsibility for her return," the admiral asked David.

"Where can she go?" I asked, interrupting. "It's an island."

"I want you to make a list of everything you gave them," he said to Miriam.

"Don't forget the forts," Max said.

The admiral eyed Max. "You are very helpful," he said with a tinge of sarcasm. "Why?"

"The Fatherland gives us great leeway in making decisions in the field. But this easily falls within my orders. A Japanese Hawaii would be very bad for die Handelsflot. I want you to win."

Chapter 8 – Carl Meets the Underworld

Max and I bounced down the streets in the back of a British army truck along with nine Australian soldiers. They'd been issued pistols at David's insistence, which seemed to be something new for them. As soon as the corporal left to sit in David's car with Miriam and the clerk, they had them out looking them over.

"You do train with those?" I asked.

Max chuckled.

"Feck no," said one.

"They're for poms and officers," said another.

"And swaggies. Me dad had one, from the army."

"Swaggie? Your dad?"

"Sod off!" he snapped back, but the others laughed.

"I guess not," I said to myself.

"We know what to do with them," said a soldier. He was dead serious.

"Hopefully they won't need them," Max said.

"The Gokudo are tough characters," I replied.

"It really depends on who we're going to visit," Max said.

"Do you have an angle on who it is?"

"No. But I think you do. Who might David know that would have influence in Iwilei?"

"That would be Ikaika, head of the Lani."

"And the Lani is?"

"Our version of the Gokudo."

Max nodded, then said to himself, "That makes sense."

He seemed lost in thought so I left him to it.

We were painfully bumping along past Fort Lono, my side throbbing with each jolt. That's no relation to Lono our cameraman by the way. Lono is one of the Hawaiian tiki gods, the god of the earth and rainbows. Our Lono, our cameraman was carefully cradling his big box camera on his lap. He had given his plate case to the man next to him.

We were driving up into the hills above Fort Nanaue, to the

land of the rich, those with a breeze and a view. But even that began to peter out as houses became fewer and fewer. I could see the road behind us though, out through the back of the truck. It was still pumiced. Our tax dollars at work. Strange for such a lonely stretch of road. David doesn't like to waste money. Strange until finally we pulled over to the side.

A soldier hopped out and undid the tailgate and we climbed out. The gravel crunched under my feet as we walked towards a beautiful low wood and stone house. He had a white painted wood tower with a tall green copper roof, I suppose to keep watch, although I couldn't see anyone in it. David asked the corporal to leave the soldiers behind.

We had to pass through a vine and wood lattice covered patio to get to the front where we picked up two big koas to escort us in. But the man himself wasn't inside. He was working in his garden in front. Just from what I could see, he seemed to like ferns and flowers.

"Aloha David," he said, standing up and taking off his gloves. He was thin with long grey hair pulled back in a ponytail, just like David.

"Aloha Palani," David said, shaking hands. "I was worried you wouldn't make it home, you were so drunk."

"I was wasn't I?" He laughed. "You know? I don't remember."

Then they both laughed.

"There isn't trouble is there?" Palani asked.

"Not between us," David replied.

"Good. That truck-full of soldiers had me worried." Then he looked at us.

"You and Miriam back together?" he said to me. He looked hopeful.

"We're still working that out," I replied. I supposed I looked hopeful too.

"Oh good," he said. "Then it can't be a bad day. Miriam and Lono I know, but who are these others?"

"Max Schuster," Max said. He clicked his heels and gave a little bow.

"Oh yes. The German at the party. And you?"

"Corporal Oliver Wendell," he said, giving a little involuntary bow as they shook hands. "The boys call me Olie."

"One of our Australians I see. Well, there must be trouble somewhere or you wouldn't be here. Let's go inside." He started walking in the front door, still talking. "You're not going to believe this mango juice my cook makes up now David. He got the recipe from the cook at that Indian restaurant next to that Haoli market . . ."

"Oh I know, *Mayua Kerala*," David said.

"That's it. They mix it with pineapple and get this, ginger."

Like I said. It's a big family. Even the criminals.

We let David and Palani catch up while we gawked at the house. He had big bay doors around the ocean side of his living room, open to let in light and the sea breeze. The polished hardwood floor was littered with eastern rungs, pottery, and overstuffed leather. Hawaiian ceilings tend to be high to keep the house cool and he had filled this space with a big fan. Something had to be powering it, I thought, but I hadn't seen any sign of a stack or a boiler. He must have gas. All the way up here!

A butler came in with a tray of glasses of mango juice, pleasantly cold of course. I sipped mine and was surprised.

"This is incredible," I said without thinking.

Palani glanced my way with a twinkle in his eye, then went back to talking to David. I could tell that Max wanted to talk to him as well, but was too polite to barge in. Actually, to be truthful, I wouldn't have minded talking to him myself. The guy had to have had a million stories to tell. Some might not even get my hands broken.

"Miriam," David called. "Please tell Palani your story."

I started to follow her, but David held up his hand so I went back to admiring the artwork on the walls. We have some great artists by the way.

I was thinking about taking a walk on the sun deck outside when David finally called the rest of us over.

"It seems," Palani said. "That we may have a common enemy. A Japanese takeover. . ." He stopped to take a sip of juice. "A Gokudo backed by the Japanese government as well, that would be a very bad thing for Hawaii. But then so would a war between

Lani and Gokudo."

"Gokudo," he continued. "Is within its rights to take contracts from foreign governments, but not if it tips the table. Kidnapping Martha was a step too far. That's not how we do things here." He shook his head and mumbled, "Breaking her leg." Then he continued. "I'm willing to help you get Martha back. Gokudo will be punished for this. If we find further evidence of their cooperation in an invasion . . ." He stopped for a second, pondering his words. "Then Lani will stand with all good Hawaiians and go to war."

ℴℙℂℛ

Orders were given in Hawaiian. Men came and went. A couple of Palani's koas pushed his car out of the garage and began stoking its boiler. I wanted to get moving, but all we did was sit down to talk strategy in Palani's patio. Miriam was sitting next to me by the way. It was hard not to keep looking at her, but she was very withdrawn. I think she was sure we were going to get Martha killed.

"Do you really want those soldiers around?" Palani asked.

"A necessary evil," David said. "They're guarding Miriam." And then he added, "And I want English observers as well."

"They might work as a distraction," Max said.

Palani looked hard at Max. "They might at that," he said. "But we'll have to hide them until we move. Iwilei is full of soldiers, but not armed soldiers standing around."

"We might be forgiven for entering the wrong building, especially if we're loaded," the corporal suggested. "Crikey, been here a year and I still get led around."

"And they could be useful carrying Martha out," I added.

"Yeh," the corporal replied. "We actually have training for that."

Miriam looked like she was about to cry again, which I couldn't take.

"This is taking too long. Hadn't we better get moving?" I asked. "We need to get down there and get organized." Damn Hawaiians, I thought. They'll be roasting a pig and pulling beers next.

"Mai hopohopo Carl," David said. "Palani has sent horseman on ahead to start things going."

"There's a trail going into town," Palani added.

They jabbered on for another ten minutes, mostly about how to get the truckload of soldiers across the bridge unnoticed. It was hard to listen. Finally, one of Palani's lugs popped in and told us the car was ready.

Max asked for and got permission to ride with Palani. It seemed they had something to discuss. It was back in the truck for me and back down the road we went, only the truck's Aussie driver was in the back with us along with Miriam, the clerk, and two of Palani's tuffs. Believe me, there was no mistaking them. They all have tattoos. Ours tend to be simpler and more geometric. Frankly, I think they look better. Angled like the islands themselves. I suppose it's a matter of taste. Criminal fashion.

We were barely down the hill when Palani's koa pulled down the flaps in back and tied them off.

"Hey, it's too hot for that," I said, in Hawaiian too.

But they just grunted back. I guess the point of it was for us not to see where we were going. And as far as that went, it worked pretty well. Judging by sound only, the best I could figure was that we were somewhere around the north side of Chinatown. The Aussies seemed to take it in stride. I guess they spent a lot of time getting lugged around in wagons and trucks without knowing where they were going.

We pulled into some sort of warehouse where we were left in the truck. The drivers dumped the coal box and vented the steam. Our truck wasn't going anywhere.

It was fifteen agonizing minutes before someone pulled the flaps back and led us to another much bigger non-army truck. This time we had to squeeze in back towards the truck cabin practically on top of each other, because we were hardly in before Chinese workers started piling boxes in after us, some of them definitely containing onions. The idea was obvious, even without Corporal Wendell's explanation. Commercial truck, hide behind the boxes. It didn't make the delays easier though. My pocket watch said five fifteen.

Once we were in the heart of Chinatown I had a pretty good

idea where we were, and there was no mistaking the river and bridge to Iwilei. We still had plenty daylight so the lanterns weren't lit, which was too bad, not that we could have seen it in the truck, because the Iwilei bridge at night is something to see.

Every class of people cross that bridge. Every nationality. It's a line of lit carriages pulled by decorated horses, many whose only business is carrying people to and from Iwilei across that bridge. Along the sides walk women and men. Not all of them were there for sex and entertainment. Some are bringing their wives and husbands their dinner or are coming to pick them up after work.

The bridge itself is lit by great glass gas lanterns, clear on the road side for light, colored glass on the ocean side to reflect in the river's surface. And dancing amid the traffic, moving with the shimmer of the water, are street performers and musicians, begging for coins. Visitors toss them from the carriages with a constant jingle and ting.

The coins only add to the music of the street. Every musician tries to play a different tune, but somehow, when you stand back on shore staring at the weaving reflections, all of the music seems to merge into one.

But we were there in the late afternoon, before dinner even. The street sweepers had barely finished their day. Worse, we were in a hurry on hard truck springs, which might as well not have been there. The bridge had settled after it was built and there were places where sections had become uneven, and it was hard to stay quiet and not whoof or grunt every time we and the boxes went over one. My side!

We turned sharply. There were grinding gears. Then we backed into someplace dark. Someone threw the flap back and the gate dropped.

"Nobody here to unload," said a woman's voice in clipped Hawaiian. "You have to climb over."

"There's nobody to move the boxes," I translated.

"Right," said Corporal Wendell. "Andrew, you first and then take the guns."

We crawled out one at a time into a dark blue twilight alley in the low sun, passing gear hand over hand, our movement shielded from the street by the truck. Soon she began to shoo us into a side door. I thought she was perhaps Pilipino, wearing a kimono. Inside, it was dark. We were standing in a hallway, precious minutes ticking by. Inside somewhere I could hear a Victrola playing music. The Aussies were still climbing out when another kimono clad woman came down the corridor with a candle to meet us. They had to be Pilipino. This one was old, her grey hair up in a loose bun.

"Follow me," she said in Hawaiian, which I translated.

"Crikey, give us a minute," said our corporal.

"Follow me or stay," she said, and began to walk back down the corridor.

"Fecken hell. Luke, you stay and help. The rest are on me."

I didn't wait but took off after her, lugging two of Lono's boxes.

As I said, the corridor was dark, lined with doors. Her silhouette bobbed up ahead. When I caught up, followed by a line of soldiers making a heck of a racket with all their gear, she had turned a corner, opening a door. There were narrow wood stairs going down. There was light down there.

"This way," she said.

"Thomas, stay here wait for the rest," the corporal said.

"Aye."

Down we clunked into a basement room crowded with men and full of smoke.

"Ah, Carl!" David called. He sounded happy. "You finally got here."

"We made a stop or two. . ." I replied, my voice trailing off. The basement was full of koas, most without shirts and pants, muscles, tattoos, and weapons in full display. Definitely a war meeting. They were standing about, leaning on walls, and sitting on crates. Two were wiping down polished steel swords with oily rags. David and Palani were sitting in wicker chairs, sipping what looked like tea. Miriam and Max were standing behind them. The soldiers were piling up behind me so I finished the steps.

"You feeling up for a little adventure?" David asked.

"Perhaps."

"We'd like you to accompany Miriam to the meeting," David said.

"Won't that tip them off?"

"We don't think so, but it will draw their attention."

"They'll want to know what she told you and who else she talked to," Palani said. "With any luck, they'll find out just before you get there." He grinned.

I frowned.

"What's wrong?" David asked.

"I'll do it on one condition."

"David!" Miriam snapped.

It was everyone's turn to frown, so I went on. "I want the story. Without any edits."

"No," David said.

"If the Japanese attack, then perhaps," Palani said.

David turned and looked at him, putting his tea cup down with an audible tink.

"David," he said, lecturing. "If they attack, it won't matter. It will be good press for us both."

"It will be the government and Lani pulling together for Hawaii," I added.

David thought for second, then smiled.

"You're right. That would be fine story," he said, and picked up his cup and took another sip of tea.

"And I want a picture too," I added.

Which is how Miriam and I ended up walking together down Iwilei way alone.

Chapter 9 —Carl and Miriam Take a Walk

They took Miriam and I back across the bridge in the truck, still full of onions, and left us. We had to catch a carriage back, on my dime by the way. I guess I'd forgotten to ask for expenses. It dropped us off at in the square at the end of the bridge, the sun setting just to the right of Quarantine Island. The usual tumble of clouds seemed thicker than before. In Hawaii, that generally means rain.

We walked for a bit in silence.

"Carl?"

"Hmm?"

"Would you have come if they hadn't given you the story?" Miriam asked.

"Yeah. I just wanted to shake them up. If I hadn't made them stop to think, they would have just said no."

Then she looped her arm through mine as we walked down an alley in the blue twilight, the building tops above us still tipped in orange sunset light.

"I suppose we're going to die," she said.

"It seems likely," I replied.

"I really do still love you," she said. It almost came out a sob.

"I couldn't stop loving you," I said back, maybe with a bit of a catch in my voice as well. I pulled her closer.

At the next cross street there were people running and scattering, but I couldn't see from what. Down the street and around the corner I heard a window break. But Miriam didn't seem to notice. She turned and put her arms around me and put her head down on my chest and started sobbing.

I couldn't pass that up and put my arms around her and held her close, stroking her hair. Somewhere along the line it had come undone, tumbling down her back in loops and curls. I pulled her hair comb loose and put it in my pocket, then went back to stroking her back while she cried. In the distance there was an explosion.

In the next alley we passed two bodies. They looked

Japanese and from the broken bones it was clear they'd met up with Palani's koas. Lua is a nasty discipline invented by the Hawaiians. It involves the use of leverage applied at critical points in the body to break bones and ruin organs. Judging from the bends in their limbs and spines, these two had met up with a master.

But Miriam walked on past. She only had eyes for me. I don't think she noticed.

A door slammed open and women in robes and kimonos poured out, some screaming. We had to dodge them as they ran down the alley behind us. Miriam turned away from them, pushing closer to keep from colliding, which was nice. It's weird, but I figured that if we were going to die, then I was glad it would at least be together.

Up ahead, gunfire had broken out, random popping echoing down the narrow roadways and alleys. It sounded like the Fourth of July and Chinese New Year combined. The air had become smoky and up ahead, a truck careened by on a cross street engulfed in flame.

"What the hell is going on?" I mumbled.

"Oh Carl, does it really matter?" Miriam replied.

"No," I said thoughtfully, then looked at her with a smile. "No, I guess it doesn't."

Finally I could make out the outline of our destination through the smoke, a three story tall pagoda nestled in a nest of ramshackle tenements painted a garish mix of colors. A regular little kabukicho. And sitting in a couple of chairs at the broken gate, out front, were three men dressed in dirty white suits. It was Lono, Max, and David. They were smoking cigars.

"Ah, the love birds finally decided arrive at the party," David said, as he took a puff. Max just grinned.

"Martha," Miriam said and started forward.

Max stood up to block her. "No, no. Not yet."

"There's still some holdouts, but she's safe," David said with a smile. "You want one?" he asked, offering me a cigar. "They're Cuban."

"Yeah," I said reaching out to take it.

"They're booty," Max chuckled.

"So you never meant for us to go in," I said.

"No, we just wanted you out of the way," David replied. "We figured you needed some time alone."

A raindrop plopped in the dirt street next to my foot, then I heard another hit my hat.

"Rain," Max grunted.

"We better get in," David said with disappointment.

They picked up their chairs and headed through the gate, with us following. I have to admit to being a bit bewildered. How was I going to write about all this if they were going to keep me in the dark?

Inside the gate there was a stretch of gravel and a stone walk. Nothing fancy. You were supposed to look at the pagoda. It had three big wide roofs, stacked like poker chips, which is good because their thin walls need all the shelter they could get. Some Japanese houses have only paper. It's true! Walls made out of a paper. One good storm and it's all gone. I have to admit that it's cheap to replace, but why should you have to? Anyway, I could hear music coming from inside.

Up the steps, past the paper lanterns which are so popular in Iwilei despite the rain, and through the double doors into what can be best described as a bar. I suspect the point was to make customers sit and buy drinks while they waited. They had a Victrola and a stack of records on the counter behind the bar itself. It was playing "Ta-ra-ra Boom-de-ay." Miriam coughed on David's smoke as it trailed behind him.

David and Max headed for the bar. Palani was already there. One of Palani's koas was wiping blood off the bar top. Max asked what kind of beer they had and if was warm. Palani asked for another scotch. I was a little incredulous.

"So you're all going to sit here and get drunk?" Miriam asked.

"You have something better to do?" Palani asked.

She frowned. "What about the attack? You know, the war?"

Max looked at her thoughtfully.

"We told the fleet," David said.

"Either they'll win or we'll all die," Palani said as a new scotch over ice was plunked down in front of him.

"It will hurt less if I'm unconscious," David added.

"Makemake au i ka green fairy."

"At least let me get Martha to a hospital."

"She's fine," David said. "They had someone set her leg weeks ago. She's sleeping."

"They gave her opium," Palani said with a grin.

"What!?" Miriam yelled.

"Apparently, she was making too much trouble," Palani continued. "Inciting the women to revolt."

"Yes, that was a surprise," David said. "Not too much sugar," he said to the bartender as the water was pouring over the spoon.

"So we're just going to sit here?" I asked.

"It's a bit early, but we could get dinner," David replied.

I had the feeling they were having a little fun with us.

"You're kidding," I said.

"Actually, I don't think he is," Max said, giving David a wry look. "I doubt the shooting will start soon so we might as well. They'll still be firing up their boilers and stowing shells. The checklists and paperwork involved are terrifying."

It was funny. Now it was a race to see who could get their paperwork straight first

"Besides, we're not done here yet," David said. There were shots still popping in the distance. "And we can go back with the Aussies. When they're through of course."

"Yes," Max said. "They seemed to be having fun when I last saw them."

"They've always been good customers," Palani added and threw back his scotch.

๛๏๛

We had dinner with the Tong. They ran a restaurant in Iwilei David liked, the Tan Chang, which they opened up especially for us. We even had Ko Chin, the Tong leader, join us. The power balance in Iwilei had been upset, not to mention a fair bit of property damage. Blood in the streets is bad for business, so David and Palani had a lot of feathers to smooth. We were lucky. The quickness of Palani's decision to strike had taken everyone, including the Tong, by surprise, otherwise it might have been a three way battle. The involvement of British troops had given the Tong pause as well.

After dinner, David, Max, and I were sent bouncing along through the streets with the Aussies in their truck. We had to leave Miriam with Martha. She couldn't have gone even if she had wanted to. The British would arrest her. She'll never be able to set foot in the British zone again. The Aussie corporal found many of their stolen documents, all certainly copied, but no Miriam or Martha.

The Aussies had acquired a case of beer, in bottles no less, and were celebrating. They carved the stoppers out with their knives, the beer overflowing out onto the truck bed. They'd left two of their own back in the hospital, but none of them had died and now they were all flying high on victory. The Gokudo are no strangers to firearms, but they don't carry them as a general rule so the Aussies had been left free to blast a bloody path through the streets, opening a way for Palani's men to hit the pagoda with complete surprise. The Lani knew all the Gokudo strongholds and had hit them simultaneously, leaving the few who escaped on the run, to be hunted down one by one by both Lani and Tong. I figured the Gokudo had probably had something similar planned for the Tong and Lani, which was why we caught them gathering at their hideouts.

"So Max," I yelled over the rumble of the truck and the Aussie singing.

"Yes?"

"Do you think the Japanese know about the Gokudo?"

"A better question might be, do they care?" He smiled. "They probably intended to be rid of them when they were through."

We went over a bump, which knocked a couple of laughing Aussies off their seats.

"You need to work on your roads," Max said.

"I keep telling David that."

"We need machinery," David said.

"Krupp can help you with that. We make the best in the world. I have catalogs."

"The problem is that you're on the other side of it," David

replied.

"That may not be such a big problem soon."

"Max," I said. "You're an unflappable optimist."

He just smiled and shrugged.

"It's too bad we can't take a picture of this," I yelled.

"I can take a picture of anything!" Lono yelled back with determination. He handed his beer to the Aussie next to him, who took a swig from it.

"I've got fast plates, but this is too close," he said, looking about. "I need to get further back."

"How far back," I asked.

"Outside the truck."

We ended up stringing a rope across the tailgate and Lono braced his feet on the edge, his back leaning way out over the moving pavement below. He looked like a jockey bouncing up and down with the truck. We passed him his camera and snapped a picture of us all raising beers in victory.

The British harbor perimeter was still closed, this time for real, and we had to wait for a runner to return with permission to let us enter. In a way, the death of the queen had been helpful here as everyone thought the base was still in mourning. But there was no disguising the smoke leaking out of their ship's stacks. One could hope that the Japanese couldn't see it in the dark. A carrier was leaving the harbor as well when we pulled up at the admiral's office. Its terraces of gondolas, envelopes carefully folded, climbing its sides. The ship's lights reflected in long lines in the water. The admiral's offices were all alight as well, despite it being 10 PM.

An aid met us in the lobby.

"You're to come up immediately," he said and turned and led us to the elevator.

The admiral was sitting in his desk, pipe in mouth, signing papers. Mrs. Stroud, as comfortable as ever, sat in big padded leather chair sipping tea.

"Requisitions," he muttered to us as we came in. "A thousand unfinished repairs all needing to be done tonight. All needing emergency supply releases!"

He looked up with a frown, his bushy eyebrows draping dangerously low over his eyes.

"I'd be very angry right now if it wasn't for the fact that you were right."

We just stood there. I don't know about the others, but I wasn't sure how to respond to that.

Then his eyes locked on the Corporal, who was standing at attention.

"Where's Miriam?" the admiral asked.

"Gone sir," the corporal said. "We lost her."

"Oh. Too bad," he said. He looked relieved. "Can't be helped, I suppose. Dismissed."

The corporal looked stunned, but managed a "Sir!" and a salute before he left.

The admiral ignored him.

"We sent scouts to the Japanese perimeter in mufti," Mrs. Stroud said.

"Yes. Yes we did," the admiral said, looking at Mrs. Stroud. "And I'll be damned if there didn't turn out to be troop movement. They're moving up into the hills through the Olepe River valley, behind the forts. Alerted the army. It's their problem. I wouldn't be surprised if there weren't landings east of Honolulu as well."

"I need to mobilize the police," David said.

"Can't let you do that. It would alert them," Mrs. Stroud said.

"There are farms out there. People could be hurt."

"Not as many as would be if they start before we're ready," the admiral agreed.

"No declaration of war yet?" Max asked.

"Not a word," the admiral replied.

"Typical," Max said. "They'll wait for dawn if they can."

"How can you know that?" I asked.

"They'll have calculated their aiming coordinates for their guns beforehand, but they won't know for sure. They'll want to see their shells fall to be certain, if they can," the Admiral replied. "Which is why we need to keep it secret. Besides, they're still moving troops. They aren't ready."

"Don't count on that," Max said.

"Quite. Of course," the admiral replied.

"Any idea of their strength?" Max asked.

"We thought they had a battalion reinforced with an engineer company and a materials company, about 1200 men, but apparently they have a great deal more. We have no idea where they hid them."

"I wondered when we were there," Max said. "They had electricity everywhere but there were no wires overhead."

"You think they've been digging tunnels?" the admiral asked, those bushy eyebrows raising in surprise.

"It would be one explanation," Max said.

"We're right next to them!"

Max just smiled back at him.

"Damn!" He sat back in his chair and said damn twice more.

"Cyril!" the admiral called.

His secretary appeared, "Sir?"

"I'm going to send out ack priority orders to all staff. I'll need runners. Get me the typist. We'll need to mimeo them, then sign them. And we'll need more tea as well."

"Sir."

HMS Hesperus

Chapter 10 –They Gird for Battle

David left with a courier to get back to the government seat. Max, Lono, and I were left to sit in the admiral's office with Mrs. Stroud, trying to stay out of the way while the man worked, drinking excellent tea. Men scrambled, paper flew. An orderly brought him his pistol belt, then brought ones for us as well. Mrs. Stroud waved it away.

"Ever used one of these?" The orderly looked at me.

I'm afraid I had to say no.

"Admiral, I'm a reporter. A non-combatant. Wearing one of these could get me killed."

"You might as well," Max said. "They will have more respect for you. It's their caste system, warriors at the top."

"We're bringing you uniforms as well," the admiral said. "We can't have you running about in those white suites. You'll draw fire. In fact, I should go change before something else comes up. I'm giving you the story Carl. She insisted." He looked at Mrs. Stroud. "Someone has to document this. But stay out of the way or I'll send you home."

The orderly was sizing up Max. I suspect he was wondering if they had any uniforms that short.

"As a representative of the Kaiser, I would like very much to stay as well," he said to the admiral. "Our interests in this run along the same lines, and who knows? If this gets out of control, Britain may need an ally."

"A German spy?" the admiral said. "I should lock you up."

"I agree with Herr Schuster," Mrs. Stroud said. "German cooperation in this will be helpful. They have more assets in the Pacific than you know admiral." She gave Max an adversarial glare. "I believe we will ultimately need their assistance. This will not end here."

The admiral looked at both Mrs. Stroud and Max. "You've been very helpful, so far," he agreed. "We may even have located one of their tunnels."

"There will be more," Max said.

Then I started to object to the gun again, but they all ignored me. Instead the admiral took another sip of his tea and got up, and frankly gave up. "Pardon, but I have to change," he said. "I'll see everyone soon."

As the admiral closed the door behind him, I looked at the pistol and muttered, "Well, they'll probably kill me anyway."

Max chuckled. "I suspect we'll wish we were dead if they catch us and don't."

"I'm afraid so," Stroud sighed in agreement. Then an orderly poked his head in and called her away. Something about a dressmaker.

The orderly came back wanting our shoe sizes and then we were left to do what all armies do, we sat about and waited. The uniforms arrived, eventually. They were kaki with black boots calf wraps. Max had to help me put them on. We had kaki cloth covered helmets too. We changed, and then we waited some more.

When they finally came for us, Max was asleep in the corner. Lono in a chair.

I couldn't sleep. Too much had happened. I had to get it down on paper. I was sitting at the admiral's desk with a pencil and paper, trying to order the day's events.

There was a knock on the door. It was a British naval lieutenant.

"Gentlemen?" He looked in and glanced about.

"Is it time to go?" I asked.

"Yes. We have to hurry."

"Hey Max!" I growled as I stood, folding my work and stuffing it in my pocket. But Max was already getting up.

"What time is it?" he asked.

"3 AM," the lieutenant said.

"I could use some tea," I mumbled.

"I'm sure they'll have coffee on board," the lieutenant said.

"Where are we going?" I asked.

"The Hesperus," he said, like that meant anything.

The Hesperus was seven blocks away, down dark crowded streets filled with marching soldiers and wagons of supplies. There were few lights and most of what lights there were, were shuttered. She was moored in a small jetty, away from the big ships. To get to her, we turned left down a dark side street, leaving the crowds to the main road. There was a checkpoint at the end of the street before we could get a glimpse of the ship herself. When they let us through and we emerged from the dark street, onto the grey star lit dock. Looming in the darkness was the outline of a warship, sleek, a gunboat with only a single small mast. No sails needed. She looked trim and probably very fast. Besides her two turrets, she had a big assembly of tubes amidships behind the bridge and the first two stacks. She had two big tubes coming out her bow as well. Judging by the sparks drifting up with her smoke, her boilers were fired and ready.

From what I could see by the lantern light on the dock, except for guards and the coming and going of runners, the dock was empty. I wondered when the moon would rise. I tried to remember what it had been last night.

The lieutenant stopped halfway up the aft gangway and saluted the ship's flag, even though no one could see it, again at the top, then he and a petty officer exchanged salutes. After that it was straight up steel steps to the grey steel bridge.

That Stroud woman was already there, on the bridge. She had changed into a simple kaki dress. No bodice, loose sleeves. The only ornamentation was a wide low collar tied with a large bow just above her breasts. Even her shoes were low heeled. She looked like a school girl sailor.

"Ah gentlemen, welcome to the party!" the captain said, turning to face us in his seat. "We're just about to make way."

"She's a beautiful ship," Max said, nodding to Mrs. Stroud, as the captain stood to shake hands.

"Now I have no choice about this," the captain said, ignoring Max. "Reporters. Civilians. A woman," he nodded towards Emily. "On our bridge, during battle no less. But I am still the captain, and if I say move, go below, or *anything else*, then you will do it. You will not get in the way. You will not ask the bridge crew questions, especially if we're engaged.

"Yes, of course," Max said.

"A German no less," the captain snapped back. Then he looked to the side at a lieutenant. "I don't think they'll be needing bunks." The officer nodded. "This will be over, one way or another, in a few hours."

"I was wondering why we didn't get spare underwear," I said.

"We're going to anchor in the west channel behind Moku' ume' ume island and wait," the captain continued. "If it comes to blows, then we'll make our run from there."

"Inside the harbor," I said. "David will not be pleased."

"I've been given to understand that he met with some delay leaving the base," the captain said.

"They didn't," I said, then chuckled.

"He'd want to mobilize and we can't allow that to happen. We would lose our advantage of surprise. I'm told he'll be delayed until sunrise. We have to keep this secret for as long as we can."

An ensign interrupted us, giving the captain a clipboard. He began to thumb through the paper.

"Oh," he said, looking up. "Don't get comfortable. We leave in twenty two minutes. If you smoke, please do it on the flying bridge." He nodded towards a hatchway. "We'll be running with lights out so no smoking after we're underway." The ensign then handed the captain a pair of black goggles.

I don't smoke, but I felt like I was underfoot so I headed for the hatch anyway. Max and Stroud followed. Inside the bridge they had electric panel lights that sort of lit things, but outside it was pitch black. Lono had pitched his camera out there.

"I'm surprised the admiral let a woman on board," I said.

"The admiral has no choice," Stroud replied smugly.

"Max mentioned an institution. Is that it?"

"I was indiscrete," Max said.

"Unusually lax of you," Stroud said. It was dark, but I think she was smiling. I know when to shut up. Max helped me out by changing the subject.

"Getting through the harbor in the dark is going to be interesting," he said.

"It could be embarrassing, especially if we run into something and Japanese don't attack." I leaned against the cold steel bulwark and worried.

"I should thank you by the way," Max said to Stroud.

"Oh, it's nothing. What good is rank and privilege if you don't exercise it once in a while?"

"Besides. I suppose we're done at this point. We can relax and have some fun."

Relax? I thought.

"Yes," she sighed, and then she smiled. She sounded excited. "All we need now is champagne."

Max chuckled. "I think the captain is waiting for the moon to rise. I doubt we have time to order it."

There was nothing above us but the glow of the stars.

"It can't be much of a moon this late," I said.

Then I heard clanging down the sides of the ship.

"Deadlights," Max said. "They're shutting the porthole hatches."

We stared into the dark for a bit. Then a figure emerged from the hatch. By the light of his match I could see he was an ensign.

"Rather a bit dark out here sirs," he said. "And ma'am." He sounded young and upper class.

"Yes," Max said. "It's for the best."

"There does seem to be some glow on the horizon," Stroud said.

"That will be the moon," the ensign said. He took a few draws on his pipe and then asked, "Are you really a German spy?"

Max laughed. "No, but I'm as good as one. I work for the German government."

"I guess you wouldn't admit it if you were," he said. "Amazing the old man let you on board."

"We share a common interest in this affair," Max said. "Besides, it's unlikely I'll get to see the important parts of the ship."

"Like what?"

"You're new Parsons turbines and your Brennen torpedoes and launchers. I saw an example of a Belleville boiler in Stockholm, but it was guarded. I would like to look at one closely."

"Hell. You are a spy," he said.

"I work for Krupp as well as the government. They are all our competitors. When it comes to our competition, I am most definitely a spy."

Our ensign almost blew his tobacco out of his pipe. I don't think he had an answer for that.

They'd pulled back the gangways and were casting off from the dock. Our ensign had stepped back inside. I could feel the engines beneath us as we slowly began to inch forward. The water glowed as it churned behind us.

As we cleared the pier, the moon topped Mo'o, Moku. Its thin light dancing across the water. Its sweet light danced on the water like syrup. I could almost hear a hula. A sailor stepped out and tied the hatch open. He was followed by the captain, who had to feel his way because he was wearing black goggles. At the forward bulwark he took them off, blinking, then rubbing his eyes. The light from inside the bridge had changed to deep red.

I hoped someone could see because, even with the thin sliver of a moon, I couldn't see a thing except the dim shape of the boat around me.

"Ten points starboard," the captain said. The sailor in the doorway repeated it to the bridge.

I could see occasional lights from shore, but we were sailing past the British sector and it was probably darker than usual. But the captain seemed to know what he was doing, calling in course corrections through the doorway.

We were out in the channel, passing the Southeast Loch, passing a fishing boat, a straggler. The captain shielded his eyes from its lanterns. It was late for a fishing boat to be coming in. Most came in through Honolulu, straight in to the fish market, which made them suspicious. If they were Japanese, I thought, they could blow the whole operation. But the captain let them go by.

Luckily, that was the last boat we saw until we rounded the south point of Mo'o. The sky had started to grey.

We spotted them as we rounded the point. Two Japanese destroyers, just like us, moored waiting to do to the British what we intended to do to them.

Our captain could do nothing. They had to shoot first. So we sailed right by them and headed up channel. Being on the far side of the island, there was thankfully no way for the destroyers to report our position. We settled in the Middle Loch in a fading pool of black. Then there was nothing to be done but wait.

හරඥ

I have to this day no idea who started it. For us it began a half hour after we took up position in the Middle Loch. It began with thunder, then great explosions, answered by more thunder until it was practically continuous. That was our queue to begin.

The ship's engines banged through the deck, fire spat through the funnels, the seaman in the hatchway grabbed me and pulled me in after Max. Lono had set up his tripod and camera and fought to stay. They finally gave up, dogging the hatch behind us. In the dark of the bridge, lit by the red panel lights and the yellow tinged thin grey of the earliest of morning, I felt the deck surge beneath us as we picked up speed, almost like surfing. Orders from our captain rolled out, answered by crisp replies, we sped out of the loch into the channel. She slid from behind the island a blue grey shadow, silhouetted by the sun, quite simply and entirely a complete surprise to the Japanese.

We were coming about, turning into the channel. The deck tipped, all of us scrambling to find things to hold on to. When she righted, we could see the Japanese docks ahead of us, dreadnoughts like a range of mountains in the distance with us still picking up speed, running towards them, the shoreline speeding by.

Great explosions and columns of black smoke were rising around the Japanese ships, ripping away great tangles of shredded iron. The ship's guns though, sealed in impenetrable vaults of iron, were answering with bursts of black flaming clouds, spitting steel, aimed at the British. The chaos was so great I could no longer make out individual ships between the explosions. Our forward turret fired, belching two great balls of smoke and fire. They enveloped the bridge as we sped through it. A torpedo spat from the bow and dove into the water.

We were so small next to what we were witnessing. What could this little ship do to monsters like those? I watched, horrified as we closed distance with them. As we began to come about around the north point of Mo'o, a second torpedo leapt out. I watched their trails through the water as they sped towards the docks. It was strange, but I thought I saw our two joined by a third and then a fourth that came out of nowhere. There were no ships about.

I looked over at Max, but he seemed to be watching battle with rapt interest. Mrs. Stroud was holding on to a pipe. She was grinning.

Then. Oh dear God. Then the first torpedo hit. The whole of the ocean lit from below. I could see the bottom blue green, brighter than day. A column of water rose from the side of a cruiser. The second struck in the dim morning twilight, lighting the bow of a dreadnought from below before it blossomed from the water. I couldn't see for all the light and water what they had done. I didn't want to see. The shells of ships are so thin. Once breached, a ship becomes a coffin.

We were turning again, hard a port, heading straight down East Loch, parallel to the Japanese docks, somehow picking up even more speed, carving a path through the orange and blue water. How can a ship go so fast? She lurched. Another torpedo sped away from the deck tubes. But I didn't see it hit because the turrets had fired and I had turned to look, the flame and smoke were magnificent.

Up until then, the Japanese hadn't fired back at us, so great was the surprise. Somewhere though, somewhere in that sea of fire and crushed metal, someone decided that we were a threat. A shell rocketed past us with a boom. The windows in the bridge burst in sending glass everywhere, in my hair and clothes. And yet the ship lurched as second torpedo left the side tubes.

I was thinking, as I tried to pull myself up from the glass covered floor that the water in Pearl is pretty warm and I'm not a bad swimmer. To their credit the bridge crew were up before me and back at the helm. Mrs. Stroud stood back up, dusted herself off, straightening her dress, before resuming her position at the pipe. She was laughing. I thought, why is this woman here? They're insane!

"We're so close, the shells are coming in with a flat trajectory," Max said, in practically a yell. "It's amazing."

"You are out of your mind," I replied firmly.

"No. It's probably the side sponsons. They can't engage the British docks. They have no one to shoot at but us."

They laughed together. They were insane.

There was another boom and the ship rocked. A pipe whistled and a lieutenant uncorked it. There was a muffled voice and the lieutenant said, "We've lost the aft funnel." But he was cut off as the turrets fired again. That was the last shot for the forward turret. I heard a shell scream by behind us and then another. Then one struck the forward turret. Metal and fire flew in the windows. Two men went down. One with half his head gone.

And yet, somehow, another torpedo left the side tubes.

Mrs. Stroud's only reaction was to look down at her blood specked dress. "Damn," she said.

Max was hanging on at the window, shrapnel be damned, to view the damage.

Then we went into another turn, our deck tipping. Around Mo'o and into the British zone we steamed, not that that made any difference. The Japanese were still shooting at us.

The British docks looked like Dante's Inferno with twisted blazing wreckage, and the water around was filled with swimming men. But their great cannon were still firing, thunder erupting defiant as their lives were torn away with the metal around them.

Ahead of us, were those two destroyers, just beginning their run – late. I saw two flashes, their forward deck guns. A shell hit the port flying bridge, tearing it from the ship, knocking everyone around. Lono, I thought. But then I remembered he was on the other side.

And here I have to apologize. The rest is missing. I must have blacked out, because I had no recollection of how I ended up laying in the corner. Apparently we took another shell. I am, however, an experienced reporter. And I'm writing this now, so you know I lived to tell the tale. The rest of the story of the battle of Pearl Harbor came straight from Max.

The two Japanese destroyers were starting their run on the British docks. The flashes I saw were their forward guns firing as we came about. Sadly, we couldn't fire back because we had no forward turret. A shell had hit the aft superstructure and taken out the rest of our missing funnel and part of another. I suppose the concussion was what knocked me down. But the captain was still standing and we had nowhere to go but forward and so it was forward at flank speed. We came at them so fast they didn't have time to fire again. The starboard torpedo tubes were still loaded so the captain swung wide of them and we fired our torpedoes into them at point blank range. Apparently we were so close one didn't have time to hit the water and arm. Naturally, I'm leaving out all the technical details which Max loves. I doubt you care about the compression to weight ratio of the British torpedo tube as it relates to water impact velocity. I swear. When it comes to weapons, Max is like a kid in a toy store.

Which, brings us to the point where I woke up in a cot below decks. I opened my eyes and it was completely quiet. I started to get up, but my head began to spin. Laying down again I waited for it to settle, which was when I realized I couldn't hear the covers when I moved. I snapped my fingers. I yelled, which brought a doctor or nurse. It didn't matter because I couldn't hear anything. He said something and I couldn't hear it!

It should be needless to say that I was very upset.

I pointed at my ears and shook my head, which I immediately regretted.

He frowned and sighed, then held up his hand for me to

wait. He came back with a piece of paper that had the words "It will probably pass" hastily scrawled on it.

So I gave him the thumbs up because I didn't want to nod my head. But then I remembered that the thumbs up might not mean the same thing in England that it does in the U.S. I think he got the idea, or maybe he didn't but didn't mind. At least he didn't try to stop me when I tried to get up. I took it slow.

My uniform was spotted all over with blood, none of it was thankfully mine, which brought a laugh that I immediately regretted.

"Do you have anything for a headache," I asked.

He smiled and held up one finger. Maybe that meant wait a minute, or maybe it meant the same as thumbs up. He came back with two pills and a cup of water, which I greedily swallowed, asking for more.

I realized the deck was rocking for real. We were at sea. I also realized I needed the head. There's no better motivation to get a man up and about. And since I was up and about, I decided to go look for Max. Doctor be damned. So I began to climb. And just like that, I could hear.

It didn't help. It just made my headache worse.

Chapter 11 – The Storming of Kane

I was surrounded by bunks filled with wounded and sleeping sailors. I suppose I should have been sleeping too, but I wanted to know what was going on. It's my job.

The Hesperus was a relatively small ship. You'd think it would be hard to get lost, but I'd only seen her in the dark, so there you go. I wandered. I passed men pushing trolleys with shells and bags of powder towards the stern. There were guys with torches and crowbars pulling open hatches. Then I found one that worked and pushed it open, stepping out on deck. The sun hit me hard. It took a moment before I could see, but when my eyes focused I saw we were close to the coast, heading into Honolulu harbor. Not Pearl.

The bridge was up above me, but the ladder near the hatch ended in wreckage and twisted metal. There was no going up that way. A shell must have passed through the deck above. It couldn't have detonated or there'd be a lot more of the ship gone.

Back through the hatch and down the corridor to the other side took me to a working ladder. This side faced the shore and the hills behind town. There were columns of smoke rising all over the city. Pearl looked like we had a new volcano. Two close reports echoed across the city from the hills above. Looking towards Kane, I could see a fireball rising. They were still fighting up there.

As I climbed to the bridge I had a better view of her damage. The bow gun was gone along with a lot of the ships superstructure. Torn right off. Behind me, the stern was obscured in smoke lazily drifting across the deck to trail behind us. With the stack gone, it was pouring out the big empty hole in the ship. No stack to lift it up in the air and out of our eyes. The ship herself, I had to guess, since we were making headway, was still seaworthy.

"Mr. Burgess," the captain said as I stepped onto the bridge. "It's good to see you up. How is our story coming?"

"I'm not sure captain," I said. "It seems I slept through some of it."

He chuckled.

"Is that coffee?" I asked.

"I suppose," he said, as he took a sip from his mug. "It's hot and black."

"That's qualification enough for me."

The sea breeze was blowing around us, blowing in through the broken front windows. Grabbing a mug from the tray sitting on the map desk in the back of the bridge, I poured. It was thick and very black.

"No crème?" I asked.

"I'm afraid we had to leave without it. You might find some on shore."

"I don't think they'll be delivering the milk today," which got another laugh. "You haven't seen any Japanese this morning?"

"Not a one," he replied. "When we dock, we're going to unload our wounded on shore, then head back out."

"Have you seen Max?" I asked. "Or that Stroud woman or Lono?"

"Onboard somewhere. Check the bunks."

"Can I go ashore?"

"I'll send a note to the OOD. Actually, it would be best. We don't know when we'll be coming back."

"Need the mug back?"

"No, no. Take it with you. Drop the left over off in the engine room. They use the coffee to grease the propeller shafts."

I had to admit. It was a bit thick and very strong.

It took some searching, but I found them. Max woke as I walked by him.

"Ready to leave?" he asked, yawning. His hair was sticking up. It was that stupid grease he insists on using. I pitied the next guy who got his pillow.

Lono was in a bunk further down, curled up with his tripod. One of the legs had been blown off. He wouldn't wake. He just grunted.

"Lono."

A moan.

"There's a war going on and you aren't taking pictures."

A grunt.

"Sit still. I'm going to shoot you in the leg," Max said and reached down to his holster and pulled back the hammer of his pistol.

Lono's eyes popped open. Then he frowned. "Noi kou kala?" he mumbled.

"The guy with the gun doesn't speak Hawaiian," I said, amused.

"Oh yeah. It's you Carl." Then he tried to roll over.

"No, not when there's the best work of your life waiting for you."

I grabbed him and tried to pull him out of the bunk. Then Max joined in.

"Nooo!" Lono moaned.

"I think shooting him is best," said Stroud, who had walked quietly up behind Max. "He's no use to us without his camera."

"You are always so practical, my dear," Max replied with a wicked smile.

"Lono, you better get up," I added. To be honest, I wasn't quite sure they were kidding.

"OK, OK, Carl. So what's the hurry?" He yawned and then stretched.

"If it's not too much trouble, we're in the middle of a war. They're blowing chunks of forest off the hillsides. And the captain says that if we don't get off, we'll have to put out to sea with him."

"That might not be so bad Carl. You should see the pictures I took at Pearl." But then he jerked awake. "Carl! I have to get back to my shop! I've got to see what I got on those plates!"

"Soon." I actually pushed him back down. "Don't worry. How many plates you have left?"

"Three." He sat up, dangling his socking feet.

"It isn't over. We need to fill those last plates."

∞∞

"I don't suppose there's any breakfast," Lono said. He yawned as we walked.

"War zones are always the same," Stroud said with a tired sigh. "They're so inconvenient. We won't find food." The wind was trying to take her hat and she had to stop, put down her umbrella to free her hands to retie it.

We were walking down the street away from the harbor, hoping for a jitney, or even better, a carriage, but the streets were full of people instead. They stood about watching the explosions in the hills the columns of smoke. A pair of police officers was walking down the street with their clubs out, watching the crowds.

The sunshine came down smoke tinted orange, which was unusual for Hawaii where the wind blows everything out to sea. Except for the cane fields, it usually it takes a volcano to set stuff on fire. There were lots of airships too, which was unusual as well.

"Are you really here to discuss immigration?" I asked her.

"No, of course not." She laughed. "I'm here about the Japanese. We, now I, were sent to assess the situation and encourage action. Mr. Schuster has been a great help in this."

"Always a pleasure," Max said. "Maybe if we tried a hotel. Mine isn't far. They serve food. Their kitchens might not be closed."

"An admirable suggestion," she said.

"I don't think this war will last long," Max said. "Without control of the sea, the Japanese can't supply their troops."

"The British fleet was destroyed," I said.

"Was it?" he asked. "What did we see? A line of old dreadnoughts. Where were the rest? And the harbor is so shallow. It might not even be possible to sink them."

"You mean the fleet left?"

He stared at me with patience.

"Those are all carrier airships," he said, pointing up.

I looked up even though I can't tell one type of airship from another.

"It better not go on too long or they'll start looting," Stroud said, eyeing the crowds.

"Yes. When the shock wears off," Max added.

Some of the airships had drifted close enough to one another to start shooting. The rattling of their gatling guns drifted down above the sound of their engines.

Then we heard another sound, a chugging motor coming from around the corner down Aolele Street ahead. As we made the intersection we saw David's car at the head of a column of police. He had somehow found them helmets and rifles. They had to be heading for Kane. When he saw us, David had the driver stop.

"There you are," he said. "I thought you had been blown up with the harbor."

"Nope," I said, with a grin. "But we were there."

"We're going to relieve Kane. Want to come?"

"It'd make a heck of a story." I grinned.

"Great picture too," Lono added.

"Well then, climb on!"

I was grateful to pile Lono's gear bags in the car.

"Max?" David asked. "You coming?"

"No," Max said. "I've seen enough for one assignment."

"Suite yourself," he said, and then waved his driver forward.

"They never ask me," I heard Mrs. Stroud say under her breath.

Max grinned. "Would you care to join me for lunch instead?" he asked.

"I thought you'd never ask," she replied, and she smiled and took his arm.

We drove away leaving them standing there.

"You'd think they knew each other," Lono said as we bumped down the street.

The siege of Kane was the kind of battle newspapermen dream of. Short but full of color and patriotic heroism. The Japanese, just as Max had said, were losing steam and all it took was David's men hitting them from behind to break them. Lono got a great picture of the charge. I figured Hawaiian kids were going to be forced to look at it for the next century or two in their school books. David actually drove his car in through the front gate as it first opened, which was another great picture by the way. That and the British wounded laying in the half demolished fort.

David left his police unit under the command of the army. There were thousands of prisoners to be watched and probably thousands still be to be hunted down. But he had to get back to city hall to help organize things. He offered to give us a ride back, for which we were grateful. Lono's equipment was heavy.

As we were rolling down the hill I realized something.

"David, can you drop me off at Miriam's?"

David laughed, "Sure thing Carl."

"Hey," Lono said. He'd been inventorying his equipment. "I miscounted. I've still got another plate."

"Well save it," I said. "We'll find something."

Miriam and Martha lived in a beach house just west of Diamond Head. I was out of the car before it stopped, heading for the door. I heard David and Lono talking about something behind me, but I didn't wait to hear. Knocking brought footsteps, then the front door flew open and she was in my arms, soft and warm with a touch of the scent of melia. It was the best kiss of my life. I'd like to say she melted in my arms, but I think both did a little melting.

Then we heard laughter. I looked around and there was David and Lono. David was stooped over so Lono could lean the broken leg of his camera on him. They'd taken a picture of us. And wouldn't you know it? It made the papers. Like I said. Just one big family.

₧℡

It took me months to write all the stories. I'm sure Lincoln was satisfied, but now I was worried. I was no longer necessary, so a week after the end of the our little war, I quit. I sent in my resignation with the last story for the U.S. Then Miriam and I rented some horses and rode up to David's.

"Alright Carl," David said, when we had settled in his study. "To what do I owe this visit?"

"I want to immigrate."

"Impossible."

"What?" Miriam said.

But David laughed. "Carl, you've been Hawaiian for years. It's just a matter of a bit paperwork."

"That's it?" I said, incredulous.

"That and a job. You're free now right?"

I nodded.

"It's time I had a press secretary. You handled the war well. To be honest, I've never looked better. I need you."

He could see we were both stunned.

"Consider it a wedding present."

Which brings us to the last curious part of this tale. It seems that while the Japanese and the British were blowing themselves and half of Honolulu to pieces, there had been a quiet revolution down in the Spanish zone. The Pilipino workers revolted and threw out their Spanish masters. It happened back in the Islands themselves too. Six battalions of the Kaiser's troops had landed in Manila to back up a nationwide revolt. The colonial government was forced to flee to Taiwan. The Philippines had become a German protectorate.

The thing that made it strange was that Max had just come from Manila. It made you wonder; who was Max really?

От Фете в в Иордании

The Féte of the Jordan

In the Green Drawing Room
sat a dead queen in black.
From her gilded quiver
she drew an arrow.
Swift it flew

Chapter 1 – Emily Meets the Okhrana

Snow laced wind tugged hat and dress as Emily stood on the train platform. Despite the shelter of her furs she still wanted to squint against the cold wind, holding back the tears as it stung her eyes. One mustn't wrinkle, she thought. The engine vented steam that fell in course crystals raking those waiting, mostly peasants thickly bundled in dower ragged colors and fur. The American diplomat, Mr. Daniels, and his entourage stood around her but were little help against the wind. They were a rude, rough crew. Their furs inexpensive, recently bought off the rack with no fitting. There was little conversation. It was too damned cold.

With typical Russian efficiency, they called for passengers to board before they were actually ready. The train men, peasants all of them, were still grunting and pulling her trunks into the upper class car, tracking in ice and snow over the polished parquet floors. She tried not to wince with each thump of their muddy boots.

With only one sleeper car, she had been forced to share her cabin with her maid, a Romanian wench she had picked up only three months before. A rough girl, barely trained, she had waved her towards the third class carriage when they boarded, but the look on the American ambassador's face had stopped her. It was a violation of his sense of L'égalité. She had laughed as if it were a joke. Tio had wisely remained passive. Emily might need that ambassador's good will before this was over. The novelty of an American might open doors.

They had travelled for weeks, so close now to their destination and yet they had stopped again, the train to be reformed once more. They were adding box cars and another third class passenger car, to be loaded with serfs, heading like she to the Saint Petersburg for Razhdestvo, Christmas. They were visiting family and friends or to looking for work helping others do the same. It took the Russians two weeks to celebrate it.

Her breath still fogged in the car, the same one she had left two hours earlier, but she was grateful for the lack of wind. The Russian cold leaked into everything like cold water trickling in through gaps and crevices in her clothing. Its passing left an aching numbness. Flexing her hands inside her muff, she followed the conductor to her cabin where she almost tripped over her luggage. It had been pushed in the door and left. Not even stowed under the seats. And, they had neglected again to change the sheets as well! The seats that passed for beds were short. They were as hard as they looked. And there was only a basin and a jug with a cork for washing.

Appalling. What must the lower classes be experiencing?

If only this had been summer and the zeppelins running, she thought longingly. An easy journey with a view and good food.

The dvornik came and checked their passports, then she threw her furs onto one of the seats, despite the cold.

"Unpack Tio. I'm going to see if we still have a dining car."

"Yes mistress."

With the doors shut, the windows immediately fogged and

Emily waits at yet another train stop.

began to drip. Out in the corridor she wiped a small circle in the glass clear to look through. Down the tracks they were herding pigs onto the train. The animal's heat drifting into a frozen fog around the pens.

The car lurched under her almost knocking her over. Damn her heels! She thought. They were useless in the snow and damn dangerous on these rocking trains. The train had rolled under her only to stop again. She could feel each car banging into the next. They advanced the train so the livestock ramps could fill the next cars. She thanked the gods that couldn't smell them.

The dining car was still there, and so was the ambassador.

"Ah, Mrs. Stroud," he called in his American twang. How very rude.

She beamed back at him out of habit and walked over. She was used to rude men.

"Mr. Daniels, Mr. Herman," she replied, slightly dipping to each.

The train chose that moment to lurch again, almost knocking her over.

"Please sit before you fall over," he said chucking.

Mr. Daniels had a cigar, and it appeared Mr. Herman was reaching for one of his own. Sadly, the train had no smoking lounge for the men. Had there been true aristocrats of stature on board, she was sure one would have been provided. No, she thought. This was the judgment of the bureaucrats who ran the line, and they had been found wanting.

"I wish they had more heat than that coal stove in the corner," Mr. Daniels said. "This is worse than Montreal."

"You would know Justin. I'm sorry we made you leave Vienna."

"At Christmas too. No one throws a Christmas like Vienna."

"If the zeppelins had been running, you could have had two," Emily said.

"Damn straight."

She had heard this conversation before. Mr. Daniels was referring to the fact that the Russians celebrate Christmas twelve days later than the Austrians. They had been travelling together for over a thousand miles, but still, she assumed an air of rapt attention.

Several secretaries and aids had followed her into the car, the tables beginning to fill.

"Missed everything. At least Natali and kids could stay."

"If it wasn't for our Mrs. Stroud, I think I'd go insane for boredom."

"Yes, the view is rather monotonous," Emily replied, acknowledging the compliment with a slight blush. "When you can see it."

He laughed. "That snowstorm in Minsk."

"I thought we were going to die," Mr. Herman said. "The train looked like some sort of frosted pastry."

"I'm often sad that I don't have a photographer handy," she said. "It would have been a wonderful picture."

"Out here they probably carve their pictures in stone," Mr. Daniels said.

"Or blocks of ice!" Mr. Herman said, laughing at his own joke. For a diplomatic attaché, he was never very diplomatic. Americans never are. He laughed a lot and she laughed with him.

The waiter arrived. Neither Mr. Daniels nor Mr. Herman spoke Russian. They didn't even speak French! She helped them, as she did every day, to order. She reminded the waiter to bring her maid her dinner, chiding him about too much cabbage. It gave her maid gas and made for difficult nights.

Their dinner, as always, was little better than stewed meat and potatoes. She managed to avoid most of it. The Americans however, being only a step away from peasants themselves, seemed perfectly at home. Her only solace was that the Tsar would provide better, and her travels would have a comfortable if not happy end.

She entertained them with false gossip, recounted carefully edited travels, sympathized with their discomforts, listened, and deflected their advances with admiration and kind flattered laughter. These men were not her target. She needed no attachments to complicate her work in St. Petersburg, but she had a feeling they might be useful. They might be her entry to court if the British consoled proved to be as ineffectual as they seemed. America was a popular novelty, a land of fortune and adventure, and the Tsar would very likely want to look them over.

She wondered again if she would see Max. This game was

important. He would certainly be there. There to defend his turf. She enjoyed their battles. She would also enjoy rubbing his face in the dirt. It was a game they shared. A treasured dance.

Europe had been dominated for thirty years by The League of Three Nations, Russia, Germany, and Austria. Britain and her shaky alliance with France were no match. The treaty was up for renewal and negotiation was going to take place in St. Petersburg, the capital of Russia. Their Majesties required that these negotiations fail. Germany must be isolated.

A tedious lunch ended. The never-ending Russian landscape rolled by. Emily, sitting in her seat in the dim grey winter sunlight, started "Crime and Punishment" for the third time.

଼ଠଔ

The Saint Petersburg railway station glowed with promise. Marble columns, gas chandeliers, and guilt scrollwork beamed with hope, as did the obsequious porters who carried her luggage. She gave them what were, in European terms, worthless coins and they seemed grateful for them. But at the entrance no one was there to meet her. She had telegraphed the embassy only two days before. What had gone wrong?

The heated sled ride to her embassy took her through wide well-ordered snow-covered streets. Tio watched through her window with wide eyes as they rolled by great houses and lacework bridges. Emily took a deep breath and almost laughed. She was back in familiar, comfortable waters.

The embassy itself was somewhat plain. She eyed it with distrust. Grey stone and a wood door on a less fashionable side street. No gilt. Not even a plaque to announce the building's purpose. Unsure, she left the cab and her maid at the curb with instructions to wait.

The servant at the door wore only a simple suit. No livery. She knew then it had been a wise decision to retain the carriage. The foyer was wood! No gas light and they were spare with their candles. The parlor, when she was shown in, didn't have a fire. It wasn't even banked in anticipation of visitors! She had been left there waiting. No tea. She shuddered. Could these be Englishmen? If they were English, then they certainly weren't gentlemen.

Finally, the door opened. It was the ambassador himself. He had opened it himself, with his own hands! He looked fat and unwell. His eyes lacked focus.

"Ah, glad you made it." He shuffled about, at a loss as to which seat to take. "Winter is a devilish time to travel here."

She laughed gently. "Yes. I'm afraid it was awful."

He laughed. A single big "Haw!" Then finally picked a chair and landed in it with a thump. She saw the dust rise.

"The whole country," he mumbled, shifting about, getting comfortable. "Flat as a pancake and just as dull."

Emily grabbed the arms of her chair and scooted it around to face him.

"Still. It's important," she said.

"You found a place to stay?" he asked. He hadn't heard her.

"No. Not yet."

"You can't stay here," he said. Rude and abrupt. He found a pipe that had been sitting loose on the table next to him without a stand.

He looked in its bowl. "No spare rooms."

"Of course. Do you have any suggestions?"

"Suggestions?"

"Yes. Where to stay near the palace?" She caught herself raising her voice, as if he were hard of hearing. She tried to smile.

"Stay." He pondered this for a second. "Oh! Stay. The Kempinski of course." Then he mumbled, "The only place."

He picked up a tobacco tin and shook it. She could hear it was empty, but he had to open it anyway. He had apparently slipped into dotage. This must be reported.

"Are you going to the Christmas ball?" she asked.

"Well of course! When is it?"

This would not do, she thought. "Do you have a secretary? I would like to make some arrangements. I could use a bit of help."

"Yes, of course. Lipovsky. Russian, but his English is passable. Do you need to see him?"

Russian, she thought darkly. Dispatches, codes, he almost certainly had access to everything.

"I'm afraid I do."

"Use the pull the rope and ask for him." He nodded towards

the pull rope next to the door.

She got up, walked to the door, and gave it a yank, and then waited patiently. When there had been no answer within a minute, she tried again. She waited two minutes, silently counting. Nothing.

Looking back, she saw that the ambassador had fallen asleep.

That left her with no choice but to wander the embassy on her own. She met servants, who shied away from her questions. She met clerks, standing together, three of them, talking politics. They turned away when she approached, apparently to head back to their desks. When she tried to ask them where the embassy secretary was, they spoke back in rude Russian, feigning ignorance. When she asked again in Russian, she met scowls and a begrudging answer. He was upstairs.

She found him in the ambassador's office, rifling through the papers covering his desk, lit only by the dim light of three candles. The ambassador's office didn't have a window. He looked up at her as she entered.

"Ah yes, you are here. You must pardon me." He continued to look through the papers, but dipped his head in greeting. "Ah, here they are." He pulled out a thick envelope. "It's your paperwork," he said in thickly accented English. She could see books on the shelves lining the room, but she couldn't read their spines in the dim light. "He must have fallen asleep on you," the secretary said.

"Yes, I'm afraid he did."

"I was hoping to have more time. He keeps papers from me. He has become quite suspicious." Opening the envelope, he pulled out a folded stack. "I'll need to go over these. You'll need a letter of introduction of course, and expenses."

"If you don't mind my asking, but what happened to the ambassador?"

"Old age I suppose. A poor diet perhaps. His decline, though, was surprising."

"But the state of the embassy . . ."

"Yes. I can't agree more. We have argued, but to call him frugal would be understatement."

He pulled two candles closer to pool their light and began

going through the pages. "Oh! I must apologize. We have been nothing but rude. Please find a seat. Let me help you."

He stood and came around the desk. Picking a seat, he lifted the stack paper off it. Then he looked at her over his spectacles. "You are English. You must be expecting tea."

Still holding the paper, he went to the door and pulled it open. "The bell ropes are broken," he sighed, then called down the hallway, "Demetri!" There was an echoing yelp. "Demetri, we need tea and biscuits," he continued in Russian.

"Yes sir," came the distant reply.

"And a lamp."

"Sir."

Emily was finally settled in her seat and they were discussing her requirements for the ball when there was a knock at the door.

"Yes," called the secretary.

"There is a young lady at the door with a carriage driver."

"That would be my maid."

"You understand Russian?"

"I'm afraid my Russian is limited, but yes," she replied in Russian.

"Oh. Excellent. Really, that wasn't bad. They've sent us someone competent for once."

"The young lady needs a water closet," the voice at the door said.

"Oh Tio," Emily sighed, embarrassed by her maid's lack of control.

"Show her where it is. The driver too!" the secretary yelled back.

"I apologize, but she's new. Romanian," she said.

"That explains it. I don't know what we were thinking letting them have their own country."

He didn't return to the desk, but gave the stack of paper in his arms a quick appraising glance, then dropped it by the door without further thought. Then he opened the door again and yelled, "Demetri!" but stopped. "Oh yes. He's in the kitchens. Boris!"

"Sir!"

Boris appeared at the door.

"We need a letter of introduction for court for the young woman. A letter of credit too. Leave the amount blank."

"Blank?" Boris visibly blanched.

"Don't worry," he said, gently cuffing the young man's head. "She could have the old man shot if she wanted to."

"Oh." The he looked at her with fear, then ran for his office.

"That will get things moving," the secretary smiled. "The rumor will spread." And then he laughed. He had to be a member of the Okhrana, the Tsar's secret police, she thought. But she liked him anyway.

The dress fitter measures with deft attention.
Ancient hands stitching a stage of qualities.
Flowing folds barely covered.
Then pearls, so soft and warm.
A silken river wandered in her footsteps!
Her blades were set.

Chapter 2 – Emily finds Max

The carriage was waiting at the door of the Kaminski Hotel, the way torch-lit by rough men and women. She emerged from the hotel doors into the flickering light, standing for a moment on the swept steps. White flakes drifted down from the heavy sky. The peasants with their brooms bowed to her from the dark corners, cowering in silence, their wide eyes following. She had heard from Tio that they all lived in the basement.

As she finished descending the stairs to the dark busy street, she felt her first footstep's touch on the pavement. It was singular. The night was open before her. The possibilities endless.

Sitting in her seat in the carriage, though alone, she arranged her dress in anticipation of her arrival. Bonfires lit the streets as they passed, warm empty draped and shuttered windows in the buildings behind. No faces looked out. Russians do not stand near their windows for fear of sickness.

Around her drove other sleds and cars, their lamps and brass glinting in the drifting trails of glowing steam which condensed and froze, turning to ice crystals in midair. She could have hired a car as well, but she loved to watch the horses work. Their breath came out in clouds. And she was only a hundred yards from the palace entrance as well, barely around the corner. Cars were so complicated. In the time it took one to start she could have

Emily makes her entrance at the Winter Palace.

walked. Through the window glass she could see them all coming. The important of the empire. The Tsar had called. It was Christmas and the The Féte of the Jordan, the blessing of the river.

Dvortsovaya Square spread itself around her as the carriage emerged from the street. The Winter Palace stretched a quarter mile around half, the General Staff Building around the rest. In the catacombs and tunnels beneath worked the Empire's bureaucracy.

The ornate walls gaily colored, brightly lit, the windows bright. The gas it took just to light the palace might have powered Paris.

She held out her hand to be helped down from her heated cab into the bitter cold, the wind stinging her cheeks. She didn't acknowledge their bows, the snow blowing in light swirls around her. It quickly speckled her fur. Two men it great coats swept the walk free of snow in front of her as she walked towards the palace.

A steward took her invitation with only a glance as she entered. It would be more carefully securitized later. Her face remembered. Her accent noted.

In her dressing room they relieved her of her furs and helped with her hair. The paper wrapped bundle brought by the servant that trailed behind her left with her furs. It was her cloak for the ceremony and would be brought to her later. She used little makeup as she was able to blush on command, but her hair was a mess after her fur hat. They fretted over it for a good twenty minutes.

Then she found herself escorted to a parlor, just off the entrance hall. She eyed it with growing anger. White plaster with painted flowers. The art all Russian, illustrations of battles and historic events. It was crowded with businessmen and city officials. She recognized it for what it was. It wouldn't do!

She stepped back outside and saw the house secretary, marked by his long scarlet robes and gold black cape. He was talking with several others of his station under the shadow of a great staircase, consulting lists. As strode towards him she was momentarily blocked by a servant asking if he could help. She laughed and walked by. The steward saw her coming. His compatriots stepped back as he faced her.

"What do you mean by putting me in a side parlor?' She snapped. "I am *the* representative of Her Majesty's government!" As if she were some visiting wife.

He wilted.

"Yes, of course, Milady."

He grasped a stack of paper from the kiosk in beside him and scanned it, leafing through the pages. That fool of an ambassador had let things slip so badly, she thought. She would see England treated with proper respect!

"There has been a mistake. We sincerely apologize." He whispered behind his hand to the man next to him in an ostrich plumed kepi. The man bowed and led her along a corridor lined with Roman and European art, glowing with white marble and guilt. She watched his peacock plume as it bobbed back and forth as he walked. She recognized a lesser Raphael in passing.

Walking down crimson carpet they stopped two hundred feet down. Another party entered the hall behind her. She assessed the quality of their clothing and found it to be correct. Behind the doors in front of her she heard music. Mozart. One of his endless small symphonies, 26 or perhaps 28. Pleasant enough. Servants in white silk livery were waiting to assist her entrance. She stood in front of the doors as they arranged her dress. Then they were briskly opened.

"Lady Stroud, representative of Her Majesty Queen Victoria."

They bowed and stepped back. Calming, she glided forward into a field of flowers, a floor awash in color.

There were uniforms, mostly Russian green, blue, and red, Chevalier-gardes. Then black and white, the suits of diplomats, mustached, some outrageously, with hair oiled, draped in colored sashes and polished gold decoration. Then the women arrayed in the usual swirls of pastel silk with far too many diamonds, as if they could distract from their weight and age! They were wives to be bent as she toyed with their husbands.

But this was the east and, unfashionably, there were full beards and men with weathered faces as well. Men who did the Empire's important business. The Tsar held them close. They were his unseverable fingers, the Cossack princes. A waiter offered her a glass of champagne. She took a moment to savor its simple sweetness. She would drink no more.

"Mrs. Stroud!" It was Mr. Daniels, walking towards her from across the floor. "I'm glad to see you're sweet face. Nobody here speaks English!" Her Americans were here. He looked at her as he walked, eyes wide with awe and perhaps lust. "You look lovely tonight," he almost stammered.

She laughed and blushed, then curtsied. "Thank you," she said, looking down, then beaming up at him, "I'm afraid that this is about as far away as you can get from English." She almost laughed. "But if you try enough people, you might be surprised. The diplomats especially." Her smile pleased him. "Don't worry. I can help. You used to be English after all. We should face the world together, at least when we aren't fighting."

He laughed. She had hit her mark.

He was dressed entirely wrong. Ill-fitting tails, a black suit with thick shoes, his hair combed to no effect. He might as well have been Lincoln's son. Simple buttons. Not a jewel anywhere to be seen. The outrageousness of it had to be devastating. She knew everyone had to be scrambling to decide where to place him in the tableau.

"Why is that woman scowling at us?" Mr. Daniels asked.

"I have no idea," Emily said. "She's German. They tend to be abrupt." Emily suspected she was the one being scowled at.

"You might be right. You know? I saw this dance they did once where they just stood there hitting themselves and each other." He shook his head. "Damnedest thing I ever saw."

"Schuhplattler. It's a very complicated and difficult dance."

"I suppose. I guess it depends on which end of the hitting you're on."

"Yes," she laughed. "Ambassador, I shouldn't worry about language. I'm sure the Tsar is arranging for a translator."

"You think so?"

"These parlors are as much for them to get to know us as we each other. We should take this time to mingle and make friends." The Okhrana were undoubtedly working feverishly at that moment to identify and categorize them.

"They look interesting," he said, nodding towards a group of rough long coated men.

"The Cossacks?"

They stood together next to the vodka, five with chin beards and long black moustaches over their weathered olive faces. Their green decorated tunics reached down to their ankles, ending in shiny black boots. Amelia was surprised they were allowed to keep their guilt sabers and bandoliers of polished silver bullets, as lethal as they were decorative. These would be the most loyal and trusted regimental commanders, probably local guard units. The Tsar relied heavily on them to keep order.

"It would be best to talk to them now, if you want. Before they have too much more vodka," she said. "But I think you ought to get to know your competition first."

"Competition?"

"Your peers. You fellow diplomats."

He sighed.

"There's the French ambassador over there," she said. "They've always been your friends. Perhaps it's best to start there?"

The French were England's ally. Her briefing had described the ambassador as pleasant, but ineffectual. She doubted if he would be any help to her, but she wanted to look the man over anyway.

Mr. Daniels turned to look at the French ambassador, a tastefully dressed elderly gentleman, but then his attention strayed.

"Oh, who's that?"

She followed his gaze to a tall thin man with a monocle. He sported a bright sash and a chest full of medals.

"The German ambassador," she said, holding back a resigned sigh. A Prussian peacock, she thought.

"Do you speak German?" Mr. Daniels asked.

"A little, but he'll speak French."

"Amazing. Let's go see."

"Lets," she said with a touch of distain.

He led her along, Mr. Herman, the ambassador's assistant, breaking off his attempts to communicate with a breathtaking woman in a green silk dress in order to follow. It was clear that their course frontier novelty would land them in one bed or another tonight.

The German ambassador, Graf Friedrich vom Stettin, was pure Prussian right down to his monocle and spats. His wife stood behind him like a bulldog, the guns of a dreadnought backing him up. She should have been wearing a monocle as well! Emily thought with a hidden smile.

Emily greeted them warmly as they approached.

"Graf Stettin, it's an honor to meet you," Emily started, in French. He was an upper order count, Hochadel, a sovereign family member whose domains had been absorbed into the German

Empire. He was essentially noble, but at ends. He had been mentioned in detail in her briefings.

"You're English. I don't believe I've had the pleasure . . ."

"I'm afraid I must make introductions for us both. I'm Lady Emilia Stroud, here as a representative of Her Majesty." She curtsied. Her knighthood left her only slightly lower than he. "This is Mr. Jedidiah Daniels, ambassador to the United States. He wants very much to meet you."

The ambassador's pupils widened just a bit. His wife's attention turned and focused in their direction.

"It's a pleasure to meet you," the ambassador said – in English! Emily felt a wash of dread.

But then he continued in thickly accented French, "I'm afraid that's about all the English I know."

She breathed a silent sigh of relief and translated. The last thing she wanted was unfiltered conversation between the American and the German. But she took it as a warning. He might know more than he admitted. For England's sake, America and Germany must remain apart.

"It's a genuine pleasure as well," Mr. Daniels said, holding his hand out to shake – ahead of Emily. How rude.

The Prussian smiled, glancing in her direction by way of apology. He took it and accepted the great tug. Then, he took Emily's silk gloved hand and kissed it. She admired the way he cocked one eyebrow, keeping his monocle in place without frowning as he bowed. He would not be an easy opponent.

"May I introduce my wife, the Countess Frieda?"

"Simply amazing," she said, smiling and holding out her hand to Mr. Herman.

Mr. Herman looked at it for a second with a frown, then grasped it, woodenly bowing to kiss it.

"How charming," she said with an amused smile.

She stood ready during their conversation to edit and alter inflection, to steer it away from sensitive subjects, but it turned out that wasn't needed. Instead the ambassador asked about the frontier and the Indians, which Mr. Daniels, now on familiar ground, was more than happy to recount. He had, it appeared, had many adventures and they quickly drew a crowd. Since Buffalo Bill had passed through Europe, the U.S. had become as exotic as India.

It was a relief when she heard someone clear their throat behind her. The translator from the Tzar, his uniform crisp and green. A young lieutenant with yellow blond hair and oriental eyes.

"Pardon your Excellency," he said, in slightly accented British English.

"Hum?" Mr. Daniels turned to face his bow. "What's this? You speak English!"

"Your translator has arrived," Emily said.

"Well I'll be balled up," Mr. Daniels exclaimed.

The translator blinked, then looked at him with trepidation.

And they were off and Emily was free to wander, the translator mangling Mr. Daniel's American slang. She made her apologies to Mr. Daniels, who seemed reluctant to let her go, and made way through the crowd, gently weaving through introductions, mostly from men, always working her way towards the Grand Duke. The Grand Duke George Alexandrovich, the Tsar's second son, had been left to attend to the higher parlor.

He was a thin wan man in his mid-twenties. A shadow of his robust father and older brother. One had the impression that his attendance was a burden of filial duty. He held his untouched drink gingerly so as not to spill it, working the conversation around him with the professional patience bred into him from birth. The plainness of his crisp blue navel uniform contrasted with the gold, diamonds, and silk sashes. Unmarried, in fact unattached, Emily frankly wondered if he preferred men. It was difficult to tell. And then there was that catch in his throat as he talked, the occasional ominous cough. It was certainly something to watch. Royals are often so fragile. She wondered if she could be brave enough to kiss him.

Then she spotted Max, behind the duke, to all appearances raptly listening. He glanced her way, barely a twitch of the eye. She, for her part, continued to scan the crowd. It was the usual collection of nobles, generals and admirals, diplomats and clergy, and of course their spouses.

The discussion had become heated, drawing her attention.

"I fail to see why modern catastrophism amongst the peasantry should be supported. If the church wants to take advantage of it, then they should do so – without government support," the duke said.

"We don't support superstition," the patriarch in his white and gold silk said, sounding quite offended. "Quite the opposite. If the people are feeling insecure, then they need our support all the more. But we need churches and priests to do that. The Motherland needs us."

"The treasury is stretched thin enough," the duke said, stopping to cough. "You have the schools. That should be enough. If they need you, then you should have no problem collecting more money without having us do it for you!"

"Yes we have the schools, but for how long? How long until we become an extension of Prussia?"

"Better Prussia than a bunch of power hungry windbags!" the duke snapped.

This drew a collective gasp from crowd. The patriarch and his attending priests looked like they were ready for a fist fight. Emily was surprised that they were so candid in public. This split apparently ran deep.

"I think we need a change of subject," said an elderly woman with an expansive corset and a rack of diamonds. She stepped forward with a pained smile. A nervous chuckle speckled the crowd. "Did anyone go to that opening at the Mariinsky?"

Another women stepped up. "Oh. It was horrible!"

The Duke and the Bishop continued to eye each other for a moment, the duke breaking contact first with a troubled frown.

"What was it called? The tale of the Nutcracker?"

"Iolanta was nice."

"Yes, we can be grateful for that."

"One never realizes how hard the seats are in that theatre until things come apart on stage."

The Duke took a deep breath and said, "I didn't think it was so bad." He even tried to smile. The priests for their part melted into the crowd.

Emilia looked over and noticed that Max had gone too. What was he up to? She spotted him heading for a corridor and followed.

"That Rubtsova woman was practically porcine!" a woman

exclaimed to much laughter.

Behind her, Emilia heard the prince reply in an amused voice, "The music was nice though." Apparently the trouble had been deflected and the evening saved.

She glided towards the corridor, only to find it empty. It ended in a smoking room, but she doubted he could have made it that far unless he ran. Cigar smoke drifted down the hallway. She blocked a sneeze.

A third the way down, a door was ajar. There was a vase of flowers on the table next to it. She pulled her eyes away from it and back to the door. Flowers are very dear in Russia, practically unknown in winter. They must have come from a greenhouse.

Moving silently around the door, keeping her shadow away from it. She peered into the darkness within but could see nothing. She heard nothing as well beyond the laughter of the men smoking and drinking down the hall.

The hinges were properly oiled, opening silently. Easing through the gap she slid into the darkness, turning her back to the corner while her eyes adjusted, her skirts flowing around her.

A fist flashed out at her, but the blow was ill timed. She deflected it and reached out encountering a shoulder, pushing him off balance then knocking him backward with her hip as she continued her turn. She had intended to throw him in the Japanese style, but he moved too fast. His arm was gone and she had no point of purchase so she chose to lash out with her elbow as she tried to turn and face him again. She missed.

He caught her arm, but the grip was loose and she broke his hold, catching his other hand by the wrist, which was up to who knows what mischief. Since she was in a turn, she kept at it, pulling him around to the wall. No longer putting up resistance and he hit it hard. Then she was on him, his wrist still in her hand. His other on her hip. Their lips met, his breath sweet. She could feel him respond. She pressed closer.

"Oh Max, I've missed you."

Divide a dark house
of crumbling towers.
A deadly waltz
wrecking borders
- they entwine.

Chapter 3 —Emily Instructs the Americans

"I can't see why they sent you," he said, pushing a stray lock that had fallen across her eye back into place. "Your mission is hopeless."

"I think they love a longshot." She smiled. "Especially when they win."

He smiled too, then they kissed in the darkness beyond the door. Like the chime of champagne glasses, it marked the start of their game. She forced herself to let go of him. There would be no more until it was over.

But that had been the memory. She was in the parlor, smiling to herself, smoothing her dress in the lost moment, someone offered her a fresh glass of champagne. Looking about, she saw the parlor spread about her like a chessboard.

He's right, she thought. The Kaiser Wilhelm, the king of Germany, and the Tsar had been bosom friends since childhood. Driving a wedge between them would be practically impossible. Still, perhaps there was the issue of the German Chancellor Bismark. Neither king liked him. He was born a commoner, but held more power than both kings together. His policies were a constant thorn in their sides, thwarting their need for absolute rule. It was Bismark's power that held the treaty in place. Both rulers wanted a treaty. Just not Bismark's treaty.

But now Bismark was dead and the two kings were left to do as they pleased. What would these friends do? Nobles, she thought smugly, could be such children.

She wove her way through the crowd, avoiding men, to return to the Duke. She wanted to see who was listening to him and why.

"We cannot be expected to pay for what is essentially, a Russian railway," a Japanese man said in thickly accented French. His wife stood behind in a beautiful silk kimono. Emily desperately wanted to run over to them to look it over. The woman was wearing wooden shoes! She tried to remember the Japanese ambassador's name. Hanabusa perhaps?

"Korea, and thus Japan, will profit from the trade." The prince said. "We will create a new silk road."

"We have railways to build on our end. Korea is a barbaric land. They resist all kinds of change. And Japan a very small country as well, with very limited resources."

"I beg to differ. Not small at all."

This is no use, she thought to herself. He was surrounded by petitioners. She would be just one more – and a woman as well. Why wasn't the German ambassador here? He surely wanted to discuss the treaty renewal. This was the discussion she needed to be involved in. The final talks would almost certainly be behind closed doors and if she couldn't find an in, then how could she influence the decision?

Suddenly, she was confronted by two servants.

"Yes?" she asked.

"Madam." They bowed. "May we have your wrist?"

She frowned, confused for a moment. Then she saw their purpose. One held a small stack of Chrismas tree shaped cards with yarn ties, the other a wooden box with pencils.

Holding out her left hand, the servant proceeded to tie a tree to her wrist. Then they bowed and moved on.

She hated this. It was her dance card. They made her work more complicated. She could already see that some were casting eyes in her direction. She had to move quickly to pick her own dance partners.

The Americans, she noticed, had drawn a bigger crowd than

the prince. And the German ambassador was there, raptly listening! She began to walk.

"Mrs. Stroud!" Mr. Daniels rudely called across the crowd in his frontier twang as she approached. "There you are."

"I'm afraid I had to attend to government business," she replied in English. She followed it with a smile. "But my duties are done." Emily noticed the translator translated her English as well as Mr. Daniels to Russian.

"I afraid I haven't earned my train fair yet."

"You're doing better than you think."

"Have you met the Chinese ambassador? We were introduced earlier," he said excitedly. "We have Chinamen in the west, but I've never gotten to meet one. Especially one that speaks English."

This drew scattered titters from the crowd.

"I swear," said Mr. Daniels. "I think I'm being laughed at."

"I think you make them nervous," Emily smiled. "They're not used to simple honesty."

Mr. Daniels frowned for a moment as he pondered that. Emily thought that he might have liked that less than merely being the butt of jokes.

"You should meet Zing. He's amazing."

He led her through the crowd, forgetting his audience, to a rotund Chinese gentleman in full western diplomatic garb, red sash and all. The only thing that marked him as Chinese were his eyes and mustache, which was long and thin.

"This is Zing Jeze. Zing, I'd like to introduce you to Mrs. Stroud, one of the finest English ladies I've ever met."

"Tseng Chi-tse," he said in English as he bowed to kiss her hand with an amused smile. "It is a pleasure."

"It's an honor to meet the esteemed Chinese minister," she replied, curtsying to him. "We have all heard of your victories."

"We have heard of some of yours as well," he replied with a sly smile.

"Nonsense. I'm merely an errand girl."

"Your rout of the Japanese has given the entire of the Pacific region room to breathe."

"Rout of the Japanese?" Mr. Daniels asked.

"The practical annihilation of their Pacific fleet."

"Now you're being too generous," she replied with a momentary frown. This was Max's work, she thought. It shouldn't be common knowledge and she certainly didn't do it alone. He was using her to cover his tracks. Fame was the last thing a spy needed. What was worse, much of Mr. Daniels' audience had followed and heard.

"Well I'll be a bag of nails," Mr. Daniels said, which drew a laugh from the crowd. He looked about in confusion.

"Honestly Mr. Daniels. I only passed along field dispatches, as any good diplomat should," she demurred, but the damage had been done. She had to admire it though. It was a clever gambit throwing the credit at her. And on the part of The Most Excellent Tseng as well, using fame to neutralize an effective enemy field agent.

"We could discuss, for Mr. Daniels' sake, your monumental part in the Saint Petersburg Treaty. As a newcomer to the city, he should meet and come to terms with those responsible for the Russian, German, Austrian alliance."

"Now you are being too generous, Lady Stroud. China is very far away and has few interests in Europe."

The world, it appeared, was destined to know of her knighthood as well.

"Yes. So true. But we all have interests in China, Mr. Tseng. Even the Americans."

The Honorable Tseng frowned.

"Our China concessions are of little consequence," Tseng replied.

"But they are. You said so yourself in your book."

"You read my book?"

"*China, the Sleep and the Awakening?* Of course! I care a great deal about my profession." There, she thought. She had regained a little of her standing.

"Pardon, but I may interrupt?"

As soon as she heard this, she knew what was coming. Someone was going to ask for her card. But as she turned she was not confronted by some horrid Cossack or court dandy, but the German ambassador himself.

"If you don't mind, if your dance card isn't full, I was wondering if there was room for me?" he asked.

"Of course," she smiled. She meant it. She enjoyed dancing with her enemy counterparts. "It would be an honor."

She knew that he noted the lack of names on her card, but politely avoided the subject.

"I'd like to put down my name too if I may," Mr. Daniels said. "Although I'm not sure that I know what kind of dances you all do here."

"You'll do fine," she smiled. "Do any of you know the dance order? We wouldn't want Mr. Daniels to end up in the middle of a mazurka."

"I suspect we won't see those until later, after His Highness arrives," Graf Friedrich said. "He does love them."

"Well then. There you are," she smiled and held out her hand for the men to sign.

"What is a mazurka?" Mr. Daniels asked.

"It's the worst kind of waltz and twice as complicated." Emily replied. Which drew a chuckle from the crowd and others forward with requests for her card.

Then came a ragged rattle and thumps as the doors that lined the east wall opened. They all turned as one to look. The sound of fifty children in white robes, each carrying a candle, singing *Angels in the Realm of Glory* drifted out of the darkness, their voices echoing in the hall beyond. There had to be groups in each parlor, she thought. The sound was unearthly.

The children entered, weaving through the now quiet crowd to the far wall to form a line and then walking forward to herd everyone towards the doors. Up until then she had seen little in the way of Christmas decoration, but in the hall beyond they entered a strange holiday wonderland.

At first the room beyond seemed dark, but as she closed with the door she could pine branches, and then a forest. A forest of cut trees bedded in white wool gauze. They wandered between them, careful not to disturb them or their decorations of tin and gold leaf that fluttered in the breeze of their passage, glinting in the light from the center for the great hall.

The gauze gave way to parquet as they entered what

appeared to be a large clearing, a pool of light that drew them inward. The great chandelier in the center of the hall had been pulled up to make way for a thirty foot tall Christmas tree. Decked in colored glass and hard wax candles. It sparkled with rainbow glints as the candlelight picked the facets off the decorations. Dark figures spilled in from every direction, the various parlors emptying, all instinctively moving towards the light, like children lost in the woods.

Following closely came servants with trays filled with plates, food, and drinks. Many, those who had not experienced this before, stood there at a loss for meaning and purpose until each was confronted by a servant. A drink in hand comforted them, giving them an anchor they could recognize.

Emily was breathing in the smell of pine and the choral music of the children from the cathedrals, when she felt a tug on her shoulder.

"Mrs. Stroud," Mr. Daniels said. "I'm afraid that I'm a bit at a loss here."

"You are meant to be," she said. "This is meant to be a memory of childhood. We're supposed to feel like it's our first Christmas."

"This ain't nothin like any Christmas I've ever seen."

"No, I suppose it isn't," she replied with a tiny tinge of melancholy. "Nor mine either."

Then she took his hand.

"But we can enjoy it anyway," she smiled.

He smiled back. "Hell yes."

A servant was there with warm mulled cider, the smell of Sri Lankan cinnamon drifting up with the steam from the cups.

The choir had given the musicians from the parlors time to coalesce and as the last echoes of the retreating children died away, the orchestra, for that's what it had become, began to play. It was *Hark! The Herald Angles Sing,* the children's voices filled the darkness that surrounded them with Russian.

They walked forward together, she holding his arm. Ahead, around the tree, people were plucking shining objects from it, little packages.

"I think there are gifts. Shall we see?"

"OK."

Emily frowned. "I'll take that as a yes."

"Yes," he replied.

They were little boxes, pink, gold, and blue, tied to the tree's limbs with colored yarn. There was a definite distinction of color, the pink being lower and the blue higher.

"The pink are for women," said a grey matron as she watched Emily eye them.

"And the gold?" Emily asked.

The woman coughed, then continued. "Either," she rasped.

"Mr. Daniels," Emily asked. "Could you bend down and pick a pink one for me?"

"Of course," he said.

"If you don't mind, one for me too please," the matron said.

"Absolutely."

He stooped down and came back up with two boxes. "Here you are."

Emily looked at her box. The pink paper came apart easily, glued only with paste. Nestled inside the brown paper box, in pink tissue, was a ring. It was a silver wire lacework surrounding translucent cuisine.

The matron sighed. "It's the same every year."

"It's lovely."

"Here, take mine. My maid already has three."

Emily accepted the ring silently.

"What did you get?" she asked Mr. Daniels, who had taken a gold box.

"A lens," he said.

"A hand glass," Emily said.

"Oh, how lucky," the matron said. "There are only a few of those."

Emily thanked the woman, who left to pursue acquaintances, tucking the rings in her purse. Mr. Daniels was looking at the ridges in his fingertip with his lens.

"His name is Tseng isn't it?" Mr. Daniels asked, without looking up.

"Yes," Emily replied.

"He called you Lady Stroud."

"Yes."

Mr. Daniels looked at Emily. "That makes you noble doesn't it?"

"No. Well, perhaps. Honorary noble I suppose. I was knighted. For service to the Empire."

"For the Japanese fleet?"

"No. Before that. I've spent my whole life in service to the Queen."

"So you're here for some reason?"

She stopped and looked at him, her face lit by the glow of the tree. He could just see the hint of a smile. He thought it was beautiful.

"We all are, Mr. Daniels," she said. "That's the reason for royal balls. We're here to look out for the best interests of our countries. Balls are a way for the king to encourage us to focus on each other rather than just him."

"The U.S. doesn't have interests in Russia."

"Then we should see about creating some."

Others joined them. In the light of the tree, the conversation followed and flowed around them. Two women had joined the conversation, clearly interested in Mr. Daniels, although he was too naive to notice. More waited in the wings. They wanted to hear about America and Mr. Daniels enjoyed telling stories, which made moving him in any direction difficult.

He was attempting to explain buffalo when Emily spied someone in the crowd.

"Mr. Daniels. You mentioned sod busters?" Emily interrupted.

"Yes. The ground is so hard on the plains that normal plows don't work."

"Then I think there may be an opportunity here."

Unease rippled through those listening.

"Plows?"

"Agriculture is very important here."

"Isn't that John Deere's work?" he frowned.

"We are first salesmen for our countries. It's our job to open the way."

Emily bowed to the crowd. "I'm afraid I must borrow him

for a minute."

"But we were having fun," a woman said. She was wearing far too much makeup. "You can't go." It was almost a whine.

"I agree," added a dandy. A young noble at ends. "These buffalo. Are they good hunting?"

"Well, yes and no," Mr. Daniels replied, frowning.

"Work or pleasure?" Emily asked.

He sighed. "Work," he replied.

She nodded again to their watchers and led him away with his translator following.

Mr. Herman, who had been talking to two young women, one with her hand possessively on his arm, hastily apologized and caught up.

They passed Max, who was in conversation. He glanced her way and she caught the meaning in it. He was suspicious.

They were heading towards the Russian minister of agriculture.

"Where are we going?" Mr. Herman asked, with a touch of pique. Emily almost laughed.

"To earn our pay," Mr. Daniels replied.

"To sell American industry," Emily added.

Mr. Herman only grunted back his displeasure.

They approached an elderly rotund man in a plain black suit talking to two Cossack officers. When he saw them approach he seemed surprised, but waved his companions away and turned towards them.

"The American diplomat and British representative. What a pleasure." To Emily, it didn't sound like a pleasure at all. Emily's briefing didn't cover the government ministries and she wasn't sure how to address him.

"Dear minister, may I introduce Mr. Jedidiah Daniels, Chief diplomat for the United States of America, and Mr. Ely Herman his attaché. I'm Lady Emelia Stroud, representative of Her Majesty's Government." She curtsied. "Do we have the honor of meeting the esteemed Russian Minister of Agriculture?"

"I am," he said roughly and followed it with a sip of what was probably vodka. "Prince Pyotr Dimitri Kropotkin.

There were then a great many princes in Russia. Every high

born son was a prince, all receiving state pensions – if work couldn't be found for them. Still, Emily had to show him proper respect.

"Your highness," she said, and curtsied once more.

Mr. Daniels stared at all this greeting, blinking, somewhat at a loss until he rallied and thrust forth his hand.

The prince looked at it for a second. It was his turn to blink in confusion. Finally, he reached out tentatively and gave it a shake.

"Sir," Mr. Daniels said heartily. "It's a genuine pleasure to meet you."

The prince's smile warmed slowly under his great bushy beard.

There was, Emily thought, a touch of the steppes about this prince. It had been the right approach.

In a dust blown field
stands a single flower.
Will you pick it?

Chapter 4 –Emily Twice Returns from the Dead.

"Lady Stroud, will you please come with us?" There were three of them. They were dressed as courtiers, but their weathered skin and blocky builds spoke of hard miles and service in difficult places. Apparently, Emily thought, the Okhrana had something it wanted to say.

"Mrs. Stroud," Mr. Daniels called. "Where are you going?"

"I have some business to conduct. I'll be back shortly," she replied cheerily.

"Don't count on it," muttered one of her escorts.

She said nothing. He was only looking for confrontation.

They walked into the forest, past couples and hidden conversations, musicians and singing children, to doors that led to a service corridor that starkly contrasted to the one she had entered through. Without carpet and drapes, their footsteps echoed down the worn red concrete floor and blue grey enameled walls. Servants with trays stepped aside, fear in their eyes, their to and fro bustle parting for them leaving a spreading quiet in their wake and a path through.

It was a long walk, the corridor dimly gas lit. The pine needles that littered the floor crunched under her feet. They had to descend steps, which were difficult in her heels and dress. Down into the bowels of the Russian bureaucracy, passing offices and a large hall filled with lantern lit desks, many of which were occupied, even at that late hour by the chin, the minor bureaucrats of the Empire. Walking on until floors again regained carpet and the walls turned from plaster to wood. They stood before a pair of wooden doors, the flickering light from a bad fixture casting dancing shadows on the carved wood. One of her escorts knocked.

"Enter."

Her guards stayed in the corridor as they closed the door behind her. Behind the desk in front of her sat a thin long nosed man with a great grey bushy beard all out of proportion to the remaining hair on his head. He was dressed in a green uniform and gold epaulets, his sash and chest covered in medals. Though clearly Russian, he wore a monocle. Apparently he had just come from the party too.

"Count Melikov."

"Lady Stroud."

"To what do I owe the honor of this audience?"

"I'm afraid there's little honor in this. We're sending you back to England."

"I'm the chosen representative of Her Majesty."

"Russia finds her choice unacceptable."

"Does Russia include the Tsar?"

"This is a delicate moment here. Your employer's intentions are obvious." He rudely spoke without eye contact, choosing instead to make corrections to several of the documents on his desk.

"You speak of the death of the Bismark."

"That and other events. These are your travel documents. I'll have formal copies drawn up. You will not return to your hotel or embassy. You will be held here until the next train. Fear not, only two hours. I believe it's bound for Helsinki."

"Finland?"

"England has an embassy there."

"The harbor will be iced over for the winter. There will be no zeppelin service until spring."

He looked up from his paperwork.

"Catch a train to Sweden."

She could see a touch of sympathy in his eyes.

"To be honest," he continued. "I would rather that we could share lunch sometime, but . . ."

"This is business."

"Yes."

"Will you wire England first?"

"We will not. I doubt we could if we wanted to. The wires will certainly be down somewhere between here and the border. Ice," he added with distaste. "They have to copy the message and then send it by train until it can be retransmitted." He looked up at the ceiling with a gesture of futility. "It can take days. By then you will be in Helsinki where there is better wire service. They have a cable to Danzig."

He was interrupted by a knock on the door.

"Yes?" he called.

"There is someone to see you," a timid voice replied.

"Who is it?"

"A priest."

"Damn! This came too quickly." He stood and gave her a slight bow, clicking his heels in the Prussian style. "If you'll excuse me."

"Of course."

He stepped outside. She waited alone. He hadn't even offered her tea.

As she sat, her curiosity grew. It had been at least fifteen minutes. One rudeness on top of another.

Standing with a sigh, she went to the door and looked out with the intention of requesting a maid and a toilet to cover her intrusion, but the corridor was empty. A walk down the hallway led her back to the hall with the desks. Chin, mere clerks, looked up at her and back down quickly in fear. Walking right through them, she continued on down the echoing corridors, lifting her dress carefully as she made her way up the steps.

She was walking down the service hallway when she heard running steps behind her. The door to the ballroom was just ahead and she thought of possibility of making a dash for it, but running was not practical in her dress and they would just hunt her down anyway. So she turned and waited.

The servants with trays had already parted for her, and were still standing heads bowed with their backs to the wall, the way being clear for the young priest as he huffed down the corridor towards her. He stopped in front of her, hands on his knees, trying to breathe.

"Your pardon malady. But these robes are not meant for running."

"I understand entirely," she replied with a smile.

"I'm to escort you back to the party."

"To whom do I owe thanks?"

"His Holiness."

"Goodness!"

"Yes."

"Why?"

"It's not my place to say."

He stood and began arranging his robes, trying to regain control his breath.

"I'm to stay by your side to see that you are not disturbed."

"With no introduction." She tisked, lightly teasing. "May I know your name?"

"Sergey malady. Sergey Simansky."

"Well Sergey, my name is Emilia Stroud." She chose the familiar to put an apparent ally at ease. "You may call me Lady Stroud."

"Of course."

"Shall we rejoin the party?"

"Whenever you wish."

"Then let's."

She found Mr. Daniels back in his crowd of followers. Mr. Herman was nowhere to be seen. She suspected he'd been dragged away into the forest.

"Mrs. Stroud! Mr. Daniels called. I was getting worried. I've been trying to find you."

"He has," said his translator. "He's raised quite a row."

"You shouldn't have," she replied with a gentle smile. "It was just business." She was fairly sure he was responsible for her rescue, but she didn't want to alarm him.

"Those men. They said they were police."

"They were, but it was only to have a private meeting. But I'm being rude. I've brought a new friend. Mr. Daniels, may I introduce Sergey. He's a priest. Sergey, this is Mr. Daniels, the American ambassador."

Mr. Daniels held out his hand. Sergey stood there confused.

"Sergey," Emily said. "You shake it."

"Just shake it?"

"Just grab it and he'll do the rest."

Mr. Daniels had gotten used to this and waited patiently with a friendly smile while Sergey tentatively grasped his hand.

"How did you and the minister of agriculture do?" she asked.

"It was amazing. Did you know that Colt designed their rifles? I can't believe we lost the contract to Krupp!"

"That won't happen again now that you're here."

"Right as rain. I'm going to need catalogs and product lists."

"And secretaries to keep track of them," she added.

"And a budget to pay them."

They both laughed. She caught sight of Max in the crowd. He looked troubled, which widened her smile just a bit more.

"Lady Stroud," said a voice behind her.

She turned to face a formidable looking gentleman in a black, his hair a wild untamed mop.

"Nikolay Berezin Milady."

"A pleasure." She curtsied.

"I was wondering if there was still room on your dance card."

"Yes, I'm afraid that I've been away."

"We all noticed and are glad you're back. May I?" He asked, holding out his pencil.

"Yes. I'd love to."

"We've had no introduction," he continued as he signed.

"No. It seems to be an evening for self-introduction. Emilia Stroud. Here as representative of Her Majesty Victoria of England." She curtsied again.

"Malady," he said as he kissed her hand.

"I am Nikolay Berezin!" He managed to add a flourish to it. "Founder and owner of the Izhevsky Arms Works."

"Then I think you and Mr. Daniels have something in common."

"And that would be?"

"You both want Krupp out of Russia."

The music, which had settled into the background, chose

this moment to jump forward as the musicians struck up an unfamiliar kolyadki. The children followed, the glow of their relit candles advancing from the trees, driving the crowd to the open doors and the next room.

She could smell food, which only reminded her how little she had had to eat. She experienced a moment of vertigo, but a strong breath, then two, within the limitations of her corset, helped it pass.

The hall, for that is what it was, was long with a high timbered ceiling, painted as only the Russians can do, in black, gold, green, and red. It held twelve long tables filled with food. Emily examined the array of polished silverware. Mr. Daniels came up behind her and looked down at the choices.

"This is important isn't it?" he said.

"I'm afraid it is."

"We're supposed to use different ones at different times."

"I'm afraid so."

"That makes no sense."

"Oh, but it does. It sets the high born apart from the commoners."

"You said you were born a commoner."

"Yes, but I started training as a child." Emily cursed herself. She had said too much, and in public as well.

"From childhood?"

"From childhood. Perhaps, sometime, I'll tell you about it. But not here."

He looked at her for a moment, his expression indecipherable. Then he pointed at a fork.

"When do we use this?"

"It's for fish."

"This?"

"Sliced meat. Notice the tines are narrower, the handle longer. Meats hold together better than fish."

He looked at her again. She looked back and tried to smile.

"I'm hungry," she said.

"Me too." He smiled back. "It's about time they fed us. And I think I'll use any fork I feel like."

She stumbled, on the edge of a faint.

Emily miscalculates.

"Mrs. Stroud?"

The priest and the translator both rushed forward to catch her, colliding. She fell in the padded nest of her dress, like a nymph in the center of a flower. It made it difficult to close with her without stepping on it. They approached her with care.

It was Mr. Daniels who lifted her.

"What do we do?" he asked, at a loss.

"They do this sometimes," the translator said. "The young ones, they starve themselves. It's the fashion you know. She needs something sweet. A drink."

"Wine?" Mr. Daniels asked.

"No. No alcohol. She'll just get a headache. Sweet tea or straight punch."

Several servants had joined them. A crowd had gathered to watch as well, as had the German ambassador.

"We should take her to one of the parlors," he said. "Away from the party and noise."

"They're bringing smelling salts," Mr. Berezin said.

"I don't think she would want to leave," Sergey said.

"I think so too," Mr. Daniels said. "It seems to me that a lot of people want her out of this room." He glanced at the German ambassador. "I think she needs to stay right here. Sergey, can you get her some sweet tea. I think she would like that."

A servant came with the salts. They opened the jeweled bottle under her nose. She frowned, then recoiled.

"Oh," Emily said, coughing. "I hate smelling salts." Her eyes were tearing.

"You back with us?" Mr. Daniels asked.

"I fainted," she said with disappointment. "I wish they didn't mix it with perfume. It only makes it worse." Then she tried to move, but they held her down.

"Sit still or you'll just be back on the floor," Sergey said. He handed her the tea. "Here. I've blessed it."

She began to laugh, but stopped as she realized her tea was precariously over her dress. "It has crème," she said.

"You need it," Mr. Daniels said.

"I suppose I do."

"Drink," Mr. Daniels said. "Then I'm going to make sure you eat."

"I'll get sick."

"That's crazy. You will eat something."

"I will."

She finished her tea, savoring the smoothness of the crème. She had woken to a crowd of onlookers but many had lost interest now that the excitement had passed. Fainting wasn't unusual for young women at balls. When the dancing started, one or two more were bound to fall. She blamed Paris fashion. She was upset with herself that she had been one of them. It had been a miscalculation.

The tea cup and saucer passed to a servant, she looked

around.

"May I get up now?"

They all looked at each other, like it was a vote! It ended with a general nod.

"Need some help?" Mr. Daniels asked.

"Yes, I'm all tangled up."

They had to lift her by her shoulders, holding her up until she could kick her feet free and set her dress straight.

"Now about eating," Mr. Daniels said. "Which fork do you want?"

"I think I'll pick the food first."

She ate, mostly fruits and lean meats. Mr. Daniels was easily deceived, passing away the worst of the food to passing servants. She drew the line at the deserts, and bluntly refused.

Someday, she thought. If I live to retire, I'll get fat.

Dinner ended with coffee. The smell filled the hall. Steam pressed, it was thick and hot in little cups mixed with bitter chocolate and spices from South America. It sent life back into her limbs and made her forget her hurting feet and cleared her head.

She had just handed her cup to a passing servant when a doorman pounded his staff on his wooden anvil. The crowd stilled and the doors they had entered through from were again thrown open.

"My lords and ladies, and all good people. It is time for the dance. Please form up for the grand march."

"Grand march?" Mr. Daniels asked.

"This will be complicated," Sergey said. "I'm supposed to stay close to you."

"Priests can dance?" Emily asked.

"My father was a Duke. Court Chamberlin."

"What do I do?" Mr. Daniels asked.

"This one is easy. Follow the person in front of you." Emily held out her arm to link with Mr. Daniels and they joined the line, which advanced into ballroom, now clear of trees. Even the smell of pine was gone.

As the line filed out towards the center of the room, Emily could see that the great chandelier had been pulled down and lit. Tall silver lacework candelabras with a dozen gas flames each were spaced around the edges of the room along with hundreds of blessed chairs of white silk and gold, just waiting to be sat in. Towering over everything were tall potted palm trees, the walls under them a jungle of fronds and flowers. Palm trees in Saint Petersburg in the dead of winter!

Mr. Daniels soon left her arm to be replaced by dozens of other men, some wanting to flirt as they walked in the dance's endless circles. The point of a grand march is to make introductions and she made quite a few.

When it was over, she made for the nearest chair. A pointless exercise as the orchestra picked up *God Save the Tsar*. The far wall began to unfold and extend from the upper balcony, forming a grand staircase as they all bowed. Almost before it stopped moving, the Tsar and Tsarina, hand in hand, began their march down to earth sparkling in jewel reflected light. Their closest courtiers and advisors had appeared at the bottom to meet them.

"Dang." It was Mr. Daniels. She hadn't noticed his approach.

"They're early," Mr. Daniels' translator added.

She watched the Tsar and Tsarina's interaction with their inner court as the stairs retracted. She could see no sign of discord or discontent.

"I've seen better," she said.

"Really?"

"Really."

The Tsar stepped forward and the crowd stilled to listen.

"My dear people. We are grateful that you could join us tonight, here in our house, for our blessing of the river, our land. May the coming year be bountiful and our land filled with peace and plenty for all. It has been a good year, with our children growing and the famine receding. Our land has suffered, but the sun is rising and all portents point to this spring being a good one. The fall rains were excellent and the seed is safely under its blanket of snow. We have much to hope and pray for tonight. Tonight we bless the blood of Russia."

The music started, Shostakovich. The Tsar took up the Tsarina's hand and made their way around and around, waltzing into the center of the crowd. Couples began to form and follow.

"Madam?"

It was Graf Stettin, bowing. Emily curtsied in return and with a true smile took his hand and around they went, the floor of the ballroom filling with swirling people at their best. He let go of her hand and she went into a spin. He came to meet her, the music pulsing in time to the swaying dancers, Vienna fast, like water in a rippling brook. She laughed as she lightly glided around the floor. He could not help but smile back. She was a beautiful woman and they both loved to dance.

"It will be sad when we lose you," he said. "These parties, Saint Petersburg, will be far less interesting."

"I will not like leaving," she said.

"You have come to like Saint Petersburg so quickly?"

"No," she laughed. "Because it will take me two weeks to leave!"

Then it was his turn to laugh.

"Then stay with us," he said. "Apply for German citizenship."

"I couldn't stay, even if I wanted to. I'm entirely too British. And you know they send me where they want. I will leave when they call."

"Perhaps it's for the best. You could turn into a dangerous vice."

"I'm not so dangerous," Emily said.

"We will see how the evening progresses," he replied.

"You're more optimistic than I."

They spun in their own circle adrift in the sea of dancers, the music soaking away their cares, easing their minds little by little until nothing was left but motion and sound. Until, at the last note, the weight of the world settled back onto their feet.

He bowed, reluctantly letting go of her hand, and she curtsied in return.

"I must apologize," she said. "I have to sit."

"Of course."

The orchestra picked up one of Bach's endless symphonies. She had no idea which one. With all the variations, Bach was worse even than Mozart. She estimated she had, perhaps, ten minutes to rest.

Looking for the Tsar, she suspecting he was at the center of the crowd at the far end of the room. Feeling at a loss, she drifted with the conversation around her. Mr. Daniels proved to be a better dancer than expected. To be fair though, it was Chopin. Two young women did faint, the servants coming with the smelling salts.

Mr. Daniels had been saying something to her when she noticed a change in the balance of the room. Its weight had shifted.

"I'm sorry Mr. Daniels, but I drifted for a moment. You were saying?"

"That's not good. You aren't going to faint on us again?"

"No, at least I don't think so."

"Coffee. You need coffee. I'll get you some."

"You forget the servants. If you do all their work, they'll be out on the streets."

He grunted. "I can't get used to them."

"We are all servants," she said with a sigh. "Even the king."

"Well said!" said a new voice. It was the Tsar! Their seats had become enveloped with courtiers and diplomats.

"We require coffee," he said, his words having an immediate effect.

Emily stared up at him. Her surprise could not be more complete. She started to rise.

"No, no." He shooed her back into her seat. "Coffee is an excellent idea," he continued. "The evening is still young. You know sir, I've been wanting to meet you all evening, but it seems work of one sort or another has been claiming my time. We've had to settle on hearing your stories second hand. I must to admit, I'm intrigued by America."

"I've found Russia to be amazing as well," Mr. Daniels said.

It was a fair response, Emily thought, but he sounded a bit dazed. He was in shock. He started to stammer.

Emily put her hand on his.

"Tell him about your hopes for trade," she said quietly.

"Yes. Yes. Trade. We, I think," he stopped to breath. "We are both countries with great stretches of wilderness."

"Good," Emily whispered.

"Both struggling to develop industry. Both recovering from great disasters. We have so much in common." He seemed to find himself. "I'm frankly amazed by how much we have in common. When I first arrived, it seemed so strange and confusing. But tonight I feel like I've finally begun to see it, the truth of it. There are so many ways we can profit by working together."

Emily stole a glance up. The Tsar was smiling. He seemed genuinely pleased. Then she felt a tap on her shoulder.

It was Count Yusupova, her next dance partner. She had found him charming at first, but as the evening progressed she had begun to realize that he could be quite disagreeable. She didn't want this dance, especially when she was finally close to the Tsar.

"I believe I'm owed a dance," he said to Mr. Daniels.

Mr. Daniels looked shocked. "You can't. Not now."

"You are doing very well," she said to him. "I'll be back."

"But . . ."

She put her finger to her lips and gently shushed him. "You're ignoring a king."

This drew scattered chuckles for the crowd. The Tsar looked like he was about to laugh, but she noticed as she was leaving that someone was whispering in his ear. His laughter had turned to a confused frown.

It was another waltz and the Count rudely started with no small talk. To Emily, he seemed almost hostile, but he moved well and was easy to follow. They drifted around the floor. As they danced, Emily realized that he was trying to lead her into one of the dark parlors. The sides of the ballroom were largely open to the parlors, some lit for those who had to sit and others not, for those who had other things in mind.

He turned them towards the darkness. She followed, at first, but then continued the turn, pushing him off balance, sending them back out into the floor.

That, she thought, should be hint enough for anyone.

But it wasn't. Still silent, now glaring, he turned her again towards the darkness. His intentions were clearly less than respectable. She felt sure she could deal with him, just not in public.

"You can loosen your grip," she said to him. "I'll follow."

His frown deepened.

"Is it debts?" she said, as she dodged the skirt of a passing couple. He was not concentrating on leading.

Anger bloomed in his eyes.

"Careful, or there'll be scandal on top of them."

There. A twitch. The ego of an impoverished noble.

Ahead, amongst the others in the darkness of the parlor, three men were waiting. Too many.

"It takes four of you to kidnap a girl?"

"British whore," he muttered.

"Kidnapping girls for pay and I'm the whore?"

"Shut up!"

She needed an incident. She needed him to attack first.

"But, I suppose kidnapping girls is the best you can do."

That was it. He let go of her to grab her properly, but missed. Then he swung at her. She dodged it easily, his hand brushing the cloth on her shoulder. The men in the shadows stepped forward into the light without thinking.

It can't stop here, she thought. Not yet.

Allowing herself to fall, she kicked out with her heel at his shin. Not hard. Just enough to hurt and his yell was entirely satisfactory.

He growled in anger and came after her as she hit the floor with a clearly audible yelp. Two others followed to grab her while she was down, but one had the presence of mind to not follow.

"Wait," he said.

"What are you doing?" Sergey yelled, coming up behind them.

"Back off," one of the thugs growled back and swung at him with the back of his hand, striking the side of his head.

They were roughly hauling Emily to her feet, the Count, livid, winding to swing again, Sergey rising from the floor to leap on them. The other thug moving to grab Sergey. When suddenly, it came to them that this was not some back alley. They were in the center of a dance floor. Around them echoed exclamations of horror and fear as the crowd broke up around them and people ran. But worst of all, there, across the parquet in plain view was the Tsar. The music faltered and stopped, leaving a silence that rang like a bell.

"What are you doing?" Mr. Daniels yelled, breaking the silence. He was up and running.

"Shit!" one of the thugs muttered, and they were running as well, dropping poor Emily back on the parquet with a painful "Oh!"

Sergey tried to grab one of their legs, but failed.

The count just stood there, confused, looking at his hand.

Emily, tangled in her skirts, couldn't move. Thankfully, she didn't need to. She was grateful the count's blow hadn't landed, but she had been preparing to take it on the side of her head, away from her nose. To others, it looked like she was cowering.

Mr. Daniels ran up and slugged the count. A great walloping roundhouse to the stomach that lifted the count off his feet and knocked him flat on the floor. A little collective scream escaped the crowd, but Emily thought she detected a certain excited breathlessness in it. Mr. Daniels, she thought, was making points in court.

Once picked, twice plucked,
legion are their hands.
Less than a feather,
they carry you
to the moment.

Chapter 5 —Emily Reminds a King of his Duty.

Mr. Daniels and Sergey were at her side. That was until Sergey fell back on his rump looking dazed.

"My head," he said.

"Mrs. Stroud, are you all right?" Mr. Daniels said. He waded towards her, through her skirt to lift her.

"I'm bruised, but well. At least I think I'm well," she said, as Mr. Daniels helped her sit up. "Sergey, what's wrong with you?"

"They hit me. Give me a minute. My head is spinning."

"They hit a priest?" Mr. Daniels asked.

"He was lucky," Sergey replied defensively.

The crowd seemed reluctant to approach them until the Tsar himself, followed by his entourage walked over.

"I must apologize," he said. He reached down to hold out his hand to Emily. "In my own house." He was shaking his head as helped Mr. Daniels haul Emily to her feet. "This is unconscionable. I don't care if you are a member of The Institution, I will not have a guest treated this way."

He turned to Count Melikov, who was standing behind him. "Mikhail, you will stop this immediately. We will have no more disturbances."

"Yes sire." Melikov dipped his head, but gave Emily a hard glance as his head came back up.

"I can't see how or even why she would want to harm me."

"Sire . . ."

"No. I'll hear no more."

"Your highness, I . . ." Emily started.

"Not another word. She will stay. I've decided."

Then he took a good long look at her.

"Are you hurt?"

"No, your Majesty." She curtsied. "Just bruises and a little confusion."

"No more of that either," he laughed. "I think our priest could use a brandy."

"Thank you, but no. I afraid it would make me ill." Sergey was holding on to Mr. Daniels' shoulder, feeling ear. "My ear is numb," he said, half to himself.

"Then we'll sit, at least." He looked about at the surrounding crowd. "Please," he called. "Let the dance resume."

He started for the side of the room and they followed, walking to where servants were pulling up chairs and bringing tables.

"Actually. I'm intrigued. Mikhail says you are a spy sent from London. You aren't going to cause us trouble are you?"

"No sire, at least I hope not. Count Melikov is correct. I am a member of The Institution, but I'm really more of an errand girl."

They sat and a servant was there with a tray of steaming cups. Belgian chocolate. Emily winced inwardly at the thought of the fat, but this was in the line of duty. She took a cup and stirred it.

"What other reason would Edward send you?"

"And how is our aunt?" The queen joined their group, interrupting. "Have you seen them?"

The dance had ended. The orchestra picked up a lovely violin work. Glazunov, she thought.

"Yes I have. We had tea before I left. She is stronger, quite busy in fact. She no longer needs the cane."

"We should visit," Alexander said smiling to his wife.

"Yes, yes. Perhaps next spring. Were you there for the funeral?"

"No your highness. I'm afraid I was in Hawaii."

"Oh yes. I heard," he replied.

The queen let out a little moan of frustration. "We couldn't go. The damn snow. I heard Willy made it there though."

"Yes, His Highness the Kaiser attended."

"Are you this stiff with Edward?" she asked.

"No ma'am, but we really haven't been introduced."

At that she rolled back and let out a great guffaw of laughter, the king following with his quiet chuckle. Naturally, the court followed.

"But they invite you to tea."

"Yes ma'am."

"So, out with it," she said. "Why'd they send you?"

"Our embassy has stopped sending reports and answering queries."

"That's it? All this way for just that?"

"Russia is important to us you highness, but your aunt had an errand too. I'm afraid it's private."

Alexandra frowned at Emily. The Tsar looked at his wife inquiringly. She looked back with a flash of concern. "Perhaps later then," she added.

"Yes ma'am."

Then the Tsar smiled. "There. See Mikhail?" he said. "She is innocent, and quite charming."

"Yes, of course your highness," The Count replied without conviction.

"No need for your heavy hand." He chuckled again. "A fight and a mystery. The night just gets better and better. Tell us more about buffalo Mr. Daniels."

Mr. Daniels picked up his story of the buffalo again. Slowly at first, but warming to the tail. Emily was entranced at first, but then doubted that such a thing could exist. So many animals, so big, living in one place. When a servant tapped her on her shoulder and bid her to follow.

The Tsarina was waiting for her in an empty parlor. There were Okhrana there, but they kept a respectful distance.

"Out with it. What did she send," the queen asked impatiently.

Emily pulled an envelope from her handbag. It was rumpled, but still sealed.

"I apologize for its condition your majesty. I've had to keep it hidden."

"Yes, yes," she said as she broke the seal and tore open the envelope.

Pulling out a letter, she turned away without a word, trying to read it, only to finally growl in exasperation.

"Damn my eyes. Get me a light!" she barked.

Okhrana jumped as if struck by lightning. A lamp was quickly produced, held up by a thug in court dress who carefully averted his eyes.

"She does hate Germans," the queen mumbled as she read.

"Yes ma'am. She does," Emily replied.

"Out of her mind," the queen continued. She looked up at Emily, "She's German you know." And then again to herself. "How can she hate them? Crazy. Just crazy."

Emily said nothing.

"I'll have a reply for you before you leave. Where are you staying?"

"The Kaminski ma'am."

"Good. I have contacts there."

There was a knock on the parlor door, despite it being open. Standing in the doorway was a servant with a paper wrapped bundle and a folded cloak.

"Is it that time already?" the queen asked.

"Yes ma'am," the servant said with a slight bow. "Will you need a maid?"

"No, Lady Stroud can attend me."

Who will attend Lady Stroud? Emily thought.

She unfolded the queen's cloak and helped drape it over her, carefully smoothing the folds over the contours of her dress. The hood was difficult. Emily was sure there would be no saving her hair. Then she broke the seal on hers, allowing the smooth cloth to spill out. She took a second to run her fingers down the course of the trim before lifting it with a shake. She twirled, spinning the cloth into the air before letting it settle around her.

"Ha!" the queen laughed and gave a single clap. "I can see why they like you."

Cloaked, they exited the parlor into a sea of women donning cloaks, helped by servants and husbands. A dais had been placed to one side of the floor, draped in gold velvet carpet. The Tsar stepped up.

"My dear people," he said. "Tonight we pray for our Russia. We pray for the harvest and we pray for our people. We have had bad years and our Russia has suffered, but with God's grace, this year will be blessed. He tests us and gives us these obstacles to strengthen us. It is a test of faith and sign of his love. We will not falter or lose sight of his light. We will continue. Our Russia is strong. Its people great."

He stopped to look over the crowd, then nodding he continued. "And we have so much more than hope. We have so much to give thanks for. Family. Friends. Our children. This beautiful Christmas. Most of all, the land itself and the blessings it brings forth. . ."

"He says the same thing every year," the queen whispered to Emily.

Emily hiccupped.

The queen blocked a laugh.

The king eyed them suspiciously as he spoke, the patriarch of Saint Petersburg stepping up on the dais next to him.

"And so we give God our gratitude for the things we've been given," he continued.

Then the patriarch stepped forward, standing in his white and gold robes, his mitre and staff, to say a rather lengthy, from Emily's perspective, prayer in a language she couldn't understand or even identify and which had sadly been missing from her briefing.

Then the last set of formerly unopened doors were opened at the back of the hall.

"We must hurry," the queen said, and dragged Emily towards the doors. The crowd was held back for them to pass into a large gold and white marble vestibule flanked by long windowed hallways. Their heels clicked across the floor as they made their way towards a cluster of uniforms and cloaked dresses gathering by windowed doors that lead to darkness. These were the inner court. She could see the Tsar and the patriarch among those let through first. Then she saw Mr. Daniels, who gave her a grin.

"Better get your hood up. It'll be cold," the queen said. "The poor men don't get to wear anything."

"No coats?"

"No coats. Ah, but wait until you see what comes next!" she said.

Near the doors were tables stacked with lamps. They had barely arrived when a servant handed Emily one and lit it with a taper.

"Do you know the Cherubim Hymn?"

"No," Emily replied.

"Then I'm afraid you'll have to wing it. Don't worry. It's mostly oooing and moaning."

Servants had taken positions next to the doors.

"Better hold on to something," the Tsarina said.

They threw the doors to the outside open and a great rush of cold blew in. Emily's teeth locked. Their group let out a collective gasp. Then, a few hoarse voices began to sing, followed by more, and followed by more still. They began to walk forward with their lamps held in front. The haunting melody echoed down the halls as those behind still lined up in the ballroom began to follow.

On the stairs, under the cold white starlight stood priests with torches. Their black and white robes blending with the ice and white stone. Before them stretched the grey white Bol'shaya Neva. A desert of flat ice that stretched into infinity as it emptied into the Gulf of Finland. A dark sandy trail had been swept across its frozen surface, lit by braziers. It ended far out to the center where there stood a great tent, glowing like an ember with light from within.

The patriarch joined the Tsar. He carried a blood red velvet pillow on which sat a substantial gold cross. It glittered in the lamplight against the dark velvet as he led them down the steps, the Tsar, a half step behind.

"Our turn," the Tsarina whispered, and dragged Emily into line to follow with their lamps, singing.

Wooden steps had been placed at the stone edge of the river so they could walk down to the thick ice. Servants and maids waited on the steps to help. Emily was grateful for it. Despite the sweeping and the sand, the steps were slippery and dirty, and her heels impossible.

Down on the ice, the wind swept snow in dry swirls. Dark

empty quiet fought against their song and the light of their lamps, the crowd of the ballroom tiny in the great dark. Cold leaked in everywhere through her cloak, the breeze swirled around her ankles. She hoped the tent was warm.

The walk was long. Emily wasn't the only one shivering as they neared the tent. She could see Cossacks with rifles, their dark figures out on the ice, guarding the tent. Two more were holding the flaps of the tent, bowing for the Tsarina.

Inside, it felt hot, but she could see her breath fogging and the ice beneath their feet was dry. They filed in, filling the tent. In the center, a hole ten feet across had been cut in the ice. White speckled, almost frozen water churned within.

Four Cossacks were tying a rope around the Tsar's waist. He looked pale in the lamplight.

"Hurry up," the Tsar said to the Cossacks. "I'm freezing!"

"The thing must be done right," the patriarch said.

"I hate this. Every year," the Tsar's teeth chattered.

"Don't rush it like last year," the patriarch chided.

"Yes, yes. As if God doesn't know what I'm thinking. At least warm the cross a bit."

The patriarch shook his head slowly.

"The thing sticks to my hand!"

The patriarch began to intone and genuflect over the cross. Then began reciting the story of the baptism of Jesus.

"And John said, 'I have need to be baptized of thee, and comest thou to me?'" The patriarch sang it. The Tsar had his hands under his arms. The Cossacks had a knot they felt satisfied with. Finally, it was the Tsar's turn.

He picked up the cross with a little, "Oh! Damn thing's cold." It was his turn to intone. "With this cross we remember the baptism of our lord, a new beginning, and a new year for our mother Russia. We pray for an early spring and rain for the fields."

The Tsar had walked carefully forward to the edge of the hole.

"For the honor and pride of the Motherland," and he tossed the cross in with a single kerplunk.

The crowd erupted in a cheer. Behind her Emily heard a man exclaim, "Great, now where's the vodka." Bottles and glasses began appearing out of nowhere. The Tsar was nursing his hand.

The Tsarina nudged Emily and held out a glass to her. "Careful with this. It was my grandmother's."

She took it and an elderly man's richly draped hand reached around from behind her with a bottle and sloshed vodka into to her cup. She looked back. It was the patriarch!

"Drink up," he smiled with glee, and lifted the bottle to his lips. He was cackling as walked away.

"To mother Russia!" someone called.

That raised a cheer and everyone lifted their glass. Emily tried to pretend, but it's difficult to fake tipping back a glass and she couldn't catch her breath things were coming so quickly. A small group of musicians picked up a Russian folk tune in the corner. There was raucous laughter nearby.

"To God and king!" someone called, and again the glasses were tipped back with a cheer.

The tent felt warmer, her breath no longer fogged.

"Your pardon, your highness. I must go."

The queen spared a moment from her conversation and gave her a smile. "Go," she whispered.

Then Emily realized that she had been talking to someone as well and someone had sloshed more vodka in her glass.

Someone called, "May we suffer as much sorrow as the drops we leave in our glass!"

A hurrah and the glasses tipped.

Emily actually felt hot. For some reason, she saw men standing next to the hole, stripping off their uniforms. Cossacks were tying rope around them. She made her way towards the Tsar.

Then Max was in front of her.

"I won't let you do this," he said.

"You can't stop me," she replied.

Behind her a chanting started and one of the men, dressed only in his underwear, let out a whoop and leapt into the water. Everyone cheered. Max's hand was on her arm.

She turned to look at him. He was serious.

"Let the lady go," said another voice. It was Sergey. "Here, have some vodka."

"You don't understand," Max said.

"But I do," Sergey smiled back. Mr. Daniels appeared behind him.

"What's up?" he said. "Oh. Mrs. Stroud. Glad I found you."

"To Grandfather Frost and his granddaughter Snegurotchka!" someone called. And the glasses were tipped.

"To hell with Grandfather Frost. I just want Snegurotchka!"

"Screw Snegurotchka, to Komissarzhevskaia!"

Everyone cheered except the first man who replied, "But Snegurotchka's a nice girl."

Max was gone and Mr. Daniels was saying, "Are you getting as tired of this vodka as I am?"

"I have to go," Emily said, and started towards the Tsar again.

"Well let's go," he said. "You OK?"

"OK?"

"You look a bit flushed."

"I am?"

"Yup."

"I suppose that's yes. I guess I am. I'm tired of the vodka too."

They were hauling another of the men from the river as she approached the Tsar.

"I'm tired of your pestering Delianov," said the Tsar. "If we must adopt the damned Prussian school plan then we must. But somehow the church must be involved."

"But we need to modernize and that means modern education. What good are factories without educated workers?"

"I don't see how it could work here. What good are workers without morals? Educating peasants the wrong way could spark a revolution! I understand the need. I just wish it wasn't such a cold sterile solution."

"The Prussian way works. Their modernization program is brilliant."

"But this is . . ." she said and realized that eyes were turned towards her. "This is mother Russia. How can you think to do this? You would have her goose-stepping like a fatherland."

The Tsar grinned and said, "Exactly!" And then to Delianov, "Would you have me wearing a monocle too?"

"No, no. Of course not."

Emily could see Graf Stettin frowning.

"But the efficiency. Think of the revenues," another man said.

"Mansein, we do not lack for organization. The Zemstvo . . ."

"Peasants!"

"They are of the people."

"Covered in mud like the livestock they herd. Most can barely add enough to compute the taxes. How can they manage a modern state?"

"Must we dissolve the Zemstvo?"

"Replace the people's rule with bureaucrats?" Emily said again.

"Yes," the Tsar blinked. "You're right. The Zemstvo has existed for a thousand years! Next you'll have me issuing clothing like it was the army."

"But the treaty."

Emily felt a thrill and focused.

"This is not the place to discuss the treaty," Graf Stettin said with finality.

"I'm tired of discussing it too," the Tsar said. "We do nothing but discuss it!"

The tent had grown quiet.

"I don't understand," Emily said.

"What?" The Tsar said.

"He's your friend."

"Willy?"

"Why do you let these lawyers and diplomats come between you?"

She heard a grunt from Stettin.

Emily could feel the moment as it passed, like she had walked through a mirror.

"That's it, what I was trying to say," the Tsar said, his brow furrowed in thought. "That's it exactly." He took another sip of vodka. "We don't need any of you for this. You can't negotiate friendship. You can't put it down on a piece of paper."

"It was the work of the Bismark," she added.

"That awful man. Yes! This treaty is nonsense! It's the work of the Bismark. He needed a treaty, but Willy and I do not."

The room had shifted. The world's weight had passed from one hand to another. The conversation continued, heated at times, but Emily couldn't be bothered to listen as the vodka took her.

ഗ∞ര

The sun had topped the horizon, a great bar of light in the frozen air. Emily climbed the steps to her hotel on unsteady feet. The vodka had nearly done her in. The doormen came to give her a hand up the steps.

Her work wasn't through. There would be more parties and perhaps even meetings. But she knew she had won. She would be there at the negotiation. The treaty was finished. The Tsar hadn't really wanted it and now he had reasons not to agree, from someone he hadn't already set his mind against.

As she passed through the doors to the warm lobby, she heard the desk clerk exclaim.

"Madam!" He came out from behind the desk. "Why are you here? Have you missed your train?"

"Train?" Emily was having trouble focusing.

"They came for your baggage and maid and took them to the station. You are checked out."

It was Melikov, she thought. Tio and her things were on their way to Finland.

Crossing the front.

The Last Mission

Explosions cut the night below as Emily gazed down through the bombardier's canopy at no man's land. The bombardier and the navigator sat behind her, across from the bombsight computer, furiously scribbling on chalk boards in the dim red light, trying to calculate their ground speed by the light of burning houses, timing their passage with stopwatches and great folds of maps. The gold of brass gears glinted and the rumble of petrol engines numbed her ears. Emily watched the clouds drift by, lit yellow orange from below.

The German offensive had taken everyone by surprise. The fall of Russia had freed a million soldiers for the western front. How could the Germans not attack? And here were the Allies, reeling back. Back again towards Paris. It was enough to break one's heart.

The bombardier and navigator seemed to agree on a solution and pushed the nob on the computer for ground speed up two clicks. She saw the gears turn, the bombsight tilting again ever so slightly.

"Looks like you'll be arriving early," the navigator yelled over the sound of wind and engines. He smiled as he rolled his maps.

"As long as it's before dawn," Emily yelled back. She edged around the computer, making her way towards the rear. She didn't think they heard her. She had barely heard them. She took a moment to adjust the cotton in her ears. She hated it. It itched.

The light dimmed to thin red outlines. They had passed the front and were heading into darkness, into Germany. The crew would switch those off few red lights soon. She would have to make her way then in pitch black, by memory and feel.

Two years of ceaseless missions mixed with immersive language training, had improved her German. It was now flawless. She could even do a French accent in German. Sometimes she even dreamt in German, which was good should she speak out in her sleep, not that she slept much. The war had been relentless. And with the way it seemed to be going these days, they would all be speaking German soon.

She stopped on that thought. No. It would not happen. She would win this game. She couldn't stop. Depression would follow and she couldn't afford that. Not when she had a jump.

Leaving the enclosed nose, passing the gunners positions, the cold wind grabbed the air from her lungs, making her nose run. Her handkerchief was already thoroughly used. They were all around her, asleep in their bunks. Airplane pilots, gunners, deck crew. She passed the twin Maxims of a gun turret, its barrels pointed downwards, the gunner's seat sitting empty. She should be asleep as well, they had given her a bunk, but the effort would be futile. Sleep these days seemed to be the only coin she couldn't mint.

The narrow Zeppelin gondola stretched back. No walls or windows except in the bow, all open to the air. It was a work of both minimalism and constructivism, the strong angular lines of aluminum and steel crisscrossing a mechanical space devoted to nothing less than earthly destruction, lit by the light of passing burning towns painting momentary ghostly shadows that drifted across the roof. It wouldn't be long before the coming day brought enough light for the crew to worry about enemy fighters. She would be gone before that.

Above, past a stack of filled bunks, up a step ladder, sat the pilot astride his control saddle, aluminum compass in front, head in his helmet attached by tubes to the navigator and bombardier, hands on the valves that controlled the engines and flaps. He and the airship were one, a great dragon that lived in the clouds. Around them flew eleven others. Dragons that flew in schools. Soon, the sky would be swarming with their children, drop fighters, and the Ruhr's children, in fighters of their own, would rise to meet them, mosquitos among giants.

Emily climbed over the bomb racks and fighter plane locks, to the stern and her bunk. It was narrow, twenty inches wide, with little padding. Come morning they would be folded up to make room. She lay down, pulling the light down cover over her.

soᗞꞇ

"Come on Gorgeous, time to wake." A hand shook her shoulder. She caught it and almost broke it. "Jesus!" The figure recoiled, holding his arm.

Emily stared up at the gunner as he scowled, her eyes finding focus. She had slept hard. The fact that she could see him told her that they were late. Dangerously late! She rolled out of bed, the gunner falling back on his ass to make room, trying to keep his distance.

"It's late," she snapped, in the dim grey, not-yet-blue, morning light.

"There's coffee," he replied.

"I need to jump."

"Take it up with the captain."

Emily grabbed her chute, helmet, and goggles from the rack at the foot of the bed, leaving the gunner still sitting on the deck, holding his wrist. Forward, the crew were rousing. Soon, their escorts would drop. The Ruhr, their target, and Emily's as well, was waiting – but she couldn't. Capture meant torture and then certain death. No one could see her jump and it was already far too light.

Still pulling the chute buckles, she found the door. Undogging it, she heard voices, exclamations. "What's she doing? Hold on!" But there was no more waiting. The door banged, whipped open by the wind. Someone tried to grab her, but she was out, stars still visible behind the grey bulk of the zeppelin's envelope, rolling. She couldn't judge her height, but did her best, pulling the slip knots on her chute. Blessed silk unrolled correctly and ever so gratefully blossomed, yanking her upwards as the ground came at her far too fast.

∞∞

Daylight! Time had passed. There were shapes looming over her. Two men, and a cow. She looked up at it in confusion as it chewed its cud.

"Hold still," one said in English. He had a beard. They all had beards. "We've got to get your pack off." Then he muttered to his friend, "She's waking up."

"Must have fallen from one of them airships."

"She jumped fool. How's the hole going?" the first, clearly in charge, asked someone out of sight.

There were more cows. Cows all around them.

"Slow. Damn ground's hard."

They were all English! Where had she fallen? They were wearing the remnants of uniforms. She must have landed in a POW camp! With cows?

"Well keep the herd around and dig dammit." Then he looked at her. "Don't worry. They're not watching us. There's too few of them to watch all the time."

"Rather hunt us with dogs instead," said his friend.

Emily tried to move, but pain shot through her. Her leg!

"Don't try Love," one in charge said. "We've just stopped the bleeding. You've got a broken leg and we don't know what else."

They had unbuckled the straps and slid the empty pack from under her.

"Damn shame to waste the silk."

"Damn shame to die for it too."

Emily blinked, then said in English, "You're British."

"A big pack of Poms, yes," the leader said, smiling.

"Where am I?" she asked.

"We're not sure. Somewhere east of Cologne we think."

"Don't tell us much. Just what to do," the friend said.

"We're going to need that helmet." They began undoing the buckles. She let them take her helmet and goggles.

"What are we going to do with her?" the not bright one whispered, with a touch of panic.

"How did you plan on getting out?" the leader asked.

"I didn't."

"I thought so. How did you plan on getting in?"

"I was going to walk."

"Well that's off. I take it you speak Bosche?"

Emily nodded.

"What can we do, George?" his friend asked, clearly worried. A third had shown up. They all were frowning. She could see them clearly in the late morning overcast.

Emily needed to take control. "You've found me," she said. "I broke it climbing a fence."

They all looked at her, surprised. Then George cracked a smile, chuckling, relieved. "Of course," he said.

His friend twitched into a smile and said slowly, "That might work."

"There's only one fence near that might do, and you'll have to explain why you tried to climb it," George said.

"I can do that," Emily replied firmly.

"You sure?" Then a look of worry crossed his face. "We'll have to carry you there."

"Do it," Emily said, with finality.

ഇൽഌ

She remembered nothing. Just dreams. Her sleep, as it often was these days, was a torturous twisting trail of memory. When she finally awoke, it was on a stretcher, coughing, trying to clear her mouth and lungs. There were rows of stretchers, the room's stone gothic ceiling echoing with a continuous low wheezing moan sprinkled with coughs. For a moment, she was lost. She had forgotten everything. There were two grey clad nurses conversing in German. Then it came back. She was in Germany. She must have blacked out. What had happened to George?

"Pardon me," she tried to call out in German, but it came out a rasp.

One of the nurses glanced at her, then continued her conversation.

She tried to work up spit, but it wouldn't come. "Pardon?" It came out a cough, her mouth dry. She couldn't focus her eyes. "May I have some water?" she managed.

One of the nurses held up her hand, motioning for her to wait. So Emily waited. But then they both nodded and parted in different directions. Emily was stunned. Then she looked at her bed mates. One was missing an arm up to his shoulder, eyes bandaged. He was bleeding through his bandage. Shot and gassed she guessed. If he was blind, then his lungs were probably gone too. The other on the other side was no better. They were as good as dead. The floor was puddled in blood and urine.

Eventually a boy, an undraftable idiot, with a bucket and dipper came by. She drank greedily.

"Careful," the boy said, annoyed. "I have others still." But she didn't care. She forced his hand to hold the dipper close. He could fill another bucket! She didn't let go of his wrist. Not yet.

When she could talk, she asked him carefully for a pencil and paper. She had to get a note to a friend.

He was angry, but afraid. "They'll come around for that. The church ladies do that."

She pulled him closer. "Listen. I have powerful friends. When they find me, you will be rewarded or killed. You will come back with that bucket regularly. You will make sure the church ladies come around. Do you understand?"

He nodded and she let him go. She never saw him again.

The water eventually beat back the headache she didn't realize she had, but she was still thirsty. She was always thirsty during her stay. Taking stock of her possessions, she found she was still wearing her walking outfit shirt, but not her shoes, pants, purse, along with her papers and money were gone. Her left leg bulged under the stained sheet and she worried they had amputated it until she saw her toes move under the fabric. Her cast went all the way up to her waist. She wasn't going anywhere.

The next day the bed pan cart came by. She had been issued a bed pan and had been expected to deal with it herself. She weakly pushed it towards the man and he left her another. He was dressed rather poorly and seemed as dim witted as the water boy had been. Dinner that night, her first meal, was thin stew, almost soup, and small piece of bread. She would die if she stayed here, she thought. She needed help. When the "church ladies" finally showed themselves, she sent a note to Max.

It took him four days to get there.

∞)(∞

Just breathing took up most of her energy. She could only lay on her back and her lungs filled while she slept until she was forced awake with quick racking coughs. Later, there came fever. She could feel it crawl over her skin. She never got enough water. She'd pay the new boy to come twice if she could just get access to her money. She told them she had money, but he said that money was no good any more.

It was early afternoon, as best as she could tell. It was always overcast. She saw him walking grimly down the aisles, past the lines of stretchers that were emptied and filled each day. There was a momentary frown as he looked in her direction and then a flash of outrage when he recognized her, but then the old genial smile filled his face as he sauntered over to her stretcher. They spoke in German.

"Hello Emily. I'm sorry I didn't get here sooner," Max said. "I was away."

"It was a long shot," she managed, before she had a fit of coughing.

He crouched down next to her.

"I'm afraid our hospitals are a bit crowded these days," he said.

"As are ours."

"I've missed you. It's been a long war."

273

"I've missed you too," she said. Her cheek itched. Was she bleeding? She touched it, looking at her finger to see what it was. They were tears. She was crying. She panicked! She couldn't cry, ever! But the tears were undeniable. It was all crashing down. The schooling, the brutal training, the years of sacrifice. It couldn't! The injustices, the compromises, the futility. Everything, the lifetime of control fell apart. She was shocked. It took only a moment for it all to collapse. Then came a sob, and then another. She cast about looking for something to hold on to as her world crumbled. She tried to rise, to run.

And he was down on the floor, ruining his pants in the filth, holding her. Saying, "there, there. You'll be fine," over and over, as she clung desperately to him, sobbing into his shoulder. Its warmth and firmness the only thing holding back the hysteria.

ℰ⍉ℬ

Max had her moved to his apartment in Essen. For the first three months she saw little beyond his guest room walls. She didn't see Max for weeks on end. Instead, there was an elderly woman who cared for her, Ulva.

A real nurse came twice a day to check her, and a doctor when needed. They had to remove her cast twice to treat infection. She lived through rattling fevers, her leg being drained, cleaned, and restitched. The endless pain. She refused opioids. It was her training. In the end there would be a terrible scar. All of it cost Max. There were very few doctors not at the front.

Then there were the bombings. Her first was her first night, when she was at her most vulnerable. The sirens, then the cannon. Light flickered through the windows, flashing like lightening down from the explosions in the sky above. Then they started below, in the city itself, one after another. They grew louder, like giants walking across the city. Coming closer. But she couldn't move. She couldn't go to the shelters. She pulled the covers up instead. The only armor available.

In the dancing shadows from the explosions she saw Max. He was standing in the doorway to her room, then in the next flash he was next to her, then with her in bed. She was sandwiched between him and the wall, desperately clinging to him through the whirlwind of explosions, the flash, the blizzard of wood and irreplaceable glass from the near miss. When they had passed, she found it difficult to let go of him.

When he was there, he cooked her meals. Delicacies bought at great expense from the black market. Real jam for her toast! She had never learned how to cook. He complemented her German and laughed as she showed off her French accent. They discussed past assignments and their hopes for the future. Emily hadn't realized that she had any. But with him, she found she did have some. She remembered her doll set, lost so long ago with her childhood.

Despite her having asked him to stay away, he was there when they removed the cast. He helped carry her wasted swollen body to the tub to soak. She wanted to scratch so, the itching beyond pain, but they held her back until they could get her in the tub, the cold water bringing blessed relief. She soaked and carefully worked her skin clean, lest she scar even more.

When she was able, she walked and stretched, and explored Max's house. He kept souvenirs. His apartment was full of them. He had glass cases. She found her dance card from Saint Petersburg. He had signed it, but she hadn't had the chance to dance with him. The silk gloves she remembered from Paris. They had waltzed then, so glorious after the game! Then she saw candies from the Moline Rouge tea house. Her cheeks were wet again. Had she lost all control? She wept, Ulva running to her as she fell. She could no longer stand. She realized she had kept nothing. She never had a place to keep things. She owned nothing other than a bank account and a title.

The war ended before she was off her crutches. She was taking too long to heal despite her constant work. Looking down at the street from the window, the celebration outside seemed almost animal, gunfire erupting around the city, people behaving very poorly, the pent up madness after the relief. A month later, once the telegraph lines had been reestablished, she took a carriage to the post office. There were no cabs because there was still no petrol. Pocking up the cracked stone steps with her cane, she sent a telegram to the Institution to tell them that she was alive and recuperating from wounds, but not where she was. It took them a month and a half to find her.

It was Kinsey, hair going grey. A note and a meeting in a park full of homeless veterans, a statue of the Kaiser looking down at them all, fall leaves covering the dying grass. He walked, she followed with her cane, ignoring his requests that they sit. It was clear to him that she would never see anything but the back side of a desk again, despite her reassurances that she would heal. She had been their last and best, practically moving mountains for the war effort, but he recognized her loss. He had seen it before. It was the most common of things since the war. She had seen a glorious run. He worried it might weigh hard on her.

He informed her that she was a widow. Leaving her with an envelope thick with solid British pounds, he told her to take as much time as she needed to recover, but not to forget them.

Her recovery took another painful year and a half.

ဢ◌ဢ

She left for England amidst riots.

Max wouldn't come. She practically begged, but they still had their lives and the game, no matter how bitter it had become. Despite all the glory, decency, and poise in the world having burned in the war.

When she stepped off the airplane, boxy, noisy, awful things, but quick. She was met by a junior agent, his breath fogging in the late winter air. He practically cowered under her gaze. So young, she thought.

"Lady Stroud?" he asked.

He couldn't have been schooled. He was too open, too easy to read. Had things slipped so far?

"Yes," she smiled, offering her hand. But he didn't know what to do!

He awkwardly looked at it, embarrassed. Then bowed and stiffly kissed it.

My God! She thought.

She asked, a glint in her eye, "And you are?"

"Woods Ma'am."

Woods the ex-agent she thought.

They put her up in a second rate hotel. The best description she could think of was, "clean," and Wood's company Vauxhall, "utilitarian." She was beginning to doubt they had won the war. Woods left her a note from Kinsey. They were to meet that evening in a pub down the street. A pub! At least her new dresses were fun. They barely covered her knees!

At ends, she searched the room and found a thread tied to the heater grate that led to a blank piece of paper. She held the paper up to the light, singed it, and dampened it, but could find no markings. A mystery.

He was waiting in a booth when she walked in, cane long gone. His grey had spread, even leaking into his eyes. For a moment they stared at each other in the dim gas light before she slid in across from him.

"It's good to see you Emilia," he said. "You look well." But she would have none of it.

"Alfred, what wrong?" she asked firmly, not caring that the answer was bad.

"What's right?" he answered with a sigh. "We're not what we were."

"So I've noticed. Things seem to have slipped."

"The Institution is gone," he replied.

Emily thought she had misheard him. The king would never let this happen.

"Nonsense. In two years?"

"There are only a handful of us left. You're the only schooled agent we have." Then he sighed. "We burned everyone and everything in that war."

She could tell that much, at least, was the truth.

Kinsey eyed her appraisingly. He wondered if they still had her. Looking carefully, he saw that she knew, but didn't believe.

"Even you," he added quietly.

The barmaid interrupted them, asking about drinks. Kinsey ordered a pint. It took Emily a moment to answer, then she said the same. She hated beer, but she was too stunned to think. All gone!

"Even the school?"

"Here or behind the front. Dead or worse." He looked so tired. "We work for the War Office now."

"That explains the hotel," she said.

"No budget. They think they don't need spies any more. The

war to end all wars," he said, rolling his eyes and shrugging.

The Kinsey she knew never shrugged. She was suspicious. This was a test.

"We fight the IRA now," he continued. "We're no better than the police."

Emily slid the piece of paper over to him.

"And me?" she asked. "What's going to happen to me?" But the bar maid had come with the glasses. Kinsey just leaned back and stared at the paper.

"Anything else?" the bar maid asked.

Kinsey said nothing, so Emily said, "No, we're fine."

"Right."

Emily watched her walk away, then turned, seeming to rise up, looming like a dark spirit, and asked again, this time with deadly seriousness, "Alfred. What about me?"

Kinsey frowned for second, nonplused, then said enigmatically, "I think you'll pass."

She sat back in her seat, mustering her patience, waiting for him to speak.

"There's one last mission," he continued with a twitch of a smile.

"Well?"

"You're going to have tea with the king."

೮೧೦೪

Kinsey left her with an account number, instructions to pick up something appropriate to wear, and some suggestions as where to look. She had a week to get ready. Ready for what, she asked. Ready for tea, he replied. The rest is up to them. She could pry nothing more than reminisces out of him as she worked at her beer. There was something about the third tailor he mentioned. She let him notice her recognition. It was another damn test. She could have spit!

The address was in Mayfair, Savile Row of all places. The shop had an old wood front with a patina of veneration. Sedwell & Son Ltd. A bell jingled. Inside they had electric light and reasonable appointments worthy of British taste. A young man appeared wearing a decent suit, sporting a tape measure around his neck. It was the first proper suit Emily had seen since arriving in London. She almost felt relief.

"May I help you Ma'am?"

"Lady. Lady Stroud."

She heard a chair squeak in the back and footsteps.

"My Lady," the lad corrected, with a slight bow.

Then an elderly gentleman in a waistcoat and a chalk pencil on his ear, bustled in from the door to the back.

"I'll take this one," he said. Emily recognized him. This was Sedwell, she thought. He had been dressing her since her first mission.

"Yes father," the lad said, a bit surprised. And now a son.

"Go in the back and finish your work."

The lad bowed, looking at Emily with suspicion as he left.

The old man watched him go, waiting until the door shut.

"It's been a long time, Malady," he said.

"Yes," she said, radiating warmth. "Yes, I suppose it has." Then she added, "For all of us. Was that your son?"

"Yes. A good boy, but he knows nothing." Then he asked, anticipation in his voice, "Is it coming back?" But a twitch of her brow brought him up short. "No, no, I'm sorry." He gave half a bow. "I know my place." Then he looked up, the anticipation still there. "Shall we start?"

Chiffon, silk, doeskin, and fur, a wardrobe evolved that clearly eclipsed her shabby German dresses. When she returned to her hotel she found that she was no longer checked in. Her things had been moved to Claridge's, and she had the use of a maid. When he made his final delivery, Sedwell, with son behind frowning in confusion, bowed and passed a paper wrapped bundle.

"These are your blades," he intoned.

She took them without a word.

They brought her in to Buckingham Palace through the south entrance, little better than a parking lot for the servants. Rather than being insulted, she was intrigued. This wasn't new. Her visit was secret.

They led her through echoing halls, then carpeted salons to the King's Corridor and the Little Chinese Room. It was just them, George and Mary, the king and queen. It gave her pause, though she didn't show it. She hadn't had a private audience since George had assumed the throne, let alone tea. They stood and came forward to greet her, an unheard of break in protocol. She curtsied low and said, "Your Majesties."

"God no," the King said. "We should be bowing to you. I remember that time the palace was invaded by anarchists. They even killed the guards! We didn't find out about it until the next day, when the carpets were gone. Had to remove the blood they said . . ."

"George!" Mary said.

"Yes, of course," he said with a sigh. "Why can't we just have dinner for once? It's just us."

"Protocol," Mary said.

"It wouldn't do," Emily added, beaming.

"He and his brother. Crazy as hatters," Mary added.

"I have better taste," he said, with an I-have-you-there grin.

"So very true," she replied, with a worn smile.

"Shall we sit? They aren't ready yet," Mary said.

"Those DMI wonks treating you all right?" George asked.

"George!" Mary snapped.

"DMI?" Emily asked as she sat on a rather hard setae. They had been designed for different fashions. Fashions with padding.

Mary scowled. "Not even small talk first?" she growled.

"I guess I'm a bit chuffed," George said.

"Directorate of Military Intelligence love," she said.

Emily allowed herself to look confused.

"The successor to The Institution. With all the losses, we're having to reform everything."

"Everything, to put it simply, has come apart," George said.

"Yes George, everything has," Mary said patiently. "We need agents and those don't just come up from the factories."

"We need you to restart the school," George added bluntly.

"The school," Emily said, almost to herself, her smile faded. All those girls gone. How many more in the years since she left?

"Well yes, the school," Mary replied, her smile gone in a flash of worry as she looked back at Emily.

"I can't," she said, for once uncertain. "I won't."

"Why?" Mary asked, now with a frown.

"Where did they go?" Emily replied. She looked up at them both, her resolve hardening. And there they sat. It was the one real secret England still possessed.

"Where did they go?" she asked again. "Where did the girls go?"

They shifted in their seats, suddenly uncomfortable.

"They're gone," Mary said.

"Where?"

"Sent to other schools," George said. Emily didn't think he believed it. There would be no more lies.

"What about the older ones, the ones who knew too much?"

"They're dead," Mary said, with an uncomfortable wave of her hand. "Buried."

"Where?"

"We don't know," George replied. "Grandma might have, but it wasn't our business to know."

"This school," Emily started. She thought of girls she knew. All lost. Lonely deaths, one by one. Abby. Max was the only one left who kept her real name now. She could still withhold her tears. Not with them. She could still choose.

"There can't be any more deaths." Emily marveled at the coolness in her voice.

"Oh no," Mary said, shaking her head slowly. "It's just not possible anymore. It'll be up to you to find an alternative."

An alternative.

She ended up accepting the position. Apparently the job merited a peerage and a spot on the civil list. To Emily though, they seemed shallow rewards.

Years later, after she had consolidated her power, her clearance without dispute, she went through the basement files in Whitehall and dug until she found the place. It was a graveyard near Chelsea, a suburb of London, called Brompton. She walked through the stones and the rough grass. They had their own area. It had started as a church yard and then later Brompton Cemetery had been built to protect it. The names on the stones were all fake of course. Three hundred and twenty years The Institution had lasted. It had been established by James I, after the Gunpowder Plot. Six thousand and twenty two girls buried three and four deep. Most without caskets. No one knew but her. She was the last one. No one knew what was beneath those stones.

In the dim blue of evening she gave them her tears. She would keep their secret.

ဆၠ

Just after Christmas, December 1932, the head of the Sicherheitspolizei, the German Security Police, showed up at her door with only his somewhat dirty well-worn suit and a briefcase.

"Max!" Emily cried. Her butler had him waiting down in the hallway and it was quite a run to fly into his arms, but he accepted her hug with his quiet good grace.

"Emily," he said, with a smile as his arms reached around her back. They had both turned grey. Both near retirement.

"Max, why are you here?"

"I want to defect of course."

She frowned at him. "You weren't followed were you?"

"It's likely," he said with a smile. "I've killed three of them, but how can you know for sure?"

"Jenkins," she said to her butler. "Arm yourself and the staff, then call the office and inform them of the situation."

"At once, Milady," he said, bowing.

"It's that Hitler," Emily said to Max.

"The little politician," he replied, with a bit of embarrassment. "I tried to hold him back, but there's no stopping him."

"This is where you belong anyway. With me!" and she hugged him again, laughing. Then she looked at the front door. "Let's get away from the windows."

They went downstairs to the wine cellar and opened a bottle of sherry. They were quite drunk when MI5 found them, laughing, trying to hit each other.

She fended off all their attempts at arrest. She outranked them.

"We can't let the bureaucrats have you," she said, drunk, almost spilling her sherry.

Max ended up staying with her. Instead of arrest, a team of technicians with wire recording equipment moved in. Max had

282

been in charge of internal security and he built them a detailed map of the power players within Germany along with as much dirt on the Nazis as he could. But with that done, he had nothing else to offer but reminiscences. He and Emily sat together working out their stories together, unwinding the last five decades of European history while the technicians sat and recorded in rapt silence.

On August 23rd, 1944, Emily Stroud died.

For security reasons, her funeral was sparsely attended, but there were wakes in every corner of the world. She had trained every operative in MI5. They were all her children. But Max was at the funeral. After the service, as they were lowering in the coffin, he approached the grave, carefully walking over the uneven dirt, and tossed in a faded cardboard cutout Christmas tree, an old fashioned dance card.

"I think we will have that dance soon my dear," he managed before they led him back to the car.

He died three weeks later.

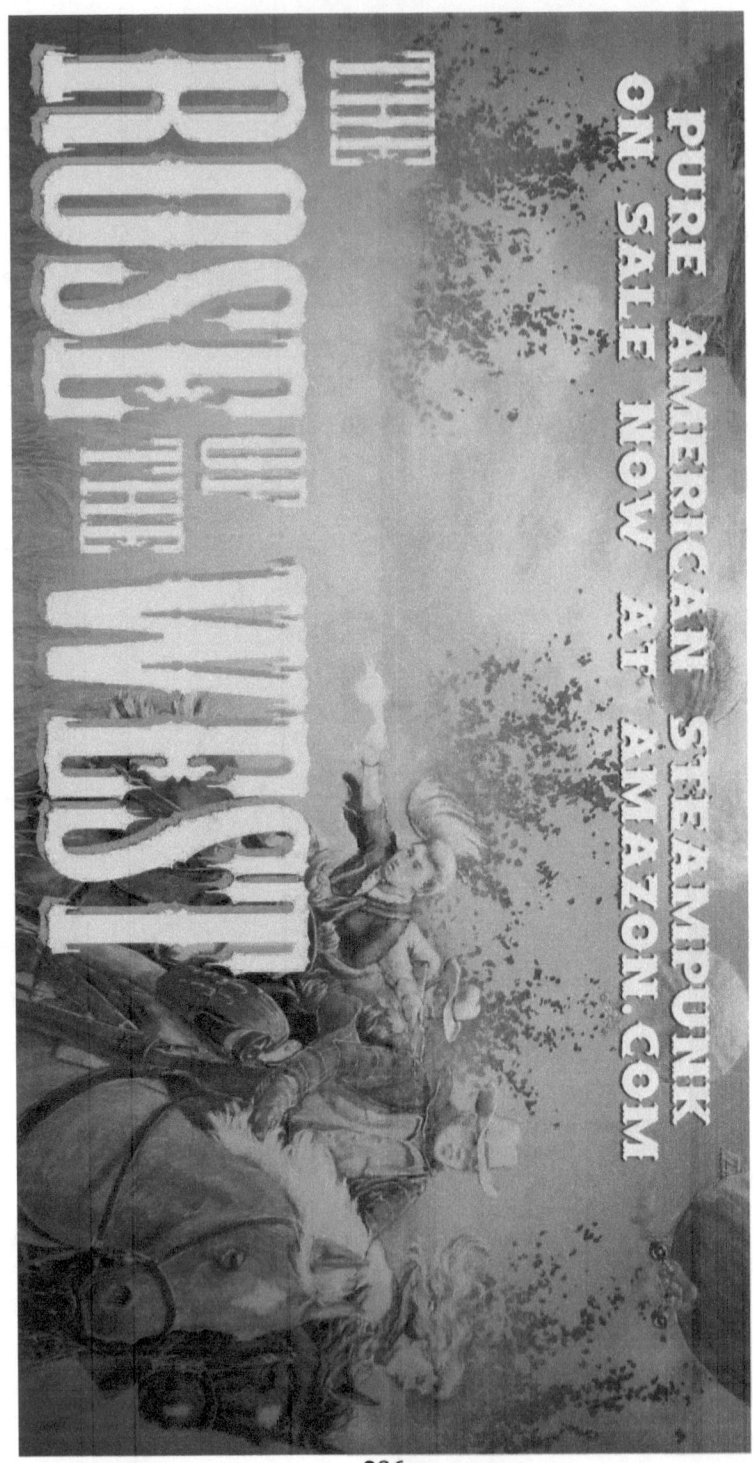

www.ingramcontent.com/pod-product-compliance
Lightning Source LLC
Chambersburg PA
CBHW031256170626
46807CB00001B/165